PRAISE FOR *IN THE* ⬛⬛⬛

"Infused with . . . fresh detail. Between the sweetness of the relationship and the summery beach setting, romance fans will find this a warming winter read."

—*Publishers Weekly*

"Fans will love the frank honesty of her characters. [Beck's] scenery is richly detailed and the story engaging."

—RT Book Reviews

"[A] realistic and heartwarming story of redemption and love . . . Beck's understanding of interpersonal relationships and her flawless prose make for a believable romance and an entertaining read."

—*Booklist*

PRAISE FOR *WORTH THE WAIT*

"[A] poignant and heartwarming story of young love and redemption [that] will literally make your heart ache . . . Jamie Beck has a real talent for making the reader feel the sorrow, regret, and yearning of this young character."

—*Fresh Fiction*

PRAISE FOR *WORTH THE TROUBLE*

"Beck takes readers on a journey of self-reinvention and risky investments, in love and in life . . . With strong family ties, loyalty, playful banter, and sexual tension, Beck has crafted a beautiful second-chances story."

—*Publishers Weekly* (starred review)

PRAISE FOR *SECRETLY HERS*

"[I]n Beck's ambitious, uplifting second Sterling Canyon contemporary . . . [c]onflicting views and family drama lay the foundation for emotional development in this strong Colorado-set contemporary."

—*Publishers Weekly*

"Witty banter and the deepening of the characters and their relationship, along with some unexpected plot twists and a lovable supporting cast . . . will keep the reader hooked . . . A smart, fun, sexy, and very contemporary romance."

—*Kirkus Reviews*

PRAISE FOR *WORTH THE RISK*

"An emotional read that will leave you reeling at times and hopeful at others."

—*Books and Boys Book Blog*

PRAISE FOR *UNEXPECTEDLY HERS*

"Character-driven, sweet, and chock-full of interesting secondary characters."

—*Kirkus Reviews*

PRAISE FOR *BEFORE I KNEW*

"A tender romance rises from the tragedy of two families—a must read!"
—Robyn Carr, #1 *New York Times* bestselling author

"Jamie Beck's deeply felt novel hits all the right notes, celebrating the power of forgiveness, the sweetness of second chances, and the heady joy of reaching for a dream. Don't miss this one!"
—Susan Wiggs, #1 *New York Times* bestselling author

"*Before I Knew* kept me totally enthralled as two compassionate, relatable characters, each in search of forgiveness and fulfillment, turn a recipe for heartache into a story of love, hope, and some really good menus!"
—Shelley Noble, *New York Times* bestselling author of *Whisper Beach*

PRAISE FOR *ALL WE KNEW*

"A moving story about the flux of life and the steadfastness of family."
—*Publishers Weekly*

"An impressively crafted and deftly entertaining read from first page to last."
—*Midwest Book Review*

"*All We Knew* is compelling, heartbreaking, and emotional."
—*Harlequin Junkie*

PRAISE FOR *JOYFULLY HIS*

"A quick and sweet read that is perfect for the holidays."
—*Harlequin Junkie*

PRAISE FOR *WHEN YOU KNEW*

"[A]n opposites-attract romance with heart."
—*Harlequin Junkie*

PRAISE FOR *THE MEMORY OF YOU*

"[Beck] deepens a typical story about first loves reuniting by exploring the aftermath of a violent act. Readers will root for an ending that repairs this couple's past hurt."

—*Booklist*

"Beck's portrayals of divorce and trauma are keen . . . Readers will be caught up in their journey toward healing and romance."

—*Publishers Weekly*

"*The Memory of You* is heartbreaking, emotional, entertaining, and a unique second-chance romance."

—*Harlequin Junkie*

PRAISE FOR *THE PROMISE OF US*

"Beck's depiction of trauma, loss, friendship, and family resonates deeply. A low-key small-town romance unflinching in its portrayal of the complexities of friendship and family, and the joys and sorrows they bring."

—*Kirkus Reviews*

"A fully absorbing and unfailingly entertaining read."

—*Midwest Book Review*

PRAISE FOR *THE WONDER OF NOW*

"*The Wonder of Now* is emotional, it is uplifting, it is heartbreaking, but ultimately [it] shows the reader the best of humanity in a heartfelt story."

—*The Nerd Daily*

PRAISE FOR *IF YOU MUST KNOW*

"Beck expertly captures the bickering between sisters, the pain of regret, and the thorny path to forgiveness. With well-realized secondary characters . . . and believable surprises peppered throughout, Beck's emotional tale rings true."

—*Publishers Weekly*

"[Beck's] heartwarming novel explores the sisterly bond with a touch of romance and mystery."

—*Booklist*

PRAISE FOR *TRUTH OF THE MATTER*

"Beck spins a poignant, multigenerational coming-of-age tale as these three women navigate their identities, dreams, and love lives. Complex and introspective, this is by turns heart-wrenching and infectiously hopeful."

—*Publishers Weekly* (starred review)

PRAISE FOR *FOR ALL SHE KNOWS*

"Women's fiction readers and series fans will be pleased with this story of friendship, family, and forgiveness."

—*Publishers Weekly*

"Like *Little Fires Everywhere* and *Big Little Lies*, this novel tackles the complicated dynamic between mothers."

—*The Hollywood Reporter*

"An inherently reader-engaging and impressively original story of friendship, hardship, love, tragedy, and redemption."

—*Midwest Book Review*

"*For All She Knows* is a must-read for book clubs! Jamie Beck's latest novel is both an insightful examination of modern-day parenting mores, and a poignant reminder of the importance of friendship and forgiveness."

—Brenda Novak, *New York Times* bestselling author

"Jamie Beck deftly crafts a riveting tale of parenthood, marriage, and friendship around a tragic event that unravels the threads that hold everything dear for two friends: their families and each other. As heart-wrenching as it is inspiring, *For All She Knows* reminds us that forgiveness is the first step to heal and Beck captures this brilliantly. A spring read every book club should pick up!"

—Kerry Lonsdale, *Wall Street Journal* and *Washington Post* bestselling author

PRAISE FOR *THE HAPPY ACCIDENTS*

"This story is an ode to girl power, making mistakes, and following your dreams. We'll race you to the bookstore."

—SheKnows

"Beautifully moving, masterful storytelling that weaves the nuances of relationships and finding yourself while facing the intricacies of life-changing decisions and their consequences."

—Priscilla Oliveras, *USA Today* bestselling author

"Jamie Beck has moved from a heavy hitter in romance to a sure thing in women's fiction, and *The Happy Accidents* shows why she can do both. In this novel, three old friends make a pact that changes everything . . . and may just be the best decision they ever made. You won't regret *your* decision to one-click this book."

—Liz Talley, *USA Today* bestselling author

PRAISE FOR *TAKE IT FROM ME*

"Many women will see aspects of themselves here in this relatable women's fiction from [Jamie] Beck."

—*Library Journal*

"[Jamie Beck delivers] an observant and compassionate story about the power of women's friendship to challenge and change us."

—Virginia Kantra, author of *Meg & Jo*

"Clever, insightful, and brimming with empathy, *Take It from Me* is Jamie Beck at her best. The story of two very different neighbors closely guarding secrets who have more in common than either woman can imagine, Beck's latest novel is a potent reminder that we *are* able to know the interior lives of those we care about—if only we can find the courage to ask."

—Camille Pagán, bestselling author of *This Won't End Well*

THE
BEAUTY
OF
RAIN

ALSO BY JAMIE BECK

The St. James Novels

Worth the Wait
Worth the Trouble
Worth the Risk

The Sterling Canyon Novels

Accidentally Hers
Secretly Hers
Unexpectedly Hers
Joyfully His

The Cabot Novels

Before I Knew
All We Knew
When You Knew

The Sanctuary Sound Novels

The Memory of You
The Promise of Us
The Wonder of Now

The Potomac Point Novels

If You Must Know
Truth of the Matter
For All She Knows

Stand-Alone Novels

THE
BEAUTY
OF
RAIN

a novel

JAMIE BECK

Montlake

Published by Montlake, Seattle

www.apub.com

Amazon, the Amazon logo, and Montlake are trademarks of Amazon.com, Inc., or its affiliates.

ISBN-13: 9781542032421 (paperback)
ISBN-13: 9781542032414 (digital)

Cover design by Caroline Teagle Johnson
Cover images: ©ganjalex / Shutterstock; © Kelly Knox / Stocksy United

Printed in the United States of America

To Brad, with love.
Thank you for sharing your good humor
to help me navigate the ups and downs.

AUTHOR'S NOTE

Dear reader,

Before I explain the inspiration behind this story, please be advised that, while it is ultimately about valuing the gift of life, the plot touches upon suicidal ideation and prescription drug abuse. The idea for this book originated in 2021, in the aftermath of an emergency surgery that saved my life. That event capped off a year in which I had endured two prior surgeries, my father's death, a broken arm, and my son's unexpected injury. The nine days I spent in the hospital following my brush with mortality were the weakest, sickest, most vulnerable ones of my life. More surprising, however, was how different I felt about my life when I went home. My terrible year forced me to acknowledge a fact we're all aware of but tend to ignore: we do not know, with any certainty, that we will have a tomorrow.

Initially, the inescapable reality scared me. The pandemic, climate change, and global politics had already made the world feel less safe, and now I had new personal challenges to boot. I felt paralyzed, questioning myself and the meaning of everything, imagining what might've happened to my family if I hadn't survived, and analyzing whether I'd spent my fifty-plus years on this earth as well as I could have. Those musings ultimately led me to embrace life's fragility and find new courage: the courage to draw boundaries, even when it is hard; the courage to speak my truth regardless of others' opinions, and to pursue that truth without fear or guilt; and the courage to put my needs equal to or, sometimes, ahead of those of the people I love.

Some of you may already have this mindset, but for those who have yet to embrace these attitudes, I hope this story serves as a reminder to fill your life with passion and gratitude, and to chase your dreams, whether they be about creating a family, a career, or a life of adventure. To live life—as Amy and Kristin might tease—with "no regerts."

Happy reading,
Jamie

PROLOGUE

A M Y   F O X   W A L S H

Mid-April
Stamford, Connecticut

The anniversary was always destined to be an awful day.

A burly paramedic throws open the rear doors, shouting through the din of heavy rain at the doctors waiting in the bay, "Patient is Amy Fox Walsh. Birth date 8/4/89. Car crashed into a tree on Route 104, north of the Merritt."

He and an EMT then maneuver my gurney to transfer it out of the ambulance. Each bump and jiggle wrenches another whimper of pain. This isn't supposed to be happening.

"Possible grade-three concussion, broken nose, and broken ribs with probable pneumothorax, based on her bluish lips, shortness of breath, some coughing, and tachycardia."

An eruption of thunder seems the perfect soundtrack for this moment. I'm nauseated but too afraid to twitch, let alone throw up. Breathing stings, as if my lungs are tangled in razor wire.

A young male doctor or nurse is taking notes on a device. His female colleague points a flashlight at my eyes, her gaze trained on my pupils. "Any others involved?" she asks the EMT.

"No other vehicles. No skid marks. No seat belt." He lowers his voice and adds, "The patient has wrist scars."

I close my eyes. They don't know me. They don't understand my history or know anything about what took place on the road today. I need to reach my sister.

"Amy, can you speak?" the woman asks.

"Yes." The effort rips through me like a sharp blade.

"Do you understand where you are?" she asks.

"Yes." God, no more questions, please. It hurts so much to talk.

"Any allergies to medication, anesthesia, or contrast dye?"

I give the barest shake of my head, searching her gaze for reassurance.

Her expression is more focused than friendly. "Is there anyone we can call?"

My sister. I can picture her face, but it takes longer to recall her name. Drawing a deep breath to answer fully makes me cough, which sends new shock waves of pain through my chest. "Kristin DeMarco. 203-555-1234."

"Okay," she says, confirming that her colleague got that info. "Let's get her inside and processed. We'll need head and chest CTs to confirm, and check for open ORs."

When they roll me toward the entry, I bite down against the pain. The doors whoosh open as I'm thrust inside, where I'm bathed in fluorescent light. The acrid scent of institutional cleaning solutions reminds me of my trip to the ER last July. Once again, Kristin will be a wreck because of me.

I might vomit after all.

CHAPTER ONE

AMY

Three months earlier
The third Saturday in January
Old Greenwich, Connecticut

This idea that you can't control life is a lie. Of course you can, simply by choosing to end it. Yes, yes, I know: then you'd be dead and your life would be over—or your life here on earth would, but that's another discussion. Even if you're repulsed by this suggestion, you cannot deny that you possess the ultimate power to control your own fate.

I find that to be perversely reassuring.

Not that I'm advocating suicide. Even during these torturous past nine months, on all but one excruciating instant when another breath felt impossible, I've tried to find some small way to make each day count. Today is a good example.

The chocolate and sugar aromas wafting through my sister's normally immaculate, remodeled kitchen are a rare treat. I blame the intimidating, overpriced, imported French oven for the cratered top of the sheet cake—something my generic appliance never did—although I can blame only myself for the poorly sliced and reassembled sections of this confection. My niece and nephew race to the large quartz island where I'm layering frosting on the bungled birthday cake.

"That's Piglet?" Livvy's face puckers. My little sidekick since I moved into my sister's guest suite in late August. She climbs onto a stool, bouncing on her knees, her black-brown curls springing around her face.

Swallowing the bubble of disappointment rising in my throat, I stare at the lumpy mound that resembles a swollen pink hornet.

"Use your imagination, will ya?" I slide Livvy a smile to mask my defeat before sticking out my tongue.

"Scotty loves him!" She reaches for the sky with the enthusiasm only a first grader can muster.

Loves. "Yes." My late son's obsession with Piglet is cross-stitched into the overall embroidery of his short life. He would be five, perhaps on the verge of losing one of the baby teeth on display in the photo I've set on the kitchen table. The tooth fairy is a tradition lost to me, but as long as I'm alive, I will honor the day he was born.

Some might find this party macabre, but I'm not the only surviving parent to plan one. Grilled cheese—his favorite—and balloons won't bring him to life, but they will keep bits of him present in our thoughts, and that's no small thing.

Luca, who's nine, swipes his finger along the base of the frosting, less interested in how the cake looks than how it tastes. Skinny but tall for his age, he's fair like Kristin, with her same pin-straight blond hair.

"Ah, ah, ah." I shake my head, pointing the spatula at him. "Not yet."

"Sorry," he says matter-of-factly, already showing signs of his father's pragmatism as he turns and walks to the family room, plops onto the enormous suede sectional, and picks up the latest Theodore Boone book.

"Are those for us, Aunt Amy?" Livvy asks, pointing at the gift-wrapped boxes on the counter near the toaster.

"Be patient." I use black M&M's for the pig's snout and eyes, then step back to see if they've made an improvement. Being an avid fan of

The Great British Bake Off does not, apparently, improve one's baking skills.

"Are you pestering your aunt while she's busy?" Kristin asks Livvy when she enters the kitchen to place a card on the pile beside the two gift-wrapped boxes. When she's not nearby, she's no doubt checking the video cameras to gauge my frame of mind. Earlier I overheard her whispering concerns about my manic mood to her husband, Tony. It's quite possible I'll melt down at some point. Probable, even. Nevertheless, my bittersweet high is enough to prove this isn't my worst-ever idea.

Livvy frowns at her mother. "I'm good company."

And a good mimic, repeating the exact words I tell her on the mornings when she crawls into my bed before sunrise.

Kristin, wearing an amused smile, ruffles her hair. "Please go get Daddy off the Peloton and tell him to shower because we'll be serving lunch soon."

I turn my back on my sister, pretending to need something from the refrigerator. What I truly need is a breather.

She means well, but her careful language has hit a nerve—not that that's hard to do lately. On some level, I get her apprehension. Caused it, even. But really, can't we call this a birthday party? It's got all the trappings. Her professionally decorated family room now looks like Chuck E. Cheese ran through it and barfed up streamers and dozens of multicolored balloons. The kitchen table is covered with a Winnie the Pooh tablecloth and confetti. The only thing missing is Kidz Bop blaring from the speakers.

"Mom and Dad want to Zoom when things get underway, okay?" Kristin raises her brows in question, although we both know I have no choice.

Four more eyeballs following my every move—yippee. I grab the pack of American cheese from the refrigerator. "Okay."

"Grilled cheese," she says gently, as if the significance of the selection has dampened her vocal cords.

I've spent my life in her shadow, with her being always a little smarter, a little prettier, and until recently, a lot wealthier. Not that she lords anything over me—the opposite, really, as if she recognizes her advantages and tries to diminish them, like when she used to stash her soccer medals and honors certificates in her sock drawer so I wouldn't see them every day. I'm sure she meant to be kind, but I was never fragile. I'm always happy for her wins, even when I cannot match them.

I open the pantry to get bread and potato chips.

"How can I help?" She flattens her hands on the island.

Funny question, considering she needs my help as much as I need hers. Not that she sees it.

"Maybe grab the paper plates and silverware?" I shrug.

Kristin lays a hand on my shoulder as she breezes past. The gesture makes me stiffen. Since my husband Sean's death (yes, I lost him with my son in one fell swoop), she's tried to be his stand-in. My safe space. The person I confide in. Sean mostly listened without judging or second-guessing. Kristin's a natural-born fixer, always more focused on what should happen than on enjoying what does, which doesn't make her easy to turn to for comfort.

On top of that, she's been edgier lately, and losing weight she doesn't need to lose. Sometimes she's nearly shaky. My lengthy stay and events like this one could be to blame.

While I'm buttering bread and compiling the sandwiches, Tony shows up, his hair still wet from the shower. He's objectively handsome—the classic Italian look with wavy, dark hair, equally dark eyes, and a strong nose and chin. A contrast to Sean's slightly dorky looks, medium-brown hair, and fair skin. A bit elfin, but sincere and approachable. Like a mirage, my husband smiles before vanishing. I blink in the hopes he'll reappear, but of course he doesn't.

"Let's see that cake." Tony glances at it and immediately covers his mouth. His torso trembles as he holds back the kind of inappropriate giggles that attack in a church pew. The epic fail on my part—and his inability to contain himself—both make me snicker, at which point even my sister relaxes long enough to laugh.

"Well, the taste is all that matters," he says. Like his son, he can't resist sampling a bit of icing. "Should I man the stove?"

His energy boomerangs to restlessness, perhaps a remnant of his earlier apprehension about the potential for this ghostly bash to spook their kids. A silly concern. Teaching kids to cope with something they'll confront time and again is at least as important as teaching them algebra.

But Tony's been patient with me. More than patient. What man wants his sister-in-law underfoot indefinitely?

I shoo him away. "Go hang with Luca. Let him tell you about that book he's reading."

I turn to the stove, but not before catching his nonverbal exchange with Kristin. The arch of his brow tells me my suggestion annoys him. It also means they've talked about this kind of thing before. If they want me to stop nudging, they should stop taking time with their family for granted.

Twenty minutes later, the remnants of our greasy lunch lie scattered across the table like branches felled by a storm.

"Cake now?" Livvy claps.

"Let's do cards first to let our tummies settle," I suggest, although this element of my plan could sink me.

Tony, who's been silent, rises to collect the dirty napkins and paper plates. Quietude is unusual for him. The first time he dined with our family, more than a decade ago, he spoke animatedly about every topic from food to travel to politics. Kristin spent that meal making moon eyes at him except for the few times she'd glanced at our parents to gauge their impressions. Back then we three were still babes playing at adulthood, blissfully ignorant of what could come. How I miss that youthful cloak of invincibility.

"You don't need to be so stoic, Tony," I say. "This is a party. It's okay to have fun, tell a joke. Otherwise, it's just plain awkward."

"We can agree on that," he mutters wryly, the subtle barb sailing over Luca's and Livvy's heads.

Kristin shoots him a sharp look and then touches my hand. "Should I grab the gifts?"

I shake my head. "I'll get them. You fire up Zoom."

She pushes back from the table and trots to the den, returning in seconds with her iPad before logging on. Mom and Dad pepper Livvy and Luca with questions while I pass out the cards.

"Hi, Mom. Dad." I briefly make eye contact, but watching them struggle to feign happiness while grieving their grandson will only pull me off track. I won't let them derail this celebration any more than I'll get sidetracked by the fact that no one from my husband's family has called or sent a card. Donning a patient-teacher smile, I ask, "Shall we jump in?"

"Me first!" Livvy stretches across the table to grab the card she made.

"I'd expect nothing less." I bop my finger against her nose before she opens the envelope. With great flair, she unfolds her artwork and displays it to everyone before turning it to face me.

"This is one time when Luca, Scotty, and me were at the beach—"

"Scotty and I," my sister corrects.

Livvy scowls and I might too. I refocus on her drawing, which depicts two figures in the water (Luca and her, I assume), and then, slightly off center by himself, is a boy in socks piling rocks on the beach.

"Scotty really liked the rocks. He piled them and knocked them down over and over. That was so funny." She giggles, her head bobbling from side to side. "We had ice cream sandwiches for lunch. It was fun."

I remember that afternoon at Tod's Point too. Scotty, then three and a half, disliked having gritty sand between his toes. The sock thing was cute, especially when Sean nicknamed him "Two Socks." That day I'd driven down from Stamford, borrowed Kristin's pass, and taken the three kids to the neighborhood beach, but none of us could coax my son into the water. Eventually Livvy sat beside him and built a rock creation of her own. She'd always played alongside him despite his social-connectivity issues. Maybe even because of them. Patience came naturally to her, unlike me, who always felt one step behind his autism.

"That was a fun day." I reach across to squeeze her hand, hiding the way memories make my insides feel like a piñata defending against batters. "Thank you for reminding me."

My praise earns me her winning smile.

We proceed around the table, with everyone sharing a memory of Scotty. Luca's letter updates Scotty on how I've been living here now, but he's not trying to take Scotty's place—something I hadn't known he'd worried about. My mother's voice cracks on her turn; so does Kristin's. Tony and Dad muscle through like newscasters reading a teleprompter. Everyone has their own way of dealing with discomfort. My request wasn't an easy one, but I wish the adults would get with the spirit. Stoic expressions aren't inspiring happiness, which is something I desperately wish to feel again.

When my turn comes, I say, "For mine, we need to go outside."

"What about the presents?" Livvy asks.

"That's next. Now go grab a coat." I stand to retrieve five of the biodegradable helium balloons from the family room. Last year it was oddly warm and sunny on Scotty's birthday. He'd been especially sensitive that day, uninterested in a party and refusing to wear the birthday crown I bought. Sean got a little pissy about wasting money we didn't have on things we should know Scotty wouldn't enjoy; then I got mad because his being right wasn't helping me make the party fun for our son. Now all I wish is that they were both here, even if we relived that same argument.

Within two minutes, the family is reassembled near the sliding doors in winter coats and hats. I hand everyone a balloon, grab the iPad, and go out onto the deck.

I tried to plan a speech, but every effort got tossed in the trash. I'm no Jane Austen, able to conjure words that could render the emotional tornado in my heart. Now I grope for a starting place while the others stare at their feet in silence.

"This party might seem strange, but even though Scotty's in heaven, he's still my baby, and I'm still his mom, and today is his birthday." These beautiful, painful truths keep me going when soldiering on feels as impossible as breathing underwater.

The kids stand dutifully, like they do at Easter Mass, waiting for instructions. My sister dabs her eyes and then grasps Tony's arm. My left hand flexes as if searching for Sean's.

It takes several seconds for my throat to loosen enough to speak again. "Scotty can't be with us today, but I thought we could send these balloons up to him so that, in some way, he's part of our celebration."

Tony's face is splotchy, his lips pressed together, zipping up his emotions. He's clasping Kristin's free hand so hard that his knuckles are white. For a second, their tension makes me question putting everyone through this.

"We'll let these go at the same time and make a little wish, okay?" I look at Livvy and Luca because they, more than anyone, keep me grounded. Livvy nods, her dimples fixed marks on her cheeks. I love her and Luca, and am blessed to be loved in return. Yet I envy that they still have their lives ahead of them. They will learn about the world and themselves as they continue to grow, graduate from high school and college, find jobs, fall in love. All the things my little boy will never experience. The not knowing who he might've become is a rabbit hole that can easily consume me.

It's still quiet except for the chattering of teeth. We huddle with our backs against the wind before we release our offerings.

As they rise, I blurt out, "I miss you so much and pray someday we'll be reunited." My voice catches, so I pause to acknowledge the yearning. "Until then, keep building rock castles in the sky."

With my face lifted to the sun, I hold my breath as the brightly colored balloons drift inland on the wind.

"Mine's winning!" Livvy points at the emerald-green one charging ahead of the rainbow-colored pack.

I pull her close, hoping her light will chase away the dark. My nose is runny as hell and my eyes burn, but I stay rooted until the last balloon disappears.

"I'm cold," Luca says.

"Yes." Truthfully, I'm more limp than cold. My big idea didn't mitigate my loss one bit. My son is still dead, and I'm still here, surrounded by my sister's family, with no one of my own. Try as I might to squeeze a single drop of joy from this day, my strength is crumbling. "Let's go inside."

"Cake!" Livvy runs ahead and throws open the door before ditching her coat on the floor and sidling up to the table.

Kristin grabs me into a hug before I cross the threshold. A silent, tight embrace that wrings out the tears I've held back. As we ease apart, she grabs my damp face, her gaze searching mine. She's scared, and it's not fair of me to be bitter. I caused that fear last summer, on a day neither of us will ever forget, and not just because my wrist scars are a permanent reminder.

I wait for her to say something, but she can't or decides not to. She drops her hands and picks up the iPad before following me inside, where Tony has already dealt with Livvy's coat and put candles on the cake.

"Oh boy. It really is hideous," I croak, half laughing, half crying. Everyone goes still, as if any movement or sound will be the trip wire that makes me implode.

Livvy's small hand slides around mine then. "You always say it's the effort that counts. Good effort, Aunt Amy."

And just like that, she defuses the gathering sorrow. We sing, and then the kids slice gigantic pieces of cake for themselves. My appetite is weak, but I force myself to take one bite to honor the custom.

I normally love cake, but today it turns my stomach. My head begins to pound.

"I need to lie down." I stand, surprising everyone with my about-face.

"What about the presents?" Livvy asks.

"Those are for you and Luca. You can open them without me, okay? I got a sudden headache."

Kristin reaches for me. "Advil?"

"No, thanks."

"I'll clean up," Tony says, smiling in that soft way he does when trying to soothe someone.

I nod. "Thank you." Before retiring, I turn to leave the kids on an upbeat note. "Don't suck the helium without me."

"Okay," Luca promises before sneaking a second sliver of cake onto his plate. I kiss the kids on the head and wave to my parents, who are still on the screen.

"Thanks so much, everyone. I love you all." My throat aches, so I dash up the stairs and close the door to my room. Perhaps Kristin was right. I've been pushing for the impossible—a joyful party for a dead little boy. Reality always catches up. The Winnie the Pooh quote "How lucky am I to have something that makes saying goodbye so hard" echoes like a message from beyond.

Luck. Something most people pray for. Something everyone cheered about when I won all those millions. Good luck. Dumb luck. Blind luck.

Bad luck, as it turns out.

Nobody who wins the Powerball imagines such luck will lead to the death of their spouse and only child. The result of a year of quietly playing the same numbers—our birth months and days—had seemed such a blessing. If only we hadn't planned that celebratory trip to Exuma.

It had been a disaster almost from the start—an overconfident reaction to our big win. I called the airline in advance for special accommodations. Scotty wore noise-canceling headphones on the flight, and I managed his food sensitivities by bringing his favorite snacks. We booked a beautiful suite with ocean views, thinking that would be soothing. Unfortunately, my son's different operating system made him prefer the company of objects to people, so the crowds and the music around the pool proved overwhelming.

The morning of the ill-fated boat tour, Scotty had spent thirty minutes yelling and then smeared his food across the table in our suite, staining his clothes with blueberry jam.

"Why can't we ever have one easy day?" It had been a trying couple of years: the managing his proclivities to reduce his stress, the fear of the unknown, the learning curves. Even before the diagnosis, Sean's reluctance to acknowledge an issue and my breakdown upon confirming my suspicions had begun to put a strain on our marriage. Sean left the daily work of parenting Scotty to me while he focused on his job and budgeting so we could afford the support our son might need throughout his life. When we'd won multimillions, we believed our problems were solved—or at least that we'd buy our way past the hardest work.

"What did you expect?" Sean shrugged.

"I expected us to have some fun. To reset. To enjoy our damn windfall."

"Then we should've come alone, like I suggested." Sean's nonchalance—his lack of sympathy for my frustration—pushed me over the edge.

"Trust me, I would've loved to have come here alone. I haven't had two hours to myself in years." My smug huffiness emphasized our tired argument about which of us was dealing with more pressure when it came to child-rearing.

Sean grabbed the beach bag I'd packed for the boat tour of the swimming wild pigs. "Fine. I'll take Scotty on the tour. Go to the spa and 'reset' so maybe we can relax later."

"He won't be able to handle the boat tour." Another of my theoretically fun ideas that would likely end nothing like we planned.

"We already paid for it. We chose this island because he loves pigs. He knows about the tour. Canceling will likely upset him more." Sean sighed. "It's a small boat, so it shouldn't be too crowded. He'll like the hum of the engine."

Scotty did enjoy things that hummed—vacuum cleaners, hood vents, fans, cars.

My skin itched. In that moment, I didn't have the energy to go with them and face other people's judgments if Scotty became overwhelmed. I didn't honestly care about seeing the pigs. I just wanted to be pampered. To drink cucumber water, get a massage, listen to spa music, and read a book. Oh my God, that sounded like bliss. "Fine. You take him. I'll hit the spa."

"Fine."

Fine, fine—our last words to each other. That and the "need" for me time simply for doing what any good mother has done for her child throughout the centuries make me hate myself most days. Had I gone, I would've died in the explosion with them instead of being stuck wrestling with the effort of living without them.

I hug their photo to my chest, flop onto the bed, curl around a pillow, and weep until I'm asleep.

When I awaken, the sun is lower in the sky and my room has grown dim. The cashmere throw from the chair is swathed across me, letting me know my sister checked on me at some point.

I sit up and catch a glimpse of myself in the mirror—thin and sallow—then decide to take a bath. Steam fogs up the bathroom as the soaking tub fills. My thoughts wander while I wait. If Kristin hadn't stopped by my house to drop off groceries at the exact moment of my all-time low point, she wouldn't have heard me slide off the toilet in my bathroom after slicing my wrists. The way horror contorted her features as she dropped to her knees—mouth gaping in a silent scream—after she opened the door and found me bleeding still makes me flinch with shame. She jumped into action quickly, wrapping my wrists tight and holding them over my head while calling 911. I should be grateful she saved me, but there are days when I almost resent it.

It's not easy to live with the consequences of my choices. To plan parties that the guest of honor can't attend. To mark time against one cruel twist of fate.

Or not.

I take my nearly full bottle of doxepin from the vanity drawer and set it on the side of the bathtub before I settle into the water.

After Kristin picked me up from my monthlong inpatient stint in the hospital in August, she first told me how much she loved me and that she was glad I was doing better. Then she said, "We want you to come live with us for a while, but I have to ask a favor."

Uninterested in returning to my empty home with all its ghosts, I asked, "What favor?"

"You won't harm yourself in my home. I love you, but I can't let Luca and Livvy witness something no child should see."

I dropped my chin, letting the weight of her words and the pain I'd already caused my family sink in. It wasn't an easy oath to make, but armed with antidepressants and fresh off a month of daily therapy, I hoped for the best.

In some ways, the months between then and now are like a long, indistinct smudge of getting from sunrise to sunset by making myself useful—doing the family laundry, tidying up, making dinners when Tony runs late. It's been tough to commit to moving on when looking forward still feels disloyal to the two I've lost.

For all my good intentions, the holidays were a brutal test. I flew to Arizona to stay with my parents rather than risk breaking down on Christmas morning in front of the kids. At least out west, nothing reminded me of home.

I've done my best to heal, but real joy is still fleeting. It's hard to feel I deserve to go on, given the reason I wasn't on that boat.

I grip the bottle of pills.

If I took them and went to bed, no one would find me until morning. It could look like I'd had a heart attack. Even once Kristin learned the truth, the kids would never need to know. She and Tony would protect them from it—I could count on that much. And while I don't want to hurt my sister or parents, they'd survive because they have everything to live for right here under this roof.

Negativity sinks its teeth into me, pulling me further down. Why stack empty day after empty day for their sake while the numbness inside—an invisible cancer—slowly kills me? An endless future of celebrating birthdays for the dead and holidays without them is too vast. Too hard. My hands tremble while I unscrew the cap. There are plenty of pills. I stare at them, tears in my eyes, escape within my grasp.

I'm starting to raise the container to my lips when a knock at the bedroom door startles me, causing me to drop the bottle. Pills plop into the tub and scatter across the floor.

"Shit," I mutter, sloshing water as I reach for the now-empty container, using the back of my hand to swipe my tears.

"Aunt Amy, can you come play dolls?" Livvy yells.

She obviously likes her new American Girl doll, as I knew she would.

"Where's your mom, pumpkin?" Hopefully she can't detect my strained voice.

"In her office."

Naturally. Weekends don't mean rest in this house. Tony's and Kristin's jobs are rarely far from their thoughts. That's why they don't notice that their careers are quietly stealing their most important—if invisible—asset: time together. Time, time, time . . . so much time spent focused on things that aren't nearly as valuable as they believe.

"Give me five minutes to dry off and get dressed." I toe the drain and let the water swirl around me, alive if not quite living. One day— one minute—at a time. It's always been my only life plan anyway.

"Okay. Come in my room."

Her love has been a beautiful gift this year. Please, God, forgive me for doing anything to disappoint or hurt her.

I towel off, knowing it's time to move out. I've overstayed my welcome, for one thing. Tony and Kristin aren't nearly as affectionate with each other as they always were before my arrival.

For months, I've searched for a reason to keep going, but if today proves anything, it's that even my best efforts will always come up short. None of my money can buy back what I need to be happy.

If I'm no longer living here, then I'll no longer be bound by my promise.

The mere decision prompts an immediate, energizing flood of relief.

CHAPTER TWO

KRISTIN

Later that evening

The kids drag Amy to the family room to goof around with helium while Tony and I deal with the dinner mess.

I want nothing more than to have faith in my sister's Julia Roberts smile, yet it's hard to shake the recent image of her huddled on her bed like a frail baby bird, her cheeks tearstained. Our family has tried to fill her empty spaces, but she's sprung a permanent leak. The sickening image of her limp on her bathroom floor, her gaze distant as blood poured from her wrists, remains my silent companion. Even now, the tension that commandeered my body that day and remained for weeks afterward can snap back like a muscle memory.

For five months, I've monitored her highs and lows to the point of giving myself whiplash. My home is no longer a respite. Whether at work or here, I'm always on call for someone I love.

Luca hops around reciting lines from *Jumanji* in a gas-altered falsetto that has Livvy's little body sliding off the sofa in hysterics. So much for our concern about the ghoulish birthday party.

Amy sucks in a lungful of helium from a red balloon. One can only imagine what she's about to say, but she's amusing our kids. She's always been much better at that than I. In a way, she rounds out Tony's and my parenting dynamic. We supply stability and discipline; she infuses playfulness. Livvy, in particular, has seemed happier since Amy came to live with us. Hard to swallow. It's wrong to hold it against my sister, and yet occasionally a corrosive envy seeps in.

I pass behind them all to remove the streamers from the built-in shelves.

"Wait! I'll help you," Amy says, her Minnie Mouse voice sending the kids into another fit of giggles. Even I have to chuckle. It's been months since we've all laughed together. I've worried our glee would intensify Amy's mourning, but perhaps I've had that backward.

I wave away her offer. She'd likely overlook a bit of tape here and there, or miss a section of crepe in some corner. One doesn't need to be Sherlock Holmes to figure out what she's done on any given day. A candy bar wrapper on the ground beside the trash can, a magazine laid open on the sofa cushion, nail polish jars shoved in the junk drawer rather than returned to the appropriate basket in the bathroom closet. Nothing has changed since we shared a childhood bedroom.

My sister would say she has little patience for perfection, although I'd argue doing something to completion isn't perfectionism. For most of her life, she's been content with a "good enough" bar that neither Tony nor I relate to. Then again, until the accident that claimed her family, my sister never needed pharmaceuticals to manage *her* life, so who am I to judge?

"Hey, Tony," calls Minnie. "Your turn!"

He places the sponge in its holder, arms folded across his chest. "That's okay."

Amy then enlists the kids in a campaign to persuade him, resulting in a chorus of high-pitched cartoon vocals chanting "Daddy, Daddy" as the kids jump around the room until he gives in. Those extra slices of cake may not have been our best decision.

Luca hands Tony a giant blue balloon and awaits his father's participation, his eyes bright with excitement.

Tony does nothing in half measures. He sucks in the helium, his broad chest expanding like the Hulk's. His eyes radiate humor. "Who wants to hike Ward Pound Ridge tomorrow?"

The tinny attempt at a bellow makes us all laugh again. I've missed that sound. Not that I heard it that often, given my work schedule.

Livvy dive-bombs her father's leg, climbing it like Boston ivy. "Me, Daddy! Me."

I let the grammar go. This moment is too precious to turn into a teachable one.

Tony bends to raise her overhead before tucking her onto his hip and kissing her head. They look so alike—her a delicate feminine version of his best physical traits. "Then you'd better get some rest so you aren't too tired in the morning."

The affection reflected in his eyes is reminiscent of his early awestruck moments during her infancy. He could hardly keep his eyes off her, opting to cradle her while I played with Luca in the yard. For the first time all day—maybe all month—I enjoy a deep, relaxed breath. Then I catch Amy staring at them—her eyes dewy—and my muscles clench.

As I gather the deflated balloons and take the party debris to the kitchen, I call, "Time for bed. Go brush your teeth and get into pj's. I'll be up shortly."

While the kids drag their feet, I empty the kitchen trash can and take the bag to the larger container in the garage. Away from everyone, I lean against the integrated storage cabinet, close my eyes, and savor the stillness.

Alone, finally, even if only briefly. Heavy exhaustion roots me in place as thoughts about the strange day come and go—my sister's mood swings, the kids' embracing the spirit of the party, memories of my nephew's serious expressions and last year's birthday party, when he'd sat in the corner fixated on the battery-operated toy drill he got from our parents. Today's gathering made missing him and Sean more present. I can compartmentalize their absence other days, whereas it must choke my sister every hour. The void in Amy's life is—well, anytime I imagine it, my body recoils as if it's stepped too close to fire.

Before losing her family, she was the silly sister who put up a tent in our childhood bedroom. The kind of girl who dyed her hair pink on a high school dare. A woman who planned my surprise bachelorette party as a glamping weekend in the Catskills. Now, despite her promise to me, I can't stop thinking she still wants to end her life.

Breathe. One minute. Two. That shitty conference call this afternoon comes back to mind. Nothing like having a client disclose a substantial contingent liability—a lawsuit filed against it—weeks before a merger is set to close.

When I was a young lawyer eager to prove myself, these challenges excited me. Now I much prefer things to go as planned. Male colleagues from my class made partner two and three years ago. Pregnancies and maternity leaves delayed my advancement because I couldn't bill the same hours or schmooze clients when I was sleep deprived and lost eight workweeks in a single year. And then this past year I took time off in September to watch over Amy when she first moved in.

My younger self had such high hopes. Salutatorian of my high school class, voted most likely to succeed. Summa cum laude graduate of UConn. *Columbia Law Review*. A legal career appealed to my innate sense of fairness and justice, and to my preference for navigating within rules rather than swimming amid chaos. For all these reasons, everyone expected me to smash through glass ceilings faster than most, not slower. Tony, especially. His eyes always light up when he boasts about my aptitude.

When I think of the sacrifices my family has made for my career . . . I don't know what I'll do if I'm passed over again.

I glance at the door to the house and make myself go back inside. The first floor is now lit by only a single lamp and the hood light over the stove. I assume Amy is helping Tony get the kids settled, until movement on the deck surprises me. The sleet stopped hours ago, making way for billions of pinpricks of light that dot the sky. My sister stands beneath them, draping a throw around her shoulders, puffs of breath fogging in front of her face. She used to crawl out of our childhood bedroom window onto the porch roof just to stare at the night sky, but I doubt she's searching for Orion or fantasizing about the future tonight.

I hesitate, debating an interruption. When she dabs her eyes, I open the door and step outside, instantly bitten by the winter wind. I rub my arms as the tip of my nose turns cold.

"Hey." I offer a sympathetic smile. "Big day."

Amy nods, her gaze returning to the sky. "Do you think he saw us?"

I don't believe in ghosts or spirits. I'm not even sure about God, given the state of the world. I step behind her and hug her tight, resting my head on her shoulder, acknowledging my own impotence. My love hasn't healed her, no matter how much I wish it would. "I hope so."

We remain on the deck as one until Amy starts to break free and wind coming off the Sound shoots between us.

"It's freezing out here. Let's head inside," I say.

"Wait," she says. "I have something to tell you."

I rub my arms, shivering. "What?"

"I've decided to move out." She's not looking at me.

I sway, thrown by her left-field announcement. "Why now?"

"My stay is taking a toll on you all. You've seemed especially jittery lately, and you're not eating as well. It's time."

She's noticed? That's not good. I don't want her feeling responsible for me when she's barely able to care for herself. "You're welcome here as long as you need."

"Thanks, but I need to be on my own." She holds up both hands. "That came out wrong. I'm not ungrateful that you care, but it creates a lot of pressure—to smile, to improve, to 'be normal' again on your schedule instead of my own."

It smarts to have all I've done for her—to my own detriment—turned around on me. "Will you move back home?"

When I took her there in October to get her winter sweaters, she sat on her bedroom floor for an hour, hyperventilating. Then again, tonight she laughed with my kids after throwing a party for Scotty. Maybe she is healing, and I'm creating a bogeyman that doesn't exist.

"No." Her voice sounds a little raw. "The market is pretty good for homes in that price range, so I'll sell it and use that money for rent."

Rent? "What about the prize money?"

With a vigorous shake of her head, she says, "Not touching that."

"Why not?"

Rather than offer an explanation, she sighs. "Can we talk about this tomorrow? I'm beat."

I'm beat too. And confused. "Fine." It's a deep freeze out here, so I cross to the slider. "You coming?"

"In a bit."

When Amy is in one of these moods, there's no reasoning with her. I go inside and make my way upstairs.

Lately I feel twice my age, probably because I've had twice as much on my plate with her here. It might've been easier if our parents were around to help, but Dad's asthma caused them to move to Arizona years ago. Mom increases my burden with daily questions about how I'm managing Amy's recovery. In all these months, she's never once asked how doing so is affecting my family and career.

My competence has always been a point of personal pride. Unfortunately, now everyone assumes I've got everything under control. I'm not sure this dynamic is sustainable for much longer, yet I'm loath to reveal any shortcoming.

Upstairs, the kids are in their beds with books. No running around or procrastinating. No breakdowns or excuses to delay the inevitable. They behave much better when Tony is in charge, possibly because he works from home part time and he almost always has dinner with them. Must be nice to have autonomy and a ten-minute commute. Mine is seventy-plus minutes.

I stand at the top of the stairs and let my chin drop for a moment before I go to kiss them each good night.

I finally enter my room, where my husband is sprawled across the bed.

We used to have fun cheering on the other's wins—me getting my job, or making junior partner, or closing a giant deal. Him starting his own development company, or breaking ground on a new site. We'd pop champagne, or I'd receive a gorgeous bouquet, or we'd leave the kids with a sitter and go out for the night. Then I hit a stretch of having no wins and getting bogged down with the little stuff. Lately I think Tony has stopped sharing his wins because he doesn't want me to feel comparatively less-than. In any case, it's been a year since we've celebrated much of anything. For the first time in my life, I'm feeling like a failure at just about everything.

He lazily looks up from his iPad. "What's wrong?"

"Amy's standing outside in the cold, staring at the stars." I cross to the bathroom to wash my face and go to the closet to change into pajamas, desperate to crawl beneath the covers and finally get some rest.

The purse I used on Friday is sitting open on a shelf. My heart skips as I freeze before snapping it closed and stashing it behind other bags. Tony wouldn't entrap me. My secret is still safe.

"She's always liked the night sky." His voice carries no trace of concern. If only I felt as confident.

"She's also ready to move out." When I reenter our room, he sets the iPad aside, eyes bright, and takes off his shirt. Gravity has not yet grabbed hold of his pecs.

"Privacy at last," he practically purrs.

It's not easy to resist his bedroom eyes, but I'm hardly in the mood after this fraught day. I peer out the window to the deck below. Amy's still standing there. Ignoring Tony's innuendo, I say, "Can you imagine how hard today was for her? Now this sudden idea about leaving. I should stay alert in case she falls apart."

"We've been on alert every day for months." He makes a face. "You can't watch her twenty-four seven. If anything, doesn't today prove she's ready to be on her own?"

"She'll certainly feel like she should be if you voice that attitude."

"What attitude?" Tony sinks back into the pillows, resigned to his failed seduction.

"Annoyance. Like it's a bother to have her here." I flinch at the memory of cradling her on her bathroom floor while waiting for the ambulance to arrive.

He sighs, tousling his hair with one hand. "I never said that, but she's been here a long time, Krissy. I know you're tired, even if you won't admit it."

I turn away from that spotlight so he can't see my guilty acknowledgment. "She's been helpful, especially with Livvy. I don't want her to feel unwelcome. I couldn't live with myself if we pushed her out and then she did something . . ." Worse, I might not forgive him.

He leans forward, pity leaching into his beautiful eyes. "I'm not pushing her out. But no matter how long she stays, you can't prevent another incident if that's what she ultimately wants to do."

Incident is an awfully sanitized description, which I'm sure is intentional.

"You don't know that," I say hotly. "Here I can keep an eye on her." Plus, she made me that promise.

"I doubt hiding out from the world is best for her at this point. It's definitely not helping us."

"What's that mean?" I frown while crawling onto the bed and loosely braiding my hair, irked that he's making this about us.

"Exactly what I said. Our sex life has flatlined because you're too tired or worried or you think she'll hear us and miss Sean. You're more concerned about how everything we do affects her than you are about how she affects all of us." His tone is casual, but the words feel pointed.

"That's not true!" I might toss a pillow at him if it weren't for an inner voice whispering that it might be a little true. "Where's your compassion? We have so much—everything she's lost."

Tony never loses his temper. He remains calm and clearheaded, which is worse when a big fight might be a good release for my pent-up

25

frustrations. "I've been totally supportive, but eventually she's got to take steps forward without being held up by you."

"Not on her dead son's birthday, she doesn't," I snap.

Tony raises both hands. "I'm just a little tired of the judgments, like I don't know what she really means when she says, 'It's too bad you missed such and such because of work.'"

Okay, that's been rough. We don't need Amy's running commentary about our parenting. "She's thinking about the kids."

"She's fixating on them." Perhaps that's true, too, but it seems like a natural response for someone in her situation. "They're our kids. We have our own style and don't need her advice."

"But your mom's advice is fine," I quip.

"My mom isn't living here." Tony often takes that wry tone when defending his mother, whose asides about my store-bought baked goods and take-out dinners goad me. Like I've got time to cook from scratch when I barely get home from work before the kids go to sleep.

I glance toward the window. Is Amy still out there?

"Listen, babe," Tony says, interrupting my musing. "You know I feel bad for Amy. What happened is unthinkable, but her wanting to leave seems like a good sign. What if she buys one of my unsold units in that fourplex in Riverside? She'll be close enough to visit every day, but she won't be roaming our halls all night."

More than once we've heard her pacing back and forth in the hallway, sometimes weepy, other times quiet except for the shuffle of her slippers.

"She can't afford million-dollar condos if she won't touch the prize money." She hasn't spent a penny of it since she returned from Exuma, now that I think about it.

"What?" His entire face screws up.

"Don't ask. She wouldn't discuss it." I hug my knees. "So don't get your hopes up about the condo, that's all."

His expression cycles from surprise to annoyance to determination with kaleidoscopic speed. "She'll spend it eventually. And a condo means she won't have to deal with the yard or roof or any of that. It's a good solution."

"It certainly benefits you." I regret my derisive tone, but it's too late. I've hurt him, possibly because he hurt my feelings, or because I don't want him to hurt Amy's. Either way, it's proof that my sister is not helping my marriage.

"I'd think she'd be happy to do something that benefits us." He stares at me, waiting for the volley. Of course that would be nice, but relationships shouldn't be a series of quid pro quo transactions. "Your reluctance to let her go makes me wonder if you keep her here to avoid being alone with our family."

"You can't honestly believe that." But his comment touches a little too close to something in my heart. Sometimes I want to escape—just for a week or two . . . or three.

He stretches his arms wide, slouching deeper into the pillows. "Okay, then let's plan a family vacation after Easter—just us. The Caribbean. Sun, sand, rum punch." When he smiles, the familiar tug of his warm gaze hooks me.

I slip beneath the blanket and roll onto my side, facing him.

"That'd leave Amy alone on the anniversary of the accident." The timing feels heartless, yet we could use a vacation. The Caribbean, however, triggers thoughts of Sean and Scotty and the horrible explosion.

Tony rolls toward me. "Your parents can come stay here to be with her while we're away."

Tony rarely pleads. He really needs this. We all do, frankly. If only I could feel excited by the idea instead of anxious and exhausted from negotiating everything in my life. "I can't take my eye off the ball at work if I want to make partner this year."

He reaches forward and touches my cheek, which stirs my blood to life a little. "Krissy, it'll be good to be just us again. We'll choose a place that has activities for the kids too. It's time."

I smile, transported back a dozen years, when planning our honeymoon. Then reality crashes on the shores of my mind. "My deal's closing date could get pushed past March now."

His brows furrow. "You need to draw some boundaries at work."

"Mm." I grunt. I can't draw boundaries when gunning for equity partnership. Or when my salary makes our lifestyle possible because Tony's income gets reinvested in new projects and illiquid assets. The deal we struck years ago to enjoy both an affluent lifestyle and also plan for retirement has become a bit of a devil's bargain. It's a little suffocating now that my end isn't turning out as I'd planned.

Undeterred, he says, "You deserve some time off—even a long weekend. Let's do it."

I hold back from shouting, *You're not hearing my concerns.* Maybe I'm not being fair either. Our family needs a reset. "Fine."

Tony smiles, stretching forward to give me a quick kiss. He hovers a second but seems to sense my preoccupation, so he rolls onto his back, grabs his iPad, and begins reading. I turn off my lamp and close my eyes, although I won't be falling asleep until I hear my sister come up the stairs.

CHAPTER THREE

AMY

The next morning

I slept soundly and woke with a sense of purpose. Knowing my days are numbered has ironically plugged me into life's energy. Everything seems heightened, from the scent of the house to the slant of the light. Each minute matters now in a way it never has before.

Last night in bed, I made a six-part plan—a checklist to earn my way to a defensible suicide. First, move out so I don't break my promise. Second, help my sister and her family embrace a "live now, not when" attitude before they waste another decade planning for a future that they aren't guaranteed. Third, make sure Kristin knows that my decision is in no way her fault. Fourth, help Livvy and Kristin strengthen their bond. Fifth, get rid of that cursed money in some way that doesn't doom the recipients to my fate. Sixth, make the most of each day between now and the anniversary of Sean's and Scotty's deaths in April—my personal D-Day.

The family is out of the house on their hike, so my apartment search can begin without my sister's "helpful" suggestions. Using Zillow, I found a cheap short-term unit available just over the

Stamford-Greenwich border, less than two miles up Shore Road. Close proximity will help me accomplish steps two through four of my plan.

In the kitchen, small cellophane-covered bowls of oatmeal, brown sugar, chopped pecans, and blueberries are set on the island next to a note from my sister estimating when they'll be home. Scotty hated oatmeal—a texture thing. Frozen waffles were his favorite. A dry, sweet, simple breakfast routine. I haven't toasted a single one since he died.

I set the cereal in the fridge and search for my sneakers, which aren't where I kicked them off last night. The human Roombas must've put them inside "my" cubby, along with my coat, knit cap, and mittens.

Once outside, the winter chill needles the skin on my face, offering an invigorating jolt. I zip up my coat and begin the stroll to the rental unit. The faint hint of seawater permeates the cold air. I meander around the miniature picket fences placed in the narrow lane to slow cars. The barren trees' branches stretch overhead like gnarled fingers. My favorite homes are the classic older Capes that haven't been remodeled.

Decades ago, this quiet community was filled with antique Asian rugs, heirloom silver, and tactful families secure in their generational wealth. I'd envied the kids whose lives looked more like a fantasy than a reality—carefree, beautiful, limitless yet lacking the showiness common today. More recently, ambitious young couples from around the globe have moved in, renovating and expanding the homes to make room for their three kids, two dogs, nanny, and the foreign SUVs that transport them everywhere. Acquisitiveness like that—once a dream—now makes me cringe.

A few houses up the road, Petra Galway, whose son is Luca's age, is outside scrolling through her phone while her black labradoodle searches for an ideal patch of grass to christen. I envy his simple dilemma.

Petra looks up and flashes a sympathetic smile that makes me feel pitiful. "Good morning, Amy. How are you?"

I slow down to be polite. "Good, thanks. You?"

"Busy as ever. Gymnastics practice, ballet lessons, walking the dog, a grocery run because the in-laws are coming for dinner."

I nod. Once upon a time my days were an endless series of colorful to-do lists. We broke each one into fifteen-minute segments because Scotty did better with a set routine. Everything from brushing teeth to naps and cleanup followed a sequence. We even covered his door with a series of photos depicting the activities so he could easily follow along. I squeezed in grocery shopping and cooking, therapy visits, housework, and other activities needed to build "a life" while Sean went to work.

"Sometimes I feel like running away," Petra says, probably referring to the pressure of providing her kids with every opportunity. Then she remembers who she's talking to. "Oh, I mean, well, you know. I'm not serious, just a little tired."

She's hardly the only parent caught in the chaos of chasing down myriad goals, often missing the beauty in the simplicity of togetherness. In turning off the noise and staring deeply into the eyes of a child you are tickling.

I spent endless hours trying to cement that bond with Scotty, whose eye contact was transitory, no matter how many therapists and articles I consulted. When he became absorbed by some item or thought, he would close off tight as a quahog and ignore my presence. Although I knew to be patient and gentle, sometimes I'd blurt out my frustrations. *Scotty, just look at me!* Afterward I'd cry to Sean about being a bad mother. Sean rarely lost his patience with Scotty, possibly because he spent much less time with him than I did. He'd also never had starry-eyed expectations of parenthood like I had, so he was less frustrated by the reality. Why did I struggle to embrace Scotty exactly as he was? To cherish his differences instead of focusing on managing them?

"Well, good luck, Petra." I smile politely and keep walking, pulling the hood up over my head as if it's a shield against darker thoughts.

Twenty minutes later, I'm standing at the end of the driveway that is home to the dingy butter-yellow rear rental unit. A far cry from my current digs, but more in keeping with my ultimate goal. The street is dotted with reasonably well-maintained small ranch homes and duplexes, except for one unkempt yard two doors down. It's quiet, too, despite being close to Fairfield Avenue. I ring the doorbell of the main house, but no one answers. Perhaps they're at morning services.

I wander down the driveway to the rear unit and step up to peer through the slats in the blinds of the living room window. It doesn't look any better in person than it did in the photographs, not that I care.

A car pulls into the driveway while I'm peeping. I freeze, worried the owner carries a gun. Planning my own death doesn't mean I want to be taken out by a hothead with a pistol. I raise my hands and turn around, offering a friendly wave.

An elderly man exits the car. Bowlegged in baggy navy pants, he squints at me, his broad forehead gleaming in the sunlight. I can't help but smile.

"Can I help you, miss?"

"Hi. I'm Amy Walsh. I found this rental online and sent a note through Zillow this morning, then decided to come take a peek. I walked over. Sorry about trespassing. I rang your doorbell first." I stop blathering, a nervous tic.

He nods, waving off the apology. "It's fine. Do you want to see inside?"

"What gave me away?" I tease. "But I don't want to impose or keep you from anything."

He reminds me of my late grandfather—short, thin, with a dimpled chin and pleasant manner. Pap always called me "turtle" because I dillydallied, but he said it with affection, so I never minded.

"Oh gosh, I'm happy for any company. At my age, there ain't much on the calendar. I'm Bob, by the way. Bob Barton."

"Nice to meet you, Bob." We shake hands. He seems kind—a decent sort of landlord. There's unlikely to be a pack of kids running around the yard or late-night teen parties. "I'll wait here while you grab the keys."

He nods, turning to open the back door to his home, into which he disappears for a moment. I hug myself for warmth while looking around the yard. It could use a little sprucing up—a flower bed or some potted plants. Yard work was my thing before Scotty was born, but now that hobby seems like part of some other lifetime. In a way it was. Maybe I'll do some planting here as something nice to be remembered by. It's important to use the rest of my days to create good memories with everyone I'll be leaving behind.

Bob returns, shaking the keys in his hand. "Now, it's not much to look at, but it's clean and safe."

"That's all I need." I follow him inside.

"The bathroom's the original stuff, but my son updated the kitchen appliances a few years ago, so those are a little nicer." He sounds apologetic, but if it were better appointed, the rent would be too high, so he needn't worry. If anything, I should be apologizing to him. When I imagine Bob finding me, I turn away and feign interest in the kitchen.

It's not the professional-grade equipment in Kristin's house or even the midlevel grade in my old home, but it's clean and it works. I'm no Martha Stewart planning fancy parties. "Looks good to me. I assume I could move in anytime?"

"I need to do a background check first." He looks at me sheepishly. "Nothing personal, but my daughter insists."

"Good daughter." I grin, picturing this man's family. Envy of his long life with them sets in quickly. I'll never get that back, but I might reunite with mine in death.

"I also need a W-2." He flashes another apologetic smile.

"Oh, I haven't worked in a couple of years." I quit my job as a staff reporter for the *Stamford Advocate* when we got Scotty's diagnosis. Our son needed extra support, so we decided one of us should be available twenty-four seven. Sean's job as a media-planning supervisor paid a little more than mine did, so I stayed at home. That led to different issues, beginning with an inaccurate budget stemming from inexperience with the costs associated with neurodiverse therapies. I also didn't realize how I'd miss interacting with adults on a regular basis. Before the changes, Sean and I had rarely argued, but the pressure of mounting debt and my loneliness proved harder than we expected. That's what drove me to buy those damn lottery tickets. Now I'm loaded and couldn't care less. I say to Bob, "I can pay in full up front. Would you consider a short-term lease?"

"How short?"

Good question. I doubt he'll go for less than six months, even though I only need three. A month-to-month arrangement would make Kristin suspicious, and if she's suspicious, I'll never accomplish steps two through four. "Six months?"

His wise gaze seems to see the mixture of sorrow and desperation I'm trying to hide. "I can do that."

Phew. "Let me write down my number. You can call me once you've done your research. Meanwhile, if you have a lease, my sister—a lawyer—will probably insist on reviewing it before I sign it."

Step one is done. There's plenty of work ahead to pull this off well.

"Oh sure. I can email a draft to you, and then I'll call you later this week."

"Deal." In a twisted way, being in motion after being stuck for so long feels like progress. If I'd been able to feel something—anything—more consistently this past year, maybe I wouldn't need this plan. But I'm at peace now, or will be once I check all the boxes.

———

On my way back to Kristin's, I detour through town to pick up something for Luca and Livvy—a little gift for when I break the news about leaving. Luca will be fine, but Livvy's become especially attached. My constant presence has weakened her relationship with her mother. More reason to get out of there.

I duck into Chillybear to pick up a LEGO set for Luca and an art kit for Livvy, then continue back to Sound Beach Avenue to finish my walk to Kristin's. After sticking my earbuds in, I am scrolling through Spotify while stepping off the sidewalk to cross the street when suddenly I'm yanked backward. My weight throws the teenager who grabbed me off balance. We both tumble onto the sidewalk while some maniac in a Porsche Cayenne flies past, honking.

"You okay?" The boy—probably fifteen—is picking up his Upper Crust Bagel Company bag, which is now smushed.

"Yes, thanks." I roll onto my knees, trembling, and grab for the Chillybear haul, my pulse thudding in my ears. Adrenaline floods my body until my veins hum. It feels so damn good—the life force and the brightness of everything as my heart pounds hard in my chest. It's the most alive I've felt in recent memory.

"You shouldn't look at your phone when you're crossing the street," he says, like some Boy Scout. Hell, he's probably an Eagle Scout, polishing up his college-application résumé by doing good deeds.

"I'll be more careful." Then again, no one should be driving through this family neighborhood at that speed either. "Thank you again. Have a good day."

I'm slightly shaken as I resume the walk home, conflicted by the thrill of the near miss—that knife's edge between life and death—that continues to thrum. By the awareness that life is precious and unpredictable. If I carry out my plan, there'll be no second chances.

Some remnant of my former self goes to war in my head—take a step, go to sleep, laugh about anything, cry, try harder, just give up. When I took that razor to my wrists, it was a dark, spontaneous urge after a morning spent poring over old photographs that brought back the joys of Scotty's infancy: the cute outfits I'd dressed him in, and the precious feedings in the wee hours, when I'd whispered all my dreams for him in his ear. The loss of our future together had become unbearable that day. Planning a suicide when I know it will devastate my family is even more selfish than that first attempt, and yet is it any less selfish of them to expect me to suffer indefinitely simply to spare themselves a period of grief?

I can't think about that. I'd rather think about how to best live out these months in a way that will make me feel as alive as I just did. Perhaps seeking thrills—taking bigger risks—can also be part of my plan to help Kristin enjoy her life more. My stride elongates as these thoughts churn. Skydiving's got to be electrifying. Anything *could* happen. That's the thrill. Plus, hello—flying through the clouds like a bird!

I pull out my phone again, although this time I'm careful to stay on the sidewalk. A training outfit up the Hudson past West Point has good ratings.

Why didn't this come to me sooner? I'll have to make a list of potential big adventures. Bungee, free-climbing, race cars . . .

When I finally return to Kristin's, I enter through the garage, kick off my shoes, and hang my coat in the cubby.

"Amy?" Kristin's panicked voice calls from the family room. "Is that you?"

"Nope, it's a cat burglar casing the joint." I toss the mittens and cap on the cubby bench and make my way to the kitchen, where my sister rushes over to me with no humor in her eyes.

"Where have you been?" She's pale, and I doubt the cold hike is the cause. I recognize that face from middle school, after she lost track of me at the Westchester mall for about thirty minutes. I realize now that she hadn't overreacted back then, but this right here—total overreaction.

Of course, I could be wrong. "Did something happen on the hike?"

"No, but you didn't return my call."

"Sorry. I didn't notice. The ringer is off." No point in having it on when I haven't been in the mood to talk to people. I've got dozens of unread email and voice mail notifications, so one or two more don't register.

Kristin crosses her arms, looking tired. "You could've left a note."

"Didn't realize I had to report my comings and goings, Warden." Our exchange erases any doubt about my decision to move out. I set the bag on the island.

"That's not fair. I had no idea what happened . . ." Her haunted expression broadcasts what goes unsaid—she thought I'd broken my promise. She'll never forget that day, and after this April maybe she'll never forgive me. That possibility makes me a little sick, as well as more determined to find some way to ease it for her.

"Well, I almost got hit by a car in town. Some kid pulled me back, but the near miss is more reason not to spend time worrying about the future at the expense of enjoying the present."

Ignoring my point, Kristin widens her eyes as she moves into my personal space. "Are you hurt?"

"Krissy," Tony says, interrupting from the sofa as he peeks out from behind his iPad. "Maybe give your sister some breathing room."

"Fine." Kristin closes her eyes, her cheeks turning scarlet. A second later, she asks, "What were you doing in town?"

I head for the comfy chair near the fireplace. "I went to look at an apartment, and then I picked up little gifts for the kids."

Kristin follows me to the family room, where she perches on the edge of the sofa cushion beside Tony. "You found a place already?"

"Yes, on Zillow."

"I didn't realize you were so desperate to leave." She looks hurt.

"It's not personal." When she harrumphs, I add, "I can't move forward as long as I'm using your family to avoid the absence of my own." Technically, this is true, even if she mistakes my "moving forward" to mean something else.

"And you'd rather rent something than return to your house?"

"Too many memories there." The good ones make me cry. Bad ones do too. Devoid of human energy, those rooms smell like sorrow, possibly from all the tears I cried last spring.

Tony, who has been quietly listening, says, "I've got brand-new state-of-the-art town houses within a stone's throw. I can walk you through one later if you'd like. They're beautiful, and they'd be low maintenance."

Kristin tosses him a hard look.

"I'm not ready to buy something either. Sorry," I answer, hoping my avoiding permanence isn't transparent even as I regret lying to them.

"A six-month lease lets me find my equilibrium before making any big commitments."

Tony's pleasant smile briefly slips, revealing disappointment and maybe a little resentment. It would be kind to buy one of his units, especially after I bailed on the sensory-friendly home he was planning for us after we struck the jackpot, but it's not like these two need the money.

"Well," he says, "I hate to see you miss out on something convenient and affordable."

I tense at the reference to my wealth. That bank balance feels toxic compared with those first couple of weeks last year, when Sean and I were surfing the tidal wave of excitement from the win. We went from scraping by and fretting about Scotty's long-term needs to knowing we could secure the best therapies and discussing a trust fund. No more worries. No more having to sit on the sidelines and watch others have everything they needed or wanted while we went without. Sean hired a lawyer to explore starting his own PR firm so he could quit working for the one he didn't particularly like. For those two months before our trip, everything seemed possible. Even his parents, who'd often criticized us about my quitting, stopped butting in.

Life was grand until I received a violent reminder that people, family, and love were the only treasures worth anything.

"I told Kristin I'm not touching that prize money."

"You'll change your mind eventually." Tony holds my gaze, confident as ever in his opinions. Of course he'd think that, because Tony's flaw—his only true flaw that I'm aware of—is his obsession with wealth building.

"No. I'll never be happy in a gorgeous home that Sean and Scotty can never enjoy. No designer belt or foreign car or diamond necklace will ever be worth what it actually cost me." My body turns red hot, but I take a breath to avoid an argument.

My sister's shoulders fall. In her softest voice, she says, "I doubt Sean and Scotty would want you to spend the rest of your life blaming yourself for what happened. It was a horrible accident, Amy. Not some punishment."

I shrug, having heard a version of this pep talk more than once. She doesn't get it, and I can only hope she never has a regret as big as mine.

A quick glance at Tony tells me his wheels are spinning. He'd probably love to get his hands on that money to invest in his business so he could build more gigantic houses that nobody really needs. I might give him all of it if I weren't worried his desire for it would bring this family the same bad luck it brought mine. Not that I'll go off on that tangent. My superstitions only add credence to the mental instability they already suspect.

"It's your choice." He smiles at me. "Of course, if you change your mind, just say the word."

Whether he means that or is saying it for Kristin's benefit doesn't matter. Allowing me the right to choose is enough. I exhale to expel all remaining stress created by this conversation. "Speaking of choices, I'm going skydiving, and I want you to come with me."

"What?" Kristin's visible alarm is almost comical. Tony's brows shoot up, but he doesn't offer an opinion.

"The adrenaline rush will be a hoot."

Tony scratches his head, while my sister sputters, "Do we have to do something dangerous?"

To get an adrenaline rush we do. "How often do you hear of skydiving accidents?"

"Seldom isn't never," she says.

"Krissy." Tony lays a hand on her forearm to get her to take a breath. Upstairs in the playroom, the kids start arguing about something. "I'll deal with them," he says.

"Maybe bring them down so we can tell them my plans together and I can give them the little gifts," I call to him.

He jogs off. In no time at all, the kids stop squabbling—a fact Kristin's face registers with some dissatisfaction. Luca and Livvy tend to walk all over her because she's a softie. Sure, she's a nudge, always on them about the little things, but at the end of the day, she comes behind us all, fixing our mistakes and problems without complaining, mostly because she does everything better and faster.

"Please come with me," I say. "I found a place on the Hudson with great ratings."

She bites her lip. "I've got so much on my plate with work."

"Why does your job always take priority over your life? I don't get it." I feel myself frowning.

"You know how much time I've put in. I've earned that partnership and can't let up when I'm so close."

"Isn't your happiness and your family's happiness more important than that old goal?"

Tension appears to grip her as she twists her neck around. "Of course my family is important, but I'm more than a mother and a wife. Having something of my own matters to me, so some of my happiness is tied to my personal goals. The more power I have in my career, the more I can promote other women. Walking away now would make everything I've sacrificed to date a total waste."

I can relate a little because some days I felt like a half self after I stopped working. "Well, I'll miss you all after I move out, so I'd really love for us to do fun things together." I'd feel bad about guilting her if this weren't urgent and important.

I can tell she's mentally weighing all the variables.

"I'll think about it. Depends on when you do it and if I can stomach it. Honestly . . . that's scary." She folds her arms across her chest.

"That's the point. Imagine the memory we'll share." I need to create enough of them to last her lifetime.

"I said I'll think about it." She tips her head to the left. "Listen, I want to apologize about yesterday—about questioning your plans for the party. You were right. It was meaningful for us all to mark the day. And you seem happier today, so maybe—as bittersweet as it was—it was a good turning point for you."

I nod but avert my gaze.

"Now, about the move. Are you sure?" She squints as if she can will her vision to see my thoughts.

I move to sit beside her, twining my fingers through hers and squeezing tight. "I'm so grateful to you guys. Honestly. Nobody could've been more loving and generous, but we both know it's time."

She lays her free hand over our clasped ones. "You're always welcome back. No matter what, okay? Day or night."

"Thank you." I grab her into a hug because she deserves that and more, and because I worry she doesn't get enough hugs in her life. Ironic, coming from me—the one without a spouse or children. The older she gets, the more Kristin holds herself apart, more observer than participant, always "on duty" in case she needs to jump in and take care of something or someone. It's not an exaggeration to say that I probably wouldn't still be alive if she weren't that person. I'm not sure how to feel about that, but I am grateful to be so well loved. Not everyone has even that much in life.

This is exactly why I must make sure she knows that nothing she did or failed to do—although, frankly, she didn't fail to do anything—is the cause of my decisions.

CHAPTER FOUR

KRISTIN

The following Sunday

"What do you want me to do?" I ask my mother. The phone is pressed to my ear while I stare out the bathroom window at Tony and the U-Haul in the driveway. He's been a good sport, pitching in all week helping Amy organize and manage the move. "She says she's ready."

"But is she?"

I close my eyes and drop the blind. "If you've figured out how to read minds, let me know. Otherwise, I can only go by what she says."

"Don't get testy, Kristin. I'm worried about your sister." She's always been worried about Amy for one reason or another—her mediocre high school grades, her getting engaged within a few months of meeting Sean, her lack of discipline and how that might impede her ability to manage Scotty's therapies.

I never wanted to cause others to worry, but maybe I miscalculated. When no one ever worries about you, it's easy to feel neglected.

"So am I, but she's been doing better. She called a real estate broker to sell her house without breaking down." In truth, Amy sounded oddly detached during that conversation, which I overheard on our way to her house three nights ago to help her sort, tag, and donate furniture. She was mechanical about those decisions, as if determined not to fall apart. "And look at how well she handled Scotty's birthday." Some heaviness at the end of that day was to be expected, given the circumstances.

"But the anniversary is on the horizon. Should she be alone for that?"

This reminds me of Tony's plea to plan a mini-vacation—something we need despite the poor timing. "She doesn't have to be alone. You and Dad could come visit that week and stay at my house."

"I would like to see the kids." A refrain I hear often despite her infrequent visits.

There's no way to avoid disappointing her, so I might as well get it over with. "We'll probably be away for a few days—nothing is set, though. We'd be here for at least part of your visit."

"You're going away when Amy is likely to need you?"

Amy, Amy, Amy. As if she's the only one who needs me—or the only one with needs.

"I'm synchronizing a lot of calendars, and I can't keep putting my family's life on hold while second-guessing her every move." I've done my best. Can't that be enough for once?

An uncomfortable pause in conversation ensues. "It isn't like you to be resentful. Are you and Tony fighting?"

I stiffen. "No, Mom. We're not 'fighting,' but we could use a break. My family has to come first sometimes."

"So Tony *is* pushing this." My mother's habit of blaming my husband for any friction between Amy and me started soon after my marriage.

It's true that our adult lives took different paths after my wedding, which seemed natural. Necessary, even, as I was investing time in my career and marriage, while Amy was getting started at the paper and hadn't yet met Sean. Tony and I also think more alike than my sister and I ever did, and even the closest sisters disagree on occasion. Just because I don't like watching Will Ferrell movies and she doesn't like to dissect Supreme Court decisions doesn't mean we don't love each other. Amy and I have always remained involved in each other's lives, and Tony has never interfered.

"I wouldn't go if I thought she was in danger, but moving out was Amy's idea. She wants space to get on her feet again. It seems like a good sign, and I won't undermine her recovery by questioning her every move."

Of course, the short-term lease gives me pause. Why only six months instead of a year?

"Well, I hope you're right." My mother's words land with that doubtful tone that always keeps me on my toes and striving. The one that will also accompany an "I told you so" if Mom turns out to be right. Not that I'd need her disapproval in order to feel guilty for the rest of my life.

Yet even now Mom doesn't ask how I've coped with the strain of juggling all my own obligations and caring for my sister. "Listen, I need to go. Tony's tossing Amy's suitcases in the truck now."

"Send some photos," Mom says before hanging up.

I grimace. Photos won't make her feel better. Even I'm troubled by Amy's choice of an apartment. Its drab walls and gray flooring could at best be described as sterile and at worst as a penitentiary. I can't believe she won't touch that prize money for her own comfort or to open new doors that might accelerate her healing.

I stuff my phone in my pocket, but not before reminders and texts pop up. Work, PTC fundraiser, carpool. Ugh. Someone is always waiting on me. My chest feels constricted. I close the toilet seat and sit, eyes closed, then breathe in and out, in and out, then eye the Adderall on the counter. The habit of getting gray-market pills from one of my colleagues, Jenna, started in November, when I hit a wall trying to manage all my responsibilities.

Down to a half bottle. I could text Jenna to ask if she can give me more. She's never said exactly where she gets them, and I've never asked—a weak sort of plausible deniability. At first, I thought it would be a onetime purchase, but months later, I can no longer pretend that to be true. My thumb hovers over the message. I close my eyes, having never imagined myself needing drugs to handle my life or keeping a secret from Tony. The little boost helps me get through the day, but maybe I should quit. Sighing, I delete the message. When this bottle is empty, that'll be the end of it.

Outside, the slam of the metal door to the U-Haul makes me jump. Ready or not, I've got to go. Refusing to overthink it, I pop one pill before leaving the bathroom and lumbering downstairs.

Livvy is crying in Amy's arms at the kitchen table. We predicted our daughter's meltdown and now foresee several weeks of backsliding.

I stand aside while my sister comforts my daughter. Livvy doesn't notice me wanting to be the one she turns to for reassurance. The glee of getting my daughter back to myself soon makes me feel as guilty as the fact that I took another pill.

"I'll be right down the street, pumpkin," Amy murmurs against Livvy's hair. "So close you might even be able to see me through Luca's telescope."

Livvy pouts, her cheeks damp. "But you won't be here."

"You can visit me whenever you want. In fact, let's plan a sleepover— just the two of us." Amy wipes Livvy's cheeks. "Come on, please stop crying, because I need your help. My apartment walls are bare, so could you paint some things for me? Maybe pictures of the ocean or flowers or whatever you want, and then we'll get frames and hang them together during the sleepover."

Livvy hiccups, appearing distracted by the idea of decorating Amy's new home. Our kids' art projects hang only in their playroom and bedrooms. It's never occurred to me to hang them elsewhere, which now seems wretched.

I'm expecting my daughter to describe what she plans to paint when she hits us with a non sequitur. "Will you get a cat and name her Gotcha?"

I muffle my laughter with one hand. Tony is allergic to cats, and I don't have the bandwidth for a dog, so she's trying another angle.

"Gotcha? That's unique." Amy grins, her brows climbing high in surprise. "I'm not sure. A pet is a lot of responsibility."

Exactly, although a furry companion would give her something to love that would love her back. "Cats are easier than dogs," I add.

My sister eyes me askance, so I raise my hands in surrender.

"I'll help," Livvy says. "My friend Carrie cleans her cat's litter box. I could do that."

I kind of love that Livvy can be relentless in her pursuit of a goal, and that she offers solutions for each objection, even if we all know she's unlikely to follow through. If anyone could talk Amy into a pet, it's my daughter.

"Let me think about it. In the meantime, paint me some pictures, okay?" Amy gives Livvy another big hug. "Now I need to go set up my new house. You can come visit tomorrow after school."

"Okay." She slides off Amy's lap. "I like fluffy white cats with blue eyes."

"*If* I get one, we'll go to the rescue center together and pick one that needs a home, so I can't promise what it will look like."

The fact that she's considering this is a good sign. A fifteen-year commitment. I'll have to text Mom later.

Livvy wrinkles her nose. "Okay."

Amy pokes Livvy's tummy. "You drive a hard bargain."

My sister is so good with kids. I pray she gets a second chance at motherhood.

Outside, Tony honks twice.

"We really should go." I cut short any further demands from my daughter as I kiss her head. "Mommy will be home in a while. Maybe you can cook dinner with Daddy tonight. I think he's making chicken saltimbocca, so he'll need someone to help."

"Yum!"

Yum is right. Tony wooed me with his kitchen skills. He was passionate about everything from which markets had the best ingredients to the plating of a meal. In the early days, he tried to teach me— explaining the virtues of *guanciale* or anchovy paste mixed into a quick pan sauce, the importance of clarifying butter, and the balance of seasonings to bring out different notes in the meal. When he realized that my interest in eating far surpassed my interest in cooking, he then used food as foreplay, smearing something on his finger for me to suckle, or across my lips for him to then kiss. Ah, the ease and spontaneity of the "before kids" days.

As Livvy skips off, I call, "Where are you going?"

"To paint."

"Don't make a mess." But she's already up the stairs.

Amy glances around as if beset by both good and uneasy memories of her life here with us. She releases a breath, fluttering her lips. "Let's roll."

"Did Brittany show up yet?" She's a neighborhood teen we hire on the weekends for date nights and other one-offs.

"She's in the den playing video games with Luca."

Luca, my easy child. I suck in a breath when it hits me that, like my mom, I worry more about one child than another. Another honk makes me start.

"Tony's getting impatient." Amy's voice pulls me from that thought. She gestures toward the mudroom, so I follow.

Ninety minutes later, we've unloaded Amy's paltry furnishings into one of the area's most depressing apartments. Worse, she's made almost no attempt to make it homey. So far, she's only set out one photo of Sean and Scotty. She wouldn't even bring her and Sean's old bed, opting instead to bring one from her old guest room. I haven't asked how she's coping, because she's made it clear that she wants to make her own decisions without me taking her temperature. It's hard, though—not knowing whether she's really recovering or just fooling herself and heading for a meltdown.

How am I to leave her here, with its small windows, blank walls, and cold surfaces? Hopefully she can't see my aversion to this place. It needs something to warm it up. She asked Livvy for artwork. Perhaps I'll have a painting made from a photograph of her family as a keepsake.

"Thanks, guys," she says, collapsing onto the sofa, her body splayed across the cushions. "That went pretty smoothly . . . and quick."

"You hardly kept anything," Tony reminds her. His wavy hair is a little damp in the front, which gives him a boyish look that reminds me of the early days, when I only fantasized that he could be mine.

"Other families will enjoy the things I donated." Amy smiles.

True. And if she does upgrade her residence when this lease ends, she can choose lovely new furnishings that aren't coated with old memories. A new chapter, one that apparently includes skydiving. I did agree to go with her, God save me. It'll be worth it if it helps her get her mojo back.

"Do you want to have dinner with us?" Tony asks. "I've got plenty of chicken."

"I'll probably regret this later, but I'm going to pass." She scrunches her nose. When we hesitate, she adds, "Go enjoy yourselves. Really, you've been more than wonderful to me, guys—but I'm looking forward to some alone time, and I bet you are too."

Her breezy tone falls a little flat, but I don't push the way I might if we were alone.

I do, however, wait for her to catch my gaze. "I'm glad you feel good, Amy. But if you get lonely, just come over or move back, day or night. Promise?"

She salutes me like I'm a dictator. "Promise."

Her attitude stings, but I don't want to part on a sour note.

"Give me a hug, and then we'll get out of your hair." I motion for her to stand. When she does, I give her an extra squeeze, suddenly wistful.

Managing her recovery has been all consuming, but amid the sorrow, we've collected a handful of lighter moments these past several months, from the November day we lay in her bed binge-watching and picking apart old episodes of *Sex and the City*, to the time we sat on a bench at Tod's Point right before New Year's.

Clad in knit caps and mittens, clasping Yeti mugs of coffee, we huddled together as we looked across an expanse of gray skies and grayer water. Although freezing, I wouldn't budge because Amy seemed preternaturally calm.

"The water looks frigid." I sipped my coffee, its warmth spreading through my chest.

"Like Maine." Her gaze was as far away as the tips of the Manhattan skyline. "Remember how cold Echo Lake was, even in July?"

Suddenly I was twelve and gliding across that lake on a Sunfish. "I haven't thought about Camp Laurel in ages."

Amy's expression turned mischievous. "How could you forget Kelly MacPherson wetting the bed every single night?"

I chuckled. The poor girl had to strip the sheets every morning. "Counselor Fran was so sour."

"She of the bad breath!" Amy looked at me. "Remember the Altoids I left on her pillow? She never took the hint."

The reminder made me squeeze my sister's arm while snickering. "Oh God, you were terrible."

"I was trying to spare us all 'death by breath.'" She cast her gaze back to sea. "Then there was Timmy Layton. We were always dodging his boogers."

We both burst out laughing.

I could picture him at the picnic tables, his scrawny index finger digging way up into his nose before he'd roll the booger and flick it away. "You have a great memory."

Amy's laughter faded. "That's part of my problem."

The truth is that I'll miss Amy's daily black humor and her extra hand keeping the kids on track. I also hate the idea of leaving her here in this box. Sean used to tease me at family gatherings—holidays, birthdays, random dinners—because while most would be enjoying a drink and joking, I would keep busy making sure things ran smoothly or checking in on someone at the periphery of the group. *We'd all be lost if you weren't around to keep us in line, Kristin.* I know he'd expect me to do more to help his wife get over her guilt. "You know Livvy will insist on visiting tomorrow, so maybe you can pick her up at school?"

"Of course."

Tony has subtly moved closer to the door, so I take the hint. "Great. Call me if you need anything. Love you."

"Love you too." She waves us both off as Tony says goodbye.

My husband remains silent until we're safely in the car. "God, why did she pick that place? I mean, fine if she doesn't want one of my condos, but there are dozens of options between what I've built and that concrete cell."

He looks out the side mirror as he backs out of the driveway.

"Obviously she's still punishing herself for surviving." Although illogical, I do empathize. I'd blame myself, too, given the whole spa-day thing. Not that it was her fault. Of course not. But it would be difficult not to feel some survivor's guilt about that. And I don't even want to imagine my life without my children and Tony. "At least this is clean and close by, and the landlord seems like the kind who'll keep an eye out for her." Bob did seem eager to befriend his new tenant, bringing us all cookies. "It's a start. Let's see what spring and summer bring. Once we get past the anniversary of the accident, she might reconsider things."

"She needs a purpose, Kristin." He looks at me, one brow arched. "She should try to get her old job back or something."

I nod, glancing out the window at the homes on the street. I'm not sure any job would make her "feel alive" or miss Sean and Scotty less. Sean was goofy and gentle. They laughed so often when they first met; I sometimes felt jealous that she and I didn't as much. Sean got her—from the way she had fun putting Mom on the spot, to her need to junk up their garden with gnomes and fountains and twinkle lights, to her refusal to commit to plans until the very last minute. It's cruel that their love story got cut short. "Maybe you're right."

"Can I have that in writing?" he teases, bestowing his most charming smile, which never fails to warm all my cool spaces.

I reach across to squeeze his arm. "Ha ha."

It hits me that maybe there's more to his little joke. Has he been feeling unappreciated? Have I been dismissive and using Amy as an excuse?

"In all seriousness, I'm looking forward to having our home back to ourselves." His suggestive lilt means he's expecting celebratory sex tonight. I hope I'm in the mood by then. I often crash when the Adderall wears off.

"Me too." I reach for his enthusiasm, but I can't stop thinking about my sister huddled alone on an old sofa a few blocks behind us.

"Hon, it's going to be okay."

I nod despite nagging doubts.

My phone pings for the fifty millionth time today. This one is from Jim Hartwell, the partner heading up the Baxter deal.

Conference call today at 4:30 with Sal Aiello about the bank warranties and this potential liability. Check email for Zoom link. Pls provide me with any new ideas or info uncovered beforehand.

Work on a Sunday—everybody's dream. As Baxter's CFO, Sal is likely to be particularly unhappy with the recent lawsuit against the company that could not only screw up the merger with Avant but also create problems with Baxter's existing loans.

Pressure builds at the base of my skull, but my little helper will keep me focused awhile longer.

"Everything okay?" Tony eyes me askance.

"I can't catch a break." I turn the phone over on my lap and swallow. My brain literally hurts, but I don't want to break down.

"What's wrong?"

"Work stuff. I'm just . . . tired." Without warning, tears begin to well. For snapping at my mom. For leaving Amy to her own devices. For the years of underappreciated dedication to the law firm. For sneaking the pills. For all the hours I miss with my kids. I try to stanch the flow before Tony notices, but I'm too slow.

"Aw, babe. Let it out. Relieve the stress, and then you'll figure out a solution, like always. I know it." He smiles reassuringly, oblivious that his confidence enhances the relentless pressure I feel to hold myself and everything in my orbit together.

What would happen if I fell apart and let someone else pick up the pieces?

Please, God, don't let that happen today at 4:30 p.m.

———

I finally join my family at the dinner table at 6:30 p.m. after a shitty two-hour conference call. My first big deal of the year could very well fall apart, pushing partnership further away. The meal smells delicious, although boiling stomach acids killed my appetite thirty minutes ago. Still, Livvy is beaming, sitting on her heels, eager for me to taste her work.

"Honey, feet below the seat," I say, then regret my impatience. It's not her fault that I'm miserable.

Naturally she doesn't heed me. Instead, she rises on her knees and points at the tray of chicken in the middle of the table. "But Mommy, I pounded the chicken with the hammer."

"Tenderizer," Tony reminds her, pushing the salad bowl toward me.

"Uh-huh." She barely takes a breath before adding, "We used waxy paper to catch all those bacterias." She looks at her dad for affirmation that she's described it right—or mostly right. I want to warn her that her approval-seeking trait won't always lead to happy places.

Tony smiles while motioning for her to sit properly, which she finally does. "You're an excellent sous chef, Livvy." When he winks at her, her grin widens. "Now let's eat."

Luca is our picky eater, preferring plain foods that don't touch each other, so saltimbocca is not drawing any enthusiasm from his end of the table. "I'm not hungry."

Tony's expression fills with banked irritation. "Fine," he says evenly. "Sit with us now. You can reheat yours later."

Luca shoves the plate away and crosses his arms. "Why do you cook stuff you know I don't like?"

"We can't survive on pizza, burgers, and fries. You need to vary your diet." Unfazed, Tony cuts into his chicken and takes his first bite with his eyes closed, as if he's concentrating on the blend of seasonings and flavor to see if he struck the right balance of sage and marsala wine. A sharp nod proves he's satisfied.

Livvy digs in, doubly excited to eat a meal that she helped prepare.

I eye Luca, worried yet understanding Tony's stance. Seeking a way out of the standoff, I try to entice Luca. Although these meds kill my appetite, I take a mouthful. "Mmm, this is fantastic. Cheesy and salty, like pizza but better. Luca, why don't you give it a try?"

Luca remains mute, shaking his head. I'm no more effective here than I was on that work call. My gaze flicks to Amy's empty seat. How is she faring? I catch myself and shut down that line of thought, aiming to stay present with my own family for thirty minutes.

We eat in relative silence, which makes me miss my sister more. She had a gift for getting the kids to laugh. I love my kids fiercely and would do anything to protect and help them, but I've never possessed the easy playfulness that helps them bloom. When I try, it comes off stilted, almost worse than if I remain true to my strengths. Sometimes I worry that my way of loving isn't what's best for them, yet I can't magically change into someone else. I'd like to think that I have something to offer by being myself.

It's a problem with life in general—the uncertainty of everything. I didn't used to notice. I used to be sure. Study hard and get good grades. Run daily and stay fit. Work hard and get promoted. Only recently have I realized that those rubrics aren't absolute. Sometimes you can work as hard as humanly possible and still not get promoted, or even get your kids to respect what you say.

"Is everyone's homework done? We want to start the school week off right," Tony says, eyeing both kids.

Livvy nods.

"I'll do it now." Luca starts to push back from the table without taking a single bite of his dinner, but Tony holds up a hand.

"No. You'll wait until the family is finished eating. And if you choose not to eat, there won't be any snacks later." He nudges Luca's plate back toward our son. "Meanwhile, procrastination is a bad habit. If you'd done it on Friday, it wouldn't be hanging over your head tonight."

Luca looks miserable, so I blurt, "Daddy makes a good point, but as long as you get it done on time, it's okay. We all need a break once in a while."

"But when you wait until the last minute, there's less time to do your best work." Tony sends me a look to signal he'd like the conversation to end here.

I eye him back. "Doing one's best is the most rewarding, but some days simply completing something *is* one's best, and that's okay too." I slide my gaze from Tony to Luca, who smiles at me. It's the very best feeling I've had all day. Again, tears build behind my eyes. I've never been so weepy.

Tony must notice because he doesn't prolong the debate.

At least, not in front of the kids.

My temples begin to throb. My deal will now require longer hours at the office at the worst possible time, given Amy's absence. Sure, we have Madeline, the after-school nanny, but it's not the same. Livvy has been less anxious at school this year thanks to my sister's daily attention. She's not clinging to her teacher or other girls like she did last year in kindergarten.

Tony sets his silverware on his plate when he finishes.

"Can I go now?" Luca asks.

Tony looks at Luca's untouched plate, but before he answers, I say, "Sure, bud. Wrap your plate and then you can go."

"Me too?" Livvy asks, and I nod.

Tony takes his time collecting things from the table, waiting for the kids to leave the kitchen. I begin rinsing the dishes and putting them in the dishwasher, gathering the will to stand my ground.

He comes up behind me and sets a stack in the sink. "Obviously you're having a day. Do you want to talk about it?"

I shake my head, too tired for this right now.

"Well, whatever's going on, let's not backslide on the way we've agreed to handle the kids. Once they think we're divided, it's over, Kristin. We need to be a unit."

I twirl around. "Fine, but you were riding Luca too hard. He's a great kid who mostly does what we ask. We can't expect perfection. It's not healthy."

"Teaching our kids to try their best isn't expecting perfection. It's about the effort, not the result."

Although I've always agreed, it's a technicality that will be lost on most kids. "Listen to me, Tony. I won't stand by and watch Luca turn into that kid who always does the right thing and never gets to mess up or, worse, who beats himself up if he isn't perfect. I know where that leads—the toll it takes—and I refuse to do that to him. It's okay for him not to like a meal, or to wait until Sunday to do his homework as long as, in general, he's doing his homework and eating well. That's it. That's the end of this discussion."

I stalk out of the kitchen and race up the stairs to lock myself in the bathroom. I've never been so dismissive to anyone, much less my own husband. I sit on the toilet, hugging my knees with my eyes closed.

Just breathe, Kristin.

Breathe.

CHAPTER FIVE

AMY

The following Saturday morning

Gravity tugs at my arms while I put the milk and cereal box away. My eyes itch too. Sharing my queen-size bed with Livvy—who twirled around wrestling the sheets all night—wrecked my sleep. In fairness, she wasn't the only thing keeping me up. Sean and Scotty visited me in my dreams again. I usually love when that happens, but not this time. They were playing at the water's edge on the beach in Exuma. When they saw me approaching, they started to walk away. The faster I ran toward them, the farther ahead they got. I called for them to wait, but Sean turned around and yelled, "Stay where you are!"

I woke up sweaty and heavyhearted, then stared into the darkness for hours, which explains why I'm moving like a thousand-pound sloth.

"Can I have more Fruity Pebbles?" Livvy asks, seated at the small dining table sandwiched between the kitchenette and the sofa. She's decked out in her Disney princesses nightgown, her dark curls darting in every direction, making it impossible not to forgive the little sprite for kicking me all night.

"Your mom will kill me if I give you more sugar." The garbage pail is already hiding the empty bag of Oreos from last night. Granted, I ate my fair share.

Livvy wrinkles her nose. "I won't tell."

A good role model wouldn't conspire in a lie of omission, but I'm not up for the lecture that would follow a confession today.

"Still a no. But we won't mention the cereal unless your mom asks what you ate for breakfast." A standard fun-aunt white lie.

I tweak Livvy's nose before taking her bowl from the table.

When she curled her warm little body against mine beneath the covers this morning, it triggered such longing. I nuzzled her, gently toying with her soft hair, wishing she were Scotty. How I'd loved those moments when he'd been contentedly sleepy and snuggly. No matter how much I love my sister's family and they love me, they are not mine. Livvy needs to start turning to her mother, and I need to wean off the opioid effect of her adoration. And yet it breaks me to imagine never hugging her again or, worse, to picture her missing me like I miss Scotty.

"We didn't get Gotcha." She sets her chin on her fists, not reading between the lines of my avoidance on this subject.

"I'm not sure I'll ever get a cat, honey. I'm still learning to take care of myself again, and I also don't know if my landlord allows pets."

Her mouth puckers into a pout. "Do you like this house?"

The space is clean and quiet. Bob is a lovely man, checking in on me to make sure the apartment is "up to snuff." He even brought me a giant slice of the chocolate cake that his daughter made this week. Best of all, he doesn't look at me as if I'm shattered. "I do."

"But you can't see the ocean. Just that driveway." She scowls, pointing toward the living room window.

I follow her gaze to the cracked concrete outside.

"That's a boring view, for sure." My old house didn't have an ocean view either—only one of our neighbors' yards, separated by a few old-growth trees and a rotting wood fence. I've listed the house with the broker who sold it to Sean and me. Other than the awkward moment when she asked about Sean and then learned the story, I haven't had regrets. After sorting through what to keep or toss—and palming Sean's unused bottle of Ambien from his nightstand drawer—I gave the broker a key. She's doing all the rest. She told me to expect multiple offers after the open house. One more box ticked. One less earthly possession tying me to a haunting past.

I smile at Livvy. "When it gets a little warmer, you can bring chalk over to decorate the driveway. But, honey, I don't need a pretty house or view. That's not what really makes a person happy."

Not that I'm an authority on that subject these days. I used to be grateful for simple things, like pizza Fridays, when Sean would grill a bunch of pizzas for neighborhood friends and I'd make a salad. We'd all hang out in the backyard with Mumford & Sons providing the soundtrack for our casual gathering. Scotty would be in the infant swing, and other toddlers would run around playing. By the end of the night, Sean and I would fall into bed sated in every way that possibly matters. That kind of lasting pleasure is beyond reach now that my family is gone.

Livvy screws up her face. "That's not what Daddy says, and he *builds* houses."

Guess I stepped right into that one. "He builds beautiful houses, and there's nothing wrong with liking something pretty. I'm only saying that I don't need that, and you don't either. The things that make you happy—a big hug, a great joke, or drawing something cool—can happen anywhere. Now hurry and get dressed. Your mom will be here soon, and we don't want to keep her waiting."

My shoulders bunch when her chair scrapes against the tile floor as Livvy slides off it. "She's always in a hurry."

I nod, then stop myself. Regardless of my opinions about how Kristin stretches herself too thin, she deserves her daughter's respect for the sleepless nights endured during Livvy's colicky stage, for the child-development books she reads in order to "master" motherhood, for the safe, stable homelife she's provided her children. "That's because she's so busy doing things to make sure you and your brother have everything your hearts desire."

"Except sugar." Livvy emphasizes the remark with a sardonic arch of one brow before she saunters off, and I can't help but chuckle. She's not mine, but those one-liners prove that some fraction of my DNA lives in her bones. Not a shabby legacy.

After pouring the milky rainbow down the drain, I set about destroying all evidence of neon crispies. One less lecture in my future.

Yawning, I wander into my bedroom, where Livvy is stuffing her pajamas into her duffel bag along with Bongo, her well-loved sock monkey. "All set?"

She zips the bag, but her shoulders slump. "I wanna stay here."

Proof that her beautiful house isn't her happy place. "You've got ballet in a little while."

She shrugs, huddled near her bag like an urchin.

I sit on the corner of the bed beside where she's kneeling. "Don't you like ballet?"

"It's okay." Her chin dips along with her voice.

I tip her head up with my fingers. On a hunch, I ask, "Is it the teacher or the other kids in the class who steal all the fun?"

Her wide-set walnut-brown eyes gaze at me while she weighs whether to be honest. "Mary Bowers and Cassidy Nolan laugh when I make a mistake."

Kids can be mean. It didn't shock me when Scotty got excluded on the playground, but other parents' discomfort or abject rudeness made it all so much worse.

"I'm sorry, sweet pea. It never feels good when people point out our mistakes, does it?" I remember that feeling well. Even when I was trying hard, an unspoken comparison with Kristin's many accomplishments loomed, invisible as carbon monoxide but just as noxious. "Is there anything you can do differently so they don't ruin the class for you?

Because I saw your last recital and think you did a fine job. And you're definitely the coolest ballerina on the stage."

That earns me a genuine smile. "Could I trip them?"

I shake my head. "If you do something hurtful on purpose, you'll feel even worse." I rub my chin like I'm thinking hard, giving her time to process that. "What if the next time they tease you, you take away their power by laughing with them? It's kinda fun to laugh at yourself. None of us does everything well all the time. When I mess up, that's what I do."

"Really?" She squints, clearly disbelieving.

"Ask your mom. In fact, I laugh so much because I mess up a lot." I ruffle her hair.

"You used to laugh more." Her clear-eyed solemnity leaves me speechless and blinking at her as if she were a blinding sun. Seconds pass before I collect myself.

"I still really miss your uncle Sean and Scotty." Unwittingly, my voice cracks. Welcome to my new normal—walking the tightrope between laughter and tears.

Livvy rises and throws her arms around me. "I'm sorry."

I squeeze her tight, taking in her scent and the power in her fierce embrace. "Thanks. Spending time with you always makes me feel better."

Another white lie, for anyone keeping track. Well, not fully a lie. It's just that the joy of my second-mom gig is glazed with streaks of heartache for what we are not. We are not mother and daughter. I didn't carry her in my womb and read to her so she'd recognize my voice when she was born. I didn't get up at night just to stare at her in the crib, overwhelmed by awe and love. I didn't fret over her fevers or get excited to see her dressed in a special outfit. I don't see Sean in the shape of her chin. And I will never have the final say in her life. That will always be Kristin and Tony—at least until Livvy is grown.

"Same." She releases me.

The doorbell rings.

"Your mom's here." I cinch my robe.

Livvy pouts and grabs her bag off the floor.

I crouch to meet her eye to eye. "Promise you'll laugh in ballet class."

"Okay."

Satisfied, I rise and jog ahead of her, expecting Kristin to hustle Livvy to the car. Instead, I open the door to find my sister balancing a rolled carpet against her body.

"Good morning." She greets us with the overly bright smile she's used for months, as if bestowing it will somehow refill my empty well. Meanwhile, the circles beneath her eyes are a shade darker every time I see her. My suggestions to slow down have been met with silence. Presently, she's searching the floor behind me. "No cat? I thought for sure you'd give in." And then her smile warms for Livvy. "Good morning, sweet pea!"

"Hi, Mommy." Livvy swings her duffel bag.

I point at the rug. "Whatcha got there?"

"Housewarming gifts. This one's for the bedroom, and there's another for the living room. A little color to brighten things up." Kristin raises her brows.

As if color is a magic elixir. "You didn't have to do that."

"I wanted to mark the occasion. It's a big step. An important one." She grabs my hand, interlacing our fingers. "We all just want you to be happy."

I jerk free. "Please stop pressuring me to be happy all the time. I'm not Tigger."

She recoils. "You could simply say thanks."

Her expression turns flinty for the first time in ten months. It's unexpected but so welcome—not that she'd understand my reaction. It's jarring—in a good way—to experience something normal, like the way we used to sometimes bicker before the ill-fated Exuma vacation.

Of course, she's right too. Kristin is nothing if not thoughtful, and prettier surroundings never hurt anything.

"Sorry. It's very nice of you, thanks." I take one end of the carpet, and then we walk it inside and set it down. She's too smart to be easily fooled by bravado. My austere apartment and short-term lease have her questioning my mental state. I roll my shoulders and smile in order to exude chill vibes. After all, I'm not offing myself today.

"You're welcome. Now, help me get the other one out of the car." Kristin is turning to go back outside when she notices Livvy's three paintings, now framed in basic black poster frames with white matting that I picked up at Target. "Wow. These look terrific, Livvy."

She steps closer to study each one. Naturally they're childish, but primary colors look great when matted and framed. The most realistic painting is of a tiny yellow sailboat with an oversize white sail. Livvy also attempted a vase filled with purple tulips. But my favorite is the modern one in which she used a wide brush to paint red and pink *x*'s and *o*'s, which she then sprinkled with glitter. *This one is hugs and kisses, Aunt Amy.*

Even now, I lay a hand on my chest in response to how deeply that touches me.

"Maybe you could paint something for me, honey. Something for my bedroom, so I see it first thing every day when I wake up." Kristin kisses her daughter's head.

Livvy perks up, looking less sad about leaving me. As it should be. "Okay."

Wishing not to intrude on their tender moment, I stand still, trying to make myself invisible.

"Great." Kristin brushes her thumb over her daughter's cheek. "Now, can you hang out at the table while Aunt Amy and I get the other rug?"

"I can help," Livvy offers.

"Hmm," I say. "How about if you push the coffee table over to the wall."

It's a cheap lightweight thing Sean and I bought at HomeGoods a few years ago. I'm not mechanically inclined, so my screwing on its legs jokingly became one of my bigger accomplishments that winter. Sean would rest his feet on the table while reading the paper and remark upon its sturdiness. No one beat a joke to death like he did, God love him. What I'd give to hear him crack that one again.

"Okay." Livvy proudly struts to the coffee table while Kristin and I duck outside.

"How was your night?" Kristin asks as we walk the length of the driveway.

"Nice. We ate pizza, played Mermaid Island, and watched *Flora & Ulysses*." When we get to the back of her SUV, I move around her while she pops the hatch.

She stands there for a moment, not moving to retrieve the rug. "She talked all week about being your first sleepover. She misses you."

My sister's conflict is plain on her face. She wants us all to be close, but sometimes it's obvious that Livvy's affection for me elicits envy too. She's worked tirelessly on everyone's behalf yet is completely unable to relax and simply enjoy any of what she's created. How do I teach her that skill?

"I miss you all too. But while we're out here, did you know that some of the girls in ballet pick on Livvy?"

She frowns. "No. How did you find out?"

"I asked."

"I figured. Why did you ask?" Her hands are on her hips, but her movements are almost jerky. Another sleepless night?

"She was dragging her feet about going."

"She's never said anything to me." My sister stiffens, glancing toward the apartment door.

"Maybe she's afraid you'd be disappointed."

Kristin turns on me, heat in her tone. "I'm never disappointed in her."

I should mind my own business, but step four is too important. "You might not express it directly, but your kids know you and Tony have high expectations."

She stares at me, her cheeks scarlet, eyes dewy—Kristin has never been a crier. I draw back, wondering what I'm missing or if something else is going on.

Her gaze skitters away momentarily as she combs her fingers through her hair. "She begged to take ballet. We didn't insist."

It was a mistake to get into this when we don't have time for a bigger discussion. "Okay, I just wanted to give you a heads-up. Anyway, what did you all do last night?"

"I had to work late." She recovers herself, grips the rug, and yanks it as if releasing her aggression. I grab the other end so we can lug it into the apartment. "Tony and Luca went to dinner at Beach House Cafe; then we all hung out reading by the fire."

That could be cozy, but she doesn't look rested. She's all jitters and furtive glances, her tone oddly detached. "Why are you so wired this morning?"

Her gaze shifts sideways. "Just busy with a million things to do."

Always using productivity as the measure of one's life. "When's the last time you and Tony had a date night? Let me come babysit one night—or a whole weekend—so you two can get away."

My sister rightfully didn't trust me to be alone with the kids this past autumn, but now she does.

"That's a nice offer," she says. The fact that she didn't immediately shoot me down proves that she's buying my recovery, a fact that would be thrilling if it didn't make me feel guilty. She narrows her eyes. "Are you happy here on your own?"

"I am, thanks." Not a lie. It's been relaxing to have my own space. To lie in bed and stare at the ceiling until ten if I need to, or to cry ugly tears while watching older videos of Sean and me without worrying someone will disturb me.

"That's good. That's all I want for you."

"Same . . . for you, I mean."

"Well, I'm not sure I can get away for an overnight, but Tony would love it. Let me see if I can make something work. Does it matter which weekend?"

"My calendar is wide open," I joke. It'd be better if she were doing it for herself and not just for Tony, but it's a step in the right direction.

She sets her end of the rug down for a brief rest. "Would you want to sit with the kids after school during the week? We'd pay you, of course. They prefer you to Madeline, and you'd earn some money while you figure out your next steps."

That she's not pressuring me to spend the lottery money is a win, but this is also a sneaky way of keeping close tabs on me and extending the duration of my promise.

She and Livvy can't keep relying on me as their crutch either. "I'm trying to move forward. Being at your house every day might feel a bit like going backward."

The combination of sharp nod and tight-lipped smile gives away her disappointment every time, not that she'd admit it. "Okay. Maybe you'll go back to work at the paper."

I first got interested in journalism in college, during the sensational Amanda Knox trial. As a college student with friends abroad, it fascinated me. I followed it closely and wrote an article for the school paper, setting my course. Reporting appeals to my nosy nature—my love of asking people hard questions and poking at inconsistencies. It was a great gig until we decided I would stay home with Scotty. During his naps, I started a blog called *The Boy Next Door*—a sort of diary about my experiences parenting a neurodiverse toddler. I managed to accumulate a few thousand followers, many of whom would write to me and share their own experiences. The connection with others in my shoes was an addictive by-product of that writing.

Sean's parents, however, hated the public nature of the blog. *My friend Martha's daughter read your blog. Why on earth are you telling*

*the world about Scotty throwing a toy at you or how you feel like a fail-
ure? People are going to judge you and Sean. Scotty will be embarrassed
later, when he's old enough to read these things. Write something else—
something that pays you.* Meanwhile, if they'd read my posts carefully
instead of worrying about what others thought, they might've built a
healthier relationship with Scotty instead of treating him as if he were
less intelligent than their other grandkids. That's what truly drove
Sean around the bend. Bit by bit their otherwise healthy relationship
deteriorated each time Sean had to defend me or our decisions, or
correct them about their misperceptions or the things they did that
would trigger Scotty. Regardless, I haven't written a word on that blog
since returning from Exuma. I wonder who all those parents have
turned to now.

"Maybe I will." Doubtful, though. Very doubtful. "Are you excited
about skydiving?"

"Is it really important that I go with you?"

I nod, using her generous heart against her.

"All right. Just know it's possible I won't be able to make myself
jump out of the plane."

"You will!" I grin, knowing her competitiveness will force her to
follow me.

We haul the rug inside and unfurl it on the living room floor,
revealing a modern and fresh pattern of vibrant orange-and-blue dahlias
against a cream field. "Wow, I love this. Thank you."

Kristin's authentic smile emerges. "I'm so glad. Let's unroll the
other."

It takes more effort to place the second one beneath the bed, but
Livvy enjoys unspooling it while Kristin and I hold the bed aloft.
Another cream field, this time dotted with faded teal-and-gold pine-
apples the size of basketballs. Quirky, like me. "Another winner. You
know me well."

Kristin throws an arm around me. "That I do."

Her embrace pulsates with energy—love, concern, hope, and maybe a little nostalgia—stirring something inside to life for a moment. I need to string hundreds of these together in the coming months.

We're interrupted when two little arms envelop our hips. "Let me in," Livvy demands.

I laugh, opening the circle and smushing her between us, where my sister and I smother her with kisses and tickles until she's giggling unabashedly, stretching this beautiful moment for a few extra seconds while my heart fills nearly to the point of pain.

As she catches her breath, Kristin fixes her hair with a sweep of one hand. "Well, we'd better get going so we aren't late for ballet."

"Okay," Livvy says without complaining, tossing me a sentient look. "I know, Aunt Amy. I'll laugh."

I wave off Kristin's quizzical glance while winking at my niece. "That's the spirit."

We say goodbye at my front door, and then I spin around, gazing at my living room. The rugs add much-needed warmth and brightness to the space, giving the apartment the appearance of a proper home, which Kristin surely intended. I'll have to admit to Livvy later that she wasn't totally wrong about pretty houses.

I traipse over to lie down on the new carpet, stretching across its nap like a starfish and heaving a giant sigh.

Kristin's suggestion about work forces me to acknowledge that I've lost all enthusiasm for reporting. I always wanted to write a book—that old dream every writer harbors. When I used to fantasize about it, my ideas had a Nora Ephron vibe. If I were to try conjuring a premise today, I'd be more likely to produce something that'd appeal to Lisa Jewell's fans. But who am I kidding? I lack the discipline and, most important, the time.

Many people in my shoes would probably use that prize money to travel the world—*Eat, Pray, Love* meets "I Took a Pill in Ibiza." That would certainly offer all kinds of escapes from my reality. New places with no memories attached. New people who have no clue about my past. There are bucket list places to visit, yet I don't have the time to both travel and also work on my plan. I do, however, need to figure out how to get rid of the money. The cursed money I wish I'd never won.

That night, Sean had tossed the remote on the ottoman, a twinkle in his eye. "I'm going up. You coming?"

I would've followed gladly except the Powerball number would be read in fifteen minutes. As irrational as it sounds, I had a feeling. Sean didn't know I wasted money on tickets, so I simply said, "Not just yet. Sorry!"

He leaned down to kiss my head. "It's all right. I'm too tired to have much stamina anyway."

"Rain check?" I grabbed his hand.

"Always." He sauntered off, scratching the back of his head, his long, lean legs taking him farther away from me.

Once he was upstairs, I snatched my purse from the bench by the garage door and rummaged for the ticket. Wouldn't it be a miracle—a godsend—if I finally won? Money to secure Scotty's future, to pay off our mortgage, to take pressure off Sean's shoulders. A taste of the little extras in life, like a bigger house, private schools, and vacations that would rival my sister's.

I never begrudged Kristin her affluence, or her perfect, handsome family with a typical, healthy boy and girl. She worked hard and was generous too. None of that meant I wouldn't have also liked our life to be a little easier and to secure my son's future.

Ticket in hand, I grabbed a Post-it Note and pen from the kitchen junk drawer and took everything back to the family room to wait. At 10:55 p.m. I tuned in to watch the drawing. The next four minutes dragged on. Sitting cross-legged on the floor, I smoothed the tickets on the ottoman.

When Michelle Lyles came on, I picked up the pen and blew out a breath, thinking, *Here we go.*

As each ball dropped, I wrote down the numbers: 01—21—08—04—09—24.

I double-checked to make sure I'd written them down correctly and then looked at the rows of numbers on my ticket.

No.

No.

No.

Nope.

Ah. 1 . . . 21 . . . 8 . . . I started to sweat . . . 4 . . . 9 . . . I shook . . . 24. 24! 24!

I gasped and, trembling, checked again. Triple-checked. Tears filled my eyes. "Sean. Sean!" I jumped up holding the ticket and my Post-it and tripped on a stair tread. "Sean!"

He came to the top of the steps. "What's wrong?"

I waved the papers in the air while sitting to steady myself. "We won. We won the Powerball!"

He rolled his eyes. "It's late for this prank."

"I'm serious. We won! Look! I just watched and wrote down the numbers and I've got them. I've got them. We're rich. We're really rich!" A shocking surge of adrenaline almost made me puke.

After a brief hesitation, he trotted down a few stairs and took the papers, looking at them and peering at me. "Since when do you buy lottery tickets?"

I swiped my cheeks dry and fudged a little, leaving out the consistency of my habit since Scotty's diagnosis. "I stopped yesterday after picking Scotty up from the SEED Center. Can you believe it? I can't believe it. Give me that ticket to put someplace safe. I don't know what to do now, except that we can't just claim it. I should call Kristin in the morning and ask her."

"Why?"

"She's a lawyer. She'll know how to claim this the right way, like set up an entity or something so we don't have crazies coming out of the woodwork to get something from us."

"Let's double-check on the computer just to make sure you didn't make a mistake. I'd hate to get excited if this isn't right." Always practical, my Sean.

I followed him to the desktop, where he pulled up the night's drawing.

01—21—08—04—09—24.

"Holy shit. Ho-ly shit, Amy." He hugged me so hard I thought he'd collapse my lungs. "Sixty-eight million dollars. Fuck yeah!"

A staggering sum. Incomprehensible, in truth. "Well, only if no one else won. I guess we won't know right away."

"Even if we share it with one or two others, it's life-changing money. I vote for the lump sum." His cheeks were flushed, his eyes wide. I knew that, like me, the relief of knowing we could finally provide for Scotty's support in perpetuity had hit him.

"Isn't that only like a third of the value after taxes and stuff?"

"But we can invest it wisely, and it will grow."

"Okay. Whatever you want. We can pretty much do whatever we want now." I grabbed his hands and started jumping as it hit me. "We're really rich!"

Sean lifted me in the air and then let my body slide down against his chest. He grabbed my face and kissed me so hard, and then our pajamas were tossed aside and we made love on the sofa.

I'd give anything to feel Sean's body again. To feel joy. To feel anything other than a distant sort of interest in almost everything in my life.

The way I see it, adrenaline-junkie options are most likely to supply a little pleasure while also allowing me to spend time with my sister. I've been watching YouTube videos ever since I scheduled the tandem skydiving jump. Everyone has posted raves about the experience.

Another possibility is bungee jumping, but the closest certified outfits are in Kentucky and Ottawa. Kristin wouldn't take time off to do that when she never has enough time as it is. In any case, what can I do today besides simply going through the motions? It's winter, but I could probably walk over to Shorelands and jump into the seawater for a minute or two without getting hypothermia . . .

I sit up, anticipating an icy awakening of all my nerves that would kick-start a little dopamine production. It's nice to smile for a reason that has nothing to do with Kristin's kids. Her friends already think I've lost my mind, so it won't even shock anyone to catch me jumping off that dock.

CHAPTER SIX

KRISTIN

Friday afternoon, two weeks later

I drop my briefcase on the cubby bench and kick off my heels, taking one final calming breath to switch gears from navigating work fires to confronting today's family crisis. I spent the entire train ride home thinking about the call Tony fielded from Livvy's school principal this afternoon. It figures that when one thing gets better (Amy), two things fall apart (work and Livvy).

Lately the Adderall hasn't felt as effective, but I'm scared to double dose because even a single dose makes my heart race. I unclip my french twist and wander into the kitchen, my scalp prickling as my hair shakes loose. Tony's seated at the kitchen island. He looks up from his laptop and offers a resigned half smile to welcome me home. Neither of the kids is in sight, which is surely by design.

After I kiss him hello on the cheek, I round the island to pour myself a glass of ice water. Tony closes out whatever he was working on before he pushes the laptop aside. It's been this way ever since my outburst the other week: polite cordiality—whether dealing with the kids or cleaning the kitchen or chaste kisses good night—each of us casting furtive glances as if wondering or waiting for the right time or incident to force the bigger conversation I dread. He's probably still a little rocked by my uncharacteristic outburst. Avoidance is fine by me because I need a little breathing room. But we leave tomorrow morning for our overnight date, so the truce might not last.

The clink of ice against my glass echoes my brittle mood. I gulp my drink down and exhale. "So, Livvy."

Tony folds his arms across his chest, wearing a stoic expression. "At least this happened on a Friday. She'll have the weekend to recover before having to face her classmates."

She's unlikely to recover that quickly, but maybe I'm wrong. "What did Ms. Goldberg say? Or Principal Jackson?"

"Nothing surprising. Livvy's been extra touchy in class these past couple of weeks, getting teary for no reason, and so on." *Since Amy moved out* goes unsaid. Why can't Tony and I help Livvy handle her emotions? "Today she heard about some birthday party that she wasn't invited to, which triggered a meltdown in the cafeteria. The teachers tried to help, but she was inconsolable, hyperventilating until she passed out. By the time I got there, she was in the nurse's office. No concussion, so that was good."

Kids can be so cruel, especially to extra-emotional kids like Livvy. My daughter used to cover her ears in the car to muffle sad songs. At four, she begged me to remove a little family-stick-figure image from my car window because no one else had one and she didn't want to be different. And when Scotty died, she cried almost as much as Amy did at first, and then told us she could see him. I talked to the doctor about those hallucinations, but he was unconcerned and said many kids have imaginary friends and find other ways to cope with death. After a month or so, she stopped mentioning Scotty, so I let it go. Tony writes her emotional behavior off to her being young and a girl, as if not having a Y chromosome automatically makes one overly sensitive. Luca vacillates between trying to soothe her and ignoring her.

Imagining her sense of rejection today makes me nauseated. I lean against the island, elbows locked so my arms act like pillars propping me up. "How was her mood with you?"

"Quiet at first. Withdrawn. She hadn't eaten her lunch, so when we got home, I threw her into a cooking project to get her out of her head. Pizza from scratch. She made a clown face with pepperoni and mushroom pieces, lots of shredded cheese where the hair would go." While he thinks back to it, one corner of Tony's mouth curves. "She seemed better after that but then crashed hard on the sofa, so I carried her upstairs. Luca got home after mathletes, but he'd already heard about Livvy from other kids at school. He was torn—embarrassed for and by her behavior. I told him that was normal and he should go do something he enjoyed while processing his feelings, but under no circumstances was he allowed to make his sister feel worse."

Good advice. Tony is the first emergency contact because he works nearby, but in truth, he's also much calmer than I am in a crisis. In that way, my being beholden to a train schedule and long commute to and from Manhattan is a blessing for our kids.

I briefly cover my face. "Maybe we should cancel our plans to get away tomorrow night."

Tony convinced me to accept Amy's babysitting offer, arguing that trusting her would be good for her sense of importance and continued healing. He then booked us a room at the Mayflower Inn & Spa in Washington, Connecticut.

"Or maybe having your sister here for the night will help Livvy. I hate to admit it, but Amy does reach our daughter on some level we don't." His cheeks flush following that concession. My husband rarely accepts defeat, so when he does, it's as unsettling as Livvy's behavior. "The reservation's nonrefundable at this point, too, but if that's what you want, I'll call and cancel."

Losing the money would stink, but so would abandoning Livvy if she needs us.

"I don't know what I want." I pitch my arms upward, my voice strained from futility. "No, that's not true. I want emotionally stable kids, a rewarding career, a resilient, happy sister—but I've got no fucking clue how to make any of that happen. Obviously, I'm doing everything wrong."

Tony's eyes widen. It's unlike me to drop f-bombs or to raise my voice. Frankly, the way my skin feels like it's peeling off my bones proves that I'm at the very edge of self-control. He circles the island, spins me around, and envelops me in a bear hug. My muscles slacken as the warmth of his body, the strength of his embrace, and the gentleness of his breath against my hair instantly support me. He doesn't immediately challenge my perspective. Having space to feel what I feel is wonderful. If only hugs were the answer to everything, life would be easier.

"Hon," he says in a hushed tone. "You've been extra edgy for months now. You're losing weight. I'm worried and think you could use a thirty-six-hour break. Staying home won't change what happened to Livvy either. If we refresh and get a new perspective, we'll be better able to handle her."

I nod against his shoulder without confessing to the bottle of pills in my purse, which is like a hidden detonator. "It just feels wrong to leave after she's had this horrible day."

"She's not exactly sad to trade us for Amy. Besides, we aren't leaving until morning, so we can spend the night reassuring her." He rubs my arms, as if instinctively aware I need to borrow his strength a bit longer. "She can even sleep in our bed tonight."

That's a huge concession. He's never believed in sharing a bed with children older than three. Neither of our parents did, either, so it seemed like the right call at the time. Now I question why we've enforced such a bright line, as if raising kids were as simple as a paint-by-numbers project.

"Let me make sure Amy's okay to watch the kids, given Livvy's current mindset." Livvy might throw another fit if we cancel Amy, but I should warn my sister that Livvy might be needier than normal.

He nods, yet his disappointment about the possibility of canceling our plans is palpable. It seems I've underestimated the effect these past ten months have had on him. He needs this trip maybe more than I do. In light of this, I don't even bother mentioning my grueling workday, but it's crowding the back of my thoughts, creating more pressure. I miss the before times, when I managed my life well and without any crutch. When I looked forward to sharing things about my day because I was proud and competent.

"I'll go change my clothes and peek in on Livvy before I call Amy." I kiss him on the cheek and then haul myself up the stairs, which might as well be Mount Everest.

My tension could make Livvy feel worse, so I opt for a hot shower first. Standing beneath the rainfall showerhead, I close my eyes and focus on my breath while the water loosens the tightness winding through me. Reminding myself of my blessings—my intelligence, my loyal husband, my children, my health—I begin the internal pep talk. *I can quit these pills. I can do it. I'm strong and smart and deserve to be happy. I'm not alone. I'm a good person and mother. We will get through this rough patch. We have love on our side. Quit the pills!* I exit the shower in a less defeated mood. After slipping into cozy cashmere loungewear, I pad over to Livvy's room and crack open her door.

She's staring at the ceiling until she hears me; then her big eyes start to water. "Hi, Mom."

I shuffle across the carpet and crawl into her bed, kissing her head. "Hi, sweetie. Did you have a good nap? Daddy told me all about your clown pizza."

Instead of bragging about her culinary artwork, she eyes me from beneath damp lashes, intent on dealing with the big fat elephant that I'm tiptoeing around. "Are you mad at me?"

"Of course not." I squeeze her extra tight, hating that her worries include my potential reaction. "I'll never be mad about your big feelings, because they mean you've got a big heart. But I am sorry that you got so upset today. It must be hard to have all those emotions."

"It's like a fire inside, right here." She sweeps her small hand over her chest and tummy.

I bite the inside of my cheek to keep from crying. That painful panic plagues me at times too. "Is that scary?"

She nods.

I keep hold of her, resting my cheek on her head. When she was two and three, I loved how she felt things deeply and had high empathy. Then in the preschool years, we got fewer invitations to playdates because her tendency to cry easily didn't go over well with other kids. I thought school would help, with its structure and emphasis on inclusion. Still, she struggles socially. It's not like with Scotty, where it was destined to be a lifelong issue. But her anxiety and way of taking things personally worry me for how they might affect her self-esteem.

I recall those first inklings Amy once had about Scotty possibly needing more than she alone could give him. A moment later, I ask, "What if I could find someone who could teach you how to control your feelings a little—a special kind of doctor?"

I shouldn't have mentioned this before running it by Tony.

"What's a special doctor?" Livvy's doubtful look is exactly what I imagine her father's will be. His parents believe that "shrinks" are for people who don't have family to help them, and they brainwashed Tony to agree. I used to share his attitude about mental toughness, but lately it's made it impossible to be honest about my own struggles. I don't know what the answer is. I only know that we seem to lack the expertise to help our daughter, as well as the time to acquire it.

"They know things about managing big feelings. They can teach you to put out that fire."

She pulls the blanket up higher, her voice hushed. "That would be good."

I cradle her against me, to comfort myself as much as her at this point. Experts say confidence comes from overcoming obstacles. Would it be better to empower her to think this through and reach her own conclusion than to coddle her? "You give it more thought this weekend, and if you want to try, I'll talk to Daddy. For now, do you want to come downstairs and hang out?"

She shrinks against the pillows. "Is Luca home?"

I nod.

"Is he mad at me?" Her wobbly chin breaks me a little. Nothing is worse than being unable to fix a child's distress.

I deflect. "He's sad that your feelings were hurt, but glad that you didn't hurt yourself when you fainted. Now come on down. I bet Daddy could use some help with dinner soon."

She straightens up in bed, her mood shifting along with the covers. "Did he show you the picture of my clown pizza?"

"No, but now I want to go see." Wearing a forced smile, I stand and extend my hand, which she takes as she crawls out of the bed. At least she's not crying. This is the most progress I've made on anything all day.

———

"Should we order another bottle?" I ask Tony upon pouring the last of the Brunello into my wineglass. All around us other couples chat in hushed tones, candlelight flickering off every shiny surface of the Mayflower Inn's Garden Room, warming its butter-yellow walls. We're seated beside a tall mullioned window, surrounded by plants. A trellised ceiling is suspended overhead. While the decor isn't to my taste, it's relaxing. Best of all, we've enjoyed an entire meal without interruptions.

He shakes his head, sampling the final course—a choco-late-mousse-like confection with poached persimmons and walnuts. "Maybe you should slow down. I'd like to extend our night past nine o'clock."

"I'm sure you would," I tease, feeling loose limbed and tingly. Day one without pills—one that began with a couple's massage. It took me that hour after arriving to mentally leave the kids and work behind. Following the massage, Tony seduced me for some unhurried lovemak-ing, after which we napped for almost an hour—such indulgences.

Before dinner we puttered around the cozy resort, sometimes talking, sometimes simply enjoying the view of the snow-dusted hills. We've ignored the difficult topics—like the kids or my moods. They can wait until morning. "It's pretty here."

Tony's direct gaze is as hot as a horny teenager's. "The view is absolutely stunning. I love to see you relaxed and smiling."

He doesn't mean for that to sting, but it skims over the good reasons I've had to be overwhelmed and exhausted. "I'm glad we didn't cancel. You were right—I needed a break from real life."

"Not all parts of it, I hope." He reaches across the table to stroke my hand. "I know it's been a rough year, but we have an amazing life, hon. Let's stay focused on that."

God knows we've worked hard to create it. Way back when, we'd get home from work at nine o'clock, open a bottle of wine, dish about our day, and tumble into bed. Tony made up a budget, and we went about planning for a future in which the family we wanted would thrive. When we had Luca, things kept falling into place. He was an easy baby—hit milestones early, ate and slept well, didn't spook easily. Madeline adored him to the point I'd joke that she might kidnap him while we were at work. Livvy was less easy. Fussy. Picky with people. Terrible sleeper. Then my career disappointments started too. At first, I used them as fuel to work harder, but that's caused self-doubts and exhaustion at levels that embarrass me.

My distorted reflection stares back at me from the window beside him. "You have to admit that things have been super hard lately."

"A little less so these past few weeks."

Amy's absence has given him elbow room but has left me with low-grade anxiety from the inability to evaluate her moods and prevent a catastrophe. My friend Rebecca thought she saw my sister crawling out of the water by the dock in Shorelands, but Amy just laughed when I asked about it. I don't know what to think. "That's not true for Livvy."

"Livvy woke up happy this morning. Your sister will call if there's any trouble," he adds.

"It's not that simple." Worrying about our children runs beneath each day like groundwater, eroding my peace of mind. "She needs help with managing her feelings."

"That'll come with age." He takes another spoonful of mousse. I can tell he's busy identifying the ingredients by the way his eyes roll upward and his tongue clicks inside his mouth.

His unshakable faith in the universe is enviable but unrealistic. I feel Amy whispering in my ear, urging me to follow my gut and go to the mat. "You don't know that. Meanwhile, she's getting a reputation at school and getting excluded from things because of it. Maybe we should take her to a therapist."

His eyes go round when my suggestion snags his attention. "Why would we do that?"

"To get her evaluated and learn why she's so . . . emotional." My pleasant buzz is fading. I should've delayed this conversation until morning.

Tony's grimace might as well be a poke at my chest. "Therapy sends a message that we don't think she's healthy, or worse, that she's some sort of victim. And we're not going to fill her with pills." He sneers with disgust, revealing how he'd look at me if he found mine. My stomach clenches. "She's empathetic and a little anxious. Let's build her a sense of confidence—instill a belief that she can manage herself."

I lean forward, holding his gaze. "But she can't."

"She's only six. Give her time." He takes one last lick of his spoon and sits back, secure in his conclusions, as if maturity and intelligence are bulwarks against mental issues. Didn't he learn anything from Amy and Sean's experience with Scotty? Early intervention is always best.

"Time could make it worse if she keeps alienating herself. What if you and I talked to someone to get advice about how to help her?"

"No one will advise us unless they've evaluated her, and once that happens, she'll already feel different."

"Well, she seemed interested in getting help," I mutter, exhausted from trying to pry open his closed mind.

"What do you mean?" He leans forward on his elbows, brows bunched together.

This will go over as well as my tirade about Luca did the other week. "I mentioned the idea last night when I checked in on her."

Tony grunts, his shoulders slumping. "I wish you would've waited until after we discussed it."

"I'm sorry." He's not wrong to be miffed. This is the second time in a few weeks that I've flouted our promise to come to mutual agreements before taking any material action with the kids. I would be unhappy if he did that to me. I'm not making good decisions lately—not for myself or my marriage. He's probably disappointed, too, because he thought we'd snap back to "normal" as soon as Amy left. "I didn't plan to cut you out. My heart was breaking—she seemed so sad and lonely."

His expression softens. "It's hard to see her like that, but we can teach her to redirect her thoughts, like I did with the pizza making."

"A great but temporary fix. She was right back to being sad and scared by the time I got home—worried about how Luca would react too. Besides, you can't always get to school right away, and I never can." I gaze longingly at the empty bottle.

Tony blows out a long breath while he sizes me up. "I'm not saying I'll never consider therapy, but it feels premature. Especially when she's doing better this year than last."

I rest my chin on my fist, the effects of the wine now dragging on my entire being. "Because of Amy."

"Not 'because' of Amy," he quips. "Sure, she helped, but Livvy's growing up. She's slowly learning to handle disappointment. Yesterday was a backslide—something we both expected because of the change in the house. Let's start setting simple goals and tasks. I'm sure, as she feels good about accomplishing things, it'll translate to more confidence. We're smart, caring parents who can handle our daughter's issues without outsiders."

I wince when considering whether I'm looking to dump a parenting issue on a therapist because I'm too tired to deal with it myself.

"I don't know how I'll find time to manage that or to read up on what's at the root of her behavior. You know my deal is crumbling. I asked Baxter's litigator, Greg Sherman, how settlement talks were going, but all he said was that these things take time. Time I don't have, given the closing date. Now the Avant execs want to renegotiate material terms. Blood in the water. It's a nightmare. I'm sure Jim and the others were working today, pissed that I made myself unavailable."

Jim knows about Amy, so he didn't question me when I claimed we had a minor family emergency. The white lie seemed necessary, given how much Tony and I needed a break. Yet I also know Jim's a workaholic who doesn't really care about family emergencies when a client is unhappy.

"You didn't create the problem. Surely Jim isn't blaming you for it." Tony tips his head left, his gaze assessing.

He doesn't understand. Other than those first few years after college, when he worked for Alliance Development, he's always worked for himself and called his own shots. As an entrepreneur, he doesn't have to deal with big-office politics. He probably thinks his show of confidence is supportive, but it's having the opposite effect. All I feel right now is alone and defeated.

"Not directly, but making partner this year rests on how many deals I bring in. If this one implodes, these past four months of work will have been a huge waste of time. Time I could've been spending with our kids."

"It hasn't been a waste of time. You're well compensated and great at your job. The kids' futures are more secure because of your efforts. They'll appreciate that someday, as I do already." He offers an encouraging smile, but it all sounds like platitudes. It's belittling, as if he understands my life and feelings better than I do. Still, I don't want to argue and then turn our one night away into a complete waste of our time and money.

"Will they?" I spread my fingers out on the table, contemplating them. More wrinkles and prominent veins. I'm aging, on top of everything else. If I died tomorrow, what would my kids remember about me, other than that I dressed well and worked hard? "Or will they hardly know me?"

Like me with my dad. I don't dislike him. I've never resented that he was always working. I understood the importance of his role in our family. But I don't really know him—his dreams, his philosophies, his disappointments. He never had hobbies. He rarely relaxed at the table or sat on my bed and talked to me—at least not during the ages when I was old enough to remember those moments. Even on family vacations, he was a background player—reading in a chair with a beer while our mother helped build sandcastles, stood with us in long lines for tickets, and played cards on the covered porch overlooking the sea.

"These doubts are coming from Amy's constant criticisms, which seem designed specifically to make you feel like a bad mother." His tone is heated, as it tends to get when he grabs hold of this particular bone.

I raise one hand and firmly say, "Please, don't."

"Don't defend you?"

"I don't need defending from my sister." I scowl.

"You're a good mother, Kristin. A great mother. A great role model for our kids, no matter what she thinks." His shoulders bunch as he stiffens against both real and imagined slights.

"Amy has never accused either of us of being *bad* parents." I run my index finger around the rim of the wineglass, wishing it were full. Wishing I felt like a good mom instead of a deceitful woman barely holding her life together.

"Fine. Neglectful, then. Either way, her insinuations are judgmental bullshit, and I hate how she's undermined your confidence. Like suddenly she has all the answers to life? Let's not pretend she was a perfect mother. Or daughter or sister, for that matter." Tony's puffed up now, hot with indignation.

"Don't be cruel. Whatever her past shortcomings, trauma gave Amy some wisdom and insight, and we'd be fools to ignore that."

"Yes, she's got a new perspective, but not every little thing going on in our family is do or die, the way she likes to frame it. It's about balance, not all or nothing. You used to get this, and I'd really like our lives to go back to normal now that she's gone." He says it all so matter-of-factly. This is his truth. My husband has never lacked the guts to be frank, and we were in sync before Sean and Scotty died and Amy went around the bend. But everything is more nuanced and complicated than he wants to admit. I wish he'd face that fact.

"Were we ever normal or balanced?" I'm half joking until Tony's mouth twitches and his gaze wanders off for a second. Oh brother. Now what?

"Kristin, what you've done for your sister, and how you did it with almost no help from your folks or Sean's, is truly amazing. At the same time, it's taken a toll. You're exhausted. You never relax, and you treat everything like a crisis. To some degree, I get it. We've all lived through a real tragedy, and we all miss Sean and Scotty too. I've tried to be supportive—I know I haven't been perfect—but I'm getting really worried about you. You're my priority, not your sister or your parents. You and our kids. So if I think someone is hurting you—intentionally or not—I'm not going to keep quiet." He blows out a breath as if relieved to have released that pent-up speech. "But put all that aside for now. Tell me what I can do to help us get back on the same page about things. How can I convince you that our family life is better—healthier—than the worrywart viewpoint you've adopted?"

His words cut like lashes, despite the truth in some of them. My nostrils flare as tears gather. I do need help but am afraid to confess. I don't want to be seen by anyone—least of all him—as weak or incompetent. As unable to manage myself and my life.

He stretches his hands across the table but stops short of grasping mine. "Don't get upset. I'm trying to take some pressure off you. Let me carry some of the weight you're shouldering. Tell me what it'll take to help you go back to being my Krissy."

For the first time, I understand why Amy gets mad when I push her to be happier. It's insulting to be told how you should feel instead of being allowed to simply feel what you feel. I also am not the same person I was at twenty-two or even thirty-two. "Maybe I'll never go back to being who I was before. What happened to Amy changed me, too, Tony. Doesn't it make you stop to consider your life a little differently?"

He reflects on this, his mouth turning down nonchalantly. "Not really. I love our life and my work. I'm not aiming for perfection—just a work-hard, play-hard way of living. I don't feel guilty that we can't spend one hundred percent of our time with our kids. In fact, I think it'd be awful for their development if they were the center of everything. How would that prepare them for adulthood? Be honest: if Sean and Scotty hadn't died, you wouldn't be taking advice from Amy on how to live your life."

Oof. That hurts so much because it's true. I was always concerned that she and Sean didn't plan enough for the future. And then when Scotty needed so much extra help, things got skewed to his needs. Between that and COVID's hit to their finances and support system, they bickered more often. I watched my sister fret about her son's challenges and even felt her envy when Luca or Livvy could relate to us in ways Scotty did not. We were all so thrilled when she won that money. It seemed an absolute blessing at the time.

"All right, all right. You win. I don't want to fight." I push the empty glass away. "I just want to go to sleep."

This isn't how either of us expected the night to end. His expression shifts, revealing my same dissatisfaction.

Great. In addition to everything else spinning off the rails, my marriage is now on that list.

CHAPTER SEVEN

AMY

Saturday, two weeks later

I jangle my keys as I grab my ID, credit card, and phone, unclear why jumping from ten thousand feet ever seemed like a great idea. Then again, my cold-water swim was exhilarating despite the frigid water's initial bite, so this, too, may end well.

If I had more time to squeeze in activities with Kristin, I would've pushed this until late spring. The skydiving company said they jump as long as the temperature stays above forty degrees. Today is a toasty forty-nine, so we're in good shape.

After blowing out three long breaths, I head out to pick up my sister for the drive up the Hudson.

"Good morning, young lady." Bob smiles at me from the middle of the tiny backyard, where he's assessing the patchy grass and unkempt flower bed. It's too early for spring planting, but not too soon for planning.

"Hey there, Bob. How are you today?" I zip up my coat as a buffer against a sudden, stiff breeze.

He pats down his comb-over with a sheepish grin. "Pretty good, pretty good. Haven't seen you in a couple days. You been sick?"

I shake my head, slightly embarrassed that I can hibernate for days and wallow. No job. No family. Nothing that requires my attention—except Livvy, that is. Even with her, the other weekend's babysitting cemented the need to step back so that she'll rely upon her parents instead of me. I'd hoped Kristin and Tony would return from their getaway refreshed. They were all smiles for the kids, but their stiff body language and unsmiling eyes told a different story.

"Just lying low for a bit," I say.

He must have questions about my life, but I appreciate that he never forces me to share my story. I doubt I will. I don't want his pity, nor do I need another person worrying about me.

"We all need a good rest now and then."

"Sure do." I stretch my arms out to the sides. "And now I'm off to skydive."

"Ooh, exciting!" He scratches his chin as if contemplating, then jokes, "I'm probably too old for that, huh?"

I laugh, contrasting his attitude with what I suspect my parents' would be if they knew. Mom would be tugging on my dad's arm, begging him to talk some sense into me. I know this from many years of experience. Her concern for my choices has heightened to extreme levels this year. "I doubt age is a problem as much as things like weight, heart condition, and stuff like that. You seem pretty healthy to me."

"Yeah, but my daughter would end up with a heart condition if I jumped out of a plane." He chuckles and I smile at his quick wit.

Small moments of levity didn't always resonate as much as they have lately. Now each give-and-take feels heightened, with my aim being to leave each conversation on a high note.

"To be honest, I worry my sister might have one." We exchange another smile. "Are you thinking about doing some gardening this spring?"

"Thinking about it. Do you garden?"

"It's been a while, but I've got an emerald thumb." I did once have a way with planning and pruning healthy gardens.

"I'd love some help," he says hopefully.

He's easy to please, but I hesitate to promise something I'm not planning on being around to see through. "Let's talk another time because I'm running late."

Before I reach my car, he calls, "I've got white chili in the Crock-Pot. Maybe you can join me at dinner and tell me all about it." Despite his general perkiness, there's something frail about him, standing there on this cold almost-spring day. Perhaps it's the loneliness in his gaze. COVID was particularly hard on old people. He probably lost friends and, more important, years of living his life freely, when he might not have that many left.

I empathize. I really do, especially now that my days are numbered too. He's not bad company either. Better than the few friends I've kept at arm's length all year to avoid bringing up old memories. And yet, this excursion might sap all my energy for the day. "That's so kind, thank you. If I'm not too wiped out later, I'll stop by around six."

He gives me a double thumbs-up along with a kind smile, which seals my fate. He's hard to resist, with his baggy pants and slightly hunched shoulders. My grandparents are all dead already. It might've been nice to have had one around this past year—old folks have a perspective that can be settling. Bob, like Livvy, has given me more than he's taken—a bit of grace that does not go unnoticed.

"See you later." I wave just before closing my door, starting the ignition, and blasting P!nk to drown out the noise in my head.

Kristin is on her front porch checking her watch when I pull up. She trots toward the car wearing lululemon joggers and a long-sleeve shirt, a lightweight jacket, and her game face. She's doing this only for my benefit, which is ironic because I planned it for hers.

"I can't talk you out of this?" Kristin asks as she slides into the front seat. Her question has been a common refrain ever since we were kids. She's always been the yin to my yang. The Monica Geller to my Rachel Green. The voice of reason that kept me from dropping out of college after freshman year to run around the globe doing odd jobs. Now I'll never see those places, but had I gone then, I probably wouldn't have met Sean.

"Why would you want to?" I throw the car in reverse, backing out of the driveway.

"Oh, I don't know. Maybe because I'd like us to be around for the next few decades."

I avert my gaze. "It'll be fine."

"Will it? We'll be hurtling toward earth with no guarantee that it'll end well." She rests a manicured hand on her stomach. Everything from her shiny hair to her clean sneakers looks perfect, as usual, except that her skin is a little pasty. Rather than recite survival statistics, I hammer at the point I want her to accept.

"No one gets that guarantee on any given day." I wait out the ensuing silence.

"I wish there were an easier way to make you happy," she mutters more than speaks to me.

Either my point sailed over her head, or she refuses to acknowledge it because she hates when I'm right and she's wrong.

"I'd think you'd be thrilled that I'm looking for ways to enjoy my life rather than ways to end it." Technically this isn't a lie. Sure, I know the how—Sean's sleeping pills—and the when—the anniversary. Until then, however, I'm determined to enjoy my remaining days. Better yet, sometimes I'm succeeding—a fact that takes me by bittersweet surprise.

"Honestly I'm not sure which of those things you *are* actually trying to do," comes her sardonic reply.

"I wouldn't make you watch me do that or spend this much money and time on it either," I tease.

"That's not funny, Amy." Her harsh tone pulls me up short. "What happened last summer was terrifying and painful for everyone who loves you. We've all worked so hard to help you heal; it feels like a slap in the face when you make light of your life."

I almost hit the brakes from shock. For three seconds, my deceit makes me nauseated. I've already stressed my family to the max, and I'm secretly plotting to do it again. Yet this day is about giving my sister a special and potentially life-changing memory. I desperately want her to return home tonight believing a spontaneous adventure is as rewarding as "success." Down the road, that gift might help her forgive me.

"I'm sorry. I didn't mean to make light of anything. I'm simply pointing out a fact." We're both quiet for a second. "Look, if my parachute doesn't open, I don't want this argument to be our last conversation. I love you. Thank you for coming with me today, and I'm sure we'll both be totally jazzed on the ride home."

She huffs. "Well, I could use a boost."

Kristin hasn't shared as much about her life since I tried to end mine. I can't let that dynamic be our legacy either. "Why do you say that?"

She stares out her window, raising one shoulder. Never before has she been this unsure of herself.

I press. "You and Tony seemed a little tense when you returned from the Mayflower. I had really hoped getting away would be a nice break for you both."

She faces me with half a smile. "It was at first, but then we argued about Livvy. I think we should consult a therapist, but Tony thinks that's premature."

My nose wrinkles before I can stop myself. "What if you simply let Livvy be who she is—a bright, sensitive little soul who is figuring out the world? I mean, I get the desire to find answers—you know how I pushed with Scotty. But Livvy isn't having developmental issues. She's just a little delicate."

"You agree with Tony?" Kristin's confused frown isn't surprising. She hates unsolved problems. Rather than respond directly to my suggestion, she pivots. "He and I used to agree about everything, but lately not so much. It's mostly my fault. I don't even recognize myself most days."

"I'm sorry," I say, heaviness settling in my body.

"Why?"

"Taking me in—all the worry—it's affected you."

Her eyes go wide. "Please don't feel bad. We love you, and look at you now. Seriously, the one thing I feel good about is having helped you." She smiles with such love and sincerity it splits my heart in two.

"I am forever grateful for your love, sis." My eyes sting. "That's why I want us to share these random wild adventures together."

She lays a hand across her sternum. "You have more random, weird things in mind?"

"Maybe." I wink. "But let's see how today goes."

I feel her gaze on me. "You've got me over a barrel and you know it, because I'll do anything that makes you sparkle back to life."

My guilty conscience almost wipes the smile from my face.

———

We rumble down the runway, my stomach flipping like a martini shaker. The Cessna's propellers grind loudly as the ground below falls away. My pulse rises with the plane. Kristin might be right—this could be idiotic.

The fact that she's here says everything about the depth of her love—her sincerity and trust. No matter how good my intentions are for dragging her along, I'm traveling the devil's road to hell.

She's behind me on the straddle bench, in front of her instructor as I am mine, so there's no way to apologize for putting her through this torment. When the plane's wings shudder like a giant bird trying to catch a thermal current, I reach out to steady myself. Oh God, she's got to be cursing me out.

To stave off instinctual panic, I recite the safety measures we learned during training and packing the rig. If my tandem instructor fails to deploy the main canopy, I know which lever to pull. There's also the emergency auto-release on the rig if we both screw up. The chances of the canopy not unfurling are minimal. We practiced a landing position, with my legs tucked up. The instructors wear helmets, but we riders don't. Not that a helmet would do much good if we plummet. My sister and I both braided our hair so it won't get in our way. I keep touching the goggles currently raised above my eyes to make sure they're still there.

Logically, I'm sure we're safe, and yet as we cut through the clouds, all my nerves tingle. It's nothing at all like training. Now it's inescapable that—on some level—we're risking our lives.

Resistance builds to being nudged along this bench and thrown out the door, falling at 120 miles per hour for the first minute until that canopy opens and slows us down. Kristin hates risk and is possibly apoplectic behind me. More than three million people per year do this, and on average, less than twenty die.

With those odds, I'm sure we'll survive.

Or not, comes the familiar dark thought.

After all, the lottery win proves people beat long odds.

Do I care? Yes. And not just because I don't want Kristin to witness my death. There are still a few things I want to do in my life, even though happiness continues to feel like a betrayal of my husband and son.

I close my eyes. Losing them seemed worse than death for so long. The bone-deep ache is always there, though not as sharp and unrelenting as last summer. Yet even on a good day, it's tough to find much meaning. I've briefly toyed with Kristin's suggestion about work, but reporting on local events or writing about grief wouldn't give me back who I need.

I open my eyes when my instructor, Gary, begins connecting our harnesses. The pilot gives the signal, and just before the door is opened, all the jumpers start hand-slapping each other in some sort of "have a good ride" ritual. I'm the second of three tandem riders. The solo jumpers go first. Unlike me, none of them appears to be on the verge of peeing their pants.

When the first one leaps, he looks like he got sucked out of the plane. I gasp, even though I know it's an illusion caused by the speed of the plane versus the speed of his falling body.

My muscles tense. It's harder to breathe, and I'm dizzy from a rush of adrenaline. There's no denying that, in this moment, I am fully alive and completely present. I thought it would feel different—more freeing, less scary.

We step up to the door. I try to catch Kristin's attention but can't make out her expression, which is hidden behind the goggles covering most of her face. Her posture is stiff. I, too, am frozen as my gaze drops to the ground below. I want to step back, but Gary yells in my ear, "Let's go!"

Suddenly we're out of the plane.

"Whaaaaaaa! Oh ho. Woo!" Half words erupt like a reflex. My stomach drops for maybe three seconds as I try to orient myself. Wind roars in my ears and my cheeks flap like the sails of a boat in high winds. In my periphery, I make out Kristin. She did it! My heart rises like a hot air balloon in my chest. I give her a thumbs-up, but she's not looking at me. She's probably hyperfocused on doing everything right, which reminds me to arch my back and bend my arms at ninety-degree angles, then bend my knees and keep my legs between the instructor's. Once in position, it's exhilarating. Even the writer in me has no words to describe it.

More like floating than falling. Like a bird looking down at the earth. The photographer somehow maneuvers through the sky taking photos of us all, which is rather astounding.

This is as close to heaven as I'll ever come during life. I'm free, weightless, and oddly calm. A burst of euphoria, like a runner's high, floods my brain and limbs, enveloping me in bliss like I haven't known since my son was born.

It ends abruptly when Gary opens the main canopy and we're yanked upward. Our rate of descent slows dramatically for the remaining four- to six-minute drift toward earth. I feel a little cheated and yet try to remain in the moment and take it all in—the yellow and brown patchwork quilt of earth's surface, the parklands, the winding Wallkill River. A view that cannot be captured by a camera lens, no matter how high def. I'm bewitched. Everything is amazing.

"Beautiful!" My heart pounds. Life can be such a fantastic ride when you push its limits.

I gaze briefly at the array of canopies as the instructor turns us toward the drop zone, carefully avoiding the others. I spot Kristin and wave, my smile so wide my cheeks hurt. She waves back. I think she's smiling, too, and hope she'll cherish this amazing experience. For an instant, I question my April goal.

Then the ground comes closer, and with it, so does reality.

Once we land, my life is still my life. This does not fill the emptiness. Nothing can, at least not for more than mere minutes or hours. The void is inescapable when my eyes are open. Although I've known that, it's a bummer nonetheless.

"Prepare to land," the instructor says.

I bring my knees up as he guides us to the ground, where we slide to a stop on our butts.

It's over.

We disengage the harnesses and I whip off my goggles, thank Gary with a generous tip, and then run to my sister, who is talking excitedly to her instructor. She turns as I approach and flings open her arms, grabbing me into a hug. "Holy mother of a dog, that was unbelievable!"

"No regerts?" A joke we have repeated after seeing a misspelled tattoo in a meme years ago.

She releases me. "No regerts. I haven't been that outside my head in, well, maybe ever. It was beautiful. What an experience. Let's go get our pictures."

We would look more badass if we hadn't been strapped to instructors, but the vantage point amid the clouds is striking.

"Wait until Luca sees this. Then again, I don't know if I want to encourage my kids to try this someday." When she laughs at herself, my heart refills.

Minutes later, we pull out of the parking lot with the sunroof cracked open to let in a bit of cool air. Seeing her with heightened color and joy makes me feel lighter somehow. Freer, even, so I try to enjoy it without examining it too closely.

"I'm suddenly exhausted," Kristin muses.

"The adrenaline ebb. Close your eyes and relax," I say.

"You don't mind?"

"Not at all." We could both use a little time to mentally replay our big adventure. I turn up the radio and tap my hand against the wheel while listening to Ed Sheeran sing about bad habits.

Today's success leads me to consider another part of my plan—dealing with that cursed money. It may sound silly and irrational, but I cannot give it to Kristin because I worry that her and Tony's obsession with wealth could doom them to my same curse. Besides, they're proud and probably wouldn't take it. They surely don't need it—not like so many others in the world do.

Plenty of charities would love millions of dollars, but they eat up a lot of the donation to cover overhead. I could make gifts to individuals, but who could I repay for a past kindness that isn't also covetous of wealth?

Scotty's occupational therapist, Josephina, springs to mind.

A godsend.

Loving, patient, and full of optimism.

Our pediatrician, Dr. Amato, referred us to her, as well as directing us to the SEED Center in Stamford. Josephina radiated warmth and acceptance, making Sean and me like her immediately. It was good for us to agree on something so easily. She'd been working with Scotty for only a couple of months before the COVID lockdown happened. We were despondent, but she worked with us remotely, and then, after the weather broke, she came back and worked masked and outside.

She not only helped Scotty; she helped Sean and me too. Gave us tips. Encouraged our hopes. She has older children of her own, including a daughter in medical school with debt that is strangling the family.

We haven't spoken since the accident. Kristin said she came to the funeral, but my mother had given me two of her Xanax, so I don't recall seeing Josephina, much less speaking with her.

Apparently my father and Tony flanked me, hooking their arms beneath my armpits to carry me down the church aisle to my seat. After the funeral service, they put me to bed during the luncheon. For several days thereafter, I drifted in and out of consciousness, screaming aloud each time I became alert and the reality of my life set in. Never to see or speak to my dearest loves again. To smell or touch them. To love or be loved by them.

The permanence—or never-everness, as Livvy might say—still chokes me, striking my throat with remarkable blunt force. In the rearview mirror, Scotty's plush toy Piglet stares at me from the corner of the rear window where I keep him.

I smile at it, as if it is confirming my plans.

Josephina. Who better to receive a windfall than someone kind who isn't asking for it? Someone like that wouldn't be cursed.

My posture straightens and my heart rate rises again. This feels right. I should make a list of potential recipients, like Lillian from the library, who always tried to create a sensory-friendly place for kids like Scotty in a quiet corner of the children's section.

Kristin wouldn't love this idea because she's worried about my future financial needs. What she doesn't know won't hurt her.

———

Bob wipes a dribble of chili off his chin. "Oh my. It sounds fantastic. I wish I'd been so brave when I was young."

"What you call brave, others might call foolhardy," I joke, glad that I pushed myself to join him tonight. Although slightly drained from the ups and downs of the day, I arrived home wanting to talk about the experience with someone. "I'm just glad my sister did it with me."

"You two seem close. I always wish my Pammy had a sister. My son, Bobby, lives in Florida and only gets back a couple times each year. It's not the same."

"Well, you spared yourself some drama. Teen girls find a million reasons to bicker." Even as I say it, anyone could tell I'm exaggerating. Kristin and I didn't bicker much, but that was largely due to her ability to forebear most things.

"Times were different in my day. Mothers did most of the care-taking. If I have one big regret, it's that I wish I'd been less stressed around my kids when they were little." He folds his arms across his chest, unaware that I share his regret.

My throat goes dry. He doesn't know my story. There's no point in telling him because it would only make him sad.

"Your kids know that you love them, even if you weren't as happy-go-lucky during their childhood as you might be if you got a do-over." I have a pang, hoping that my son knew I loved him despite my shortcomings.

"Parenting is the toughest job I ever had. Maybe someday you'll get your chance." He winks.

My face goes blank. I'm unable to form any words until I give myself a mental shake. It's time to be alone. "Thanks for dinner. I'd chat longer, but I'm wiped out. Let me help you clean before I go." I stand with my bowl and spoon. I hate lying to Bob, but there's no reason to burden him either.

"I've got it, dear." He rises too. "Thanks for the company. Renting to you was the best decision I've made this year."

I heat with shame because he won't think that by late April. "You're very sweet. I hope you know how fond I am of you."

With that, I make my exit so he doesn't catch me crying.

CHAPTER EIGHT

KRISTIN

The following Monday

Taking half my Saturday to pacify my sister and jump from a plane led to a long Sunday workday, but the exhilaration and Amy's giddiness mitigated that stress. This morning I'm staring at my reflection in the microwave glass, clipping my hair back into a low barrette while the juicer whirs, and trying to ignore the bags under my eyes. Another restless night—a consistent theme on weeknights. My brain jumps from client problems to career issues like a frog hopping lily pads. I expected sleep to improve four days ago, when I swore not to refill my pill bottle, but my experience has not borne that out. If only life could be as free as I felt falling through space.

I butter Livvy's pecan pancakes, hand Luca the carton of almond milk for his cereal, and chug lukewarm coffee. My train leaves in twelve minutes. "Where's Daddy?"

"I don't know," Luca says, barely looking up from his bowl. I hand him and Livvy each a glass of fresh-squeezed orange-and-carrot juice.

"Mommy, there's no chocolate chips," Livvy says, frowning. Ugh, the grammar.

She's been more demanding since I gave most of my Saturday to Amy. I wish I could split myself into three people: one for work, one for home, and one for Amy.

"We don't start school days with chocolate. Now hurry up and eat. Daddy has to put you on the bus soon, and Mommy has to run." I kiss her and Luca on the head and call aloud: "Tony? I'm leaving."

He bounds down the steps. "I'm here. Go, go." He busses me on the lips, the perfunctory action making me yearn for the before time, when physical touch felt imperative. "Have a good day."

What a joke. I can't remember the last good day I had at work, not that I say that. He's been lying low to give me space while we've been focused on Livvy. I should be honest about how badly I'm struggling but fear admitting it aloud will make everything worse. "Thanks. See you all later."

I trot to my car, knowing I might not see the kids before they go to bed. After I make partner, I won't need to prove myself. I'll finally be able to work from home part time and keep more reasonable city hours.

On the train, I dig into my purse for my phone. My email inbox makes me wistfully think of Adderall.

I hold my breath and open the one from Baxter's litigator. Dammit—they lost the motion for summary judgment. Litigation will drag on unless they settle, and either way, it's not good news for our merger talks.

Next up, a note from Luca's teacher. I frown.

Mrs. DeMarco,

I'm sure you know Luca is a pleasure. He's kind, studious, and gets along with everyone. I wanted to make you aware, however, of something I'm seeing in the classroom. Generally, we have to remind kids to compromise and cooperate. Luca, on the other hand, is so quick to do those things, some others are starting to take advantage of him. I've caught at least one boy getting Luca to do some of his homework. I've also seen Luca give away his lunch to anyone who asks. I've spoken with him about healthy boundaries, and wanted to alert you to these things so that you and your husband could also reinforce these concepts. I don't think there is cause for alarm as I've not witnessed bullying. It's simply a matter of other kids recognizing that Luca has trouble saying no and then they manipulate him.

Please feel free to call me if you have any questions.

Sincerely,
Miss Diaz

I stare ahead, my stomach tight. Darwin would have us believe weak traits die off. But no, here comes too-eager-to-please Luca, ready and willing to sacrifice his time and food and God knows what else, ensuring that he is the only uncomfortable person in a room. I don't want him to end up like me. Is it inevitable due to genetics, or is he learning these bad habits from my behavior?

I sigh and forward the email to Tony, suggesting we talk later. As I'm doing that, my coworker Finn Larkin texts me to ask when I'll be in because he has questions about some UCC filing. My head begins to throb, and it's not even eight o'clock.

This is shaping up to be a long day. It's possible to get through it on my own, but getting through is not excelling. I need to excel this year. I also need to be alert when Tony calls—probably at lunch—to discuss Luca. Guilt and self-pride call out these justifications, but I can always quit the pills after these matters are resolved.

When I get to my firm, I beeline for Jenna's office and close her door behind me. Jenna is two years younger than I am but looks half my age. Glossy black hair and bright blue eyes give her that sharp, attractive look that commands attention. So does her Balenciaga artist-doodle neck-scarf blouse.

"Good morning, Kristin," she says; then her expression shifts. "Uh-oh. What's wrong?"

I bite my lip, wishing I were stronger. "Would it be possible to get one more bottle of Adderall? Or even just a handful of pills? I swear, this is it. As soon as the Baxter deal is closed, I should be able to catch my breath."

"No need for excuses. I've been on them for two years now." She opens her top desk drawer and retrieves a bottle. "There are only about ten left. Take the bottle." She tosses it at me. "I've got more at home."

"Are you sure?" I peel fifty dollars from my wallet and set it on her desk.

"Yes." She pockets the cash. "If you want more, let me know. But these'll cover you for the week."

I grip the bottle tight in my fist. "You're a lifesaver!"

"Happy to help." Her smile is genuine and guilt-free. It's a relief to not be made to feel worse about what I'm doing.

When I exit her office, I leave the door open and walk directly to my office to set my things down before getting coffee from the kitchen. Finn is there, refilling his cup. He's only a few years younger than me, but unmarried and with no kids. His boundless energy isn't proof that he's smarter or more driven than I am. It's simply because he has no one else to consider but himself. Who wouldn't sleep well and have loads of time to work under those circumstances? If he were using that time wisely, he wouldn't need to come to me with so many questions.

"Did you get my text?" he asks, all sleek in well-cut trousers and a crisp blue shirt.

I position one hand over the tiny syrup drop on my skirt. "Yes, but I just got in. Give me ten minutes to clear the decks, all right?"

Once I'm back in my office, I close my door, open the bottle, and down a pill before I have time to reconsider. For the second time this morning, I catch my unflattering reflection in glass. I'll quit when this bottle is finished. I mean it this time.

———

"Not today, honey." I skim the marked-up stock-purchase agreement that recently landed in my inbox while Livvy is on speakerphone.

Between meetings and client calls, I've dealt with multiple personal calls. Tony called about Luca, tossing out questions I couldn't answer. He agreed to follow up with Miss Diaz for clarifications and email me the details. Emailing about our children isn't A-plus parenting, is it? Amy called about taking a trapeze class in Brooklyn sometime. This is Livvy's second call of the afternoon. The pill is wearing off, and I have at least two more hours of work before I can go home.

"Why not?" my daughter whines.

"Because we can't impose on Aunt Amy without asking first. She might be busy this afternoon. Besides, you probably have homework. When you finish that, ask Kerry to come over to play instead." Kerry lives four doors down the street. Tony's refusal to consider therapy has forced me to do some reading on childhood anxiety. Those books make me feel inept. In any case, we're trying a few changes at home. If Livvy plays with kids her age more often instead of relying on grown-ups for entertainment and direction, she should learn to navigate friendships better. That should increase her self-confidence, which in turn could reduce her anxiety.

My gaze snags on some new language in the survival clause that would extend Baxter's liability beyond what we previously agreed.

"I want Aunt Amy. I never see her."

I stand and close my office door for privacy, pressing two fingers against the vein pulsing in my neck. "You just saw her Saturday, when she visited after we skydived, Livvy, so don't exaggerate. Please, honey. Mommy's really busy right now. I don't have time to argue."

"You never have time to argue."

My mouth falls open before I cover it with my free hand to stifle a surprised laugh. As preposterous as her reply is, she's right. And yet somehow, during the weeks since returning from the Mayflower Inn, Tony and I have lived around each other like polite roommates—him cooking, me folding laundry, him paying bills, me coordinating sports carpools—without once discussing anything substantial. Meanwhile, I imagine Livvy tucking one hand under the opposite armpit in a defiant stance while holding the phone to her ear.

"Is that what you want, honey? To argue with me?" I ask. "I'd so much rather you want to be nice to me."

Rather than soften her outlook, she comes back with, "Be nice to me too."

"I'm nice to you all the time. Just this morning I made you special pancakes." A time suck that left me no time to eat anything myself.

"That's what all moms do."

I blink at the phone while picturing her scowling. Is this what all kids think, or is Livvy utterly spoiled? Perhaps I deserve this attitude because Amy is right and my priorities are screwed up.

"I want a cat," Livvy adds.

I glance at the clock. I'm due in Jim's office in five minutes, and perspiration is breaking out all over. "Honey, you know Daddy's allergic to cats. Now listen, I have to go to a meeting."

"Will you be home soon?"

"I don't know." Probably not. "I'll try." The silence at her end somehow blares in my head. "Livvy?"

"Fine. Bye."

I imagine her little finger punching the off button as she hangs up without an "I love you." Am I the only working mom who hasn't figured out how to balance things so that my kids don't suffer?

A jarring knock at the door precedes Finn's entry. I grew up with guys like him—smart, socially savvy, a little entitled. We share a paralegal, whom he both hogs and flirts with. Well, *flirt* may be too strong, but he butters her up so he can shoehorn his work in before mine when he's pressed for time. "Ready?"

Not really. "I just got the requested changes from Avant's counsel, so I haven't given it a thorough review." Or any real review.

"Yeah. I focused on the reps and warranties."

Now I'll look less prepared than him in front of Jim. If Livvy hadn't been dogging me, I could've gotten to it a little sooner. I can hear Amy in my head. *Your daughter is more important than work, isn't she?* Of course she is, but why is it an either/or proposition? I've worked damn hard—in law school and at this firm. Aren't I entitled to be more than someone's mother? To have my own goals and needs in pursuit of my interests and ambitions? No one expects Tony to step back from his goals. I deserve satisfaction—the recognition and rewards for my work—the same as anyone else. Frankly, I deserve it more than any man who conveniently relies on his stay-at-home wife to manage all family matters.

I grab my notepad, preferring paper notes to a stylus and iPad. "Let's go."

Jim is seated behind his desk when we get to his corner office. He's aged a lot these past five years or so. The balding, the bags beneath his eyes, the slight turkey neck—all signs of a man advancing in age without enough exercise or sleep. A peek into my future if I continue down this path.

Finn and I each sit in the chairs opposite Jim's desk.

"I just got the revised purchase agreement—" I begin.

Jim holds up a hand. "Doesn't matter. I just hung up with Sal. His board won't sign off on the concessions. They'd rather dispose of the contingent liability first, which they're convinced will cost less than Avant's estimation. At that point, they'll decide whether to go hunting for a new merger or not."

Months of work go up in a puff of smoke so fast I almost cough before my posture slumps like a candle in the sun. I introduced Sal to Jim and have been running point on almost all aspects of this transaction, yet Sal called Jim to kill the deal? My limbs go numb even as rage blazes in my chest. "I knew Sal was unhappy, but I didn't think he'd walk away before we finished negotiating. Are you sure he's not trying to call their bluff?"

"That's what I thought at first, but no." Jim steeples his fingers. "Sal doesn't want to keep churning fees and playing games. He's soured on them in general."

"I don't blame him," Finn—the king of testing which way the wind is blowing and then adjusting his sails rather than risking an original thought—says. "Assholes tried to screw him out of the bargain they made."

Jim nods, and while I knew Avant's backpedaling from agreed-upon terms spelled trouble, if I were *its* counsel, I probably would've tested those waters too. After all, Baxter's liability, while contingent, is not immaterial. If Jim were being honest, he'd admit this too. "Had the potential liability been known from the outset, the original deal terms would've reflected it from the start. Isn't part of our job to advise our own clients when they're being stubborn? On the whole, I still think these companies are a good fit."

"Think what you like, but you aren't the client." Jim makes a face to signal that I'm not to press Sal.

"Well, guess this frees me up for that NFT project," Finn announces, standing. "Should I ask Linda to close up this file?" he asks me.

"I'll take care of it, thanks." I start to rise.

"Kristin, hang on a minute," Jim says, waving Finn off.

Finn closes the door on his way out.

"What's up?" I sink back onto the edge of the chair to appear eager, although it's taking all my energy not to sigh.

"I know you know that losing this deal is a blow. But Kristin, you've been edgy this past month or two." He's looking at me for an explanation, but he won't squeeze a confession from me. Amy and Tony have also noticed a personality change. The way my clothes hang on my hips is the other sign that the pills are a problem, but right now they're my only solution. I just need to hold on until things fall into place. No way I'm giving up at first and goal. "I know you've got a lot going on with your sister—"

"We're coming out of that now." I cut him off, clenching my teeth. He would never imply that personal problems were an issue for Finn or any other man. "If I've been edgy, it's my frustration with this Baxter problem."

"Its collapse poses a problem in terms of your personal goals."

My entire body goes taut. *Oh, hell no!* sounds off in my brain, but I cannot show any sign of weakness. If I crumble, it's game over. "Jim, why does my decade-plus of service here—my excellent work—count for nothing?"

"Not for nothing, but it doesn't count for as much as you'd like it to. And before you get pissed off, look at it from the partners' perspective. We expect our associates and junior partners to be excellent. To work hard and produce winning results. That's the minimum requirement for employment, not the bar for being considered for equity partnership. As you know, full partnership comes down to money. To how much you're billing, closing, and bringing in in terms of new clients."

He didn't ask Finn to stay behind for this talk, and Finn thinks he's in the running this year too. Did he get some secret handshake that I missed? I'm honestly ready to throw a chair through a window. I might quit if I weren't so damn determined to force this place to acknowledge my value.

"I've brought in many new clients and billed tens of thousands of hours throughout my career. I'm also a team player."

"All true, but the demands on partners are high. You've got young kids. You're no longer logging weekend hours like you once did. I get it. I'm not criticizing. But no one can have it all, Kristin."

No woman, he means. Plenty of dads around here have made partner. Our department has forty-two equity partners, but only six are women, and only one woman has been promoted in the past three years. "In other words, even though it's only March, I can basically kiss partnership goodbye again?"

"Unless you bring in a big fish or two—even if on projects you hand off—you've got an uphill climb." He leans forward, clasping his hands together on his desk in a patronizing fatherly manner. "You know I've always liked you. That's why I'd rather shoot straight than see you blindsided."

I hesitate to move or speak when I'm trembling with both fury and also shame from his pitying tone. "Well, I appreciate your honesty. You've given me a lot to think about, so I'd best go do that."

One brow rises, as if my attitude has unnerved him. "To be clear, your job is secure, as is a healthy bonus. I'm talking strictly about equity partnership."

"Yet I suspect Finn is being considered despite having less experience and fewer new clients than I did at his year." I channel my husband's ability to remain calm and fix my gaze on Jim. "If that happens, it would seem that the criteria are . . . unequal."

There. We both now know I'm not willing to ignore gender discrimination if younger men get promoted over me again.

Jim clears his throat, tapping his fingers on his desk. He knows the optics of a public accusation wouldn't look good, so I don't push and risk creating a bigger problem for myself and HR. He says, "Like I said, go hunt an elephant so we don't have any disappointments."

I nod. Got it. I have to bag an elephant, while Finn merely has to kiss enough ass and bill more hours than is humanly possible, the unethical little shit. As I'm leaving Jim's office, I resist the temptation to slam his door shut.

When I return to my office, I close the door and lean with my back against it, looking out at the Manhattan skyline. Golden sunlight bounces off the glass buildings, making the entire city glitter. The dazzling view has always given me a sense of purpose and power—a passion for working in one of the most important cities on the globe.

I've missed out on school plays and lacrosse games to compete with some of the brightest legal minds. My first interest in becoming a lawyer sparked when Sandra Day O'Connor retired—all that news about her being the first-ever female justice of the Supreme Court. I thought I would become a judge until law school taught me that I'm not suited to litigation's confrontational nature. Transactional work is better because negotiation and compromise come naturally.

My new career goals were plotted with friends from our cramped Morningside Heights apartment during our three years at Columbia Law School. My revised goal of becoming partner at a big firm in Manhattan had seemed more attainable too. Now look at me, still stuck with my nose pressed to the glass ceiling.

Of course, Tony had pursued me so hard that I married him right after I took the bar exam. He'd been so proud and supportive. His work was in White Plains and mine in the city, so we rented an apartment in Yonkers to split the commute. Then I got pregnant eighteen months later—unintentionally—which took me off track that year. When I got pregnant with Livvy two and a half years later, Tony thought it was time to move to Connecticut. He wanted the kids to have easy access to his parents and Amy and Sean, and he liked the familiarity of the schools and parks and communities there.

Although that extended my commute, the life he envisioned looked beautiful. I thought, *Why can't I have it all?* A home near the shore in Old Greenwich, with my sister and Tony's parents in neighboring towns. Weekend picnics and safe, walkable neighborhoods for the kids. I was young and energetic and didn't foresee years of banging on a locked door trying to have my efforts recognized by these partners. Or how the long, harried days of negotiating and thousands of hours on the train would affect me and my relationship with my children.

Quick math puts my aggregate commuting time since then at around seventy-four hundred hours. How different might my relationship with my family be if I'd spent even half of those hours with them instead of working on the train?

And what have I gained for all that I've given up? Money. Piles of money that we spend almost as quickly as I make them. Not only don't I have it all; I'm losing what I have. Am I being selfish to hold so fast to *this* job, to the detriment of everything else in my life?

I spin my chair to look at the city again while my body processes amphetamines and I question pretty much everything. The view glitters, but what's the true value of a diamanté illusion?

CHAPTER NINE

A M Y

The same day

Josephina will be waiting for me at the restaurant soon, yet step five of my plan suddenly seems more awkward than anticipated. What amount is too big a gift? And if I choose one that's more palatable for the recipient, how will I ever get rid of all the money in time?

I tear a half-million-dollar check from the booklet. It's a generous sum that she might reject, so I won't let her open it in front of me. Josephina deserves this because she lives her life making people a priority. It feels good to do something unselfish—although making myself feel better is hardly altruistic.

Decision made, I stuff it in an envelope, seal that, and then scribble her name across the front. I drop the envelope in my bag and sling it over my shoulder on my way out the door.

It takes fifteen minutes to cut through downtown Stamford to get to High Ridge Road, a main thoroughfare that runs north and is littered with retail strip centers. My left knee bounces the closer I get to Luigi's Restaurant.

By Scotty's first birthday, I had an inkling he wasn't typical. Sean wasn't concerned, so I stuffed my new-parent anxieties into a little box and hoped for the best. As Scotty's second birthday approached, my instincts kicked that box open, and I called Birth to Three for an evaluation. When we got the autism diagnosis, I berated myself for not acting sooner. Josephina calmed me, assuring me that all would be well. She helped me, and now I can help her.

On the passenger seat, my purse is like a stealth bomber carrying one scrap of paper that will change a life. I hope it brings Josephina only happiness, although that isn't always the case with money. While it does relieve some types of stress, I'd go homeless if doing so would buy back Sean's and Scotty's lives.

Shortly before noon, I pull into the parking lot and take a moment to settle myself. This meeting requires strength and presence. Piglet stares at me from the back seat, so I wink as if he were Scotty and open the car door.

Inside, Josephina is already seated and scanning a menu. She looks up and smiles, standing with open arms as I approach the table. The missing little soul who first brought us together is inescapable, making us both teary within seconds.

She's the first nonfamily member I've hugged since last April. Her embrace is oddly comforting, as is the powdery scent that triggers many memories, including how Scotty instantly took to her singsong voice.

Those earliest sessions were eye-openers. Until Scotty's diagnosis, I felt like a failure after having watched Luca and Livvy sail through infancy while meeting milestones. They and other kids smiled at their parents and responded to hearing their names. They didn't push away from hugs. They babbled constantly, and their faces were lit with glee and curiosity. They tried different foods and didn't experience discomfort over the slight scratchiness of wool blankets or linen shirts. Mostly, they craved their parents' attention. All the while, I grappled with Scotty's apparent disinterest in me.

Kristin and Tony made suggestions—introduce things slowly, let him pick a book, and so on. Nothing worked. Conversely, within Josephina's first session, she taught me how to get Scotty in his "just right" feeling about his body and sensitivities before any learning could happen—whether that meant dimming lights or finding the right fabrics for his clothes or keeping the sounds inside subdued. Bye-bye, Baby Einstein videos; hello, birdsong.

She also explained that repeating his name over and over, especially when paired with demands to look or come or whatever, wouldn't get him to respond as well as if I used his name less often and only when paired with a positive reinforcer. Every week, her work unlocked a new doorway of understanding about my son's way of experiencing the world so I could meet him there and be a better mother to him.

By his third birthday, after I'd begun to stop judging him and myself, I knew that he loved warm pavement and long cool grass, so we would picnic in the yard. He liked marching up and down stairs, so I'd sit at the bottom and hum songs while he worked his little body to exhaustion. I stopped expecting facial cues and paid more attention to his words and pointing. I even found the patience to read about Piglet for hours at a time. Learning the ways he filtered the world allowed me to slowly relax and help him grow. I wish we'd had more time to get to know each other. I wish I knew for sure that he felt my love, despite how long it took me to get things right.

As my gratitude for Josephina's assistance swells, I hug her extra tight.

"You look wonderful," I say as we take our seats. I don't think she knows about my stint at Silver Hill. I tug at my shirtsleeves so my history won't detract from my intentions today. "I was nervous on my way over, but it's really good to see you."

"Same, Amy. I've thought of you often, and I've missed sweet little Scotty." Her voice quavers on those words. "How have you been?"

Going straight to the heart of the matter is why she's an excellent occupational therapist. Throughout my life, I considered myself brave because I always took the dare or sought humor in adversity, whether when grounded for throwing a party in high school, being put on academic probation in my sophomore year of college, or managing

Scotty's therapies. The truth is that, until this year, I had never faced real adversity.

"Better now." Talking about myself is my least favorite thing to do, especially in light of my bigger plans. "Of course, I've struggled. It's lonely without Sean and Scotty, although in a way they're always with me, like silent ghosts. Sometimes not so silent."

She's nodding. "Grief is painful. You think you're healing, and then you're blindsided by some memory. Maybe it helps to expect healing—like children—to go in a crooked line. Everything has its own path; you just need to follow the cues."

"You're so wise." In truth, my grief loops like a figure eight, always bringing me back to the beginning. "My sister and her family have been a great support."

"How is Kristin?" She smiles, having been impressed with my sister's intelligence and curiosity, her fastidious attention to detail.

"The same. Efficient. Devoted. Maybe a little overwhelmed lately. But her family is all fine. Healthy." Alive.

"That's good. People who love you are a blessing. Not everyone is so lucky."

A truth made more evident by comparison with Sean's family. His older sister, Leslie, lived in Oregon for most of our relationship, so we rarely saw her. His parents—in New Jersey—were fun loving in the beginning, but then came the comparisons and doubts. *Leslie's kids were walking by one—you should put things up on a table so Scotty has to rise to reach them. Little Lizzie was stringing words together by sixteen months—aren't you reading to Scotty? When he throws those fits, you should ignore him, or he'll just keep manipulating you.* Their uneducated advice, refusal to respect our parenting choices, and the COVID lockdown eroded our relationship. That should bother me more, I think vaguely. I liked his mom, Jane, when Sean and I first married. She'd been considerate and giving in ways my mother—who worried about us more than she actually did anything to help us—never was.

"All true," I say.

"Are you still in your same house?" She sips her water.

I shake my head. "I downsized. It went on the market the other week and got four offers. I donated the furniture and lamps I didn't take when I moved, but there are still things in the attic and basement storage area to deal with." I'd gotten through the move thanks to Tony's and Kristin's presence and efficiency. I haven't been alone in that house since the day my sister took me to the hospital. I'm not sure I'm ready to be there on my own, but I'm running out of time.

She nods, tapping her fingers against her lips. The waitress stops by our table, so we order two salads and a "thinny" pizza to share. It was a staple in our house for years, but I haven't eaten one since before the trip to Exuma.

"How are your kids?" I ask, biding time before explaining the purpose of this lunch. Now that we're here, qualms rattle me. She might think I've lost my mind.

"Good, thanks. Marissa is in her third year of medical school already, if you can believe it. The boys are in high school and, well, you know teen boys." As soon as she says that, her expression shifts to that of someone who's just sworn in the middle of a sermon.

Jokes about parenting woes can rub me wrong, yet I used to laugh at them precisely because they weren't meant to be taken literally. It's not like she thinks I'm lucky to never have to deal with a teen son.

"I know." No, actually, I'll never know, but I let that thought drift past. "I gave my parents a good run in my teens."

"That doesn't surprise me," she jokes, which does raise a genuine chuckle from me. "Sometimes I catch myself wishing for the time when they're all out of college and I can worry less and retire. Then I feel guilty for not enjoying the moment." Again she winces, catching herself. Yes, I'd give everything for the chance to muddle through maddening parenting issues, but that doesn't mean she shouldn't get to discuss hers.

"Pretty sure that's called human nature." Perhaps that's something to remember when I get irritated with Tony and Kristin.

She shrugs, sipping her beverage. "It is, but you were always good at celebrating the little wins and taking things in stride."

"Was I?" That's not my recollection. I'd hung up with the Birth to Three team more resigned than shocked. Then came the anxiety, the heartbreak, and the natural fear of someone who was uneducated about neurodiversity.

I'd grabbed Sean's arm as I set the phone down. "Can he still go to preschool, or does he need a special program?"

"Let's ask the preschool." He patted my hand, acting calmer than I felt.

"Will he be able to assimilate? Will he be able to manage his own life and fall in love and have a career and do all the normal things?" My eyes got watery. "Or will his whole life be difficult and lonely?"

Sean tugged me to his side and wrapped an arm around my shoulders. "Honey, there are a lot of people on the spectrum. People understand it more, and there's less stigma than when we were young. I can't see the future, but we'll take it one step at a time and give him the best support available."

"Where will we find the money and time? Maybe Kristin's been right all along. We should've been smarter about budgeting and saving. And even if we had enough money, am I equipped for this? I've been bungling motherhood almost from the beginning."

"You're not bungling anything, Amy. We didn't know what we didn't know, but you noticed something and pushed to get him evaluated when I resisted. If anyone isn't equipped, it's me. Have some faith. We've got a lot to learn, but we'll be okay. Scotty will be okay. We love each other and him, and together we can handle anything."

I took a breath, closed my eyes, and laid my head against his chest, listening to his strong heartbeat. It calmed me in the moment. And then Josephina came into our lives.

I smile at her now. "I owe any good mothering to you. I loved my son, but you know how often I was confused by what he needed or why, and distraught that he had to cope with all these extra struggles. I'm ashamed to admit to how often I fell into bed wishing for it all to be easier. Sometimes even envying families with typical kids."

My cheeks heat in the face of the naked truth. I might be extra hard on Kristin when I see her making some of my own mistakes—her bowing to that insane pressure of trying to do the "right" things instead of simply enjoying the child as he or she is.

Josephina taps my hand, which is resting on the table. "You're too hard on yourself, Amy. Every mother doubts herself sometimes. But you could laugh and roll with the punches. And you worked so hard with Scotty. I saw the love in your eyes when you were with him, and I'm sure he did too. You were a good mother. Your son was well loved, even if your time together was tragically cut short."

My skin prickles as the hairs on my neck and arms rise. "Thank you. It's nice to hear, even if you exaggerate."

"I don't. Trust me. I've worked with many families, and not all parents are like you and Sean. Rest assured, I have only good memories of you all."

She's handed me the perfect segue just as our salads arrive. "As do I of you. That's actually why I called."

"I was wondering . . ." She smiles, picking up a fork.

"You mentioned retirement earlier. What will you do when you stop working?" I also take a bite of the salad, with its garlicky Caesar dressing.

"We're not sure. Probably volunteer somewhere, although I look forward to having more free time too. I love to knit, and my husband and I enjoy kayaking. We've also discussed moving somewhere less expensive so we can enjoy our lives with more breathing room, but I worry I'd miss my friends. He likes the Carolinas. We'll see."

"It's fun to fantasize. I'm sure you'll settle on a good compromise."

Our pizza is delivered, so I take advantage of the distraction to work up to the gift. Two bites in, I set down my slice. "Josephina, I've been meaning to thank you properly for everything you did for Scotty, and for me. Honestly, I can't imagine how we would've fared together without you."

"That's kind, but I don't need thanks. Working with kids like Scotty is my privilege. I love helping them acquire new skills."

"It shows. Seriously. You're so selfless—with my family and other clients. I've felt terrible that I didn't return your calls last spring. I wasn't in a good headspace, not for a long time. But I did appreciate your thoughts. Now I just, well, I want to show my appreciation." I pull the envelope out of my purse and slide it across the table.

Her brows rise. "What's this?"

"You made my life a little easier for a few years, and now it's my turn."

Her gaze jumps from the envelope to me and back a couple of times. "Amy, I don't need thanks for doing my job. I already got paid for it too."

Exactly the attitude that makes her deserving.

"I know, but this is something I want to do. The prize money—I hardly need it all." Nor do I want it. "Giving gifts makes me happy. You've not only made my life better; you also make the world a better place, so I am starting with you. Please accept this for what it is—nothing more or less. Don't open it now. Put it in your bag until later, and know that it comes from my heart." I pray her awkwardness will give way, because I need this little win—a chance to do some good of my own in the world before I'm gone.

Josephina pats her breastbone a few times. "Okay, I guess. I didn't mean to be ungrateful."

"I know. Please trust me, I'm doing this for myself as much as for you. Being generous is one of the very few things I've had to smile about this year."

On that note, she takes the envelope and puts it in her purse. "Thank you. It's unexpected but much appreciated."

I breathe a sigh of relief and smile. "You're welcome."

She's probably guessing it's a few hundred—or possibly a few thousand—so she might freak out later. It makes me giddy to imagine how she and her husband will celebrate once the shock wears off. That first week after I won, Sean and I shook with excitement anytime the wonder of it all hit us. Oh, the plans we'd made. The excited phone calls.

Of course, we didn't know what was coming. But Josephina won't have my bad luck because she's never made her life or wishes about money.

Life does go on, doesn't it? People come and go, and a few like her leave a significant impression. I wonder who I've affected outside of my family without realizing it. Should I add more to my plan—perhaps a road show of sorts where I contact people from the past? No. It's better to sit deeply with the few I hold dear . . . and sweet Bob. Why stretch myself too thin?

———

With my reunion with Josephina boosting me, I mentally retest the idea of going to the old house while my mettle is relatively strong.

It's not as if my life with Sean and Scotty—the memories of that time—are trapped solely within the home's empty rooms. They're unavoidably pressed like cave art into each chamber of my heart, where they belong.

When Sean and I were first dating, we went camping in Vermont and spent a day at a quarry outside Manchester Center. He dragged me up to the tallest cliff—maybe twenty feet high—and coaxed me into jumping into that dark, icy water. Holding hands on the way down, we shrieked when we popped up from the frigid depths, and then warmed up at night with a campfire and vigorous sex.

I miss him. And sex. I blink, my lips parting on that thought. Anything intimate and pleasurable has seemed too taboo to consider this year. Perhaps handing Josephina that check has unearthed a buried piece of my soul.

Well, Sean, you'd coax me into the deep end of the dark waters now, too, wouldn't you? Decision made, I reroute for the old house. When I arrive, I sit in my car and stare at the small, blue, 1950s clapboard colonial that had been cream colored when we bought it seven years ago. Sean loved this house more than I ever did, a fact that somehow makes selling it now chafe.

After learning we were pregnant with a boy, Sean painted the house Prussian blue. Chasing runaway emotions was such a him thing to do. We settled on white trim and a yellow front door.

That rolling ball led to hours of DIY home-improvement projects like jungle decals on the nursery walls and a swing set in the small backyard. For the most part, it was more fun than work—our life motto to that point. One I've failed to live up to since he died. He would not be pleased about that.

I shiver before glancing up and down the street. It's probably best that no one's outside, although some kind of goodbye is in order. Notes to the few neighbors we knew well should suffice.

My keys jingle in my hand as I stride along the short walkway to the front door, where I'm hit with the memory of bringing Scotty home for the first time on that frigid winter morning, swaddled stiffly in the tiniest snowsuit known to man. The world's cutest baby. Chubby folds on all four limbs. A tuft of cinnamon-colored hair. A dimpled chin. Slobbery, pouty lips.

I hold my stomach, light-headed but still standing.

After Sean opened the door that day, I touched my nose to our son's and said, "We're home, little buddy." Sean teased me about how often I talked to Scotty those first few months, as if the infant understood me. I knew he didn't, but that didn't stop me from narrating each moment of every day. I wanted my child to know me. To know our home. To know himself. How can you know anything if no one talks to you?

With a held breath, I step inside and close the door behind me. The oak floors are slightly sun damaged, darker in spots that rugs used to cover. If it weren't for the seller's market, I would've had to refinish those before listing.

One won't find sleek, monochromatic color schemes and smart-home features, soft-close cabinets, or a gleaming quartz island here. No fine art either. That stuff never mattered much to us. Boggle and BBQs. Failed cooking experiments and cheap bottles of wine. Rocking Scotty to sleep. Birthday parties and anniversaries. Laughing at a favorite sitcom or bingeing Netflix on a rainy day. Smiling across the room. Being held when I cried. What made this home beautiful was the love inside these walls.

I give myself a mental shake, tuck the keys in my coat pocket, and head upstairs to the pull-down attic steps. The hatch springs yawn as I yank the string and unfold the ladder. Clicking on the phone's flashlight, I begin to climb, poking my head into the musty space to reach the cord and turn on the light bulb while ducking to avoid the spiderwebs.

I hoist my body up until I'm standing—ducking—surrounded by boxes and garbage bags. Those bags stop me. I'm pretty sure Tony jammed Scotty's plush toys in them and then stuck them up here while I was in Silver Hill. He and Kristin thought it might be best to remove some of the reminders, but they did so only after getting my permission. Granted, I was semicomatose at the time, but their hearts were in the right place.

There's no good reason for these toys to be tossed into the garbage when other kids might enjoy them. Perhaps the local nursery school or church would distribute them. I open one bag to determine whether the items are in good enough shape to donate. A colorful choo choo train. A fuzzy football. A beagle and chihuahua. All gifts from family and friends. Scotty loved stroking soft toys. I rub at the tightness gathering in my chest, then run my hand over the lifeless figures.

The only truly meaningful one is the Piglet in my car. It was my son's obsession. So much so that I redid his bedroom in a Pooh motif when he was three, eager to elicit any joyful reaction from him however

I could. But oh, how often I envied that pig. I physically ached for more of my son's affection. For that occasional big smile and eye contact. When they came my way, my feet practically left the ground. None of my accomplishments ever compared with my son's hugs and smiles. Hugs and smiles we'll never share again.

A sudden shift in the air—a coolness—settles around me. The hairs on my arm and the back of my neck rise. I look around. "Hello?" My cheeks heat. How silly, talking to thin air. And yet it feels like I'm no longer alone. I sit with the sensation, my heartbeat heavy, and listen. For what? A whisper, perhaps. Or simply for a sign. "Sean?"

Poof. The cool air diffuses, and I'm back to being hot and itchy in this dusty attic, eyes now misty. I need to get moving.

I've gone without this stuff for more than a year, so there's no reason to sift through it and make myself sadder. I grab a few bags to bring down the ladder with me and then organize a staging area in the garage—one for donations and another for the dumpster.

Then I remember Lillian, the librarian, so I go back to the attic in search of Scotty's books. I peek inside the lid of one box to find *Love You Forever* on top. That book always made me cry because I'd imagined that day in the future when my son would be a man who cared for his ailing mother. When he'd love me to the depths of his soul as I already loved him.

Our story didn't end that way, but this book reminds me of a time when I looked forward to the future. When I celebrated life and love. I stare at the illustrated cover image of a little boy sitting on the bathroom floor amid a mess, happy as can be. My throat turns sore. Scotty could lose hours examining inanimate objects. I swallow hard, stuff the floppy book into my purse, and then tuck the cardboard folds of the box with the remaining books back together and lug it to my car. I can't stay in this house that no longer feels like my home.

There's no corner of the earth that will ever feel like this place once did. Nowhere to outrun grief and regret.

When I get to my car, heaviness pins me to the front seat, my shoulders slumped. Always two steps forward and one step back. I'm running out of time to make sure my sister and her family are okay. If I don't figure that out before I go, my sister will forever question every choice she made when helping me this year. How could I live with that? Of course, I wouldn't be alive, but that's not the point.

Kristin agreed to join me on the flying trapeze. Getting her to do frivolous things—watching her stress melt away for an hour—makes me ridiculously happy. I hope that playfulness sticks and that, in my absence, she'll plan her own adventures with Tony and her kids.

Thinking of saying goodbye to them all is brutal. I can't be honest about my intentions, but I so want to plan something poignant for us all. I haven't figured what that could be, though, because every time I try, I cry.

CHAPTER TEN

KRISTIN

The same evening

"I'm sorry I wasn't home for dinner, Livvy. Trust me, I would've rather been with you than at work." I tuck the covers snugly around her little body before kissing her forehead. I would've had to catch the 5:14 train to get home by six thirty, which is nearly impossible when no one clocks out before six thirty.

"You always say that, but you're never home."

A failure at work and at home. It's hard not to cry. "I'm doing my best. I'm sorry my schedule makes you feel bad. I promise I'm not avoiding you."

She pouts before rolling over to face the wall, her tiny figure buried beneath the covers. Not yet seven years old and hurting, unable to comprehend the demands of adulthood and careers and the fact that I have only so much energy on any given day. Even as my heart breaks, each of my muscles turns rigid with the restraint needed to stop myself from stomping my foot.

"I love you." Defeated by the ensuing silence, I turn off her bedroom light and then go to Luca's room, where I need to weigh in on Miss Diaz's email.

Naturally he's already brushed his teeth, packed his backpack, and set out his outfit for the morning. "Hey, sweetie. How was your day?"

"Good." He climbs into bed with a Percy Jackson book. "I got an A on my math test."

"Adding fractions? Great job." I sit on the edge of the mattress. Tony said Luca understands the problem, but I'm unconvinced, partly because I doubt Tony honestly understands it either. How could he when I hide my similar struggles from him? "Daddy said he talked to you about an email from your teacher."

Luca wrinkles his nose. "He says I'm not allowed to give away my lunch, and that I can't do their homework for them because I could get in trouble."

"Well, yes, but it's more than that."

"What do you mean?" His brows gather.

"Well, when you do someone else's homework for them, you rob them of a chance to learn. More important, though, is that it's not your job to make everything easy for other people. If someone doesn't do their own work, then they need to suffer the consequence." Something I should remember when Finn relies on me to do his legwork. "Same goes with lunch. Daddy puts a lot of effort into making sure you and Livvy have healthy meals. If other kids like what you have, they should tell their parents, not take yours. You don't owe them that. Do you understand?"

"But I'm only being helpful, like how you are with Aunt Amy."

I'm stunned by his instant association between his behavior and mine. Proof that I need to make changes. "Aunt Amy is family, and she wasn't being lazy or selfish. She was grieving. It was a special time that required special care." I lean forward and kiss his forehead. "I love that you want to be helpful. That's great, as long as you're not nicer to other people than you are to yourself. Or than they are to you. And as long as it isn't making you unhappy."

A simplistic take on a complicated topic, but I'm in my thirties and still trying to discern those lines.

"But I don't mind."

"As you get older, the asks will get bigger. Some people will take advantage of you if you don't learn how to say no." It isn't much, but my words could start a subtle shift. I feel it in me already—this deep questioning of whether I'm spending my time in the best way versus in the way I've convinced myself I should.

"But you always say we shouldn't be selfish." His expression is a picture of confusion.

"It's not selfish to say no when someone is asking for too much, like cheating on homework or taking your food. Be kind and generous, but not when it requires you to do something that makes you uncomfortable. Does that make sense?"

He shrugs. "I guess. Can I read for a while?"

May I, I think, glancing at the clock. "Fifteen minutes."

"Thanks."

I turn off the overhead light, leaving him in a circle of lamplight. Parenting is confusing. I thought I was modeling a good work ethic for my kids, yet each of them is taking something different from my example. Something less beneficial than I hoped too.

When I descend the stairs, Tony is sitting by the fire with his beer in hand, poring over plans for some development project.

The first time I ever saw him, it felt as if I'd been plugged in and turned on. Tony, however, was a senior who didn't know I existed until I got invited to Brody Kingsman's graduation party by his younger sister. I spent the evening spying on Tony, who laughed with his friends, picked up trash other kids had strewn in the yard, and confidently spoke with parents.

When he caught me watching him, he beelined for me with an intent gaze that made me so nervous I almost peed my pants. We debated everything from the worst teachers at school to dream vacations. I was certain he'd ask me out, but when Brody called him away, he leaned close and said, *I'm leaving for college in a few weeks, so the timing's bad, but I hope we meet again in a few years, Kristin.*

It was the very best and worst thing he could've said, yet it cemented a truth about him: he was an intentional person with integrity. I spent too many nights fantasizing that we'd kissed before he'd sauntered off, and compared each boy I dated to my impression of Tony. We did finally meet again the summer after I graduated from college, while I was waitressing at Rowayton Seafood before law school started. He came in with some friends for lunch one Saturday, and the rest—as they say—is history.

I've never second-guessed our decisions until recently. That intention and integrity that I admire can also make him rigid, and these days we could use a little flexibility.

He didn't hear me come downstairs, so I hold still and survey our home. Ten-foot ceilings and extensive windows. High-end gold and nickel fixture finishes. Sumptuous Tibetan rugs. A Mark Grotjahn original hanging in the dining room. Fit for a magazine spread. I'm proud of how hard we've worked, and yet what's the point of all this if we aren't around enough to enjoy it, or even enjoy each other?

I sigh, then sit across from him and stare at the fire, thinking about how to reach my husband without confessing everything.

"What's the matter?" Tony sips his beer.

What's not the matter? Work. Home. Amy's unpredictability. Everything is out of balance.

"I talked to Luca about Miss Diaz's observations."

"I told you I handled it." His tone is pragmatic, like he ticked that box so I wouldn't have to.

I shrug. "I'm his mom and want to be involved. Besides, he takes after me this way, so I thought he would appreciate my empathy."

Tony's expression is hard to read. "So why do you look so upset?"

"Livvy scolded me." I tuck a throw pillow against my abdomen, a weak substitute for the hug our daughter denied me. "I'm worried she's starting to hate me."

He makes a disbelieving face. "She doesn't hate you."

"Okay, she resents me. She's making things personal because she doesn't understand my career. Honestly, I'm starting to wonder why I'm sticking with it." I glance again at the hypnotic flames, letting the heat warm my face after the shock of that confession.

"You've always loved your job."

I cast him a sideways glance. "Firm politics are making me crazy. I wanted to scream when Jim started in again with the 'maybe next year' bullshit."

"Sorry. Maybe focus less on that and more on the negotiation and strategy you enjoy."

It's not a terrible suggestion, except that it feels like giving up. And while I've been proud of my job—proud of what it says about my acuity—things have felt different ever since Sean and Scotty died. Amy's constant commentary has made me more irritable that I haven't made partner despite everything I've sacrificed. The work itself has taken a back seat to achieving my long-held goal.

"Even so, the commute is a killer. Is that the best way to spend my time?" I put my feet up on the hassock. "Maybe I should quit," I quip, and yet it doesn't feel like the halfhearted joke I intended.

His expression registers some alarm. "You can't quit, Kristin."

The command makes me nearly cry. What's with me and the tears lately? Do I even want to quit? "I'm so tired. Tired of proving myself. Tired of spending three of my waking hours commuting every day. Tired of missing out on school events. And really tired of seeing the disappointment in my daughter's eyes. If she's not going to therapy, maybe I should be here after school. Be part of the kids' daily lives while they're still young enough to want me to be involved."

He rubs his chin before staring at the ground. The crackling fire is the only sound breaking the heavy silence. Have I said too much or too little to gain his support for some changes? Balance always eludes me.

Finally, he lifts his gaze to mine. "I hear that you're tired, but it's not even two months since Amy left. It should keep getting easier now. I've known you a long time. Being at home might sound like a dream when you're this frustrated, but you'd be climbing the walls within three months. You've always said you want to be defined by more than your relationship to the kids and me, and I agree."

"That's true, but I wouldn't mind a break from being a lawyer in the city." I watch him take that in with some surprise. "Maybe I could volunteer at the schools or at a local nonprofit for a year, just for a change."

"PTA politics?" Tony grimaces, his head shaking. "It will feel like playing tic-tac-toe after running point on multimillion-dollar mergers."

"Maybe tic-tac-toe is what I need right now." My voice is sharper than usual.

He twists his lips in thought. "From a practical standpoint, we've built our life around dual incomes. If you quit, we'd have to pull the kids out of their private school, for starters. We also can't afford this mortgage if you've got no income, since mine gets reinvested in projects to grow our asset base for retirement. Is that really what you want?"

My insides feel like boiling lava. "Maybe we don't need all this." I gesture around the spacious living area we designed. I love it, but it's just stuff.

Tony scrubs his hands over his face, conflict in his eyes. He loves me and cares about my feelings, but he also wants us to stay the course. "So you want to change all our goals because it's been a rough six months? To sacrifice the kids' best education and their beautiful, safe neighborhood? And what about our plans to retire young enough to enjoy life after the kids graduate from college? We agreed that these things were important to us, so I think you'll regret giving it all up in a moment of exasperation."

Fair points, although he doesn't know about the pills. About the sleepless nights. The deep exhaustion. I'm not Superwoman, and yet a part of me loves that he has always seen me that way. My fall from grace is humbling, and I'm not ready to fully face it. How's that for infuriating self-sabotage?

I turn the anger at myself on him. "So I'm trapped?"

"Trapped?" His eyes reflect hurt feelings. With a heavy sigh, he concedes, "It's been a shitty year, and you're burned out. I get that loud and clear. But maybe we try less extreme options before we blow up our lives?"

For the first time in my life, I don't care about logic. I want to run away and hide for weeks. I want someone to make everything easy for me. I want to be irresponsible for once in my goddamn life. "I'm so unhappy. Sal pulled out of the deal. Worse, he called Jim—not me—to deliver the news. Jim then had a sit-down with me, during which he basically told me not to expect partnership this year. Again. What the hell am I doing giving so much time to a firm that doesn't value me?"

Tony pushes off the sofa and comes to kneel beside me, rubbing my thighs. "Babe, that sucks. I'm sorry. I truly am. You deserve better and Jim's a fool. I hate that this is messing with your confidence, but with or without partnership, you still work at a top firm on complex projects, which you enjoy. You're highly compensated for that work too. If you want out of there, find another firm first. Or, if you want to stay where you've built your reputation knowing partnership is off the table this year, then tell Jim you plan to work remotely a few days a week for a while. That cuts your commute and would let you spend more time with the kids without sacrificing everything you've worked for."

I hadn't thought of that. Prior to the pandemic, it wouldn't have been an option. During lockdown, it was impossible to get through a workday at home without multiple interruptions. Would it be better now that the kids are a little older? More important, is accepting remote work as a consolation prize for my failure enough? Not that he even realizes what he's suggested. "Would you be satisfied working as a runner-up?"

His face contorts like I've tossed water in it. "That's not what I'm saying."

"It sort of is, Tony. But I can't keep talking about this tonight. I'll think about what you've said. Maybe there's a compromise I can live with." I'm officially more confused and exhausted than when I sat down.

Tony smiles, sensing that he's convinced me not to do anything drastic. Part of me wants to pinch him. The other part sees his side. Seeing all sides has always been my problem, though.

Tony rises off his knees. "Let me get you a glass of wine, and we can watch whatever you want. Unwind and let the day go. Think about some options, and then let's see where we are."

As if a rom-com and merlot will solve my problems. I nod without enthusiasm.

Maybe he's right. Pulling the kids out of a school they love and away from their home and neighborhood friends doesn't sound like a move in their best interests. Yet in the long run, they might be better off if I weren't self-medicating. If I were more available and less exhausted.

Lately it seems like my only real choice is to decide which of all my options will make my family resent me less.

My phone chimes.

Excited for our trapeze date on Friday! I'll drive in so you don't have to deal with subways and trains to get home.

That should push me over the edge, but instead our plans make me smile. It's the only thing on my calendar this week that promises any kind of fun. Better yet, it's helping my sister find joy again. She's moving past the worst of her pain, which is a gigantic win. Maybe that fact will help me sleep better tonight.

———

Mats, gym equipment, and chairs are scattered throughout the expansive white industrial gym space. Overhead hangs a huge net and the trapeze swing. Amy's face is bright with anticipation, which helps offset the sick feeling I have about skipping out of work early to join her.

All week I've been contemplating Tony's suggestions, yet I can't swallow the remote-work consolation prize. I'm a good lawyer. Smart. Disciplined. Ethical. I need to reset my game. Complaining, breaking down, begging for help—none of those inspire confidence or admiration. This week I deserve an Oscar for how well I'm playing the roles of devoted wife and mother, supportive sister, and enthusiastic lawyer as if undaunted by recent setbacks. Projecting strength will hold things steady while I map out a fresh way forward.

I'm here now, so I may as well throw myself into swinging from the ceiling. This should be a cakewalk after jumping from a plane. Maybe all the blood rushing to my head will invigorate me.

The instructor, Matt, is probably thirty—fit, with overgrown sandy hair and see-through-blue eyes. He's flirting with Amy, which she's either ignoring or not processing at all. She can't imagine falling in love again, but she's lovable, so she won't be able to fend men off forever.

"Okay, ladies. We've run through all the training. Any questions before you go up?" Matt says to Amy.

I raise my hand, which makes Amy snicker and bat it down. I'm probably blushing, but old habits die hard. "Quick recap: We get up there and hold our left hand up, hips forward, shoulders back, then reach out to grab the bar with both hands, lean forward on our toes until you say 'Hep,' then we jump?"

"Yeah. Jump off the ledge like we practiced here on the mat; then you'll try to hang from your knees. It's easier than it sounds because the motion of the swing and gravity will disperse your body weight. After a few swings like that, right yourself again, pump your legs for momentum, and then drop off into the net. Easy."

I raise my gaze to the platform above. *Easy* isn't the word that comes to mind, but the net makes it less scary. Beside me, Amy rubs her hands together in excitement. Honestly, I can't get enough of seeing her this peppy.

Tony is right about one thing—my sister's mental state most definitely affects mine. There were so many days this past year when I lost hope of ever getting my sister back. It's made me aware of how much I rely upon her mirth as a counterbalance to my restraint. It's why I joined her on that skydive, and came here today. I should thank her for breaking me from my cage. For reminding me to make fun important—another thing I want Luca to understand far sooner than I have.

"Who wants to go first?" Matt asks.

"Standard operating procedure?" Amy asks, donning an impish smile while holding up a fist.

Ooh, it's been years since we've done this. I nod and raise mine for a rapid round of rock, paper, scissors. Best of three—how we always settled these decisions as kids.

"One, two, three, go!" I throw scissors to her rock. I don't like to lose, but in this case it might not be the worst thing to go second.

"One, two, three, go!" I throw a paper to her rock.

"One, two, three, go!" I throw a rock to her scissors. "Ha!" I say, caught up in the win, until I realize that I now must scale that ladder.

"Okay, Kristin. Chalk your hands and then let's climb." Matt flashes his winning smile, which reminds me of being young, single, and having all options wide open. Not that I'd change my life with Tony, but I do miss that sense of "anything could happen" that permeated my teens and early twenties.

I drag my hands through the bowl of pulverized chalk and then begin the climb, with Matt following behind.

"Woot! Go, girl," Amy calls from below, her phone raised, taking photos or video. From here, she looks ten years younger and devoid of all her grief. Perhaps these outings are helping her reconnect with hope. With a future that could be as filled with love as her past. I smile to myself.

When I get to the platform, it's pretty high, and this time I'm not clipped to an instructor. I reach out and grip Matt's arm in a dizzy moment of vertigo, then crane my neck to peek over the edge at the net below while he hooks my safety belt to various bungee cords.

"All set," he says.

I creep toward the edge, grab the trapeze with my right hand while raising my left with my shoulders back, then reach my free hand to grab the bar and lean forward on my toes while Matt holds the belt. Time's up.

"Hep!"

I close my eyes and jump, then open them during the freefall. "Ohmygod, ohmygod, ayeeeeeee!" My grip is so tight it hurts. The bar swings faster than I anticipated, and unlike the skydive, I have to keep my wits at all times. A breeze catches my stray hairs while I glide across the room like a pendulum.

I'm swinging backward when Matt calls out, "Raise your knees!"

Oof. It's clumsy attempting this while swinging backward.

"Yay, Kristin. You got this!" Amy's gleeful voice makes my discomfort worthwhile.

With a burst of agility, I hook my knees around the trapeze bar. Now comes the scary part: letting go. *Shit, shit, shit. Let go!* I close my eyes and release my hands, then sail across the room upside down. I open my eyes as I fly past Amy. "Ohmygod. Whoaaaaaa!"

Fear fades quickly as I revert to being a ten-year-old hanging upside down on a playground, the whole world a giant circus of opportunity. Amy yells something, but I'm not paying attention. I'm staying present for once and taking in this personal win—the risk and reward of letting go. It's comforting to feel daring yet safe at the same time—a little like falling in love with the right person. Tony and I need to get back to swinging in sync. I miss our harmony. Being off-key is as much to blame for my current struggles as anything else.

"Okay, now reach back up and bring your legs down," Matt says.

I'm reluctant to end my turn so quickly, but Amy is waiting patiently, so I right myself and release, plunging into the springy net.

My heart is pounding. I'm sweaty and overstimulated yet bubbling with delight.

Amy races to the side of the net as I inelegantly tumble out and grab her into a hug. "Thank you for making me come on these absurd adventures with you."

She hugs me so hard. For months, I've yearned to see any hint of her old self. My eyes water with gratitude that we are here together, sharing another special moment. My Amy is coming back, and even if it lasts for only an hour, it's a start. A real start.

"I took video so your kids can see and hear you. I think they'll love it." She's bouncing on her toes.

It dawns on me how rarely they've seen this side of me. Honestly, I've been my own worst enemy in this regard, always assessing, always being responsible and safe. Amy might be onto more than she realizes by guilting me into these adventures.

When we ease apart, she hands me her phone. "My turn to kick ass. Don't mess up the video."

While she chalks up and begins the climb, my heart settles back to normal. I can't stop smiling, giddy with childlike feelings of energy and silliness. Of pure fun. Would Tony do something unexpected—something that doesn't have a specific goal—just for the experience? We could use more of them in our lives. I hope the video will inspire him.

"Hey, are you paying attention?" Amy calls from above. Hallelujah! Her saucy impatience is another trait I welcome back into our lives.

"Sorry. All set." I hold the phone up, hit record, and watch my sister fly.

CHAPTER ELEVEN

AMY

The following Wednesday

I'm trotting toward my car after donating the box with Scotty's books to the library and handing Lillian an envelope containing a generous check. She didn't open it, per my request. I prefer to imagine her reaction than to see it. Kind of the way it's fun to shake presents and guess what's in them in the days leading up to Christmas.

I sink behind the steering wheel, pleased to check that item off my to-do list for the week. Other items include revising my will, signing the real estate sales agreement, setting the closing date, extending the list of who to give money to, and so on. No one is more surprised than I am to realize that working my plan would bring such a sense of satisfaction.

My phone rings. Jane? I stiffen. It's been months. My innards sizzle like butter in a too-hot pan. She's my connection to Sean, and yet his parents sometimes hurt us with their ignorance and meddling. I close my eyes and inhale. Whatever Jane's flaws, she raised the man I adored. For that, she deserves some respect.

I picture my husband's face and answer. "Hello, Jane."

"Amy!" She sounds surprised that I answered. "How are you?"

My grip on the steering wheel tightens, as if the wheel will offer emotional support.

"Hanging in there. How about you?" Keep it light.

"About the same."

We both fall silent. It's been easier to avoid her wistful tone than to confront my discomfort. How can I not know what to say to the only other woman who loved Sean as much as I did?

Jane finds courage before I do. "I called because of the anniversary next month. We bought a bronze angel to put on the graves, if that's okay."

Unbidden, I picture the charcoal-gray granite headstone with etched flowers surrounding each of our names. I close my eyes to erase the image, but not in time to stop the resulting ache. The tchotchkes people buy for the dead to make themselves feel better make no sense to me. "Of course you can."

"Oh good. Are you planning anything to commemorate them?"

Them. We're speaking of Sean and Scotty without saying their names, as if leaving them off the table somehow makes it all more palatable.

"I . . ." I've been so focused on my own plan for that day that I haven't considered what others who loved them might want. In the moment, I lie. "I haven't thought that far ahead. It's all I can do to get through one day at a time."

I can't have others showing up, at least not in the morning. I plan to go to the cemetery early with my bottle of pills. That way the groundskeepers will find me instead of Kristin or Bob. Even so, it makes my stomach hurt to put anyone in that position. Sean's parents and their bronze angels are a complication I hadn't considered.

"It's hard, I know." Her voice splinters, breaking my heart a little. "Sometimes I still wake up and, for a few seconds, forget that my boy is gone. Then it hits me again. It's unnatural to outlive your child."

It sounds like she's forgotten about Scotty, but she probably spoke without thinking. My bitterness gives way to envy. Jane hasn't given up on life despite losing a son and grandson. She presses forward for the rest of her family despite grief and despair. I wish I were as brave, if not for myself, then at least for my family.

My eyelids feel like sandpaper when I blink.

Had Jane's and my relationship remained healthy, we might've consoled each other this past year. Instead, we stand on either side of Sean's ghost, each wishing for an alternate reality. And while I might blame her for the distance between us, her son is dead because of me.

"I'm sorry." The memory of Sean and Scotty leaving that hotel room makes me flush. People walking by the car peer through the windows, increasing my self-consciousness.

"It's not your fault," comes her sincere reply.

Everyone says that, but platitudes aren't truths. What happened wasn't my *intention*, but my decisions—to buy the lottery ticket, to plan the vacation, to skip the boat tour—were the nexus. I am, therefore, the cause of both deaths; ergo they're my fault. "Either way, we're all mourning."

Another pause ensues. "Mike and I should've visited when you got out of the hospital. Things were so strained; I didn't know what was the right thing to do. It also seemed like your family wanted privacy when things were so . . . hard. But we were thinking of you and worried."

It isn't an apology for the "before" times, but it's the closest she's come. Her effort unfolds a petal in the battered bud of my heart. Haven't we all made mistakes? "It's better that you didn't come. I was in terrible shape and barely spoke for weeks. I'm still finding my way." My days have been busy lately, structured around my end goal. The fact of my impending expiration date causes a momentary panic—a sense of things unfinished. A sudden reluctance to give up on life's beauty.

"I guess we made the right decision then." She sounds relieved. Before I can find a polite way to end the call, she asks, "Are you still at Kristin's?"

"No. I moved out at the end of January."

"Oh, then if we come up, maybe we could stay at the house one night and take you out to dinner?" They live in Parsippany, New Jersey, so they could come and go on the same day more comfortably than we could endure a sleepover.

"I sold the house—the closing is before the anniversary."

"I didn't realize. Sean loved that house." Whether intentional or not, her words make it sound as if I am maliciously throwing away something he loved. His love for the home is partly why I couldn't bear to stay there again. Wait, is she sniffling? She adds, "I'm sorry. You caught me off guard. I didn't realize I'd never see it again."

I clench my teeth because she's making this about her. It was my house. My family. My life that got most destroyed. Should I live in a mausoleum that makes me sad just because she might want to see it one more time? Pressure builds until it feels like my head is a cork about to pop from a bottle. "It was too hard to be there alone, Jane. It's hollow without Sean and Scotty." There. I said their names and didn't spontaneously combust.

"Where are you living now?" She sounds concerned, making me regret expecting the worst from her.

"I rented a one-bedroom apartment near my sister."

"Rented? But you have all that money . . ." Her voice keeps shifting tones, up and down, as she bounces from sorrow to shock with each twist in the conversation.

"I'm not ready for big commitments."

"I'm . . . surprised."

"Why's that, Jane?" My shoulders tighten. I don't owe her or anyone an explanation. My visceral response could be more reflex than fair reaction at this point.

"You and Sean were thinking of building that house on the shore, and Sean mentioned maybe a second home elsewhere. He loved Mexico. I imagined you'd use the money to live out some of those big plans—all the places you two wanted to go—you know, since he can't."

Is she high? We never once talked about a second home in another country. How could we have managed that when Scotty still needed regular support, and routines and familiarity were keys to his comfort? But perhaps Sean had private conversations with his mother, during which he fantasized about things that he didn't feel he could say to me. After all, we had our own rough patches that last year. On any given day, something unexpected could crop up and cause a little blowup.

"He bit me, dammit!" Sean barked once while restraining Scotty in a chair. Our son's screams had brought me running from the basement laundry room to find his arms and legs poking out from around his father, seeking escape.

"Let him go, Sean. That's not helping."

Sean shot me an angry look. "If I let him go, he'll bite me again. Or start banging his head on the wall, which is what I was trying to stop in the first place."

"Did you try a pillow first? We shouldn't use force. That always makes it worse." I turned off the overhead light and grabbed a throw pillow.

Sean raised his hands overhead. "Fine. You handle it since I always do everything wrong." He ducked, barely missing one of Scotty's flailing legs.

I scowled. "I didn't say that, but what a convenient excuse to let me manage . . . again." I knelt by Scotty and set a pillow beside his head, lowering my voice and speaking calmly so that he could work himself into a more comfortable state of being. "Honey, you're safe. Everything's okay. Let's try some deep breaths so you can show me why you're upset. I want to help, but you have to be calm first."

In my periphery, Sean watched, his posture slumped, defeat contorting his features. The week before, I'd overheard him telling Jane that he sometimes got depressed that our family was turning out so different from what he'd envisioned. Even as I understood his frustration, it hurt so much I could barely meet his gaze that day.

Since his death, I've suppressed the less-than-perfect elements of our life together. It occurs to me that some of my negativity toward Jane could be related to the fact that Sean sometimes complained to her instead of talking to me. I can't argue about that with him now, but it's not fair to dislike his mother for supporting her son.

"Well, I'm not planning to spend the money on myself. I'm giving it away." The car is getting stuffy. I need to end this call.

"To whom?"

"People who deserve it. People who helped Scotty."

"Not to family?" There it is again, that sneaky judgmental tone that creeps into her voice when she disapproves. The same tone we used to hear when she and Mike questioned our therapists and other child-rearing decisions that they didn't understand.

"My family doesn't need it."

"Surely if Sean were alive, he would have wanted to make his sister's life easier too. Not just hand it all to strangers."

He never said anything like that to me. We had temporarily parked the winnings in an investment account while we conferred with lawyers about setting up a trust for Scotty's care. We probably would've gotten around to being generous with our siblings and parents—big gifts like new cars or college tuitions for their kids and such.

Who knows what might have been if Sean and Scotty hadn't died so soon after winning that money? But they did, the money is mine, and I have no interest in helping his sister when she couldn't even drop me a note on Scotty's birthday. "I'm giving it to people who really need it. Leslie and her family are financially secure. Besides, they haven't called me since the funeral. She didn't even send a text on Scotty's birthday." *Neither did you* remains unspoken, but I'm sure she's heard it loud and clear.

"That's because none of us knows how to act. It's all been so difficult for too long, and I don't know how to fix it." Helplessness tinges her tone.

"Neither do I, and maybe that's okay too. The past is what it is. We both wish we could do things differently, but we can't, so maybe we accept that and just . . . move ahead. Sean would support rewarding people who've made their lives about helping others. I'm sorry if you don't agree, but it's my money, so it's my choice. It's not a punishment of you or Leslie." My blood is simmering.

"I didn't call to argue."

"Of course you didn't, and yet we often end up this way." I sigh, not wanting to later regret arguing with my mother-in-law, or for her to think that she is in any way responsible for my planned final act. "I'm sure it's my fault, so I'm sorry. I told you earlier, I'm still not good company. Don't take it personally. I wish your family well, really, but I'm fumbling to manage my own life these days, so I don't want to have to defend the choices I'm making to try to get closure."

"All right, Amy. Mike and I will make our own plans to visit the graves." Most likely they'd arrive after lunch, so they wouldn't be the first to happen upon me. "If you change your mind about seeing us, let me know. My son adored you. We both loved him, and between us we hold all the memories of his life. Whatever our past sins, I don't want us to disappear from each other's lives completely."

Her shaky voice makes me teary. If I hold half of Sean's memories, then my death will be another slam to her. The burden of not hurting others weighs heavily against my plans.

Fuck it, I don't want to start sobbing. I look upward with a quick apology to my dead husband. "Sean will always be alive in my heart, Jane. Always. Thank you for giving me more time and space. I'm glad we talked."

"Can I call you in a few weeks?"

What can I say without telling the truth? "All right. Take care."

I turn on the ignition after we hang up, my entire body humming with guilty energy. I've made everything worse, because we won't talk again before the anniversary, and after that . . .

Am I fooling myself to think that my contemplative death plan will mitigate the pain I'll cause everyone? Is it an elaborate justification to make myself feel less selfish and weak? If I could expect any twenty-four-hour period that did not involve a degree of regret or longing for the past, maybe I could imagine a future worth fighting for.

I aim north up Bedford Street to 104 and eventually turn onto the Merritt Parkway to work off the unpleasantness that call kicked up. It's a beautiful stretch of road—two lanes each direction, divided by a tree-lined median. No commercial trucks allowed. Hills and hidden bends make it something of a natural roller coaster, a lot like my life these past several weeks.

When I was young, friends and I would cut class to speed along this road midday when the traffic was light. We'd race well over the stated speed limit because there weren't emergency lanes or graveled areas for cops to lie in wait. That's changed slightly in the intervening years, but it's still easy to speed without getting caught.

I need that now.

The speed.

The adrenaline.

Anything to leave the past in the rearview and make me feel present.

I switch to the passing lane and floor it. 65. 70. 75. 80. 90. 93 . . . Trees and guardrails blur in the periphery. It almost feels like flying—though not quite like skydiving. This is riskier.

My Nissan groans and rattles in warning, but I'm chasing a high. I grip the wheel tight, staring straight ahead, whizzing past cars that are probably traveling at seventy miles per hour.

I holler into the empty space of my car, feeling powerful. Feeling daring. Feeling the fragility of everything, which delivers a needed surge of adrenaline. Up this hill, down the next.

I zoom up to the car in front of me. When it doesn't move out of the way, I start to shift lanes until a horn's frantic blast sounds on my right.

My heart cinches as I yelp and veer back into my own lane before pumping my brakes.

Every part of my body trembles. My heart takes up all the space in my chest as it kicks in protest, making each breath burn.

What the hell am I doing, putting other people in danger? There could have been a family in that car. In any of these cars.

The back of my throat fills with the bitter taste of bile. I'm a sick, selfish woman with a death wish, like Kristin probably still suspects.

As soon as it's safe to change lanes, I pull off at the next exit and park in the first parking lot I can find to let my heart rate slow down. Tears leak from the corners of my eyes, even though they're closed.

Luckily nothing worse than this fright happened, but I can't apologize to the poor person who honked.

I open my eyes and stare into space. None of that therapy I got in the hospital made a lasting impact. Despite glimmers of reprieve, there's no cure for what ails me. Not the gifting. Or the adrenaline fixes. Or selling the house. I can't get myself right in the head and latch on to a foolproof reason to keep going.

My text notification pings.

See you at dinner.

I'd forgotten about my plans with Kristin tonight. I'd cancel, but I sense that she's coping with more than Livvy's problems, and I would love to help her for a change.

See you at eight, I reply.

Settled, I turn the car on and head toward home, determined to hide this mood from my sister.

I grab my mail on my way into the house, sifting through it quickly, expecting it to be all junk. My fingers stop on a handwritten envelope with Josephina's name and return address. I start to sweat, praying she didn't return the check.

After tossing the rest in the trash, I take her note with me to the sofa, where I carefully open it. No check falls out, so I release a breath and start to read.

Dear Amy,
There are no words to express my gratitude for your extreme generosity. Honestly, I considered returning the check, as it is more than anything that seems fair to take. But after speaking with Ernesto about all that you said and what you've been through, I can see that you are trying to fill the hole in your heart by using what you have to help others. I understand that urge, and I also know from experience that helping others is always the best way to heal yourself. So I want to thank you from the bottom of our hearts for choosing us as one of your recipients. I promise we will not be frivolous with your gift. It will help offset my daughter's medical school loans, and give Ernesto and me a little nest egg for our retirement. I did, however, allow myself one special gift. I bought a solid gold cross necklace and will think of your family—especially our little angel in heaven—every time I wear it.
God bless you, Amy.
Fondly, Josephina Gonzales

I swallow thickly while wiping wet cheeks. Happy tears are an odd phenomenon. It actually hurts my face and chest to smile and cry at the same time, but the pain quickly gives way to a burst of euphoria. I eased the burden on an entire family. If I needed evidence that Jane is wrong about how to best spend my money, I've got it now.

I press the letter to my chest and slink down into the sofa, closing my eyes. A sort of afterglow—a warm tide washing through me—makes my entire body relax.

———

I beat Kristin to the restaurant and order us each a drink while I wait, thinking about our new rhythm. She's trying new things to appease me, yet she's also enjoying them. She's stopped monitoring my every move, which suggests she's letting go of feeling responsible for me. Having that bit of space has helped me feel more in parity for a change. A nice change.

Our momentum, coupled with the goodwill I got from Josephina's note, might be something I could build on. Are small bursts of happiness with my sister's family or Bob enough foundation for a lifetime? Sometimes it seems so, but in all cases I'm a fifth wheel with everyone else's family. Nothing is really mine. That's the sticking point—what do *I* have of real value?

A bejeweled lady at the next table yammers to friends about some "unfair" country club policy. I roll my eyes, not caring who sees me.

"Sorry I'm late." Kristin flashes an apologetic grin while hanging her purse over the chair, then sits down and picks up the menu. Her outfit is chic. Layered silk shirts beneath a lightweight navy wool jacket, cinched with a thick, knotted brown leather belt. Powder-blue-and-camel houndstooth slacks with brown suede ankle boots. Her face, however, is haggard, with purple circles beneath her eyes. Sure signs of stress, which is unfortunate because I want to vent about Jane.

"No worries. I ordered cocktails."

"Liquor? I hope your day wasn't worse than mine." Although her tone is teasing, a hint of concern flickers in her eyes. She tries to cover it by scanning the menu, which she knows by heart, considering how often she's eaten here.

"Jane called."

My sister's eyes go round as she lays the menu aside. "Really? What'd she want?"

"To come up for the anniversary and spend the night. Like we're all chummy or something." I immediately regret being bitchy. Jane had decent intentions.

"I'm not surprised she wants to mark the day. Maybe it'd be good for you two to share it in some way."

My lie of omission about that day grows heavier each hour. Where's my drink? "We can't even have a simple conversation without twenty layers of subtext. We're hardly ready for a sleepover."

Kristin grimaces. "Did you argue?"

"Sort of." I recite the conversation without skewing it in my favor.

"Oh, Ames, I'm sorry. I understand how you feel, but it sounds like she wants to make amends. I'm sure you understand her desire to hold on to any connection to Sean."

I flinch. "So I was wrong to turn her down?"

"I didn't say that. But what if forgiveness helps you both heal?" Her gaze is soft and warm, but I am cold. I can't be honest with her, and I already feel bad enough about that call. In response to my silence, she says, "Let's change the subject. Did anything good happen today?"

I won't mention my almost-crash on the Merritt or the gifts I've made. If she learns I'm giving away my money, she'll get suspicious and might even put two and two together. "I donated Scotty's old books to the library."

Her lips part. "The ones Tony and I stored in the attic?"

I nod. It's suddenly warm, so I sip my ice water.

"When did you get those?" She's blinking like she doesn't recognize me. It's a change to see me not falling apart from handing his belongings over to strangers. I'm oddly numb about it. Either I'm getting stronger, or I'm not upset because I'll be seeing them soon. I try not to overthink it. Life is easier that way.

"The closing is coming up, so I had to deal with that stuff." Seeing me doing well helps her relinquish responsibility for me and my life. That's critical for her own sanity as much as any other reason.

"I would've helped you—or done it for you, honestly."

"I need to do these things for myself."

She reaches across the table and lays her hand on mine. "It's a lovely way to recycle the books. I'm sure they were grateful."

"Yes. The library needs all the donations it can get."

Kristin sits back, head tipped, a gentle smile in place. "You had a big day, yet here you are, steady. It's wonderful to see. Your thrill-seeking ideas are working. Should we pick another?"

I smile, uncomfortable with her praise although pleased by her enthusiasm. However, my Speed Racer incident has me rethinking the adrenaline plan. Danger aside, temporary highs don't endure. I need to create special, intimate memories that only sisters can share. As for the rest of my plan, I don't know enough people to gift away $20 million in my original time frame.

I tense, wanting to be better for my sister, for my parents, for my niece and nephew. I've squeezed out a laugh here and a moment of grace there, but the effort has yielded fleeting rewards. Meanwhile, duplicity gnaws at my conscience like a termite. If I were making the right choice, it wouldn't be this hard. That truth's getting harder to tune out.

The waitress brings our Sun Kiss cocktails. "You ladies ready to order?"

Kristin nods, so I gesture for her to go first. "I'll take the salad special, please."

"Fish and chips for me, thanks." I hand off the menus and, once the waitress walks away, raise my glass and say, "Cheers."

"To little wins, wherever we find them." Her hopefulness almost makes me confess my darker thoughts.

Instead, I ask, "Are you afraid of death?"

"Isn't everyone?"

"No. In fact, I'm curious about it."

"Curious?" She sits forward, jaw tight, eyes alert. "What are you trying to tell me?"

"Nothing. I guess Jane's call got me thinking about it," I fudge. "I think our spirit outlives our bodies. Maybe it continues right alongside us all, like a parallel universe." I lean across the table and whisper, "Sometimes Sean and Scotty talk to me."

Her face pinches as she glances at the nearby tables to check if anyone's listening. Then she murmurs, "You hear them talking to you?"

"Only in my dreams," I say to reassure her that I'm not hallucinating. "Although sometimes when I'm awake, I get a feeling—a phantom tingle—like they're nearby. It happened when I was packing the attic."

Her shoulders bunch as she carefully considers my claims. "I guess anything is possible."

"I hope I'm right." I've rendered my sister speechless.

Within a moment, her eyes get that light they do whenever she comes to a clever conclusion. "If you believe in spirits and eternal peace, then Sean and Scotty are happy and free now in a way none of us on earth are. That should go a long way to bringing *you* a kind of peace, right?"

Her conclusion—a perspective I hadn't considered—pushes me deeper into my seat. Thrown, I frown. "Fair point."

"Well, thanks. I haven't had many of those lately." The dark tone of her joke matches those circles under her eyes. She hasn't mentioned Livvy yet.

"How are the kids?"

"Okay. Luca's been sweet and helpful since Livvy's cafeteria meltdown last month. So far there haven't been further signs of distress at school. I still question whether a therapist would help."

"Maybe give changes at home time before getting an outsider involved."

"You still agree with Tony?" She pulls back.

"Think about all that's happened in a year. She lost a cousin and uncle, then had a depressed aunt living in her house for months, all of which made you more high strung. The drama has increased her anxiety. Things should continue to settle each week, and if you and Tony focus on her for a bit, I bet it will sort itself out." I'm suddenly queasy, knowing my plan will heap more trauma on those kids. Livvy's little smile pops into my head, making me ashamed.

"Maybe." Kristin stares into her drink. "Luca's being taken advantage of by kids at school. I've told him to draw boundaries, but he's confused because I've always taught the kids to be generous and helpful." She holds her temples, shaking her head. "I'm the worst mother."

"You're a great mother, Kristin. But maybe the best way to help your kids relax and draw boundaries is for you to do the same." I hold my breath, awaiting the backlash.

Kristin shrugs one shoulder as she takes a long pull at her drink. "Easier said than done. And how can I relax when Livvy's bitter with me?"

"Sorry. I know I haven't helped matters."

"What?" Her brows gather.

"I was around all the time, which comparison probably fueled some resentment." I sip the bubbly orange beverage.

Kristin looks at me, but her gaze is unfocused. "I don't regret helping you. In the long run, I'll work things out with my kids."

In the long run. My skin breaks out in goose bumps.

"Assuming you get that time." I take another sip of my drink. Her eyes start to shimmer. Making her cry isn't my goal. "Kristin?"

She dabs at her tears. "Dire warnings hardly help. I resent that being responsible—at work, at home, my whole damn life—hasn't made anything easier. I'm damn tired, too, so I don't need you to pile on by pointing out the ways you think I'm failing."

I've seen our mom get teary in public a dozen times or more, but never Kristin. To break down here means she's in far worse shape than I—or Tony—understand.

"I never said you're failing." Not directly, anyway. It suddenly strikes me that I've treated her like Jane has treated me, and oh, the irony jabs. "I'm sorry I upset you. Honest."

She inhales sharply to reboot. "Your heart's in the right place, but nothing's as simplistic as you want to make it. There's a lot to consider. I can't turn my back on all my commitments and live only for the moment based on the remote chance that tragedy might someday fill us with regret."

She would never say that so lightly if she had any idea of what living with real regret is like. "Are you trying to convince me or yourself?"

She twists her neck both directions and rolls her shoulders. "I'm saying it's complicated. I get your point, but I'm not you. I don't make snap decisions. Dismantling my career and upending my entire family's life requires analysis."

"And yet you just said that doing everything right hasn't made you happy. What if you're this worked up because your gut is telling you what to do, but your head is stopping you?"

Her neck and face are flushed. She's never liked to be challenged. "Well, if I had multimillions in the bank, maybe I could afford to follow my gut. But again, I'm not you."

She might as well have thrown her drink in my face. I'm dumbstruck for many reasons, not the least of which is that Kristin has never before been deliberately cruel. Money not only didn't solve my problems; it created bigger ones. But perhaps I deserve that slap. Does the fact that I'm not trying to hurt her matter if I am, in fact, hurting her? My limbs feel heavy.

Kristin abruptly pushes back from the table and heads off, presumably to collect herself in the ladies' room. Seconds later, the waitress delivers our meals, knocking Kristin's purse off the chair when she does.

"I'll get those," I say, quickly moving to collect my sister's belongings. Her phone. A pen. A prescription bottle. Wait, what? Adderall. I stare at the label, my heart ticking up slightly. She doesn't have ADHD. When I snap out of the daze, I shove her things back into her purse, hang it on her chair, and take my seat. Now the jitters and weight loss make sense. Does Tony know? He would never approve of this. Is this my fault?

Kristin returns, looking more controlled. "Sorry, Amy. That wasn't fair. I . . . I didn't mean it."

"Maybe you did a little." I dip a fry into the ketchup, pretending my world didn't just tilt on its axis. I need answers, but it's been too long since I've had to dig for information to be much good at it now. "Listen, I'm worried about you. You haven't been yourself for a while. I know you're juggling a lot, but is there something else you want to tell me?"

"No." She stabs her salad. "I'm fine. I'll be fine."

Normally I'd let it go, but this is affecting her health. I set down my fork. "When you left the table, the waitress accidentally knocked over your bag, and stuff spilled out. I saw the pills."

She flushes, her gaze now in her lap as a stony silence ensues.

"Since when do you need Adderall?" In the face of continued silence, I ask, "Does Tony know?"

Kristin looks up sharply. "No, and he doesn't need to. It's a temporary fix. That's all."

"When did this start?" I think back to pin down when I first noticed small changes in her behavior. A few months into my stay. Thanksgiving, perhaps?

"It doesn't matter."

Obfuscation is her way of protecting me from feeling responsible. I bury my head in my hands, unable to bear the weight of guilt and sorrow.

She quickly says, "This is the last bottle. I swear. Now that my deal is dead, I'm not on an immediate deadline."

I shake my head. "That damn job isn't worth your health. God, Kristin. Think about your kids."

"I am thinking of them and all the things they need. Their tuition, their lessons, the life they're used to." She's rigid, with a tight grip on her fork. "Not to mention my own goals."

A year ago, I thought that way—that life with Scotty would be easy and happier if only I were rich. That the quality of our days would improve with more cash to fill them with more stuff.

Looking back, other options seem so obvious. I could've gone back to work part time, bringing in a bit more income and giving me the adult interaction I missed. Or we could've moved somewhere less expensive. Or any other choice we never discussed because it seemed easier to deal with the devil we knew than risk making a decision we might regret. "I've never been as smart as you, but I know for sure that money isn't a panacea. Besides, you and Tony have plenty. You've got options."

She looks away. "We've got a high burn rate, and Tony's business is illiquid."

Sell everything! I want to shout. But it wouldn't be easy to turn her back on her goals and her desire to smash the patriarchy in her profession. She isn't asking for my money, so perhaps the curse won't extend to her. "All right, then. If money is the answer, take some of mine."

"No, thank you." She shakes her head vehemently. "I would never do that."

I slouch back, offended, even though I suspected she'd be too proud. "Why won't you let me help you?"

"How could I ever enjoy that money when you resent it so much you won't spend a penny on yourself? I appreciate the offer, but Tony and I will be fine. Besides, money won't buy me that partnership I've earned. I need to solve my own problems. What you can do is give me emotional support." She downs the last of her cocktail. "But please don't worry."

Now I have an inkling of how helpless she feels—and how distrustful—when I tell her not to worry about me. It sucks, by the way. Like acid in my gut. I wait for her to look at me again, my own plans adding a sense of urgency to everything. "Promise me you'll stop using those pills now. I mean it. Don't make me tell Tony."

"I said I would, okay?" We are locked in a staring contest until she switches directions. "Since we're talking about money, what do you plan to do for income?"

"I don't know and don't feel pressure to figure it out tonight." If anything, tonight is making me question abandoning her at a time when she's turning to me.

"Okay." She takes another bite of her salad, so I eat some of my fish, and we chew in silence for a moment. Kristin tilts her head. "For someone pushing changes on me, you're not keen on living by your own advice. I mean, attempting to defy death in creative ways might be fun, but it's not meaningful progress in terms of rebuilding your life."

I can't lie to her face, and I can't tell her the truth. But I also think she's wrong. Our outings have helped me remember how happiness feels.

"Our situations are different. You aren't grieving." Everything in me, including my voice, is hardening.

She sets her silverware down, scowling. "I am grieving—I loved Sean and Scotty too. And beyond that, I miss *you*, Amy. I miss us—the way we were. I know that we'll never be exactly who we were before, so I've given you space. Helped however I could. It hurts when you run away or get irritated when I ask questions. And while I know you were never much of a planner, it concerns me when you won't even discuss the future, yet you fling yourself from planes and then sit here speaking rapturously about the afterlife . . . and you know why."

Those loaded words hang in the air, suspended like an unpinned grenade. My breath comes up short and tight. The pressure in my head makes it hard to hold upright. Who the hell am I to give advice when I can't even make sense of my own life? I bite my tongue so hard I almost yelp.

"We've both had a crappy day. Let's stick to lighter topics while we finish dinner." I dredge two fries through more ketchup. Then I can't leave it, because whatever happens in the future, I cannot have her stressing about me. Not when her own life is falling apart. "But first, one last thing. I appreciate everything you've done for me and how much you care, but it's time for you to stop worrying about me."

"I love you, so I'll always worry about you."

"I love you, too, but you've got your own issues to resolve now. Whatever my choices, they have nothing to do with you or anything you've done or not done. You can't control me. You also can't will me to want what you want for me. So please take me off your list of obligations and rest easy knowing, whatever comes to pass, I'm living life my way, and that's more than most people do. From now on, just be my sister and friend, okay?"

She raises her hands. "Got it."

I hope that's true.

CHAPTER TWELVE

KRISTIN

Sunday morning, eleven days later

Livvy's seated behind me petting her new guinea pig, Snickers, so named for his black, caramel, and white patchy fur. After considering Amy's suggestions and reading articles about how pets help children cope with anxiety, I talked Tony into this little guy. I would've bought one for Amy, too, if she hadn't ordered me to butt out of her healing process. It's best, really. She's doing better, so now I can redirect my energy to my family and career. "You happy, sweet pea?"

She nods, smiling at me in the rearview mirror. Surprising her with her first pet has been a big hit. Luca wasn't as interested because he didn't want more responsibility. Drawing that boundary around his time is something I could never have done at his age. As a reward, I promised him a game of Scrabble later.

"Can he sleep in my room?" she asks.

"Maybe on the weekends. I don't want Snickers keeping you up on school nights." When we pull into the garage, I turn off the ignition and open my door.

Livvy scoops Snickers from the cage and nestles him to her chest. "Wait till Daddy sees."

He'll smother his little princess with all the praise she requires. For all his big talk about discipline, he's softer with her than he is with Luca. Gender discrimination in action, but since my dad was never gooey with Amy or me, I won't rob Livvy of being the apple of Tony's eye, especially not at this tender age.

Lately Tony and I have showered attention on the kids rather than address our disagreements. My career frustration festers like an open wound, but I haven't raised it again. I know where he stands, and like Amy said, this is my issue to resolve. It's my career, my goals, and my choice, not Tony's or even Jim's. This is no time to feel sorry for myself.

Of course, that raises the matter of the pills. I broke down and took another early last week to help me juggle the kids' demands with drumming up new business with old clients and hunting for that "elephant." I'm chipping away on all fronts, praying that everything will turn out well.

I duck into the back seat to undo Livvy's child seat and then let her slide out of the car before grabbing the cage and other supplies and closing the door. Livvy skips toward the mudroom door and then bursts inside, calling out for her father. While hanging up my coat and purse, I pause and hold my stomach. It's been queasy for twenty-four hours, probably because I haven't taken a pill since Thursday to prove to myself that I'm not addicted. This feeling should make me want them less, but that's not the case.

Around the bend, Tony fawns over Livvy and her rodent.

"Boy or girl?" he asks.

"Boy."

He smiles at her. I've always loved his smiles—toothy, dimpled, warm—and miss being on the receiving end of them. Tony's been deliberately low-key, giving me time while he takes over more of the housework to lighten my load. I appreciate that, but it's left me feeling lonely. "Does he have a name yet?"

"Snickers!" she cries with delight, at which point Tony reminds her about the responsibility of cleaning his cage and giving him food and water. Luca comes downstairs to check out the newest member of the family.

"Wanna hold him?" Livvy offers in a shocking moment of magnanimity.

"Yeah!" He carefully takes the trembling animal from his sister and strokes its back. Both kids are practically bouncing on their toes. I want to hold this moment—this joy—for as long as possible. Just the four of us together, relaxed and happy. We can build on this.

Luca hands his sister back her pet. "He's cool."

"Why don't you help Livvy set up the cage in the playroom? I want to talk to your mom about taking a little beach trip," Tony suggests.

"Really?" Luca's eyes light up.

"Let's see what we can work out." Tony squeezes Luca's arm.

"Awesome." Luca looks at his sister then. "Come on, Livvy, let's go before they change their minds." While Livvy cradles Snickers, Luca puts the supplies inside the cage and then lifts it, demonstrating his natural organizational and planning skills. My son, through and through.

I enter the kitchen hoping water will settle my stomach. In January, I agreed, generally, to consider a trip, but we never got around to planning it. Despite wanting to do this with my family, as I predicted, the timing sucks. "Are we off to the Caribbean?"

"I found two luxury resorts with plenty of kids' stuff to do—one in Antigua and the other in Anguilla. I sent you an email with some links. We're last-minute planning, though, so we should act soon if we want to get away, even if we only do a four-day trip after Easter."

His mentioning a short trip means he's willing to compromise. That's a start.

My smile feels tight. "I'll take a look."

Tony rises from the sofa and comes over to give me a kiss, then touches the back of his hand to my head. "You look a little pale. Are you feeling all right?"

"I'm fine." I glance at the counter to avoid his gaze.

Wearing a doubtful expression, he loosely wraps his arms around my waist. It almost feels like old times, except for my secrets and anxiety. "I have other news."

I drape my arms over his shoulders, eager to change the subject, and going for the "fake it till you make it" thing. "Oh?"

"Luca and I bumped into Dan Lewis when we ran out for breakfast sandwiches." Dan's a college friend of Tony's and the CEO of a sizable private-equity firm based in Greenwich. "While we caught up, he expressed dissatisfaction with his firm's outside counsel. I reminded him of your specialty, and he said you should call him."

She should call me sounds like tepid interest, but it certainly would be a coup to reel in Guerrilla Investment Group. A possible ticket back to partnership. My commute would still suck, but I'd rather quit at some point after making partner than slink away in shame. Better yet, as equity partner, I'd have more autonomy to work from home. A delicious pop of hope fizzes. "Thanks, honey. I'll call him this week."

"Attagirl." He winks and kisses me again. For a second, it feels like we're back in our little place in Yonkers, at the beginning of everything, when we were spurring each other on to new conquests. Deep down I know we can't return to that youthful, starry-eyed outlook. We probably shouldn't try if we want to evolve as people and a couple. "Livvy seems happy. Your morning went well?"

"She wanted every gerbil, hamster, and guinea pig because she felt sorry for all the ones stuck there. You're lucky we didn't come home with a small petting zoo. Hopefully cuddling Snickers will help her self-soothe. Caring for him should help her mature. It's unlikely a full solution to bigger issues, though."

His hands drop away, and I can tell he's restraining an eye roll. "All right. But it's a step in the right direction."

Unlike him and Amy, I'll keep my mind open to therapy. "At this point, I'll take the thawing of her freeze-out, no matter how temporary."

"Change takes time. Let's stay the course." "Stay the Course" could be the theme song of my life, which would currently be played in a minor key. He squints at me, hesitating. "So, did you see today's local paper?"

I shake my head. He points to a stool, so I take a seat.

"Uh-oh . . ." I wrap my arms around my waist in preparation for whatever is about to punch me.

He shakes his head. "Nothing bad, but it looks like Amy's giving away her money. She gave some librarian in Stamford a bunch, and that lady then donated part of her gift to the library to create a permanent sensory-safe space in the children's section. It'll be called 'Scotty's Corner,' and they'll also lend things like noise-canceling headphones, fidget spinners, and other things to help kids enjoy the library experience."

I'm momentarily stunned. Amy hasn't mentioned any of this to me. Maybe it's not my business, but the only reason to hide it would be if she's plotting something I wouldn't like. She was overly interested in the afterlife the other week. Yet she's also been more engaged lately. I hate not knowing whether she's doing better or simply putting on an act.

"Wow. Why'd she make a gift to a librarian rather than the library itself? I mean, it feels backward. I wonder if she's given money to other people too."

"Are you wishing she'd give us some so you could quit?" He tips his head as he eyes me carefully. I'm frankly surprised he brought up the *q*-word instead of pretending that conversation never happened.

If he knew she'd offered, he might be upset that I declined. I pray he can't read my face. "I couldn't enjoy her money when it's so connected to her grief. It would feel wrong."

He shrugs, conceding that point, unaware of my omission. Amy's hiding things from me. I'm hiding things from Tony. Is Tony hiding things from me?

"So why do you care who she gives it to?" he asks.

"It's not the giving—it's the secretiveness that gives me a bad feeling." I stare out the window as if the answer will pop out from behind a shrub. She's still young, and when her grief subsides, that money could really come in handy. Randomly giving it away reeks of fatalism. She's been so insistent that I back off. That her choices are out of my control. Is that all a veiled warning?

"I admit, it's odd," Tony says, interrupting my dark musing. "Why not give money to charities instead of acquaintances? Especially if she thinks it's cursed. It makes no sense, but that can be said of a lot of your sister's decisions." He makes a wry face after his little joke.

I toss him a cautionary glance so he doesn't run with that line of thinking. I'm allowed to criticize my family, but I don't like him speaking ill of them. I don't like his sarcasm either. "Maybe this gifting can be tied to something bigger. Something that would give her a real purpose, like you mentioned weeks ago. The librarian had a nice idea—honoring Scotty's memory. Maybe Amy could start her own foundation to honor Sean and Scotty while also giving back to the community." I sit forward, latching on to this idea as a real way forward for my sister. A true and meaningful goal that might give her something lasting to live for, unlike thrill seeking.

He frowns doubtfully. "She's got no nonprofit experience."

"She can hire experience. I know a nonprofit lawyer, Declan MacAfee, who could help set it up and advise her. It's worth a conversation, isn't it?"

"I hate to see you get your hopes up, Krissy. That's a lot to take on, especially for someone still in mourning."

I won't give up on anything that could help her rebuild her life. "I'll call Declan and suss it out before mentioning anything to Amy. But a local foundation dedicated to helping families like hers feels like the perfect legacy."

Tony's wrinkled expression stops me.

"What?"

"Your mind is a thing of beauty." He kisses my forehead, and I absorb every ounce of his pride. "Pouncing from idea to planning and staffing in minutes is where you shine, and yet you've been so tired lately. Is adding to your plate a good idea?"

Look at me, just like my son, piling more on my shoulders without thinking about myself. It isn't the right time to take on more, and yet if Amy is planning something untoward, time isn't on my side. "I'll make the suggestion and introduction, that's all."

"Mom, I'm ready for Scrabble," Luca interrupts us, having come downstairs while Tony and I were talking. He offers a devilish smile. "This time you're going down."

I need a few hours to map out a plan for approaching Dan and calling Declan, but my son—my family—should come first. "I'll never let you win."

"I've been playing online and learning tricks. You'll see."

I raise my hands. "I've been warned. Grab the game from the cabinet and set it up on the kitchen table. I'll fix us a little snack."

He gives a sharp nod and then dashes back upstairs in search of the game box.

"You might go a little easy on him today," Tony says.

With my hands resting on my hips, I say, "I can't believe you, of all people, would suggest that. Besides, my mom never let me win, which made me a better player."

"He's been working hard to improve. A little win could reinforce the benefits of hard work. Don't throw the game, but maybe don't play for the kill." He hikes one shoulder.

I grimace, acknowledging my miles-wide competitive streak when it comes to Scrabble. "We'll see."

He looks at me, bemused. Who could blame him? Lately my behavior is as inconsistent as internet service in Montana. Even I can't guess what will come out of my mouth next. Tony says, "I'm going to work out."

Working out is something that I've let drop off my to-do list lately, so I envy that release. I text Declan a quick note and then send one to my sister as Luca returns and begins to set up the board. Want to come for dinner?

It's a risk. We've texted a few times since our dinner out, but we haven't gotten together again. This gifting stuff has me concerned. Getting eyes on her will lower my anxiety, especially if she likes my foundation idea. Of course, she might mention the pills to Tony if she thinks I haven't quit. I will soon. If I land Guerrilla, my career will get back on track. Kids take Adderall for years. I can do it for a few more weeks.

Setting the phone on the counter, I pull a bowl of red seedless grapes and two seltzer waters from the fridge. My phone pings as I set the snacks on the table.

Amy.

Sure. I miss Tony's cooking.

I smile, my shoulders relaxing as my plans come together. Tonight, I'll need to approach Amy artfully. Do I applaud the gift to the librarian and expand from there? Do I pretend not to have seen the article?

Luca draws an *E* tile while I pull an *M*.

"Me first!" He rubs his hands together.

I let the grammar go.

"Let's see what you've got." I look at my own tiles: *A, I, I, Y, K, M, X*. Not a great start. I might not have to throw the game after all.

———

The good news: while Livvy was thrilled to show off Snickers to Amy—and Amy was relieved to no longer be pushed to get Gotcha—Livvy didn't hang all over my sister and beg for her attention like normal. The bad news: Amy scrutinized me all evening, trying to catch me out about the pills. I can't react and risk Tony asking questions, but my body feels like a human fist. She must've tired of my constant scrutiny this winter, but I had greater reason to worry than she does.

We all sit at the table patting our distended tummies, thanks to my husband's homemade manicotti feast.

"I can't even make jarred sauce and pasta without overcooking it." Amy sits back. "How do you do it?"

"Practice helps." He sips his wine and eyes the kids, lest they missed that comment. We all know it wasn't a chore for my husband to learn to cook at his nonna's side. Food is his love language now.

Livvy licks the sauce off her fork before setting it on the empty plate, then turns toward Amy. "Can we have the treat you brought?"

"It's up to your parents, but luckily it comes from a bakery instead of my oven," Amy says.

"Can we have some, Mom?" Luca asks. "To celebrate my win."

I pretend to pout about losing. "I could use a consolation prize."

His win was mostly legit. I held back from supercharged words on only one occasion, my options often limited by having too many vowels or uncommonly used consonants. His online practice has taught him to strategize making two words at once whenever possible, which also helped him. Best of all, while we played, Luca talked to me about a new teammate, his interest in outer space, and some video game. It felt the way time with a child ought to feel. Happy. Easy.

Tony winks. "Kids, clear the dishes while Aunt Amy gets her dessert."

They leap off their chairs as if they were spring-loaded.

"Careful!" I brace for a dropped glass or dish in their rush to complete the chore. Tony and I share a satisfied silent exchange across the table. While our problems aren't all solved, it's been a good day with the kids. I'd be feeling hopeful if only my sister's true state of mind were clearer.

Amy sets the red velvet cake from St. Moritz Bakery on the table. Luca grabs paper plates and forks for everyone, while I hunt for a cake spatula.

"This looks delicious, thanks." I cut into it, then hand Luca the first generous slice.

Tony waves me off. "My metabolism is catching up to me."

Hardly. He simply prefers to waste calories on cheese and good wine rather than sugar.

"Mine is, too, but I need comfort food after my big loss," I tease my son, who smiles with lips shiny from the cream cheese frosting.

"I want a big piece just because," Livvy declares, fork in fist.

"'Just because'?" Amy repeats, tickling her side. "That's my favorite reason of all."

Livvy giggles with her aunt. Months ago, their closeness concerned me because Amy's suicidal thoughts had the power to devastate my daughter. Livvy's well-being is another reason to help Amy find new purpose.

The kids devour dessert in record time, which will mean stomachaches at bedtime. This cake is so delicious; it's probably worth it.

"Haven't seen you eat this well in months," Amy says to me, staring like a hawk.

I brush it off with a shrug, although I want to bug my eyes.

"Go brush your teeth," Tony tells the kids as he refills my and Amy's glasses with wine. "I need to jump on a call with my architect. You two relax and enjoy the wine."

He makes himself scarce so I can approach my sister with the foundation idea.

"You're in a much better mood than the last time I saw you." Amy doesn't touch her wine, instead swirling it from the stem. "Have you kept your promise?"

"I'm off the pills," I murmur, which is technically true today. I don't owe her further explanation, and I didn't invite her here to be judged. "We had a good weekend. Livvy loves her new pet."

"Brilliant compromise with the guinea pig, by the way." Amy relaxes.

I'm tempted to lick the leftover icing off my plate like a kid. "Her enthusiasm for the responsibility will likely wane, but I'll take the win for now."

"Good plan. And what's up with you and Tony, and you and work?"

Time to rip off one bandage. "We're planning a mini-trip to Anguilla in a couple weeks."

"That's great!" She shows no sign of being upset that we might not be around as the anniversary approaches, which only raises more concern that she's planning something terrible that day.

"As for work, I'm regrouping." If I mention Guerrilla, it'll provoke another argument. Best I stick to sharing my overarching goal rather than each step toward getting there. "I'm trying to create balance on the weekends and holidays."

My little rebellion—pushing aside working at home unless it's a true emergency. Of course, if I bring Dan in, it'll be back to long hours until the partnership vote.

Amy pushes the wineglass away. "A good start."

I nod at the faint praise as I prepare to broach the topic I asked her over to discuss. "Speaking of starts, I have an idea to run by you."

"Uh-oh. This feels like a setup." She eyes me.

"I had a thought about the lottery money."

"You'll take some?" She leans forward with her hands stretched across the table toward me, eyebrows high.

"No, no." I wave her off. "This is about you."

Her expression hardens. "I told you, I'm not using it."

"Not for yourself, I know." I hold up a hand. "But I have an idea to honor Scotty and Sean and help other families like yours."

"I'm already doing that."

I'd best begin with a little honesty. "Yes, I saw the article in the paper. That's what gave me the idea."

She hesitates, and I can feel that old rivalry—the one she creates in her mind—brewing. "What's *your* brilliant idea?"

"Start a nonprofit to help families with special-needs kids pay for services and equipment or whatever else they need. It could offer group programs, or take grant proposals and hand out checks."

Amy grimaces. "That sounds complicated."

I shake my head. "Only until you get the hang of it. Imagine it: the Walsh Foundation, or SAS Family Foundation, or whatever. The point is, it gives Sean and Scotty a real legacy." I smile, hoping that concept hooks her. "Think of how rewarding it would be to help thousands of people instead of a handful."

Her mouth twists from side to side. "So you think my way is stupid."

"No, but you can increase your impact. A foundation could go on for decades." Thus tethering her to this life so she stops flirting with the afterlife.

Amy crosses her arms, eyes narrowing. "Just admit that this dinner invitation was an elaborate ruse to convince me to do things your way."

"It wasn't." Maybe a little. Okay, a lot. "I wanted a reset after our dinner last week. You know I don't like tension." Then I can't help myself. "If you're set on making personal gifts, consult your accountants about gift taxes, which will start to eat up the money you have left."

"Who cares? When it's gone, it's gone."

I press my lips together, when what I really want is to shake her. "You're barely thirty-four, Amy. What if someday you want another child? Won't you be sorry that you didn't keep any safety net?"

My sister's posture turns rigid as her face drains of color. In a tone as brittle and clear as fine crystal, she says, "I'll never have another family. Never. Don't even think that, Kristin. I mean it."

Hearing her close herself off from the possibility makes me further question her recovery. My chest aches with doubt. It also occurs to me that the surprise painting of her family I'm picking up later this week could upset her. "Regardless, it wouldn't hurt you to keep a little safety net for yourself. But forget that and think about how rewarding it would be to build a community foundation in your family's name."

Some pink returns to her cheeks. Full-blown fight averted.

"I'm not sure I'm ready for such a huge commitment." She's making marks in the leftover icing with her fork, avoiding my gaze.

Short-term lease. Haphazard gifting. No job or big commitments. Despite sparks of hope these past couple of months, might she have a grand plan of her own? One I wouldn't support? I should raid her bag to see if she's still taking doxepin.

"Would you at least meet with my friend Declan to discuss the idea? Find out exactly what's involved before you reject it. You could always hire someone to run it if it's too much work for you."

"Declan?" Her tone is harsh, filled with disgust.

"What's with the face?"

"I just told you I'm not interested in meeting other men, Kristin. God."

I roll my eyes. Sometimes dealing with her is as difficult as dealing with Livvy. "It's not a fix-up. Declan's a dozen years older than you and raising a teenager, since his wife died two years ago. He used to work at my firm, and nonprofit law is his expertise. He works in Stamford now. I reached out this morning just in case you were interested. He said he'd be happy to help and has a little time on his schedule tomorrow afternoon if you were free."

"Oh." She relaxes, and we sit in silence for a minute. The fact that she's thinking makes me optimistic. "I'll admit, I love the idea of a legacy for Sean and Scotty. But what are the chances I could set up something like this without screwing it up?"

"Meet with Declan before you sell yourself short. I could come, too, if you want. Then if it feels like too much, I'll drop it. Promise."

She eyes me. "You've got enough to manage. I can talk to him on my own."

Despite the slap across the hand, I couldn't be more exhilarated from winning this concession than if I'd been made partner and put on my firm's executive committee. She's considering this, which suggests that she isn't committed to suicide.

"Terrific. I'll introduce you by email, and then you can take it from there." I grab her hand, relieved tears welling behind my eyes. "This is exciting. Maybe Tony can help you find some inexpensive office space."

"Don't get more people involved. I'm not even saying I'll do it. I'll talk to Declan. Period."

"Okay." I can't stop smiling. Declan is a lovely guy who was eager to help after hearing her story. I'm sure he'll convince her to agree. This is it. Building something in Sean's and Scotty's names will keep her with us. "Pass the cake. This calls for a second slice."

"Holy shit, the world must be coming to an end!" Amy jokes, sliding the cake toward me.

I stick my tongue out like I used to when we were kids, then cut another sliver. Things in my family are finally—slowly—turning around. Once I get my career on track, my marriage might also find its new normal.

It's all within my grasp, if I can push a little harder to bring it all together. I'll call Dan to gauge his interest. If it's genuine, I won't rely purely on Jim's goodwill and empty promises again. I need to be smarter and more confident. Leverage the opportunity. In other words, take a page from Amy's old book and make my own rules.

CHAPTER THIRTEEN

AMY

The following day

The children's library quickly installed flexible soundproofing partitions in one area to create Scotty's Corner, which is filled with beanbag chairs, noise-canceling earphones, and other items to help neurodivergent kids feel comfortable. The beautiful gesture and the looks on all the moms' faces fill me with pride, increasing my commitment to explore the foundation idea with Declan today. Establishing one would stall my larger plan, but I can't disregard a chance to honor my son and husband.

Kristin's proposal proves she'll never stop trying to reengage me. I am loved, even after all I've put her through, so I can't be angry at her refusal to let me go. If our shoes were reversed, I wouldn't give up on her either.

Standing at the podium, I face the small crowd of employees, parents, and children who've come to the dedication. This resource would've been wonderful when Scotty was alive. It should be easy to make a short speech now, but the thirty or so sets of curious eyeballs staring at me are making me wither. The idea of talking about my dead family in public plants a thick lump in my throat.

I cough to clear it. "First, I want to thank Lillian for honoring my son, Scotty. This library was a special place for him. It was here he first discovered Piglet, his dearest love. I lost track of how many times we read the Winnie the Pooh series. And yet, as some of you with neurodiverse kids know, a trip to the library can sometimes be a challenge due to the many distractions, bright lights, and people. I'm eternally grateful to Lillian's generosity and ingenuity in creating Scotty's Corner, and hope it helps many other families better enjoy their reading experiences here. I also hope my son is somehow aware of this gesture, and that he's got his own little reading corner in heaven. Thank you." I back away from the podium, straining to keep my chin up.

The round of applause makes me uncomfortable. Kristin would've been more eloquent. She would've recited a beautiful quote, thanked more people, and maybe even told an affecting story about Scotty.

I quickly take a seat near the back of the crowd while another staff member says a few words. Although it's likely my imagination, it feels as if everyone is looking at me, whispering pitying asides to one another. This might be easier if I weren't alone, but Kristin is working and my parents are in Arizona. I thought to invite Bob, but he doesn't know my history. It's been nice having one friend who treats me like a normal person, so I've resisted being honest.

Suddenly folks are milling about, their kids testing the different apparatuses. Life races forward even when I stand still.

Lillian approaches me. "I'm still overwhelmed by your gift. Are there charities that you or your family care about where I can make another donation?"

I lay a hand on her arm. "This is enough. Honestly, it's bringing me joy to make gifts to people like you. Please accept it without reservations."

Her eyes get misty. "I don't know what to say. Thank you. I guess we'll pay off our mortgage so we can put more money into the kids' college funds."

"Terrific!" This happy feeling would repeat often if I set up a foundation. That might make sticking around bearable, preventing me from devastating my family. It's getting harder to not want to be around for Kristin and her kids, for Bob, and for all the parents who could benefit from my generosity. The appeal surprises me even as it presses on the tender spot of survivor's guilt resting in the bottom of my heart.

"Will you stay for cake?" she asks.

"Sorry. I'm due across town in fifteen minutes. But again, thank you for naming this cozy space for kids after Scotty. I know he'd love it."

"I hope to see you here again in the future."

Perhaps she, like my sister, assumes I'll have more kids someday. Though well intentioned, that wish affects me like a splinter beneath my fingernail. "Take care, Lillian."

It takes only five minutes to drive to Summer Street. Declan's office is housed in a classic gray-and-white Victorian home that reminds me of the dream houses of my youth, with its gingerbread embellishments and welcoming front porch.

I park the car and sit, knee bouncing, hands tight on the steering wheel. This will be my first serious conversation with anyone outside my family in months. If this guy knows anything about anything, he's going to see how preposterous this idea is—me, a foundation owner. Me, making decisions that affect other families.

I shouldn't have shot down Kristin's offer to get involved, especially if she might ultimately be the one tasked with keeping it going. Perhaps I should also involve Jane, who'd want to see it succeed. Sean would've liked that.

Despite my flagging confidence, thinking about a legacy in Sean's and Scotty's names has my knee bouncing.

After locking my car, I tug at my shirtsleeves. My history is mine to tell when I'm ready.

The hinges of the oversize wood-and-glass front door squeak. In the sunny entry, a brass directory announces the three professional offices—a lawyer, a shrink, and an architect. There's a joke in there somewhere.

Declan's office is to my left. The door unlocks almost immediately after I hit the buzzer. When I step into the inviting reception room, my very being exhales amid the earthy comfort of mahogany wainscoting. A thick Tibetan carpet in reds, blues, and golds absorbs sound, creating a cozy ambiance. Light filters through slanted wooden blinds that obscure the busy traffic outside. But what makes it singular are the plants. Ivy hangs off a bookcase behind the receptionist's desk, while ferns, spider and zebra plants, ficus, and bromeliads for a pop of color transform the space into a tiny rainforest. The room is alive and bursting with a loamy aroma. My soul responds as if overdosing on fresh air.

The receptionist—a cute twentysomething with bright eyes that have yet to know trauma—smiles. "Can I help you?"

"Yes, please. I'm Amy Walsh. I have a two-o'clock appointment with Mr. MacAfee." I clutch the purse strap on my shoulder like it's a climbing rope dangling over a cliff.

She looks at her computer to confirm. "Great. I'll let him know you're here. It'll just be a minute, if you want to take a seat." Without fanfare, she returns her attention to typing something. I sink into one of the two handsome leather wingback chairs and continue studying the plants while drumming my fingers against the chair's padded arms.

My sister's colleagues typically have been intimidating, aggressive, and dismissive—an arrogant trifecta. I'm bracing for another uncomfortable conversation when a stately man emerges from the door to my right. He's tall and slim, dressed in gray slacks and a pink striped shirt. His salt-and-pepper hair is beginning to thin only at the temples. What strikes me most are his eyes—they've known deep sorrow. Still, the crinkles fanning from the outer corners when he smiles suggest he's also known great joy.

He offers a hand. "Mrs. Walsh?"

I rise. "Amy, please."

"Amy. Nice to meet you. Shall we go chat?" He gestures toward his office. Efficient. Pleasant. Businesslike. This is perfect.

"Yes, thanks."

His office decor resembles the reception room. Sumptuous rich, deep hues and a dozen more plants. It feels more like a psychologist's office than a lawyer's. He catches me taking it all in. With a sheepish grin, he says, "A bit much, perhaps?"

"I like them. A little old-fashioned, but in a good way. Now people use fake plants or big designer ones as statement pieces. But this here"—I gesture around—"this isn't for show. They're thriving. This takes devotion."

He points to one of the two chairs in front of his desk, and then, instead of sitting behind his desk, he chooses the other one so that we are seated side by side. His informality tears down yet another of my invisible walls.

Glancing around at the assorted pots, he then looks at me with a shrug. "The truth is that they were my late wife's great love. She had a flair for gardening. Our yard hardly has any grassy areas for all the beds and shrubs. I brought most of her indoor plants here after she died because it's easier to care for them when they're clustered together this way. It's also better for me to keep the reminder here instead of having our daughter live in a jungle mausoleum."

I'd forgotten he was a widower. He blushes, suggesting he's surprised himself with his easy confession. Vulnerability is not something I've come across often in men other than Sean. I instantly trust Declan, even as the reminder of Sean scoops out my heart.

"I'm sorry for your loss. There are just no words for it, are there? I suppose Kristin told you about me." I tug at my shirtsleeves again.

"Only the basics—the lottery win, the tragic accident. I'm so very sorry. It's quite a testament to your strength that you're considering this bold new direction." He reaches forward to squeeze my hand but pulls back as if remembering we've only just met.

"Thanks." I haven't felt bold in so long that my eyes fill with tears I can't identify—happy, panicked, sad, a mix? Perhaps hope is a blend of all those emotions. "It's been a challenge. You're lucky to have your daughter to keep you grounded." I've often shamelessly latched on to Luca and Livvy like a substitute mother who craved being needed and useful. All the years I'll never get with my son rise like a rogue wave to suck me under fast and hard. I can't catch my breath.

Declan doesn't look away, choosing instead to sit in my pain with me. Perhaps his being a decade or so older than I am gives him that patience. Being provided space to collect myself as the dreadful ache recedes is a gift. "She's the center of my world, although getting her through the loss of her mother while I'm also grieving has presented its own challenges."

I hadn't considered that aspect. Grief gathers like smoke in my lungs, but we're not here for a mutual pity party. "Well, I don't know what Kristin shared about her idea—and this is her idea, not mine—but I'm looking for basic info that would help me decide whether to do it."

"Yes, that's what she said. Of course, she's as enthusiastic as ever. I can only imagine having her as a sister." He chuckles, acknowledging her momentum when she's motivated.

"She's driven. Pretty perfect by most measures. But if you ever need blackmail material, I'm your girl." I wink. The truth is that there isn't such material because Kristin has always followed the best practices, so to speak. Well, other than taking those amphetamines. She said she stopped, but it's hard to tell.

"Good to know," he says. "Her idea would make a lovely tribute and a viable community resource."

"My main concern is that, well, I'm not a driven brainiac or even very organized. Running a foundation sounds way above my pay grade."

"I'm confident you could manage. Let's dispense with the easy stuff first. Filing the paperwork, opening the bank account, even leasing a small office space—that's all straightforward. As for the administrative aspects and record keeping, you can hire an assistant to manage that if it isn't a strength. A good executive assistant for a small foundation in the nonprofit space in this area might run around forty grand per year. But let's back up. We're talking about a foundation rather than a charity. A charity takes public money and is viewed a little differently by the IRS than a private foundation. Within the realm of foundations, you'd be relegated to one of two types—a private foundation or an operating foundation. A private foundation is generally set up by a benefactor—you—and that money is then used to further some mission in the form of grants or other payments."

"Got it." It's got to be more complex than that, but I like how he simplified it.

"Great. Now, to qualify as a 501(c) entity, a foundation needs to spend five percent of its total assets annually on the mission. An operating foundation is more nuts and bolts. It would run its own programs—perhaps educational ones for parents or therapeutic ones for kids, or a combination. Obviously, that's the more complex type of foundation. Given your concerns, I'm guessing you'd prefer to stick to a private family foundation. In that case, once the entity is legally formed, you'd set up criteria for gifts—like an application form—which people would then submit, and you'd choose who to help and how much to give. It would take some time to think through the criteria and perhaps set some caps—per family, per annum, et cetera. But once that's set, the whole thing should run rather smoothly."

"So I'd be handing money over to strangers with no way of knowing whether they'll use the money to hire the therapists or whatever?" That sounds elitist, and yet there was real comfort in knowing that Josephina and Lillian are civic-minded people.

"Perhaps you could set it up so that you send the money directly to the end user designated by the applicant. The only rules are that the grants be for the charitable purpose, that the purpose is authorized by the organizational documents, and that there is no self-dealing. You could require an application and interview to help you get a better sense of potential recipients. These are all details that you'd decide up front and would be known by applicants in advance."

His measured tone and straightforward language make it seem like an easy choice. I mean, it's basically formalizing and expanding my plan of giving the money to deserving individuals.

"That sounds like a lot of paperwork." I look at my lap. "The truth—what Kristin doesn't get—is that I still struggle some days to shower and make breakfast. I still question the purpose of everything most days, which can quickly drag me down." It's the most honest I've been with anyone in months, and it feels so good I could cry.

He's nodding. "That first year, I lost track of how many times I reached across the empty bed before the cold spot made my heart collapse. If it hadn't been for my daughter, Gracie, I could've easily holed up for months. That said, this plan would give you a reason to get out of bed even on bad days. Another thing that helped me was joining a grief group."

I must've grimaced at that suggestion, because he adds, "I know it sounds awful. A former coworker dragged me to the first one, but it was a great decision. I still go once in a while—like on my wife's birthday or our anniversary. Sometimes I go to support others—paying it forward. It's a comforting community, particularly among those of us grieving unexpected or too-early deaths." He then makes a face and holds up a hand. "Sorry. Didn't mean to pontificate. That's not why you're here."

"It's okay. You really get it—better than a doctor or my family, who all want me to be better now, if possible."

He nods, a knowing grin in place. "Family support can unwittingly create pressure. Grief is a long journey, but in my experience, things do improve. Slowly. Painfully. Never exactly fully. But Gracie and I are in much better places now than we were two years ago, or even last year. So, for whatever that's worth . . ."

I've always known that most people recover from this pain, but Declan's encouragement makes it feel more tangible. Granted, his choices didn't result in his wife's death. That's the sticking point that pops my balloon whenever hope rises. "It's worth a lot, thanks. Sorry my being here is bringing up painful memories."

"Not at all." He shakes his head, again gesturing to his wife's jungle as a reminder that he's never not surrounded by her ghost.

Ferns, stuffed toys, photographs. Why do we cling to the last remnants of the people we loved when the sight of them can sometimes feel like a pillow over our faces, our lungs burning and gasping for air? I blink twice to clear my eyes. "So, back to the foundation. How long does it take to form?"

"Filing the entity paperwork and opening bank accounts could happen quickly—a couple weeks at the outset. The rest depends on how much time you put in to get things rolling. How much money were you thinking of using to fund it?"

"All of it—or what's left."

His jaw goes slack with surprise. "You're not reserving anything for yourself?"

"No. It's . . . no." I close my eyes while shaking my head. If I spout my curse theory, he'll think I've lost my mind. Other than revising my will to leave a little surprise for Kristin, I want nothing to do with that money.

He presses his lips together while studying me, but he doesn't ask for an explanation. "Well, once you fund the entity, you'd invest the capital in some conservative instruments that throw off distributions. As I mentioned, you'd need to spend five percent per year. That figure includes any operating costs like rent and salaries, including your own."

"Oh, I could draw a salary?"

"You should, in fact, especially if you're not keeping any assets for personal use." His sober expression reveals his concern about that plan.

"That makes sense. And would you act as an adviser after the initial legal work is done?"

"You could engage me as legal counsel with a small annual retainer. I could also serve on your board."

"I need a board?" Me leading a board. Sean is rolling around on a cloud right now, laughing his ass off. I smile myself, picturing that. I always loved to make him laugh.

"Yes. Nonprofits are legal entities with corporate-governance requirements. Your board could be simple—you, your sister, me, maybe someone else with special knowledge related to the mission, like a therapist or doctor. It'd meet once or twice a year to oversee certain decisions."

"That's good—I mean, if something were to happen to me, there'd be a structure in place to keep things going." As soon as I say it, I regret my habit of thinking out loud.

His gaze narrows, and his face fills with concern. "Is there a reason to think you wouldn't be around? Are you ill?"

Holding his gaze while being less than fully honest makes my stomach tighten. "No, but, like, if I hate running it or something. If I decide to move to Italy," I joke to deflect from more probing questions. Meanwhile, the board offers perfect roles for Kristin and possibly Jane. I could kill several birds with one table, so to speak.

"Ah. Well, yes. Having a decent board helps with any transition. Of course, you'd also need to appoint a new director if you decide to vacate the position."

"Vacate the position." That has a nice distancing sound compared with "offing myself." *Don't be sad, Kristin. I'm merely vacating my position on earth and will see you again someday.* Somehow I doubt that would alleviate her grief, and I loathe the idea of causing her more grief.

"Well, you've given me a lot to think about. Let me take a few days to consider everything. It sounds doable, as long as you and Kristin are willing to help me out in the beginning." I frown then, thinking of how overwhelmed Kristin has been this year, and how—despite her offer—it's selfish of me to throw more on her plate. Another reason to involve Jane, who has too much time on her hands.

"Absolutely."

It'd be easy to spend the rest of the day in this comfortable chair, swaddled in his snug office, breathing the supercharged oxygen. But he has other clients to meet, and I have decisions to make. There's no denying the fizz of excitement about doing something substantial with that damn money.

"I'll call you soon and let you know either way, and of course, if I proceed, I'll hire you to do all the work."

"Thank you. It'd be my honor to make this happen for you and your family. It'd be an exceptional way to honor your love for the departed. Building something that will give to others for decades to come—I can't think of a better way to spend your time."

I stand and shake his hand again. "Thank you for your advice and for sharing your personal story. It's been nice to meet you."

"You too, Amy." He walks me to his office door. "I look forward to hearing from you."

I wave goodbye to him and his assistant, and then exit the building and pull up my collar against a stiff early-spring breeze. On my way to the car, a whisper that sounds like a little boy's laughter slides up the back of my neck like a breeze.

"Scotty?" I whisper, stopping to look around, although no one is there. Thin branches with tiny green buds waver overhead. It's a sign, I'm sure.

Despite my hesitation, I know what must be done. It would be criminal not to help thousands of worried parents, especially if the only reason not to is a selfish desire to end my own suffering. If everyone is right, then this focus could lift me out of my self-pitying spiral. As much as it pains me to imagine being happy after losing my family, if Sean had been the survivor, he would've done this if given the chance. And I would've wanted him to live. To thrive.

Healing fully sounds as impossible as holding a rainbow, yet Declan works surrounded by his dead wife's plants and is moving forward. Every day people lose family members and recover. I will never forgive myself for the reason why I wasn't killed with my family, but perhaps if I can atone for it, I might eventually recover too.

CHAPTER FOURTEEN

KRISTIN

The following day

The late-afternoon sun's reflection transforms distant skyscrapers into a dense forest of lit candles. Daylight savings grants us an extra hour of daylight now, which will make the evenings spent at my desk less noticeable—to me, anyway. The kids will still note my absence at the dinner table.

Today's circus of client title problems, breached loan covenants, and contentious negotiations made me fall off the wagon and take another pill. I'm not proud, but the energy boost sustained me during my enlightening conversation with Dan Lewis, who is quietly speaking with several firms. After listening to my personal experience and learning of this firm's expertise, he wants to meet with our team.

His compliments bolstered my wilting mojo, reminding me that I shouldn't need to jump through ever-shifting hoops. No more handing clients over and hoping it will be rewarded, either. It's time to draw my line in the sand.

In order to catch a 5:14 train to make it to Livvy's dance recital this evening, I need to speak with Jim now. I could've allowed more than thirty minutes for this conversation, but honestly, if his answer is no, I only need five. My only niggling concern about this approach is the sense of frenetic emotion gathering inside. I'm fired up, but not in a strategic sense.

I shut down my computer, pack up my briefcase, and then set it just inside my door before walking down the hall to Jim's corner office, shaking out my arms to release the jitters. The combination of nerves and amphetamines isn't ideal, but it's go time. Jim's door is open. I rap on the jamb before entering.

When he looks up, I ask, "Got a sec?"

He nods, gesturing to a seat in front of his desk. "What's up?"

I remain standing. If I sit, my leg will bounce, and that isn't a power move. "I have a lead on a big client who's shopping for new outside counsel. It's only beginning stages, but after my preliminary conversation, the door is open."

Jim leans forward, elbows on the desktop, expression eager. "That's great, Kristin. Who is it, and when are they coming in for a pitch lunch?"

"Before I set that up, I need a promise that, if we land it, I'll be made an equity partner."

He frowns. "A promise?"

I nod, keeping my poker face firmly in place. "You said if I bagged an elephant, I'd be in good shape."

"I was speaking in general terms."

"General terms, like in each of the past two years when I've brought in clients yet been passed over? Jim, I cannot watch another group of younger lawyers pass me by. I'd be better off taking this client someplace that will bring me in as a partner."

My heart thumps in the wake of that bluff. I have no assurance that Dan would consider exploring representation with me if I were no longer with this firm and its storied M&A reputation. Maybe, maybe not. But it's the only play I've got at this moment.

"You're asking me to make a unilateral decision, but that's not how this works, and you know that." His mottled neck and cheeks always flare up when he's caught unaware. I don't hate the powerful feeling it gives me. "We have a partnership process. The voting happens in December."

"What I know is that 'how this works' isn't working for me. I won't list all my accolades because you already know them, but I'm done accepting pats on the head and another 'maybe next year.'" My reputation would make it easy to make a lateral move to another great firm. Netting a partnership elsewhere would most likely happen with a smaller firm, which isn't my first choice and might not excite Dan. And either way, I'm still on the train every day. A small inner voice questions the value of any of this, but I can't shake off wanting the recognition I've earned.

Seconds pass with us locked in a staring contest. Having worked with him most of my career, I know this tactic. He wants to rattle me so I'll say something he can use against me. I hope my expression doesn't reveal anything other than a patient smile.

Finally, he breaks. "Is this client big enough to support your demand?"

Naturally, money trumps everything, including our personal and professional relationship. I can imagine Amy rolling her eyes at that sickening reality. "I think so."

His gaze narrows. "Who is it?"

I shake my head, knowing he just wants to go around me and get to it on his own. "What I will share is that I'm talking seven figures per year in billings."

His eyes light up. He leans back, his chair mechanism squeaking in protest beneath his weight. "I admire the hard-nosed approach, Kristin. I'll give you that. But could you wrangle a client that size on your own? I suspect you need the backing of this firm to reel it in, so you might be overplaying your hand."

He's never been stupid.

I force my shoulders and spine to relax so as not to appear ruffled. "This isn't the only M&A firm in the city. I've fielded plenty of

headhunter calls over the years, so I've got options, especially if I introduced this client along with my other clients." A somewhat toothless
threat without having an actual offer in my pocket. I'm beginning to
regret my risky approach.

"So we're at an impasse." He raises a single brow and folds his hands
across his belly. "I won't make a promise I can't keep, and you won't
move forward without it."

That's it? That's how little my dedication is worth?

A burst of rage ignites as all my kids' milestones that I missed flood
my mind. On top of that is the cumulative revenue I've billed, which
far surpasses my compensation. I am quaking inside from the restraint
to keep from unleashing a string of expletives. I've spent my career—
my life—being the good girl, following the rules, trusting the people
I served to appreciate and respect my effort. I've been a fool, giving
away power instead of claiming it. Amy's right—I've made too many
decisions based on trying to control the outcome rather than trying to
meet my own immediate needs.

Fuck it. "Oh, I'll be moving forward, Jim, but sadly, it looks like
I won't be moving forward here. Consider this my notice. Thank you
for everything you've taught me. I'll contact the clients on my current
caseload and hand off clients who choose not to follow me as seamlessly
as possible." Adrenaline and Adderall surge through my veins like water
through a fire hose. Honestly, I'm a little faint. I grip the back of a chair
to steady myself.

Jim rises, signaling for me to calm down with his hands. "Kristin,
hold up. No need to get hysterical and overreact."

Hysterical? That dog whistle snaps my last reserve. "It's not hysteria
to know one's worth. But if the partners here don't agree, it's time to
go someplace that will. That's all. I'm not overreacting. I haven't even
raised my voice."

"You've always been valued here, and you know it. I can't stop
you from leaving. I can, however, insist that we come up with a joint

communication about your departure so that clients aren't concerned or confused." He's turned formal now, his gamesmanship mode.

"I know the ethical obligations, Jim. I'll write up a statement and send it to you in the morning for your review, and once we're *both* satisfied, we'll send it out. I assume no one will suggest that my departure is anything other than a professional decision made with careful consideration. If that happens, I'll be forced to take action, including exploring why two male lawyers were made full equity partners last year—both of whom have less experience than I do, and one of whom has brought in fewer new clients too. I'm also aware that Finn is being considered this year—also a man with less experience and fewer new clients than I'd brought in by that same point in my career."

His upper body jerks back as if I've body-slammed him. "Jesus, Kristin. What are you insinuating?"

"It's not insinuation. The firms' salaries and partnership demographics are hardly even among men and women, and to be clear, numbers are not hysterics either. They're simply facts from which a judge or jury can draw their own conclusions." Oh my God, it feels amazing to finally say what I've been thinking for years. To speak up for myself and other female associates in this department.

For the first time since I walked into this office, doubt clouds his eyes. I'd rather see remorse, but I'll take what I can get.

"Let's not make things ugly. For the record, we do not discriminate. I get that you're disappointed and it's easier to blame us than to face what you don't want to face." He's leaning with his hands planted on his desk. "Now you've put me in a position of having to alert HR on top of all this."

"I reject your characterization. I'm not hiding from anything or pointing fingers at nothing. I'm also willing to part on amicable terms, as long as no one tries to screw me. Neither of us will benefit from a public fight." A fact I hate because it is exactly why discrimination continues to flourish. The truth is, I don't have the mental energy for a legal battle that history proves I'm unlikely to win. Better to channel my rage into finding a better situation for myself and my family. I glance at the time. "I'm sorry to run out, but I've got someplace else to be now. We can discuss transition details in the morning."

His shoulders fall, and for the first time, I sense some genuine disappointment on his end. "I'm sorry it's come to this."

The mentorship he's provided tempers my anger. I could let him off the hook, but Livvy's little face sifts through my thoughts along with the cost this job has extracted from my personal life. His sorrow is another useless platitude, and I'm done with those. "If you really valued me, you would've at least offered to speak to the partners instead of summarily dismissing my request. Yes, there's a process, but you also acquire partners from outside firms on an ad hoc basis. There's always a way to make things happen when it matters. We both know that, so again, let's respect each other enough to be honest."

His chin juts forth, and he throws his hands up. "And yet, if you truly believe the partners here discriminate against women, I can't imagine why you'd want to stay. We'll talk tomorrow."

A bullshit argument only a man would make.

"Good night." I leave his office, forcing myself to smile at people I pass in the hall while acting as normal as possible despite my quaking insides. I snatch my briefcase from my office door before making my way to the elevator, my cheeks aching from the charade.

When the doors close, I lean back against the wall on wobbly knees, and a sheen of perspiration breaks out over my scalp.

What have I done?

I convinced myself that a bluff that big would be effective and then blew up everything without a real plan or a job offer from another firm in my back pocket. Tony will freak. On top of that, I don't have a commitment from Dan Lewis or any other client. I feel sick for letting Jim's indifference needle me. For letting emotion overrule reason. The amphetamines probably didn't help.

I grab my forehead, which is throbbing. A new job search takes effort and energy that I'd rather put into my family. And yet, while I mishandled this situation, nothing I said was inaccurate. I do deserve better. And so do my children.

At the very least, I'll get to spend some extra time with them while I'm regrouping. I've earned that after the year we've all had, haven't I?

———

The train ride was a grueling exercise in restraint as I held back tears, still shocked by where impulse had led me. My sister's experience and influence—everything about this year—have affected me more than I realized. That's the only explanation for my quitting after Jim didn't care enough to push for me.

Why didn't he want to push for me? That's the question that keeps stabbing me behind the eyes. I've worked for years to make myself invaluable. Turns out the so-called barriers I've climbed over didn't help one bit. My mindset—this desire to please and be given pats on the head—isn't healthy. Not for me, and not as a model for my son. Quitting isn't the worst thing when viewed from that perspective.

I could scream, but Livvy goes onstage in thirty minutes. I'm also not ready to face Tony's reaction.

"Livvy, hurry, honey. We need to leave now," I call while tossing Luca his jacket. He's so much like me. Always ready on time. Always patiently doing his part. Never demanding much of anything. God forbid he waste a decade of his career waiting for his due. "I appreciate that you're always ready on time. But just so you know, I won't love you less if you aren't perfect."

The surprised smile stretching across his face gives me a reprieve from my crappy day.

Tony finally emerges from his office, having been in the middle of a call when I got home ten minutes ago. I glance away to hide my chaotic emotions.

"What's wrong?" he asks. "You look especially tense."

"Do I?" My voice is too high—a dead giveaway. I force myself to make eye contact, hoping to throw him off the scent.

He narrows his eyes, hands on his hips, then turns toward our son with a bright smile. "Luca, go buckle up in my car, okay, buddy?" As soon as he's out of earshot, Tony says, "Something happened. You're an open book."

I wish his approach were more comforting than inquisitive. "Yes, fine, but let's discuss it after the recital."

Livvy is likely spending every last second possible with Snickers—one recent decision I have no regrets about.

"Oh boy. It's that bad?" He rubs his forehead.

"Depends on how you look at it." I remind myself of the major upside—time at home with the kids.

He holds his breath for a moment. "Just tell me. I promise not to discuss it until after the kids are in bed, but give me a chance to digest it first."

I don't want to do this here and now, but he won't stop asking. Livvy is coming down the stairs, so I murmur, "I quit my job."

Tony's eyes bulge. The way he shakes his head is so cartoonish that I might laugh if I didn't want to throw up. "Are you joking?"

I shrug, then smile widely at Livvy, who floats into the kitchen—a cloud of powder-blue tulle—her hair in the tight bun that our nanny must've fastened before she left. I grab my chest, my eyes filling with proud tears. She's growing up fast and is utterly adorable. "Honey, you're the sweetest little ballerina ever."

"You came home in time." Her eyes are bright with pleasure. Another little win with one of my kids when I need it most. Being here when they get off the school bus will be a much-needed gift, which gives me the courage to face down Tony later.

"I promised I would, and I always keep my promises." I reach for her hand without looking at Tony, who most definitely wouldn't agree with that sentiment, considering how I've been breaking some of ours these last couple of months. "Now let's go."

Tony has fallen silent, but his dark expression shouts his thoughts. He tries to fake excitement for Livvy when kissing her forehead. "My little angel."

The seven-minute drive to the recital would be awkwardly tense if not for Livvy's nonstop chatter about where she'll be standing and what side of the stage we should sit on. She's also sharing that last time Mary and Cassidy bullied her, she laughed when they did, just like Amy told her to do. I'm grateful Amy's helped my daughter be bold. If only my sister's intrusion into my life had begotten her desired results too. Instead, I'm on the verge of a major blowup with my husband—someone whom I rarely disagreed with before last autumn.

"She's coming, right?" Livvy asks.

"Of course." I didn't confirm it because I'd been preoccupied with replaying the conversation with Jim. But Amy would never miss something this important to Livvy. Come to think of it, I should've confided in Amy, who'd be happy I quit.

When we park, I volunteer to run our daughter backstage, and ask Tony and Luca to grab four seats.

Dozens of young girls and the teachers are buzzing about backstage. The two mean girls are huddled together about ten feet from us. Despite her brave talk, Livvy clutches my shirt and leans close to me.

I crouch to be eye to eye and smile. "Sweetie, Aunt Amy gave you her trick for taking away mean girls' power. Can I give you mine?"

Livvy nods, her gaze hopeful.

"Okay. Well, mine isn't as easy as Amy's because you need to answer a few questions. Can you do that?"

Again she nods.

"Are you a good person? Do you treat others kindly?"

"Yes."

I poke her tummy gently. "I know that and am glad that you do too. Next, do you pay attention in ballet?"

"I do!"

I smile. "I'm sure you do too. And lastly, do any of the other kids here always do everything perfectly?"

She thinks for a second, as if searching her memory for evidence of others' mistakes. "No. Some even get yelled at by the teacher."

That's a different but important conversation for later. "Okay, so if you know that you're kind, that you pay attention, and that other people make mistakes, then you can feel very proud of yourself, even when you make a mistake. In fact, you should be as proud of yourself as I am of you. Don't let anyone make you forget that you're wonderful, okay?"

Livvy hugs me so hard that I worry it will loosen her bun. But I squeeze her back just as tight before kissing her forehead and then wiping away my lipstick. To earn her love and trust right now is a powerful reminder of the value in rethinking my priorities.

Once I'm sure she's got this, I hand her over to the teacher and go hunting for the rest of my family. They're in the seventh row, center section of the auditorium. Luca is seated beside Tony's jacket, which is spread across a chair.

"Hand me your coat," Tony says. When I do, he spreads it across two more chairs. "Luca, sit tight and hold these seats for us, okay? We'll be right back. If you see Aunt Amy, flag her down."

"Okay, Dad." Luca fidgets in the chair, already bored. Most nine-year-old boys would rather do homework than attend a first-grade ballet recital, but this show of support is part of being in a family.

Tony looks at me, hitching a thumb toward the lobby. "Let's talk for a minute."

"Now?"

A sharp nod is his only reply. So much for his promise. My stomach is as hard as a rubber bullet. He's only ever been this terse with me once before, when we were engaged and I came home drunk after an evening with coworkers. He first suspected one of the guys had drugged my drink, and when I assured him that it didn't happen—that I'd done a couple of shots—he was mad that I'd been so careless with my safety. *You can't put yourself in such a vulnerable state on the train, Krissy!*

We stroll up the aisle; then Tony gestures to a corner of the lobby to get away from the crowd. He runs a hand through his hair.

"What happened? I mean, did Jim or someone do or say something so inappropriate that you had no choice?" His eyes are questioning, his expression twisted into a tight knot that reminds me of when his mother's diverticulitis took a bad turn and she needed surgery. I could remind him that he said this conversation would wait until we got home, but that could make things worse.

"Dan Lewis and I had a good conversation, so I tried to leverage it to get Jim to guarantee that I'd make equity partner if I brought Guerrilla in. He didn't even offer to speak to the partners—just said no promises—and I snapped. I'm done with the firm's bullshit. I'm done putting my family second. I'm just done." As the words tumble out, I find some strength in them. At some base level, buried beneath disappointment and a touch of panic, I really am done.

Tony flings his hands sideways. "Why quit before finding a new job?"

"Look, I know it was impulsive, but honestly, if it weren't for worrying about *your* reaction, the sense of freedom I feel—the sense of power, even—is liberating."

"I'm the problem here? That's convenient," he mutters. "You quit your job after we talked about other options like remote workdays—and you did it without warning or any plan—but I'm the bad guy? Do you think I wouldn't love to walk away from the stress of my job sometimes? That I never feel disappointment and a desire to escape, especially now, when my office park project has been losing money?"

Now it's my turn to reel from shock. "You never mentioned any trouble. You never act stressed either." Questions form, but we're in public and the show will start soon.

"You've been exhausted, losing weight, and edgy for months. I didn't want to add to your plate. But trust me, things aren't great. I'm resisting throwing it into bankruptcy because that could impact future lending options. I thought I could count on you to keep us going while

I work things out, like we've always agreed. I thought we were a team. How could you disrupt everything without even calling me first?"

I heat up. Granted, this isn't the same as letting Luca off the hook for homework or getting a pet. This is a massive break from our normal way of handling things together—from our agreed-upon plans. Still, I'm not a child. I'm entitled to make my own career decisions. I'm about to say that when Amy shows up.

"Hey, guys, everything okay?" She takes in our tight expressions. "Livvy's not too nervous to go on, is she?"

Tony closes his eyes and breathes through his nose like a bull. "I'll see you at the seats." He turns and leaves, which is uncharacteristically rude. It's a little scary, frankly.

"Did you tell him about the pills?" Amy's eyes are wide.

I glance around to see who might've heard her, and then scowl and raise my finger to my lips. "No."

I watch Tony's back as he goes through the auditorium doors.

"Then what the heck is wrong?" she asks.

I roll my neck around. "I quit my job unexpectedly. Tony's pissed."

That's hardly fair to him, as if it's unreasonable for him to be upset. It ignores our prior conversation about this, when he proposed moderate steps to alleviate my stress while buying me time to regroup.

Amy grins despite my frown. "Oh, Kristin, that's terrific news. The kids will love having you around, and you deserve some time off. A chance to reset. Tony will be fine once he sees all that."

A simplification, to be sure. "We can't afford for me to be out of work for very long, and leaving the way I did—in a huff and without any plan—won't help me win over a new employer. I'll have to spin some story when I go job hunting."

"Don't rush back. Besides, anyone would hire you, Kristin, so set good terms for yourself." She squeezes my shoulder, full of confidence and reassurances.

But if I had that much control, I wouldn't be in these shoes. "Apparently Tony's having some business trouble. If I'd known that, I wouldn't have quit today." I run my hands through my hair, tempted to tug at it in frustration. "In any case, I should've planned this all better."

"Look, if money will smooth this over, let me give you guys whatever you need. More than anything, I want you to be happy and healthy." She eyes me, her reference to the pills not at all subtle.

"I already told you, your money can't make my life better when you won't use it to improve your own. And honestly, this isn't about money—not really. For me, it's about self-respect and what I deserve. What I've worked for. And in my marriage, it's about renegotiating some things, I guess. I'm not sure. It's complicated."

"I get that." She tips her head sympathetically. "Whatever Tony's flaws, he loves you. I've never doubted that. Things will work out. Don't feel guilty for quitting. You did what you needed to do for you. Your well-being is as important as anything else. Life's too short to waste at a job that makes you miserable."

Another form of this lecture isn't welcome right now. "Can we not go down this road? Seriously, enough with the 'life's too short' comments, when sometimes I'm not sure you even want to live at all." I cover my mouth. What is going on with me today? Everything around us gets hazy as my brain replays those last words. Although it is my truth, I want to fall to my knees in apology, but I'm frozen with shock. "Sorry. That was just—I'm sorry. I'm not at my best tonight."

Amy stares at me, looking stunned but not broken. "I can take it. Besides, you're not entirely wrong."

What's that mean? Like whiplash, the images of her bloody wrists and agony-twisted face race into my consciousness, making my stomach flip. "Amy—"

An usher comes into the lobby to notify us stragglers that the show is about to begin.

Could all these things have happened on a worse night? I need to be present and smiling for my daughter. "I don't like the sound of that, but we can't miss the show. We'll finish this conversation later."

We cross to the auditorium doors, taking our seats just as the lights dim. I cast a sideways glance at Amy, who doesn't look distraught or depressed. I had hoped her meeting with Declan would be the hook into a new purpose, but she hasn't said a word to me about what she's thinking.

Tony sits beside me like a hunk of granite, lost in his own thoughts. I've pushed him to places he never saw coming, and he probably also thinks he's failed me. I lay my hand on his forearm. His muscle tenses beneath my palm, but he doesn't withdraw. We're headed into new territory. My whole life is, it seems. This isn't me. I don't feel secure without a plan. I've got to pull myself together before everything falls apart.

Livvy isn't onstage until the third piece, at which point Tony's posture finally softens. He leans forward, smiling. She's clearly searching for us, so we all give her a little wave.

I try to keep my focus on each plié, relevé, and sauté in order to compliment Livvy later, yet Tony's behavior distracts me. This cold man beside me is not my husband, nor is the man who didn't feel he could be honest about his work troubles. I'm angry that instead of being my rock, he's making me feel worse. I'm also sad that my behavior this winter has made him feel like he couldn't lean on me. Possibly the most surprising thing of all is the fact that, despite these mixed feelings, I'm not truly sorry for quitting.

Hours later, after we've put the kids to bed, changed into pajamas, brushed our teeth in silence, and climbed into bed, I am sitting against the headboard, watching Tony check his messages and set his alarm.

"Can we talk now, please?" I've been chewing at the inside of my cheek for hours. It's an open wound now, like my heart.

Tony and I faked "normalcy" in front of the kids after the recital, focusing on giving Livvy the praise she expected. Out of their earshot, his silence has been painful.

He sets down his phone, barely glancing at me. In a cool, even tone, he says, "The time to have talked would've been to strategize together after you spoke with Dan and before you went to see Jim. We could've worked out scenarios—like waiting to talk to Jim until after you quietly spoke with one or two other firms to explore options. Or done an A, B, C series of options—if he says no to a guarantee, then what else could you ask for and get, or whatever. Now there's nothing to say. You did something so rash that I honestly don't even recognize you. You've been changing since Christmas. I thought it would get better after Amy moved out, but it's getting worse. Jumping from planes, quitting your job?" He shakes his head. "I'm exhausted and have a big day tomorrow. It's obvious you've got a lot of thinking to do to figure out what exactly it is that you want, because I'm not convinced you know anymore."

And then, without giving me a chance to reply, he turns away and sinks beneath the covers, ending the conversation.

I stare at his back, blinking. My anger is diminished only by my secret pill habit, which has surely contributed to our problems, even though for so long I thought they were helping me. But the things I've done with my sister have been freeing and have also helped her. I won't feel guilty for them.

I didn't want to ruin my career. I don't want to hurt my husband or upend our marriage. I just want to be happy. To experience more joy. And to be appreciated for all that I do by the people I do those things for.

Why are my simple goals so far outside my grasp?

CHAPTER FIFTEEN

AMY

The following day

Last night, Livvy stole the show with her sweet smile and enthusiastic jetés. Her pride was the only thing that wiped the scowl off Tony's face. I've never seen him in that state. All this time I've pushed Kristin to make changes hoping to improve her life, not to cause marital problems.

I type out a text. Checking in. Everything okay?

The dots dance on the screen, so I wait, biting my thumbnail.

Things aren't great. Tony's holed up in turtle mode. I can't undo what's done, so I'll tie things up at work and go from there.

I blow out my breath. In Kristin-speak, "things aren't great" means they're disastrous. I text back. Would it make you feel better to learn that I'm creating the foundation?

I'm waiting to see the dots, but the phone rings. It's Kristin. "Hey," I answer.

"Amy, that's great news. I'm so proud of you. You're going to change so many lives." She sounds almost weepy, but in a good way that makes my throat catch too.

After a couple of months of planning my way out of this life, the decision to stick around long enough to launch this foundation and get it to run smoothly makes me feel a bit like a fawn taking its first awkward steps. In truth, my sister's current crisis is another reason to stick around. It'd be cruel to cut out after inadvertently causing some of her problems. "Thanks. It feels wrong taking compliments for your idea, especially when I've made everything in your life worse."

"Stop that. I chose everything I've done this year. Maybe it'll be a good thing in the long run. I hope so, anyway. Right now, I'm thrilled by your decision. I can help, too, while looking for a new job."

"I wish I could help you with that."

"Your good news is help enough." Her sincerity reassures me that I've made the right decision. "Hey, I'm about to pull into Grand Central, so I'll talk later."

"But what about Tony?" I flatten one hand on the counter and worry my lip. "I've never seen him like that."

"Neither have I." The phone cuts out.

"Kristin?" The line goes silent, so I hang up thinking about how unexpected changes and pressure can test any marriage, like Scotty's needs did for mine. I rub my stomach, concerned that the fallout from Tony and Kristin's tension could affect Livvy and Luca. Now that I'll be around longer, I can distract the kids while my sister works through this rough patch.

Feeling calmer, I glance through the window. Bob is sitting in a folding chair outside his back door, drinking coffee and reading a newspaper. Wisps of hair blow in the breeze. He looks adorable in his plaid flannel shirt and worn Levi's. I make myself some sweetened Earl Grey tea and then go outside to join him. It's unusually warm for the end of March despite a light spring breeze.

He looks up with those smiling blue eyes framed by white eyebrows. "Good morning, my dear."

"Good morning, yourself." I sit on the railroad tie that hems in the small flower bed of daffodils against the back of his house. The happy blossoms bow toward me in a cheery welcoming. Sharing this peaceful morning with a dear old man is another welcome boost. "We need to plan the rest of this garden. I think we can squeeze two hydrangea over there, and maybe that sunny patch will be good for tomatoes?"

"I hadn't thought about vegetables." His expression turns enthusiastic. "I like it."

"Well, it's a little early for planting, but I'll make a run to Home Depot soon to get some things so we can get the soil ready. After Memorial Day, we can get things in the ground." *After Memorial Day.* It's jarring to think that far ahead when, not long ago, I was convinced that I wouldn't be here by then.

"What are you up to today?" Bob asks.

"Pulling the trigger on a huge commitment. It's scary, but I can't find a valid reason not to try." I blink, somewhat surprised at myself for sharing something that still feels intimate.

"Scarier than skydiving?"

I laugh. "Yes! That was a one and done. This will require a ton of time and effort, and a learning curve to boot."

"Sounds important." He tilts his head in curiosity, yet still not forcing me to share more than I am willing.

I lucked out with this kind new friend and landlord. It makes me wonder if fate put him in my orbit because it had bigger plans for me all along. "I'm starting a charitable foundation to help families with neurodiverse children afford the special services available to support them."

Bob sets his paper aside, his eyes wide with awe. "Well, missy. That sounds like quite something. May I ask what's motivating this?"

I stare into my cup to buy myself a moment, then gaze at his friendly face and take the leap. "I lost a son with ASD and my husband last spring in a terrible accident that happened a couple months after we won a massive lottery payout. At first, I didn't want to go on—couldn't imagine ever being anything but miserable. I lived with my sister's family for months but then knew I had to go because, well, a variety of reasons." A wave of hot prickles moves over me from shame about my cavalier plan to kill myself in this man's residence. "I still have bad days, but lately there've been good times, too, like this one. Still, I'll never ever enjoy that money myself. The foundation was Kristin's suggestion. Now those funds will help thousands of families while also honoring my husband and son."

Bob nods. "I confess, I read a little something in the paper a couple of weeks back about the library. I didn't say anything in case there was another Amy Walsh out there."

I push his knee. "You've got a good poker face, Bob. Remind me not to play with you."

He throws his head back, chuckling. "I'm terrible at cards, but I love backgammon."

We sit in silence, sipping our beverages. I'm pleased that he isn't needling me with questions or sending me pitying glances. Talking about the past hasn't devastated me or changed things between us. Am I getting better, or is Bob simply the easiest man in the world to open up to?

"For what it's worth, I'm sure your personal connection to the mission will make you good at running it." He sips his coffee. "Whenever I'm down, I've always found comfort in helping others. It gets me outside myself, you know?"

"I do. Thanks for believing in me, and for not making me feel pitiful."

He makes a "forget about it" face. "By my age, you learn that grief, like everything else, is a phase—a 'growth opportunity,' as you young folks might say. It isn't something to pity. You'll be all right. I know that much."

His certainty almost has me convinced. "I should call the lawyer and set up another meeting before I chicken out."

"This calls for a celebration. I'll teach you how to make a good pierogi!"

"You'll make me fat!" I tease, standing to slap my hip. "I can live with that. Have a good day, Bob."

"You too, Amy."

I go inside to email Declan, feeling buoyant. In a way, this will be an extension of the support network I created with my old blog. Perhaps I could reincorporate it onto a website for the foundation. Something to consider.

If this kind of foundation had existed when we got Scotty's diagnosis, Sean and I might not have struggled so hard trying to make ends meet. If I hadn't been so desperate for money and played the lottery all the time, they would still be alive. Through that lens, this foundation might not only improve lives; it might save some.

I'll need a team, though. Kristin said she'd help, but I can't ask her to run to my rescue when I should be riding to hers. Then again, our working together might make her happy while she's making new plans.

Josephina might be willing to consult now and then, at least at the beginning to set up criteria and options. When I ponder others who might care, Jane returns to mind. I suck in a breath. She was hardly willing to learn about autism in the past. On the other hand, she worked as an executive assistant for some CFO for two decades. She's organized, and she would devote herself to making sure this entity was a success. Most important, Sean would want me to invite her, a fact I cannot overlook.

On impulse, I dial her number.

"Hello?" she answers.

"Hi, Jane, it's Amy."

"Hi, Amy. I didn't expect to hear from you so soon. Have you changed your mind about the anniversary?" She sounds hopeful.

While my personal plans have changed, I still don't want to spend it with her—maybe not with anyone.

"No, but I wanted to invite you to help me with something." I fill her in on the idea for the family foundation. "I thought you might want a role, perhaps helping go through applications and such."

At first, I think her silence spells trouble; then a sniffle comes through the line. "Oh, Amy. That's a beautiful idea, and I'd be honored to be part of it. Sean would be so proud. Thank you for asking me. I promise, I won't overstep either."

I sit at the table, my body flooding with warmth. Forgiveness of her and from her—who knew it would supply a small sense of the peace that's been missing all year? "You're welcome, Jane. I appreciate the help. Who knows, maybe this work will mitigate some of our grief."

"I think it will. How soon will this come together?"

"Maybe a month? After the initial paperwork is filed, we'll set a first meeting with the team."

"I can't wait to tell Mike."

"Well, go on then. I'll be in touch." I hang up and slide the phone onto the table and stare at the paintings Livvy made for me. *This one is hugs and kisses, Aunt Amy.* Pure love in my home, every day, right in front of me. For all my lectures to Kristin about what matters in life, how have I taken this for granted?

Yet optimism worries me. The last time I got excited by big dreams, it ended in a big disaster.

My phone pings. Declan has suggested a meeting. I reply and then text Kristin. Meeting with Declan on tomorrow afternoon if you want to come. No worries if you don't.

I haven't had to wait more than a moment for any reply from her since I attempted to take my life. What a burden that must be. I must repay her somehow.

I'll try to be there. This is an amazing gift you are giving the community and I could not be prouder of you.

I stare at those words and then type, You could never be as proud of me as I have always been of you. No one tries harder or does more for other people than you. I have not come close to thanking you enough for a lifetime of love and support. I don't want to meddle and risk making things worse, but know that I am here for you to lean on now if you need me. Love you.

The dots appear and disappear twice, as if she's typing and deleting and trying again, so it is a surprise when her text comes through and simply states, You could never know how much that means to me. Thank you.

I almost set the phone down and leave it at that, but something about the exchange nettles. It isn't just me who takes her for granted. Our parents always have. And I suspect Tony may also take her for granted at times, despite how much he loves her.

I promised not to meddle, but now that feels like a cop-out. I open my laptop and compose an email to my brother-in-law.

> Tony,
>
> Let me begin with an apology for overstepping. Know that it's coming from a place of love and empathy for both you and my sister.
>
> It's obvious that my trauma and choices have placed an unfair burden on your entire family this year. Kristin would never admit that to me because she worries about my state of mind. I am deeply sorry that my problems have put a strain on your family and your marriage. At the same time, I'm also deeply grateful for both of your unwavering love and support, and your forgiveness for putting you through so much.
>
> I know you and I are very different people, but I also believe that we love and respect each other enough to be honest. I understand why you are upset by Kristin's recent decision to quit her job, but I'm more concerned about her mental health at this point.

I pause, considering whether to bring up the pills, then decide not to because Kristin said she stopped taking them, and I won't risk making things between them even worse.

> Please go easy on her. For years, we've all relied upon her superhuman ability to juggle seventeen things at once and shoulder stress levels that would cripple others. But this year has brought her to a breaking point, and I'm convinced she doesn't presently have the bandwidth to cope with everything if there is also a breakdown in your relationship.
>
> We both love her and we both want to see her happy. I'm asking you to set aside your disappointment for now and simply support her. Have faith that she will—with your love and support—find a solution that meets everyone's needs, as she always has.
>
> Again, I'm sorry if this is out of line. Perhaps it's simply that I look back on so many arguments with Sean that I wish I'd never started, and now hope to spare you that same regret. In my experience, most things are not worth making the person you love feel worse about.
>
> Love, Amy
>
> P.S. She has no idea I'm writing to you and hasn't shared any details beyond the basics. I just know her well enough to read between the lines.

"It's settled. I'll prepare the filings for the Walsh Foundation 4 Autism. Once we receive confirmation from the state, we'll apply for an EIN and open a bank account, into which you'll deposit twenty-two million dollars." Declan pauses there, as if hoping I'll decide to reserve a little something for myself. I just nod, comfortable with the half million I'm keeping to leave to Kristin's family someday. Even if I never intentionally end my life, I won't want anything to do with that money on a personal level. "Okay. For now, you're the sole owner of the foundation, so I'll draft appropriate bylaws, with your board being yourself, your sister, your mother-in-law, and me." Declan's gaze goes from me to Kristin, whom I invited to join us this afternoon.

She's been quieter since the recital. Checking in with me less. Putting off any discussion about her marriage by claiming to be busy closing files, updating her résumé, making calls . . . all things that ring true but are hardly the whole truth.

It's got me more concerned about her and Tony. He replied to my email with a simple "I appreciate your concern and would never intentionally hurt my wife."

My sister squeezes my hand. "I'm sure you'll manage this foundation with compassion and good humor."

It's similar to Bob's remark. Some moments I feel ready. Others less so. Compassion requires a beating heart, and mine still goes numb at times, like a foot that has fallen asleep with only occasional tingles to suggest it might find its way back to normal.

The longing for Sean and Scotty persists. I never wake up without reaching for them in more ways than one. Or go a single day without at least one "remember when" trigger, like yesterday, when while flipping through television channels, I came across *Lady Bird*, which I dragged Sean to see despite his protests. I knew he'd like it if he gave it a chance, and I was right. And yet, despite the lingering grief, I appreciate the people here and now who love me. Who even need me to support them through their problems. With each day, I recognize how lucky I am to not be alone and am sorry to have been cavalier about that this year.

Declan stands. "Let me go speak with Janice for a second. I'll be right back."

Once he's out of the office, I turn to Kristin, who seems to be studying Declan's office forest. "Hey, real quick, how are things at home?"

In person, she doesn't brush off the question or reply with a quick "Fine." Instead, her gaze falls to the floor somewhere beyond her own feet as her spine rounds. "Cordial. I'm updating my résumé and networking. Some of my clients plan to follow me, but not as many as I'd hoped, mostly because I don't yet have a new firm to support their work." She blanches a bit on that comment and then clenches her jaw. "I screwed up. There's no way around it."

I want to hug her and delve deeper, but Declan will be back any second. In this moment, the best I can do is show that I'm not worried.

I tease, "Well, if you screwed up, pigs are flying somewhere."

She looks at her lap without smiling. Unlike me, Kristin doesn't joke her way out of a crisis. Actually, I don't really know how she handles a personal crisis of her own making because she's never made one that I'm aware of.

I nudge her nearest foot with mine. "You're usually the one explaining things to me, but it's my turn now because I know about screwing up. No matter how bleak something looks in the moment, it will get better." I stop when she glances at my wrists. Oh yes, that's some first-class irony, isn't it? And yet, I honestly believe what I'm saying. How's that for progress? "One rash decision will not undo a lifetime of measured ones. It won't empty your brain or destroy your reputation. So take a breath and then another. Try to enjoy the downtime and new opportunities that might come from your so-called mistake. And have faith that you and Tony have what it takes to find a better way forward together. I do."

Declan walks back into the office as I'm finishing my little pep talk and now wears the awkward expression of someone who's overheard a private conversation and isn't sure whether to acknowledge it.

Kristin relieves him of the burden—a pleaser to the end. "Sorry I've been a little preoccupied today. I'm at loose ends after unexpectedly quitting my job."

He sits down, his eyes reflecting mild surprise. "Well, having worked there, I can't say I'm sorry to hear it. That grist mill will grind you down. Being on my own took some adjustment, but I like the pace and autonomy. I wouldn't go back even if they came begging."

I sensed Declan's kindness the first time we met, and each conversation since has only confirmed it. He'll make some woman a lovely partner someday.

Kristin replies, "I just wish I'd made a plan before quitting."

Declan nods. "If you need any references, let me know. I've got some connections at firms in Stamford and Greenwich, if you're ready to leave the city. I'd be happy to introduce you."

Kristin smiles. "I may take you up on that, thanks. But let's get back to the foundation, because I need to run soon. Is there anything left to decide today?"

He shakes his head.

"Okay, then. Let me know when it's time for next steps." My sister rises, rubs my shoulder, and then waves goodbye to Declan. "Have a nice day."

After she leaves, I ask Declan, "Is there anything else you need from me?"

"No. I'll email you paperwork to sign, and we'll go from there. I have a fairly good idea of what you want, so I can start drafting the operating agreement too. Your homework is to come up with some initial criteria for grant applicants."

I wrinkle my nose. "Homework? Ugh."

He nods. "Yes, homework is something we never outgrow."

"Needless to say, it was never a strength." But this might be different because I'm invested in this foundation's success and am also a bit of an expert on this topic. "I'll call Scotty's old therapist, Josephina, to generate ideas. Maybe she'll even help—on a consulting basis or something."

"Sounds perfect."

I slap the arms of the chair and start to rise. "Well, guess I'll get out of your hair too."

He holds up a finger. "Before you go, I'll be attending my grief group tomorrow evening at six. If you have any interest in joining me, shoot me an email. I think it could help you, and you could help others as well. It's very symbiotic."

Me, helpful? I've fooled him into thinking I'm coping much better than I am. He's not seeing me stare at the wall for an hour at a time, or wake up from another nightmare about a boat explosion, or cry when an unbidden memory of my son winds around my heart like a rubber band.

My knee-jerk reaction is to decline his invitation, but given what I'm about to undertake with this foundation, and the fact that doing it well will require me to function better than I do presently, I resist the urge. "Let me think about it."

His grin widens. "Wonderful. Speak with you soon."

I leave him and his cozy office behind, tempted to swing by Kristin's to visit the kids. But Tony will be home from work soon, and I don't want to walk in during the middle of a spat, especially when I feel partly responsible for the situation now causing problems.

———

The sun is dipping below the horizon, splashing gorgeous purples and vivid reds against the dark blue sky. Declan is waiting for me outside the Center of Hope on Old King's Highway. I exit my car and wave.

"I'm glad you came," he calls as I approach.

I nearly turned the car around twice on my way here, breaking out in perspiration when thinking about having to sit in a roomful of mourners and "share my feelings." That said, a source of emotional support to help me stick out this commitment to the foundation is worth exploring. "I feel awkward."

He nods. "That's normal. You might be the only first-timer tonight, but everyone's been in your shoes. This will be the most awkward it will ever be."

"That's one convoluted pep talk," I tease.

He shrugs, grinning. "I'm a lawyer, not a salesman."

"Lucky for you." I laugh a little too hard to cover my nerves. Part of me would prefer to simply have him teach me how he clawed his way back to the land of the living. Another part is afraid that other people's stories—their pain—will cause a setback. I remind myself that Declan wouldn't steer me wrong, and not only because I met him through Kristin. He's like the older brother I've always wanted.

"Shall we?" he asks.

I nod.

The lobby is pleasant if spare. We come to a room where a few people are taking seats. I shouldn't be surprised to see a teenager. Not everyone who loses someone is an adult. Some women are older than me, and one looks to be about my age. There are fewer men than women, which doesn't surprise me, though that stereotype is probably as incorrect as any other.

An attractive blonde woman in a crimson A-line skirt and lightweight cardigan comes into the room wearing a lanyard with a name tag. Dr. Sarah Connors. She quietly greets a few people I presume are regulars based on their familiar body language and comfort with one another. Declan also exchanges a friendly nonverbal greeting, at which point Dr. Connors speeds over, her expression extra sunny.

"Hello, Declan." She touches his arm as she turns my way. "Looks like you've brought a friend. I'm Sarah, the discussion leader." She has warm brown eyes and a slight gap between her two front teeth. Her manner is calm and breezy, but her ringless hand lingers on Declan's arm for an extra second. I think she likes him. Is she why he keeps coming back? The thought makes me smile.

"Hi. I'm Amy." We shake hands.

"Welcome, Amy. So, how do you two know each other?"

"Through my sister. I needed some legal advice."

"Well, we're happy to have you." She glances at the clock, then back to Declan, her eyes lively. "We'd better get started."

Declan and I take seats in the circle with the others.

"Good evening, everyone. It's good to see so many familiar faces, although we do have one new participant this week." Sarah turns to me. "Would you like to introduce yourself, which may or may not include what brings you here tonight? No pressure."

Any hope of lurking is dashed. Then again, I'm weary of cowering. It's never been my nature, and somewhere inside, the old me is kicking the basement door, demanding to be let out.

I clear my throat and recross my legs. "Hi, everyone. I'm Amy. From Stamford. Nearly a year ago, I lost my husband and only child in an accident. It's been challenging to find reasons to go on since then, although lately I've been doing better. Declan encouraged me to come tonight, but I'm here to observe more than share at this point." The suicide attempt is TMI for strangers. I fall silent because my throat is tight and I feel hives rising beneath my skin.

A chorus of "Hi, Amys" resounds. I squirm in anticipation of questions, but Dr. Connors opens it up to the group. "So, would anyone like to kick us off? Any news to share? Breakthroughs? New coping tactics?"

To my surprise, the scruffy-faced teenager across the room with shaggy hair peeking out from his baseball cap raises his hand and leans forward, elbows on his knees, expression solemn as he bows his head.

"Joe, what would you like to share?" Dr. Connors prompts.

Joe looks up at me. "Everyone else already knows I lost my mom this year. Breast cancer. It sucked."

"I'm sorry," I say, instantly concerned for the teen, who appears to be here on his own.

He nods. "She suffered a lot at the end, so it almost felt like a good thing when she was finally out of pain. But then it was just weird—like this numbness. She wasn't there in the morning to poke me for sleeping in, or to make sure I signed up for stuff on time, or make me my favorite snacks, or do my laundry—she was really good at folding laundry—or to hug me and cheer at my games and other stuff.

"Now the house is just sad. My younger sister, my dad, it's all so quiet and weird. What's gotten way worse is how, lately, I've been remembering all the times before my mom was sick, when I told her to leave me alone, to stop nagging. Told her all the things she got wrong about me and my friends." His eyes glaze with tears, triggering my remorse about arguments with Sean, particularly that last one in Exuma. It feels like an anvil is sitting on my chest. "I mean, now it's too late to thank her or tell her that I loved her, or tell her I was wrong about so much. And I'll never be able to do that. I can't talk to my dad because he's already sad, so I'm stuck." His voice cracks, and everyone in the room is nodding.

The urge to fling myself across the room to cradle this kid almost catapults me from my chair. I get it, truly get it. I hate myself every time I recognize that I have it within me to hurt someone I love. And yet Sean hurt me sometimes, and probably Joe's mom did nag a time or two. None of us makes it through any authentic relationship without upsetting the other person now and then.

This poor kid needs to go easy on himself.

"Joe," I begin, haltingly, glancing around at others as if seeking permission to continue. I feel a little like I'm sitting there in only my undies, but I persist. "Perhaps I'm not the right person to offer advice, but as a mom, I'm confident that your mom knew that you loved her. She was a teenager once and probably pushed back on her parents the same way you did. It's pretty typical behavior when you're trying to figure stuff out for yourself, which rarely matches up with the way a parent sees things.

"I also believe that when people die—like in those first moments as they drift off to heaven or whatever you believe—they're enlightened in some way. Perhaps they see into the hearts of the people they love or they see the world from a perspective we can't even imagine. If so, your mom knows your heart. Maybe that sounds weird, but no matter what, your mom loved you unconditionally, and she wouldn't want you to punish yourself for behaving like a normal teenager."

I stop talking then because it feels hypocritical to lecture about healing when I'm sitting here hiding my wrist scars. Joe is looking at me appreciatively when a coolness tickles the back of my neck, like when Sean would run his hand up my nape while we snuggled on the sofa watching TV. I freeze, my eyes darting around as if he were here. Is he saying he forgives me like I'm telling Joe to forgive himself? My heart thumps a few extra beats.

When Declan clears his throat, the feeling vanishes. "My teen also argued with her late mother, so thank you for sharing your thoughts, Joe, because now I know that maybe she's struggling and afraid to tell me. As a father, I bet your dad wants to be there for you if and when you decide to share these feelings with him. Holding pain in never makes anything better for anyone. I've found talking about my wife helps me more than it hurts."

Joe swipes a tear from his face, and a shy grin appears. "Thanks."

Dr. Connors is smiling appreciatively at Declan too.

Of course Declan found a way to show gratitude to this boy, which instantly would make the kid feel better without having to ask him to feel better. Does that just come more naturally to some?

Then again, I do that with Livvy, just not with myself or my sister.

An elderly woman speaks up next. "When you live long enough, your relationships get tested. You learn to live with the mistakes you made, too, which isn't always easy. I miss my daughter all the time and could kick myself for how I criticized her. I didn't see it as criticism at the time. Helpful advice, in my mind. Yet it created a wall between us that I could never quite break down. It kills me to think that she didn't know, always and deep down, that I thought she was an amazing miracle. Now she's gone, and so I'm trying to be a better grandparent than

I was a parent. In a way, Joe, you're lucky because you're young enough to learn something it took me too many decades to figure out."

These stories are making me sweaty. My parents might be kicking themselves every day because of what I attempted, which is a fact I hadn't really considered until right now. I need to be more patient with them. More flexible. Each one of us is doing our best, and that's what really matters. The energy in the room—grief tinged with hope for healing—is not an instant game changer, but I do feel less isolated because these people can empathize in a way my family cannot.

My thoughts wander as others speak up. I'm grateful that no one is asking for details about Sean and Scotty. I'm not ready to share more. Hell, I didn't expect to say anything at all, so points to young Joe for dragging me out of my shell.

I sense Declan looking at me. He mouths, "You okay?"

I nod.

Thirty minutes later, the meeting ends. People are standing and saying goodbyes when Dr. Connors makes her way over to Declan and me. "I hope you're taking something good with you from this, and that you'll join us again."

"It was better than I expected. Not as scary, I mean." I'm an idiot, so I stop talking.

She touches Declan's arm again. "Good to know we're not scaring people off. Well, I hope to see you both again soon."

She turns and crosses the room to greet a quiet elderly man whose name I don't recall, so Declan and I head for our cars.

"Would you like to grab some dinner?" he asks.

I flash hot and cold. Is he asking me on a date? Have I sent him some mixed signal? Oh God. I have to shut this down. "Honestly, I'm a little beat now. But I bet Dr. Connors would love to join you for dinner." I elbow him playfully.

He rears back, eyes wide. "Why do you say that?"

"I got a little vibe." What if I'm wrong? What if putting that thought in his head makes him uncomfortable coming back? Oh man.

"I could be wrong, of course. But she's lovely and single. You know each other, and she'd be understanding of your need to keep your wife in your thoughts."

His gaze trails over to her, and then he shakes his head. "I'm not ready to date."

Now I feel like a moron. "I see."

He tilts his head, eyeing me. "To be clear, I wasn't asking you on a date either. I just thought you might be hungry."

"Oh, I knew that," I lie to keep things from getting more awkward between us. "Another time, okay? I'm a little wrung out now."

"I promise the meetings get easier and more helpful each time."

"I can imagine. Thanks for pushing me to come. I'll probably come back."

He smiles. "I'm glad. Well, have a good night, Amy."

"You too." I leave him on the sidewalk and go to my car.

It's been a comfort to talk to someone kind who gets what I'm going through and knows I can't be rushed. To befriend someone who isn't directly connected to my past with Sean and Scotty and yet who shares a similar loss. I care about what happens to Declan and hope he doesn't miss out on someone equally nice by keeping himself off the shelf. I frown, supposing this is how Kristin feels about me.

The only man I feel completely comfortable letting into my personal life right now is my landlord. We are lonesome for different reasons, sitting on our sofas with only the actors on TV as company. For whatever reason, Bob and I click. On my way home, I pass the bakery and pick up black-and-white cookies—his favorite. He's happy for even five minutes of my company, and I always leave his in a better mood.

My thoughts veer to Kristin, who's likely feeling isolated despite being surrounded by people she loves. Butting in with Tony doesn't seem to have made much difference, which makes me hesitant to try again. And yet, if she hadn't butted in on me last summer, I wouldn't even be here. Can I afford to sit back and wait?

CHAPTER SIXTEEN

KRISTIN

The following Tuesday

Tony's mother's car is in our driveway. If Rita's here after Madeline clocked out, Tony must be dealing with a work crisis. He'd claim to be keeping these things to himself to spare me, but it feels like he's pulling away. I've been walking on eggshells for days, waiting for him to make time to have it out. Instead, he's locked himself in his office for hours and kept himself busy with the kids, workouts—anything at all to avoid a bigger confrontation.

It may be for the best. It's been easier to keep the fragile peace than to risk an argument I'd likely lose. That said, I wish I knew what he's told his mother. He shares more with her than I do with my parents, perhaps because he doesn't have a sibling. Either way, he and Rita have the kind of closeness I'd like to share with my kids someday.

On my way into the garage, I give myself a pep talk while wondering which Rita will greet me this evening—the cheerful, somewhat boisterous one who can be the life of the party, or the fretful martyr.

When I enter the house, garlic's pungent aroma affects me like smelling salts.

Rita calls, "Is that you, Tony?"

I place my briefcase in my cubby and kick off my shoes. "It's just me, Rita."

"Oh."

Guess it's the martyr.

We've enjoyed a mostly loving relationship since we first met. She liked my need to please more than my ambition, though, particularly after Luca was born. Not that she would tell me so directly. Instead, she dropped hints: *I'm surprised you don't want to stay home to make sure Luca is raised with your values instead of leaving that to some nanny.*

I inhale before entering the kitchen, where she's breading chicken cutlets and has laid out ingredients for pasta aglio e olio. Oil simmers in the frying pan, awaiting the chicken. Unlike when Tony cooks, the island is littered with basil stems, stray bits of garlic, a clump of parmesan, and drips of oil. Not that I'll criticize. "Looks delicious."

She smiles politely. "Thank you. This is an easy quick meal. Have you ever cooked Milanese?"

"I'm better with breakfast foods. Tony does most of the real cooking."

Her brows rise in that "of course he does" expression of hers. "He's a good cook."

"A great one." I look around for something to do. "I'll set the table."

"Wait." She sets down the fork and leaves the breaded chicken sitting on the wax paper—something Tony never does because the bread crumbs get pasty—before turning off the stove. "Can we talk for a minute? I'm concerned about my son."

My insides go taut in response to her somber tone. I perch on a kitchen stool. "Concerned why?"

She plants her hands flat on the island and drops her chin, eyeing me like we are talking about a critical illness. "He sounds very stressed."

Well, yes.

"I suppose he told you that I quit my job." I can't blame him for going to his mother for support and advice when I've turned to Amy these past few months.

"He mentioned that, yes. I'm surprised, honestly. To change your mind like that"—she snaps her fingers for emphasis—"now, when the kids are older and in school."

"I didn't change my mind." I still have personal ambitions. "My firm didn't value me as it should've. I deserve better."

"That must be a big disappointment for someone as competitive as you." She's watching me carefully. I almost ask why she makes it sound like being competitive is bad—at least when referring to me—but don't. Needling her would drive another wedge between Tony and me. "So what happens next?"

The million-dollar question. "I'm wrapping things up this week, then I'll figure out my next move."

"I hope you figure it out soon." Her gaze remains on the chicken.

I clench my jaw to hold back a snippy retort. My husband sold me out, but I bet he didn't share the extent of his own problems. He never wants her to think he's failing. I'm tempted to expose him, but that would feel good for only three seconds. Petty games won't fix my marriage. "At least my being home for a while will be nice for the kids. We could all use more quality time together, like our upcoming trip."

Her expression shifts. "Oh. I didn't think you were—" She stops talking. "Never mind."

"You thought we'd cancel?"

She averts her gaze, which means Tony discussed this with her as well. I used to consider it sweet that he'd bounce everything off her, from what to get me for Christmas to her opinion on our plans for this house. His respect for her opinion is something I've credited for why he has always been respectful of women's opinions in general. What cuts now is that he's gone to her before coming to me. No matter how tense things are, this can't become our new dynamic.

"Ignore me," Rita says. "I'm just a worried mother. I offered Tony some money to tide you over, but he got mad."

It's my turn to raise my brows. "Rita, thank you, but we're fine."

"Are you sure?" Her doubtful tone nettles.

"Yes." I'm frustrated by the picture Tony has painted. I've made a lot of money in my lifetime. We aren't paupers on the verge of losing our house. "If I choose a different career path, it may require some lifestyle changes, but we'll be fine."

"Lifestyle changes?"

I raise one shoulder because this is not her business. "Priority shifts."

"Hmm." She dredges another chicken breast through the bread crumbs, the corners of her mouth turned down in thought.

"I'd think you'd embrace this, honestly." I cross my arms. "You've always wished I were a more traditional wife and mother."

She raises both hands, her expression one of comedic denial. "I only want you all to be happy. What I think doesn't matter as long as you and Tony are happy. But when you aren't, then I worry."

There is no easy comeback to that statement. I worry too.

Couples go through rough patches as relationships evolve and life throws curveballs. I'm not perfect and shouldn't need to be. "I love Tony. Nothing is more important than my marriage and family. Hopefully you know that about me by now." I cross my arms.

"Of course I do. But being a mom is a constant worry. Little kids, big kids. Doesn't matter. You'll never stop worrying about Livvy's and Luca's happiness, and I'll never stop worrying about my Tony." She presses one hand against her breastbone.

It sounds exhausting, and while it's probably true, there are reasonable degrees of worrying about adult children. Or maybe I'm jaded because my own parents never worry much about me. "I understand."

"I'm glad we had this talk." She smiles, clearly feeling better for having gotten things off her chest, a trait Tony shares. I'm not like them, so now, like always, I'll replay every word of the conversation and note what I should've said differently. "I'll go home since you're here and can finish the chicken."

"You don't want to eat with us?" This conversation aside, it's nice for the kids to spend time with grandparents.

She shakes her head. "Rossi is waiting for me for dinner."

Tony's dad would wait two hours rather than fix himself something simple to eat.

I gesture to the food. "Well, at least take some of this with you so you don't have to cook twice."

"I'm fine, dear. I'll just go up to say goodbye to the kids." She wipes her hands on a dishrag and makes her way across the family room.

"Send them down when you leave," I call while turning on the gas to reheat the oil.

Forty-five minutes later, the kids have eaten and shared their school stories with me. It's a nice change to spend a relaxed weeknight evening with them. We enjoy a casual dinner conversation about the Scholastic Book Fair and Luca's winning four square strategy before they leave the table. I'm finishing wiping up the counters when Tony walks in, and the tension between us rises like fog.

His peck on my cheek feels more obligatory than affectionate. I hold my breath, unsure how to proceed.

"Hey, hon." He unwraps the plate I set aside for him, grabs a knife and fork, and stands at the counter.

"Don't you want to reheat it?"

He shakes his head. "Room temp is better. Chicken never reheats well."

I can't go another day without dealing with what's going on between us. "It was nice of your mom to go to all this trouble, although I was surprised to find her here."

His mouth is full, so he shrugs and mumbles, "Meeting ran long."

"She quizzed me a bit—she's worried about you." I lean forward against the counter. "What exactly did you tell her?"

Without lifting his head, he eyes me evenly. "Just that you quit your job and I've got a lot going on."

I suspect that's a half truth. The weight of what's unsaid sinks me onto a stool. "Did you tell her we weren't going to Anguilla?"

Seconds tick by as his head remains bowed. Finally, he slouches onto a seat. "I think we should cancel today so we get most of our money back. The hotel, I mean. We'll have to bank the plane tickets and use them within the next year."

He's acting like we're broke. Is he hiding more from me?

"Our finances aren't that dire, are they?" Do I really want the answer? I can't take any additional stress, and yet I'm worried what it says about us if he's kept me in the dark about more than I suspect.

"We have no idea how long it will take you to find another job, or what kind of income you'll end up with. The kids' tuition and our mortgage and bills are hundreds of thousands per year, plus the market is down, so I don't want to sell stock now. If I don't sign a big tenant for my office park soon, I may have to pull from our savings to keep that project from dragging others under. With the uncertainty, we should cut out all extras until you land somewhere and we know what we're dealing with." His tone isn't accusatory, just resigned. The pressure tugs at the corners of his eyes, his mouth, and at his shoulders.

It's quite a jigsaw puzzle we've constructed. If we stay the course and I go to another big firm, we can retire at fifty with a very comfortable lifestyle based on his then-projected stream of rental income. But is another fourteen years of that commute worth it, especially if I'm not a partner for several more years? If he'd been more open about his problems, I would've been more thoughtful about my options. He says he was protecting me, but that's not the kind of marriage I want.

"I wish you'd shared all that sooner. We've always been partners, and I don't want that to change."

"Yet you quit without talking to me. Obviously, you've been unhappy for a long time but only recently told me." He shrugs.

"When I did, you didn't take me seriously." I shouldn't be so snarky when I've also hidden my pill habit.

"Had I known how bad it was, I would've. You said you were upset about one deal, not your whole career. When you mentioned quitting the other week, you said you'd explore remote or part-time work." He looks at me, waiting for me to confirm those facts. "Honestly, given all that happened this year, I chalked your frustration up to the chaos and figured you'd go back to normal once your sister stabilized."

There it is—the refusal to make room for any evolution of my thoughts or needs. I feel like I'm whooshing down a sliding board with no way of stopping before hitting the ground. I rub my forehead to stave off the first hint of a stress headache. "Why do you assume I'll always keep in lockstep with you?"

He raises his hands, palms up, from his sides. "Why's that a bad thing? We've always been in agreement about things. You've enjoyed being a lawyer. I had no reason to think otherwise."

"It's a lot of pressure to juggle everything with a smile on my face— particularly when things around here have been rocky. Am I not allowed to change my mind about anything?"

"How would I know you're struggling when you never ask for help? Even when I ask if you're okay, you skim the surface. So I give you a pep talk because it seems like that's what you want, Krissy. What else can I do if you don't let me all the way in?"

"I let you in!" I clamp my mouth shut because it's not true. I have shut him out, even if I didn't mean to. I turned to pills instead of him. I pushed myself harder rather than let him think I couldn't hack it.

"If that were true, I wouldn't have been blindsided." Tony slurps down some of the linguini. "And for the record, I support you telling them to go fuck themselves. I just wish you'd had an exit strategy in place first."

My role in our fracture is bigger than his, but he has also kept things from me. "We've both withheld things, so let's not lay blame. We've got to get on the same page."

He huffs, nodding. "Fine, but there's no point in burdening you with my business shit. You don't need to fret about another thing you can't control."

"What's that mean?" I rest my hands on my hips, scowling.

"You still have one eye on your sister, even though only she can find her will to live."

"You think I've been wasting my time?"

He lays one hand on the island as if grasping for patience. "That's not what I said. You rescued her in July, but ultimately the choice to live is and will always be hers alone. I think it's time to accept that. Otherwise, you'll continue to be only half here with us, and your stress will stay sky high."

My hands ball into fists as little shock waves shoot through my limbs. "You're right about one thing. I'm exhausted. The commute. My sister. Livvy. Something had to give, and of all the things that matter to me, the easiest to let go of was my job, not my sister or the kids."

"Obviously." His enigmatic tone is hard to interpret.

My stomach is on fire. I slap a hand on the counter. "You want me to share my feelings, fine. I'm not sorry I quit. I can't wait until Friday. No more commute. A chance to spend some time at home, where I can take care of organizational projects and do things with the kids after school. My sanity is worth something."

He pushes the empty plate aside and leans his elbows on the counter, gazing at me, his voice hot. "Do you think I don't want you and the kids to be happy?"

"You're hardly making it easy for me."

His expression reveals surprise. "Other than my initial shock, I haven't said a word."

"Exactly." I raise my hands overhead, losing control of myself. "You haven't asked how it's been at the office these days, or how I've been treated by Jim. You haven't validated my reasons for leaving. You've worried more about money than my feelings. You won't consider reevaluating our overall plans. You're focused on the negatives without acknowledging any of the positives—and there are positives. However long I'm home, I can continue my progress with the kids and take some stuff off your lap, like cooking and groceries and other things you usually do because of my commute. That'll free you up to focus on your business."

He makes a face. "I'm not unwilling to reevaluate anything. But if you're telling me you want to be a stay-at-home mom—which I honestly don't think you'd enjoy for more than a few months—we need to sell this house and put the kids in public school next year."

Again with extremes, as if I'm suddenly someone entirely different rather than someone looking for compromise. "I never said I won't work again, but I might decide to work at a local firm with a short commute, or some other option that gives me some flexibility and autonomy. Maybe that won't be as lucrative, but it also won't be for peanuts."

He sits back, arms raised in submission. "Look, we have some leeway before major changes have to be made, okay? I don't want to argue, so whatever you need, do it. You have my full support."

"It doesn't feel that way. It feels like you've given up or you're repressing your real feelings. This isn't you at all." I gesture at him like he's an inanimate object, which is sort of how he's acting.

"I can't win." He hops off the stool and paces, his face a mask of repressed fury. "When I bring up alternatives, I don't support you quitting, but when you talk about those same options, it's different? If I tell you I'm unhappy about what you did, I'm not supportive. If I choose not to argue, then I'm also not supportive? Jesus Christ, Krissy. Give me a break. You aren't the only one in this house whose life has been turned upside down by Sean's and Scotty's deaths, but I've been here supporting you and your sister and your parents, working in a rough economy, doing laundry and cooking and anything else I can think of to make it easier on all of you without asking for one goddamn thing except that I can count on you to keep your promises and build the life and family that we always agreed on—*not* the one your sister envisions for us."

I'm temporarily stunned by his outburst and glad the kids are upstairs. "So you have resented Amy's presence."

"Don't put words in my mouth. I never resented her presence. I only got sick of her criticisms of my parenting. It's not her business, frankly, and I didn't want the kids to hear it and start to think ill of me just because she did. If anything, I wish you had defended me more."

I suck in a breath, having never seen it from that perspective. "I was caught in the middle, seeing both sides."

"And look at where that's gotten us."

A standoff, which scares me. I don't want to push him away, but I also don't want to capitulate completely. "If you had ever once considered Amy's and my opinions instead of shutting us down, maybe things wouldn't be like this now."

"I'm not obligated to consider Amy's parenting advice. She's not my wife or the mother of my kids. And in what way haven't I considered your opinions? Is this because I thought you were overreacting to Livvy's temporary anxiety issues when you wanted to cart her off to a psychiatrist like she had a serious mental health crisis? Isn't the fact that she's doing better now that our house has returned to some semblance of normal evidence that maybe I was right? Or am I ignoring you because I want Luca to try different foods and learn not to procrastinate? Are you going to stand there and tell me you don't believe those to be valuable lessons? Or is this all because I'm not throwing a party over your quitting your job with no backup plan after we talked about alternatives? Enlighten me about how I'm not hearing you, because in all cases, I've put the long-term welfare of our entire family first. First—unlike you, who has made Amy's crisis your top priority and then decided nothing that we always agreed upon made sense anymore."

I'm shaking from his verbal assault, although unable to hit back as quickly. "You're being condescending and oversimplifying everything."

He starts to laugh. "Okay. Cards on the table? The real reason why I've kept quiet since you quit is because your sister told me to give you space. To be supportive. How's that for more proof that her advice, however well intentioned, doesn't work for us." He rakes a hand through his hair while I recover from the shock of that revelation. "We always had our own way of working through things. Whatever worked for her and Sean doesn't work for us. That much I hope we can both agree on."

This revelation requires a second to collect my thoughts. "I didn't know Amy reached out to you. And I'm not minimizing how she's affected us. I appreciate everything you've done to help this year. I'm scared, though, because I love you, but I'm not the same person I was at twenty-five or even thirty. I need to know that your love isn't conditional on my behaving and thinking exactly as I used to."

He inhales deeply and slowly exhales, his expression softening. "My love has never been conditional, Krissy. But it feels like you've been on a mission to challenge me at every turn, contradicting me in front of the kids, this stuff with your career, et cetera. I've never once made a U-turn without consulting you." His voice is broken now. Beaten down and defeated.

I feel unsupported and he feels betrayed.

I look down, as if the solution to fixing our problems is on my shoes. "I'm sorry. I guess I felt like you weren't giving me space to change, so I stopped turning to you and did what I wanted."

My apology shifts his energy to something calmer. "It's no secret I don't like change. I'm sorry you thought I didn't care about your opinions. All I can say is that I'll try to do better." He rolls his neck around, and I can hear it cracking with each rotation. "Can we table this and talk about something else now? It's been a long day."

"Sure." I wish we were hugging but won't force it. We both have some thinking to do and adjustments to make.

"When are your parents coming?" he asks.

The timing couldn't be worse. "Sunday around lunchtime. I thought your parents could take the kids to church for Easter Mass so you and I can prepare things before mine show up. They'll be here for eight days to be with Amy through the anniversary. If we're not going to Anguilla next week, perhaps we should plan a small family memorial. A brunch or something." Is that asking too much, given everything he just said?

Tony shrugs noncommittally. "What does Amy want?"

"I haven't asked." This reminds me that she went around me to Tony, which I need to quiz her about. In an effort to be more honest, I add, "We've been having growing pains too."

One brow quirks upward. "Really? You seemed closer lately."

I still don't tell him about the pills or Amy's offer to help us financially. "Yes, but then I said something awful at the recital."

"I can't believe that."

I screw up my face. "I accused her of still wanting to die."

"Wow." He's blinking at me as if trying to recognize who I am. "Why, after you've been so careful of her feelings all year?"

"She made one of her judgments, and I snapped because I was overwrought from quitting and disappointing you. That must be why she wrote to you. Anyway, the foundation should be a healing force for her. Thanks for that suggestion."

"You made it happen. She's lucky to have you in her corner. That's why I get pissed when she criticizes you."

"It's coming from a place of love." Unlike his mother's criticism of me, not that I say this.

He shakes his head. "It's coming from a place of fear, Krissy. Understandable, given what she's been through, but I don't generally operate from that place." He steps closer and holds my hand. "I know we have some work to do, but I don't want us making life decisions based on statistically improbable events. You and me, we rely on logic and goals. I'd really like to stick to that. So, if you're burned out and need to step way back, we'll find a way to make it work. That's okay with me, but it could require short-term changes, because I'd like to keep our long-term goals intact."

"Well, I'm not sure how to get what I want."

"That's also unlike you."

"Doesn't make it less true." I shrug. "I want better balance between my job and our family. At the same time, I don't want my life to get better if it means yours or the kids' gets worse."

"I'm not good at hypotheticals. Think about your ideal plan—whether that's part time or full time but local or whatever—then we can have a meaningful discussion about how to make it all work, okay? Now I have a little work to finish up for a meeting tomorrow."

Hypotheticals are meaningless. I have to figure myself out first, and he has to carry us until I do. I'm grateful he's able to do that for me. "Can I help you at work now that I'll have free time?"

He raises a hand on his way to his office. "The best thing you can do is figure out what you really want. In the meantime, you picking up more of the housework will let me focus on my business."

"Okay." A compromise. We have work to do, but all is not lost.

I rise from my stool and put my dishes in the dishwasher, rubbing my arms to ward off a chill. I down two aspirin because the headache is pulsing. One more week of work and my parents' visit to get through. Can I manage it without drugs?

Tony put his cards on the table, but I'm still lying, and not for his protection so much as my own.

Speaking of protection, Amy cannot stick her nose in my marriage again. I pick up my phone and call her. "Hey, you have a minute?"

"What's up?" she asks.

"Why did you go to Tony behind my back? If you thought that would help, it didn't."

Amy hesitates. "I'm sorry. You were upset after the recital, so I wanted him to give you time to process things."

I walk toward the window and look across the yard to the water, frowning. "Well, meddling in my marriage won't help me. I can't confide in you if you don't respect my boundaries."

Amy makes a miffed sound. "Like you've respected mine this year?"

I roll my eyes, even though she can't see me. "You tried to end your life, Amy. I had reason to be concerned about your ability to manage yourself."

"You've been using drugs to cope with yours, so I have reason too." Her triumphant tone affects me like cymbals struck beside my ears.

I almost say it's not the same, but that isn't exactly true. "Just please don't go behind my back again."

"I won't. So . . . is everything okay now?"

I don't know. I hope it will be. "We cleared the air."

"Do you want to come over?"

"No. But is there anything else you've done that I'm not aware of? I don't like being blindsided."

"I haven't said anything else to anyone. Listen, I only want you to be happy."

"As you like to remind me, I'm the only one who can make that happen. I'll talk to you later this week. Mom and Dad will be here Sunday, so we should make some plans."

"I wish they weren't coming. Mom will stare at me all week, chewing her lip off."

"Well, it's not the best time for company for me either."

"What did Mom say about your quitting?"

"Surprisingly little." Mom's never understood my personal goals or shown much interest in what I do. She'd be far more upset to learn about Tony's troubles than mine. Whenever she calls me, she mostly asks about the kids and Amy. "She's focused on the anniversary."

Amy groans. "I was glad you'd be traveling so I could be alone that day."

Her wanting to be alone might make sense, but it also makes me concerned. "We're canceling our trip, so you won't be stuck with Mom and Dad by yourself."

"Why are you canceling?" The shock in her voice mirrors the way I first felt when Rita alluded to the idea.

I whitewash it, wanting to end the call. "There's too much going on with Tony's business and my quitting. Listen, I need to tuck the kids in. Let's talk later."

"All right. Give them a kiss from me."

Amy enjoyed being part of the bedtime routine. It reminds me how alone she is now, and how, no matter how much she seems to have improved, there will always be little setbacks. Despite Tony's opinion, reassuring her that she is part of this family does give her a reason to go on. "They miss you. You should stop over one night and read with them."

"I'd like that."

———

"Where's Daddy?" Livvy asks while helping me arrange fresh-cut white roses in a few vases to place in the guest room and elsewhere to welcome my parents. She's coming down off her jelly bean high. Luca and she were probably fidgety in church this morning with their other grandparents. I owe them for that favor.

Tony and I have settled into a peaceful truce while I've been wrapping up work and figuring out my next step. That said, neither of us would choose to have my parents here for eight days at this point in time.

"He went to the airport to get Nana and Pops." I smile at her and snip more stems. Flowers won't improve the timing of their company, but they do boost my mood.

"Wait until they meet Snickers!" She smiles at me.

"They'll be so proud of how well you take care of him. I'm really impressed with how clean you keep his cage."

"I love him!" Joy beams from every pore on her face.

I grab her into a hug. "I love *you*."

She giggles, hugging me back. "I love you too, Mommy."

Those words seep into the cracks in my heart and fill me with warmth. I have nothing but respect for my peers whose careers require them to be less available at home, and yet I'm looking forward to sharing more of my young children's days with them for a little while. This is the right choice for me after the year we've all suffered. We ease apart and take the vases to the family room and guest room. When we come back downstairs, the garage door rumbles to life.

They're here. Time for my game face. I text Amy to let her know that we'll be over within the hour.

My parents bustle through the door, with Tony following behind carrying their gigantic suitcase, which he immediately takes upstairs. Mom and Dad hug Livvy while I call for Luca.

My mother's gained ten pounds since I last saw her in person. My father's hair is grayer, or maybe it's his extra wrinkles that have aged him.

"Nana, Nana, come meet Snickers!" Livvy tugs at her arm.

"I will in a minute, honey," she says. Luca races in, so my parents pepper him with kisses and questions about school. Eventually, I get a moment to give them both a hug.

"You look too skinny, Kristin." Mom scowls as her gaze roams my figure. "Isn't Tony cooking anymore?"

"Yes, he's cooking. It's been a busy time, so I'm not eating as much." A lie to keep the peace. I swore I wouldn't touch those pills again, but this week may test my resolve.

"Where's Amy?" she asks.

"I thought we'd go to her apartment and give Tony a quiet house to get some work done."

"Can I come?" Livvy asks.

"Not this time. But you'll see Aunt Amy later tonight. You and Luca can watch a Harry Potter movie while we're gone."

"Yeah!" Luca pipes up.

It's nice when things go smoothly. I'll need to hide their remaining Easter candy before we leave, or we'll all be miserable later.

"How's your sister?" Mom's intent stare would intimidate anyone.

"Surprisingly good. She's befriended her landlord. Between him and the foundation, she's been in a pleasant mood."

Mom claps her hands together in front of her chest. "That's wonderful. Let us go freshen up and unpack. We'll be back in a jiffy."

"First you have to meet Snickers," Livvy commands, taking them both by the hand. Dad winks at me, and then they wander off. Despite their attempt to act normal, the strain of grieving their grandson and their enduring concern for Amy hangs on them like a heavy coat.

Luca trails behind, and I search for Harry Potter on Peacock, then take the Easter baskets to the walk-in pantry and set them on the highest shelf.

Tony reappears and goes directly to the kitchen to check his list. He's planning a big feast tonight. I wander over to him.

"Can I help—maybe a grocery run?" I rub his back.

He shakes his head. "We've got everything. I brined the bird last night. If you don't mind, I want to sneak away to my office to make some calls."

"Of course. Thanks for doing all this to make my parents feel welcome."

He drops a quick kiss on my nose. "We're family. They're always welcome."

My spine softens at the reminder that his love is true. "I'm taking them to see Amy's apartment. I've teed up a movie to occupy the kids, so enjoy the quiet while you can."

Tony makes a face. "Your mom's gonna die when she sees that place."

I grunt an acknowledgment. She's unlikely to get through the visit without offending Amy.

Livvy comes downstairs, frowning.

"What's wrong?" I ask, ruffling her hair.

"Nana called Snickers a rodent!"

I cover a laugh. "Well, technically he is a rodent. Nana's probably a little afraid of him, honey. She's never really liked pets."

"Why not?"

I shrug. "I don't know."

My mother bustles down the stairs with Dad behind her, so I put my finger to my lips to signal to Livvy to drop it.

Mom's applied some fresh lipstick and has her purse in hand. "All set."

"Let's go. But remember, it's a temporary pit stop. Lower your expectations, and try not to upset Amy," I say.

"I would never upset your sister," Mom replies.

Dad pats her shoulder and winks at me. "Not on purpose, dear. Not on purpose."

Tony works to suppress a grin as he waves us off and picks up the remote to get the kids settled.

"Don't act like I don't know how to conduct myself. I've made it into my late sixties with more friends than either of you have." She huffs and heads toward the garage.

I can't argue. My colleagues aren't dear friends. We don't socialize outside the workweek or share intimate confidences. My law school friends keep in touch via social media, but we rarely get together now that everyone has kids and is spread out over the tristate area. I should start to build actual friendships in my community while I'm unemployed.

"We won't be gone long." I kiss Livvy's head and then go to the car. Five minutes later, we park in front of Bob's house.

Mom eyes Bob's Cape-style home from the back seat. "It's tiny, but it looks well maintained."

With my hand on the driver's door, I say, "This is the landlord's house. Amy's unit is in the back. Watch the cracks in the driveway so we can avoid the ER."

"Oh my," Mom mutters.

Amy's expecting us—*dreading us* is probably more accurate. Still, she answers the door with a smile. "Welcome to my humble abode."

Our mom embraces her in a death grip, and then Dad gets his turn. "You look good, honey."

While Dad tweaks Amy's nose, Mom cranes her neck to peek at the inside.

"Come on in." Amy steps aside so we can enter, giving me a pleading look after our parents pass her.

I sit at the kitchen table, freeing up the comfortable seating on the sofa. At least the new carpets keep the place from being completely depressing.

"Want a beer, Dad?" Amy asks.

"Of course I do." He sits in the recliner with his hands folded on his lap and waits for her to serve him.

Mom wanders through the unit, inspecting the space, the windows, the bathroom. At one point her classic cluck of disapproval sounds. In order to undo her frown, I say, "Look at the artwork Livvy made for Amy. Isn't it sweet?"

She glances at the wall without enthusiasm. "Yes, they're lovely."

Amy sits in one corner of the sofa, her foot jiggling. Meanwhile, Mom peers at her like a biologist looking through a microscope. "Are you sure you want to sell your house?"

"Yes. Besides, the closing is tomorrow. No backing out now." Amy shifts from foot jiggling to drumming her thighs.

She'd insisted on dealing with the move by herself. Honestly, it was nice not to have to organize and otherwise oversee that. I'm learning that everything doesn't have to be perfect, especially when it isn't my stuff.

"Did the final broom sweep this morning." Her face pales, but she quickly recovers without the blank stare or clenched jaw that typically signals a breakdown. She swore selling would be a relief, but it had to be hard to say goodbye for the last time.

"If you want company tomorrow—" I begin.

She holds up a hand, shooting me a sober look. "I've got it."

I nod, letting the rebuke roll off my shoulders. *It's not only about me*—a mantra I've been repeating in my head lately.

Mom finally sits, her posture erect, her purse on her lap. She could not look less comfortable. Her expression pinches each time her gaze lands on some new part of the rental unit. "Maybe a coat of paint— something pretty, like a pale peach."

"Ooo, how very 1980s," comes Amy's dry response. The sarcasm misses our mother completely, based on her pleased expression. I try not to laugh.

"Kristin says you've got a nice landlord," Dad says between sips.

"Bob's very sweet. He's probably ten years older than you, but he treats me like a granddaughter. He's good company when I'm feeling social. We're planting a few tomato stalks next month."

Planting a garden suggests she's looking forward to summer and fall. Another positive sign.

Mom nods. "I see some spring flowers out there. We'll buy you a nice outdoor glider so you can enjoy the, er, yard."

"I can buy my own patio furniture, Mom, but thanks."

"Mm," Mom says. "Well, tell us about this foundation. How's that going?"

"I've enlisted Josephina to help me write up information and resources for the website, which should be ready to go live soon. She and I have also begun crafting application questions. On Friday afternoon, I signed the organizational documents that will be filed with the state tomorrow. I'm having lunch this coming week with my lawyer to celebrate and talk about next steps." She's rubbing her thighs at this point. It's a lot of responsibility, and that's never been something she's embraced. Yet there's determination in her eyes—a mother's determination. My own grow watery when I imagine her gratification from building a legacy for Scotty and Sean.

"You're making a positive difference, Amy." My dad clears his throat as if he, too, is affected by its significance. "It's a terrific idea."

"It was Kristin's idea," she says.

"That's not important," I say. "You're the one doing it."

Amy shrugs. "It's a little worrisome—all the families asking for guidance and money for different programs could be triggering. My personal experience might also make it difficult to say no to anyone, so this could be the shortest-lived foundation ever." Sarcasm doesn't hide her discomfort.

Those decisions would carry an emotional burden for anyone, let alone someone with her lived experience. Although she's made it clear she doesn't need my help, I can't stop myself from trying to solve her problem.

"What if you structure the grants to be given out biannually to give yourself breaks throughout the year?" I suggest. "Or form a committee to go through the applications and come to consensus on who gets money. That'd give you emotional distance from the final decisions."

"Waiting six months for help is too long for most people. Early intervention is critical," Amy says.

"Oh." I hadn't considered that. "Maybe quarterly, then?"

She presses her index fingers to her temples. "Thinking about this is already making me nervous."

It was smart to involve Josephina and Jane.

I'd thought I was supportive when she was learning about Scotty's needs, but I was too busy with my own kids, career, and marriage to be fully plugged in to Amy's daily struggles. And she wielded humor like a giant shield, so I saw only what she let me see. I guess we're the same in our ability to project the image we want to, something I haven't noticed until now.

"No charity can help everyone, Amy," Mom says with authority. "Focus on the good you're doing, not the challenges. Your sister isn't working, so she'll be climbing the walls looking for ways to help. I'm happy to serve on a committee too."

I'm still choking from my mom's assessment of me when Amy replies, "Thanks, Mom, but you live thousands of miles and a few time zones away. Plus you're at the stage in life when you should relax and tick through your bucket list."

"Well, don't kill us off. We're not even seventy, for goodness' sake." Mom looks at Dad to see if he's as affronted as she is. "I'm as organized as Jane. I served on many school committees in my heyday."

Mom loves Amy and would be happy to help if asked, but I suspect she's jealous of Jane's involvement, or perhaps views the work as a way to remain relevant. Or maybe I'm projecting to how I might feel decades from now.

"I'll think about it, Mom, but let's stop focusing on me. I'm not the only one in flux, for a change. Kristin's at a crossroads too."

My pulse kicks up as my parents stare at me. "I'm fine—looking forward to a little break. I'm considering local firms and general counsel positions to cut down on the commute."

"That's good," my sister says. "More time with your family."

That's the upside. The salary cut is a downside. I'd rather not have this discussion now, so I pivot. Mom has made it clear to me that she won't let Amy be alone on the anniversary and wants me to pave the way to some compromise. "Listen, Ames. We've been wondering if you'd like to do anything special on the anniversary next weekend. A little affair, like we did for Scotty's birthday."

Amy twirls her wedding band without looking at any of us. "I don't know. I'm not sure how I'll feel that day."

I'd want to be around people who loved me and shared my memories, but Amy and I are different. Her vague reply raises my concerns that the date could take her to dark places. If she's surrounded by love, she'll be less likely to harm herself. That's my goal—keeping her alive. She says it isn't my job, but it is my wish.

"No pressure," I concede for now. "We can leave it open—a loose plan. Brunch if you're up to it, and a visit to the cemetery. The important thing is that you know you don't have to go through the day alone—"

"Honey," Mom interrupts, "it'll be a hard day for all of us. If we're together, we can lean on each other. We should invite Sean's parents, too, and maybe some of your friends you haven't seen in a while."

I want to bury my head in my hands at our mother's heavy-handed approach.

"It's not a celebration, Mom," Amy snaps.

"It could be." Mom is undeterred, having had years of practice butting heads with Amy. "A celebration of their lives and of the foundation.

Of your turning the corner. These are all good things, honey. Things that deserve to be recognized."

Fair points, but Mom's methods are never quite effective.

"I'll never 'celebrate' the death of my husband and son. Shame on you for saying that." Amy tenses as if ready to flee the room, maybe the house. Proof that her progress is incomplete. She's gotten better at hiding her grief, but it still pulses beneath her skin with every heartbeat.

I reach over to touch her arm. "We only want to make sure you're okay and to come together that day in remembrance."

Dad is predictably quiet, finishing his beer. Mom folds her arms across her chest. I'm holding my breath.

My sister pats my hand, her eyes watery. In the ensuing silence, she squeezes my hand. "Plan a brunch, but I want to go to the cemetery alone."

A compromise relieves me. "All right. Did you want to invite anyone outside of our family?"

She shakes her head. "Sean's parents lost their son because of me. I can't face them in person just yet. Not on that day, anyway."

Guilt is corrosive and spills over to me because, in all these months, I've failed to get her to accept the accident as something beyond her control.

Mom chimes in: "Amy, Jane's going to be part of your foundation. You'll have to see her sooner or later, so why not do it on your turf surrounded by your family? And really, you know they don't blame you for the accident."

I make eyes at Mom to shut her down.

Amy gives her a long look. "If we invite them, then I'm not only locked into coming, but will also have to manage my feelings about them on top of my own feelings about the anniversary. You just said we would keep it loose."

Finally, Dad pipes up—an action rare enough that it elicits our instant attention. "I like Sean's folks, but we can't make their feelings more important than Amy's. Send them a nice note that day that you are thinking of them—that you look forward to working with them to make the foundation a success—and then we'll do something simple with the family. You can leave quickly if you can't stay."

"I like that plan." Amy sighs, smiling at Dad. "Thank you for being the voice of reason."

Absently I think Dad's advice sounds a lot like something Tony might suggest. They share a sort of pragmatism, which is something I may have subconsciously found comforting about my husband from the beginning.

"Do you want to help me make up a menu, or—" I begin.

"Whatever you want is fine. I doubt I'll be hungry," Amy says.

As much as I wish she were further along, I do understand why that date will always be hard and that I can't take her pain away. "We'll plan for ten o'clock so you won't have to spring out of bed. You can eat a good meal and have some company before you go to the cemetery." This schedule leaves open the option to go with her if she ends up wanting support.

"Fine. Now, can we please talk about anything else? Dad, how's that jerky neighbor—the one whose fence is falling down?"

Dad starts to fill her in on the latest tit for tat between him and their new neighbor, who moved to Phoenix from California, while I take a cleansing breath. Big topics addressed. No major tears. No fighting. Dare I hope that the worst is behind us all?

CHAPTER SEVENTEEN

A M Y

The following Friday

My to-do list today gives me a break from sitting with my family yet again. They love me and mean well, but daily doses of them, their spouses, and their children are making me feel my losses more keenly this week.

So does tomorrow's anniversary.

A few months ago, it was to be my last day on earth, yet somehow the steps I planned to get there ended up steering me away from that goal. Each act—from forcing Kristin to do crazy stunts, to talking to Joe at the grief group, to sharing meals with Bob—has led me to finding the gumption to create a foundation. I'm even looking forward to getting back to gardening. Go figure.

Before I hit up Home Depot, I sit in front of my laptop and navigate to my blog for the first time in a year. The cursor blinks, impatiently awaiting the first keystrokes of a new *The Boy Next Door* blog post.

Greetings, old friends.

I've spent two weeks trying to find the right words to apologize for ghosting you all last year, and for taking away the support and community many of you counted on. In the end, the naked truth is all I can offer—I lost my sweet Scotty and husband, Sean, last April in a terrible accident. I then lost the subsequent few months to grief so deep I almost didn't survive. With the love and support of my family, I have crawled out of that dark hole and found the strength to begin to move forward on my own. Despite my absence, I've thought of you throughout the year, and hope you can forgive me. An important step of my ongoing journey is to rekindle this community for myself and all of you.

On that note, I have an announcement that may be of real value to some of you. I've started a charitable foundation—The Walsh Foundation 4 Autism—

whose mission will be to provide financial support to help families with neurodiverse children obtain the services they require. More information will be available on our website soon (www.thewalshfoundation-4autism.com), so please check that out and spread the word. At this time, I'm planning to ensure that at least fifty percent of the annual grants go to families in Fairfield County, Connecticut, but the foundation will accept applications from elsewhere in the state.

I hope that, during the past year, each of you and your families have made great strides together, and that you are looking forward to what lies ahead. It is a relief to honestly say that, although I miss my family daily, I am—for the first time in a year—looking ahead with some eagerness too.

Fondly,
Amy

I reread the post, wishing for more eloquence. This, however, is sincere, and pretty words wouldn't make the message itself more meaningful. I hit "Post" and then grab my car key and head out the door.

When I pull into Home Depot, my first win of the day comes in the form of a parking space near the door (a true miracle). Next, the gigantic cart I choose doesn't have a single wonky wheel. Lastly, I locate a gardening-tool basket set and seedlings without having to lap the warehouse in search of an elusive orange-vested employee.

I trudge to the checkout line with plenty of time to spare before I'm due to meet Declan for our celebratory lunch. There are three people ahead of me—a middle-aged contractor in steel-toe boots and stained painter pants, a young woman balancing a ceiling fan box on her hip, and a mother with her young son, who is sitting in the cart wearing noise-canceling headphones. He's truly gorgeous—dark hair and darker eyes that draw me in. It's then that I'm stricken.

He is intently sucking on a plastic hammer, appearing unaware of my presence. Unfazed by my gaze. He's completely absorbed by the toy in a way I recognize so viscerally that I push my cart aside and stride out the door, gulping in shallow breaths.

A year. It's been a year since my son took a breath. Since I helped him get dressed and comb his hair. Since I talked to him or held him or lay beside him in the cool grass.

I unlock my car and sit there without turning it on. People pass by, their heads doing double takes while I grip my steering wheel and cry. Sob, actually. The ache to hold Scotty again—to touch his face instead of seeing it in my dreams—swells so fast, my lungs become heavy weights that don't function well. With sorrow, I think of Sean, whom I miss every damn day. My friend and lover. My best audience.

Without them, it's lonely, lonely, lonely. Especially at night, when I lie awake in the bed, hugging a pillow and wishing it were my husband. One year later, the loss can still suffocate me like a plastic bag thrown over my head.

The emotional onslaught causes doubts to crop up like mushrooms. I let myself get roped into commitments by somehow believing everything would change, yet founding a charity won't give me what I most need. Life on earth can't reunite me with my husband and son.

I want to run away, yet I'm also afraid to be alone.

I hunch forward, head to the steering wheel, and draw several deep breaths. My phone rings. Mom. Absolutely not taking that call now. She's been overstepping every boundary possible this week. I'm exhausted from defending myself, my choices, my moods. Everything. All of it.

They must also be weary from the worrying they've suffered this year. The trauma of the accident and my response. Even now I feel them evaluating everything from my house to my moods, cautious optimism breaking through their wary haze. It might honestly be easier on everyone if I weren't around. Sure, they'd grieve, but the fussing and fretting would end. They'd help each other heal and then they'd get on with their lives, minus the stress of checking on me and my moods.

Of course, I'd miss out on seeing Livvy and Luca become adults, and saddle them with another loss so early in their lives. That thought makes me hot with shame. So selfish. I'm so damn selfish. I need to be stronger and more grateful for what remains.

I sit back, my chest rising and falling as my heart rate slows. That mom and little boy walk behind my car. He's now less docile, banging his hammer against the cart and stiffening his little body as if he's determined to break out of his skin. She's harried, trying to soothe him while shooting apologetic glances at whomever is watching and judging. I recall that panic, too, like that time Scotty kept screaming in the pediatrician's waiting room. I tried to contain him on my lap, only to wrestle strong, tiny arms and legs flailing to find freedom. He'd thrown anything his fingers could grab, while other mothers tried to ignore us or sent me pitying glances. The fact that I felt embarrassed then elicits a dozen mental apologies to Scotty now.

I reach for the door, thinking to help, but that could be unwelcome. She'll be okay once she gets home to some support, unless she's a single mom managing on her own. Exactly the kind of person who'll benefit from my foundation. And just like that, the source of my pain becomes the proxy for the thousands of families who could use the hand I'm willing to extend.

I must get through today and tomorrow's anniversary without doing anything rash. In a frustrating moment of clarity, I understand that attending brunch and pretending to be okay to alleviate everyone else's concerns will keep me safer. Kristin knows this, too, I'm sure. Once again, her chess skills have put me in checkmate.

The inability to break free of pain and obligation—even if only for a moment—can still make me feel trapped. I crave one truly peaceful breath. But there's no time now, because Declan will be waiting for me at the restaurant soon.

———

"You don't seem as excited as I hoped," Declan says while laying his napkin across his lap. Behind him is a wall of glass overlooking the marina in Stamford. The sky is a flat, steely-gray color, signaling the storms moving in overnight.

"I'm sorry. I had a weird experience before coming." I fiddle with the silverware.

"Oh?"

I quickly recite what happened at Home Depot without breaking down—a small victory.

"I wish I could promise that'll never happen again, but of course, you know better. If you'd rather do this another time, we can leave." Declan smiles patiently.

"No, I'm okay." Someday I'll easily surf the occasional waves of heavy sorrow knocking me over today and be glad of this accomplishment.

"Good, because starting a foundation deserves a little bubbly."

"Champagne always helps." My joke falls a little flat, but I give myself a mental shake.

Sean and I didn't often enjoy fancy lunches, especially after Scotty came along. When we did indulge or escape responsibilities for a while, we could finish each other's sentences and laugh at the same things. He would hold my hand or pinch my ass or give me a saucy look that was a promise of things to come. A year is a long time not to flirt and be kissed and told I looked pretty despite how my bedhead made for prime meme material.

To break an extended silence, I tease, "Do all your clients get the white-glove treatment?"

"Only the ones with a sense of humor." He grins, adding, "Seriously, I'm awed by how you've channeled your grief to help others. I didn't manage as well during my first year without Melinda."

Shared grief would never be my first choice of basis for a new friendship, but in this case it works. "I doubt that's true."

"I may look like I've got it together now, but my first year was rough." He gestures to his hair. "Lots more grays. But as for you, this venture will change your life in all the best ways."

His optimism lets me forget—for three seconds—that tomorrow is my personal D-Day. It helps me handle the fact that my life—this half life—isn't at all what I'd planned.

"That would be a nice side effect," I admit. Several months ago, suicide seemed my only option. The foundation puts that option on the back burner, which on its own qualifies the decision as quite literally improving my life immeasurably. I'll probably be grateful at some point.

For now, I'll focus on the families I will help, and my family, who are desperate for me to find joy again.

The waiter opens a bottle of champagne and pours us each a flute before leaving the bottle in the ice bucket.

"Guess you aren't planning on doing much work this afternoon?" I tease.

"No. I'm headed home from here. My daughter has her driver's test late this afternoon, and I want to be there for either support or celebration, depending."

It's nice to talk about something ordinary for a change. "Is there a chance she'll fail?"

"She's the only teen I've taught to drive, so it's hard to know if she's terrible, or if she's normal for her level of experience. I confess to having lost a few years of my life while riding shotgun." His voice is full of love and gratitude, notwithstanding this critique.

My mom couldn't tolerate the passenger seat, so Kristin had taken me out for driving practice before I got my license. She'd remind me to keep both hands on the wheel, to turn down the music, to keep my eyes on the road. I would act obnoxious, even though I secretly felt safer with her beside me. Our dynamic hasn't changed much in all these years, although I will take credit for getting her to be a little more daring lately. It's caused short-term friction for her at home, but in the long run, I still believe it will make her happier.

Meanwhile, driving lessons are another among a million normal things I'll never do with my son. The thought threatens to spoil my mood, so I quickly raise my glass. "Good luck to her. I hope you can keep celebrating tonight."

We clink our glasses, and I down my first glass like a shot. Declan's eyes reflect surprise—maybe even mild alarm—but the waiter reappears to take our orders. I use the interruption to pour myself another glass. Getting buzzed might be the key to getting through the rest of this day without falling apart.

After the waiter leaves, Declan dips some torn focaccia into olive oil. "Any progress on the grant criteria?"

"Josephina and I are meeting next week to try to refine the draft." I gulp half the glass, eager for the sedative effect of the alcohol to take over.

"Terrific. Have you thought of renting a small office space?"

I wrinkle my nose. "That seems unnecessary."

"I don't know. Given the work you'll be doing, it might be worth separating it from your homelife."

"Why?" My second glass of champagne is nearly finished now.

"At first applicants might trigger difficult memories. It could be better to keep your home a little sanctuary."

"Oh gosh." I laugh. "If you saw my apartment, you'd never refer to it as a sanctuary." Although as I joke, an image of Bob and the garden we're planning together surfaces. Despite my fail at Home Depot, I'm looking forward to digging my hands into soil and harvesting beefsteak tomatoes fresh from the vine come August.

"Just something to consider." He smiles and sips his champagne. I love how he never makes proclamations. His advice is always buffeted with cotton batting and left for me to unspool at my leisure.

"I'll think about it." I eye the champagne bottle and decide to wait for salad before pouring a third glass.

"What about the grief group? Will you return?"

My shoulders tense. "Not sure."

"I'd be happy to join you again if that would help. There are multiple meetings per week, some of which are for more specific groups, such as parents grieving children. Perhaps there's a meeting tomorrow."

The mention of tomorrow upends me like a massive wave. My ears ring a little. "Tomorrow's the anniversary."

Saying it aloud makes my stomach turn. I must've winced because Declan reaches out to cover my hand. "I'm sorry, Amy. That's a tough one. All the more reason a meeting might help."

"You're probably right, but it feels like too much." I slowly withdraw my hand and pour that third glass. Perspiration gathers around my hairline and along my spine. God, I'm out of practice with normal socializing. "Honestly, as much as I feel I've improved, there are days like today—here, celebrating a big event—when it all still seems pointless without Scotty and Sean. It makes me crazy, this wondering if I'll ever feel normal again. Or happy." A sigh escapes. I rest my chin on my hand. "Joy. Do you think that's even possible?"

"I do. Not easy, mind you, but possible. Melinda was my first real love and a wonderful wife and mother." He places one hand over his heart, but I'm struck by his use of the word *first*. He believes he'll fall in love again. For his sake, I hope he does. "Part of me will always and only be hers. But I want a full life. I want my daughter to see me recover. To see me fall in love again so she learns that a broken heart can mend, and that there is more than one person we can love in our lifetime."

More than one person we can love in our lifetime. I sit back, polishing off my third glass of champagne while taking that in. His aren't particularly novel goals, but they're deeply sincere, which moves me in some inexplicable way. "You're so healthy."

He chuckles. "It's taken work."

Our meals come as a pleasant sort of wooziness kicks in. I feel floaty. The next forty minutes pass more comfortably, and I knock back a final glass of champagne.

While Declan pays the bill, he says, "I don't think you should drive."

"I'm fine, thanks. I just ate that pasta."

He shakes his head. "No, Amy. Trust me. You drank most of that bottle, and you can't weigh much. Let's be safe. I'll zip you home, and you can Uber back later for your car."

"Oh fine." I stand and sway, proving him right.

He comes around to take my arm to keep me from pitching into other diners. "Off we go."

It's strange to be touched by a man who isn't Sean or Tony or my father. The warmth of his grip, the hint of citrus cologne, the innate strength of him. I lean against him, partly because I am very tipsy, and partly because of the yearning—not for him, but for the feeling of being part of something more than just myself.

He gets me seated in the passenger seat, and then we spend the next few minutes driving to my apartment, letting Brandi Carlile fill the silence. I stare out the window, guilty yet unable to ignore the fact that I miss sex too. I went until last month without thinking about sex. I wish I weren't thinking of it now, but everything about this day has snapped me wide open. The ups and downs, the champagne, the kindness of a sympathetic man.

Lord, I'm a disaster. I need to get away from Declan before I humiliate myself further. He pulls into the driveway and parks the car.

"Thanks," I slur, unsuccessfully trying to open the door.

"Hang on, let me help." He unlocks it with a button and then exits the car and zips around to catch me before I hit the pavement. "Up we go."

He tugs a little harder than I can keep up with, so I fall against him again, but now I'm crying.

"Did I hurt you?" His gaze fills with alarm.

I shake my head. "I'm embarrassed."

He smiles and begins to lead me down the driveway. "Don't be."

"But I am. I'm drunk. And lonely. And having weird thoughts." I look up into his kind eyes. *Don't!*

"We all have weird thoughts sometimes. We all get lonely. It'll be okay, Amy. One day at a time."

"Do you miss sex?" I blurt, then my cheeks ignite.

Declan clears his throat and wisely lets that one go. My humiliation is complete. "Let's get you inside, where you can drink some water or maybe coffee."

I wipe my nose, but the tears keep coming. "You're not going to fire me as your client, are you?"

He laughs. "No. Absolutely not."

Bob comes out the back door. "Everything okay?"

Oh boy. I was wrong a second ago—now my humiliation is complete. Tears burn and I want to disappear.

Declan waves. "She just had a little too much champagne at lunch, so I brought her home. She'll be fine."

"Why're you crying?" Bob asks me, unwilling to simply accept Declan's explanation.

"Because everything is too hard. And tomorrow is one year—but it feels like twenty. Can I keep this up? Sometimes I just don't know. It's too much." I'm slurring a little and struggling not to turn an ankle in these wedges.

Bob looks at Declan for clarification. "One year?"

"The deaths," he replies quietly, and then it hits Bob.

Bob's eyes fill with compassion. "Oh my. Here, let me help." He takes his keys from his pocket and opens the door, then fills a water glass while Declan guides me to the sofa.

"Here you go." Bob hands me the water and then looks at Declan. "If her car isn't out of your way, maybe you could take me to it now and I can bring it back for her."

Declan shrugs. "Fine with me if it's okay with you, Amy."

"You don't have to do that, Bob," I say.

"Happy to. You might need it to go to your sister's later, right?"

The kindness of my new friends slices through my haze and touches me deeply. I nod and fish through my purse for the fob. "Thank you."

"No problem." Bob smiles and heads for the door.

Declan crosses his arms. "Do you need anything else before I go?"

"Yes. Please, please, please forget everything I said since we left the restaurant." I pitch sideways and grab a throw pillow to hide my face.

He laughs and snaps his fingers. "Done."

I peek out from the pillow. "Thanks."

He nods and then crosses to Bob and closes the door behind them.

It feels impossible to face Declan again, let alone work on the foundation. I shouldn't have trusted myself to have lunch today. Should've known the sinking feeling that's been building this week in anticipation of tomorrow would not be easily overlooked.

I stare at the ceiling, wishing I could drink enough to black out and forget the last thirty minutes. That won't happen. I'm not that lucky. And now I'll be hungover tomorrow for my family memorial brunch too.

Please let me get through the next thirty-six hours without doing anything more reckless.

CHAPTER EIGHTEEN

KRISTIN

The following day

After packing up my office yesterday morning and handing in my key card, I stared blankly out the window for the entire train ride home. Numb. A little dejected. I'd put off calling Dan at Guerrilla to inform him that I'd quit, hoping to first land elsewhere. While a few competitors were interested in bringing me in, only one—a small boutique firm—was willing to consider equity partnership if Guerrilla committed. The weight of having spent a decade working toward a goal I failed to achieve rippled deeper within me with each mile of track that took me away from the city and home to an uncertain future.

My ride was made worse when Declan texted to suggest I check in with my sister because she'd had a bit too much to drink at their lunch. Apparently she seemed embarrassed by her behavior—not that he held it against her, but he was worried about her state of mind. When I called her from the train, I played dumb.

"I'm in the pits and need a boost. Please tell me you had fun celebrating the foundation," I said.

"I'm hungover," she rasped.

"Sounds like quite a party," I teased, holding my breath while waiting for her reaction.

"Not exactly." A yawn came over the line. "Congrats on your last day. How do you feel?"

"A little dumbstruck, honestly."

A second passed before she said, "It must be hard, but try to enjoy the time off." Amy yawned a second time. "Listen, I just woke up. Can we talk later?"

Her attempt to get me off the phone raised a little red flag. "What if I swing by and grab you for dinner? Mom is probably dying because she hasn't seen you all day, and I could use a buffer after the day I've had."

There was a pause, during which I assumed she was considering my plea. "I'm sorry, but I wouldn't be any help. I'm tired and grumpy."

She didn't sound weepy or fragile, just impatient. I would've felt better if I had eyes on her. "Maybe the kids can help you ungrump."

Amy chuckled. "I'll see you all tomorrow, okay? Bob's checked in twice already. I'd like to spend some time alone. Like you, I had a long day."

In recent weeks, we'd respected each other's boundaries, so whatever had happened with Declan earlier, she seemed to have it under control.

"All right. See you in the morning." I closed my eyes, dreading tomorrow, anxious about how she'd feel when the sun came up. "Love you."

"Love you too."

The one bright spot when I got home was Tony's compassion. As soon as I entered the house, he tugged me into his office and hugged me. He said nothing, just held me for what seemed like ten minutes, although it was probably only two or three before Livvy pounded on the door. When she did, he kissed me and said, "I know today was hard. I'm sorry you feel hurt and defeated, but this is not the end of your story or your journey. A year from now, I'm sure you'll look back and be happy about the decision."

"Mommy!" Livvy called from the other side of the door, so I simply kissed Tony as a thank-you for words I needed to hear. "Come see what I made."

Tony and I smiled at each other.

"Coming," I called back, then more quietly said "thank you" to Tony, touching his cheek again.

My mother spent last evening fiddling with her jewelry and tuning in and out of conversation, clearly preoccupied by Amy's absence. Having them here to witness the end of my tenure at Watkins, Glenn & Arpad hasn't been a picnic either. They'll be gone by Monday. We'll have crossed this anniversary milestone together as a family. Better days are just around the corner—I hope.

This morning I woke with a nervous stomach thinking about my sister. Did she sleep? Is she all right? I won't breathe easy until she arrives.

I'm sitting on the bed, fastening my sandal straps. Outside, the dark skies spit rain, and rumbling shudders in the distance. Maybe it's better if we can't visit the graves today . . . if we're stuck inside together where we can keep Amy distracted.

The painting of her family sits on the dresser. A modern gilt frame surrounds the sixteen-inch-square artwork and pale-blue matting, giving it a quiet beauty that I hope she'll appreciate.

"Should I wrap this or set it up somewhere for Amy to see when she arrives?" I call to Tony, who is in the bathroom shaving. He doesn't answer, so I stand and cross the room. "Did you hear me?"

When I get to the bathroom, he is standing, towel around his waist, holding a bottle of pills—the Adderall.

My limbs weaken, so I set down the painting and grab the vanity for stability. I want to avert my gaze, but I'm frozen in place, too horrified to move. Although I made it through the week without taking any, I removed them from my purse yesterday and stashed them just in case I ever needed a little boost. Why is he rooting through my side of the vanity?

His expression tightens as he stares at the bottle, confusion shifting to a dawning understanding. He glances up at me, his face a picture of dismay. I almost double over as every bit of goodwill we've been building since our last argument goes out with the tide. My fault. All my fault. Seconds tick by, him thinking of something to say, me bracing for impact.

"I was looking for extra shaving cream. Where did you even get these?" He shakes the bottle, his expression grim.

Nothing comes out when I open my mouth. I clear my throat and try again. "Last autumn was so hard. I got backlogged at work after taking September off to settle Amy here. I was fumbling trying to manage her, the kids, and my work. In November, someone at work offered me some after finding me asleep at my desk. They gave me so much energy—it felt like a miracle. I could stay awake and focus. They helped me keep everything on track, so I kept buying them."

"You've been taking these for months?" He turns away, cursing under his breath. "Now it makes sense—the weight loss, the edginess, the impulsiveness. Why didn't you talk to me?"

I wrap my arms around my waist, fighting against tears. "You would've wanted Amy to leave, and I couldn't have that."

"Now you're thinking for me too?" He tosses the bottle onto the counter before scrubbing his hands over his face. "First, Amy's been gone for a few months, yet you've still been taking them. Secondly, I would never have kicked her out, but I would've insisted on hiring help, Krissy. Or maybe a dozen other options that were safer than taking drugs without a doctor's supervision. This is basically speed."

"Shh!" I glance over my shoulder to check whether our bedroom door is closed. My mother's legendary radar for tension could spell disaster. Not to mention her disappointment being the last thing I need today. I already feel horrible enough. "I know. I'm sorry. I shouldn't need them anymore. In fact, throw that bottle away."

As if this gesture is somehow bold or brave after having been caught red-handed.

"I will." He removes the cap, dumps the pills into the sink, and turns on the faucet until they've all washed down the drain. A momentary panic erupts inside, but I tamp it down, shaken by my reluctance to get rid of them.

His shoulders slump as he throws the empty container in the trash. Do I reach for him, say nothing, apologize? Not that he'll believe anything I say at this point. I've screwed up my life, and yet having the truth out is making me feel free for the first time in forever.

I remain frozen while he lets a deep sigh loose. "Don't you know how much I love you? How devastated I'd be if something happened to you? Promise me you'll go to the doctor and get a blood test or whatever and make sure that your heart and everything is okay. God, I'm stunned. I'm furious with you, honestly, but as furious with myself for not seeing what was happening. It makes me sick to learn yet again how much you don't trust me. That you don't feel like you can turn to me for help."

Seeing his eyes bright with tears breaks me a little more.

"I'm sorry. I thought I had it under control." That's not precisely true, but I thought I could handle it all. "I was wrong, but I can't undo it. We are where we are."

"Where we are scares me. A year ago, I wouldn't have foreseen any of this—the secrets, the recklessness, this distance. I don't know what to do. Help me know what to do." He's turning in a circle with his hands out from his sides, as if seeking advice from invisible onlookers.

He doesn't believe I have the answer, and I can't blame him. Will this be the straw that breaks us? Why did this happen today of all days? Part of me wants to lock us in this room until he forgives me. The other part knows we must go put on a false face for my parents and Amy. None of that changes the fact that my choices have led us here. "I don't know, Tony, but we can't hash it out now. Amy should be here soon. My parents are probably wandering around the house looking for us. We've got to get the ham in the oven."

"Fuck," he mutters, hands on his hips. "At least tell me the truth about one thing—are you feeling okay today? Physically. Mentally. Are you okay?"

"Not really, and not just because I'm worried about Amy. Now I'm worried about us and how you're looking at me." Honesty, at last. "I swear I haven't taken any pills for several days. Other than some headaches and an uneasy stomach, I've been all right. I'll call my doctor on Monday morning."

His head is bowed and he says nothing, locked inside his own thoughts.

"My parents leave tomorrow night, and then we'll finally have some privacy. We can talk this out, but right now, can we please pretend like everything is fine so we don't make this difficult day worse for everyone?"

"I'd never do that, although the truth is we're not doing much better than Amy is, are we?" The defeated tone in his voice is so unusual that another note of panic rises.

"Tony." I reach forward.

He waves his hand. "Let me get dressed. I need a few minutes alone to get my game face on, please."

I hesitate, moving to hug him but sensing his resistance. "All right. I love you, and I'm sorry I've hurt you again."

He nods without looking me in the eye.

I turn around and grab the painting, suppressing the desire to throw up from regret. I've never understood how good marriages fall apart, but looking back over the past six months, I haven't even noticed how my own has been slowly crumbling beneath the weight of pride and lies.

When I get downstairs, my mother is standing at the island, looking at Tony's to-do list. She's overdressed, wearing a long-sleeved lilac dress and pearls despite knowing we aren't going to a church service. She's eyeing my beige slacks disapprovingly, but when she looks me in the eye, she must see that I'm in no mood for a critique.

"This brunch menu is fit for a queen." She waves Tony's paper list in the air until her gaze drops to the artwork in my hands. "What's that?"

"A gift for Amy. Now I wonder if she'll resent getting a present today. Should I just leave it out instead of wrapping it?"

"Wrapped or not, it's still a gift." She pulls that face she makes when she thinks I'm being obtuse.

I twist my mouth up. "Maybe it's less awkward if she's not unwrapping it."

"Then you've answered your own question."

It seems that everyone's nerves are frayed. More thunder rumbles, moving closer. It's going to be that kind of day. I set the painting on the coffee bar and tell myself to keep breathing.

"What's keeping Tony?" Mom asks, glancing at the ham, potatoes, and other things that have been laid out. "I preheated the oven because this stuff needs to get cooking."

I rub my temple, picturing him upstairs pulling himself together. He's torn, furious at my recklessness, yet beating himself up for not realizing how badly I've been stumbling. I should be happier about that last part. For years, I've privately lamented that no one ever asks how I'm doing, but the truth is that I've hidden my struggles. I've wanted to be everyone's superhero, so they've seen what I've revealed. Joke's on me. "He'll be down in a second."

"What's wrong?" She's perched forward and twitching with those hawkish eyes. "Is he mad about this brunch?"

"No, Mother. He's not mad about the brunch."

"Then what is he mad about?"

My drug problem. "Mom, please. Today will be tough enough without looking for trouble everywhere." I glance at the time so she can't see the truth in my eyes. "Have you heard from Amy yet?"

"No. Have you?"

I shake my head, my body taut from a bolt of worry, then shoot my sister a quick text. Should I have gone to her house last night? Bob was checking on her. She wouldn't do anything to devastate him, I convince myself. I put the phone down and prep the fruit salad to help Tony.

"I'll go see what's keeping your father. I swear, he gets slower every year." Mom waddles away, muttering to herself. As soon as she's gone, I plant my hands on the counter, step back, and inhale. I feel drowned by the confluence of the anniversary, my parents' scrutiny, my career implosion, and my marital strife. If I haven't already destroyed Tony's trust, the only way forward is to manage my life more truthfully.

The kids tromp downstairs behind Tony, who can barely meet my gaze. I smile at Livvy. "You look pretty."

"I love these dots!" Wearing a giant grin, she pokes at the little pink dots on her cotton dress.

"You look darling, Livvy." My mom reappears like a stealthy cat.

Luca, in contrast, is a picture of restraint. "Mom, can I ask a question?"

"Of course."

"Why'd you quit your job?" On closer inspection, Luca's eyes dart back and forth between Tony and me, and his mouth is tight.

On top of everything else, my actions are causing my children stress. I can't possibly explain everything when I'm still trying to understand how I got here. "You guys are growing up fast, and I got tired of missing out on everything because of my long commute."

"So you didn't get fired?" he asks.

"Oh no, honey. No, no. Why would you think that?"

"You guys canceled our trip, and you and Dad seem unhappy. Brendan Trainor's dad got fired last month, and now he might not come back to school next year." The pity in his voice almost does me in, especially knowing that my kids could also be pulled from their school if I don't secure a high-paying job.

"You should've taken Amy up on her offer for some of that prize money," Mom says.

Tony's gaze cuts to me in disbelief, making my entire body go hot. Another piece of information I've withheld from him. Frustration rolls off him in waves, but he doesn't cause a scene. If I could make myself melt into the floor and disappear, I might. Seeing the doubt and questions, the disappointment, in everyone's faces is something new to me. Something awful. Losing my career is bad, but losing my husband—my family—would be intolerable.

I crouch and brush my son's hair from his eyes. "Sweetie, please don't worry. I'm just rethinking how to balance my life. Everything will be fine, you'll see." I hate that my choice has made him worry. Everything I've done lately is wrong—the pills, quitting without a plan, refusing my sister's help. My entire life is slipping out from under me, and yet I must hide my fear from my son. "The good news is that, at least for a little while, I'll be around all the time."

He nods, his forehead smoothing as he relaxes.

What I'd give for a few minutes to myself. I need to figure out how to salvage my marriage without the pressure of my parents' presence and wondering about Amy.

"Now you can come to story time," Livvy says.

Focus, Kristin. "Yes. I can volunteer in the school library too."

Livvy's grin briefly offsets Tony's black mood. And then, with lightning speed, she shifts gears. "Is there cake for the party?"

"It's not a party," Luca says.

"Is too."

"Is not."

"No bickering." I rest my hands on their shoulders, taking the moment to reset myself for this day. Everything else must wait. "Today is about supporting Aunt Amy and remembering Uncle Sean and Scotty. Aunt Amy will probably be sad, so please don't beg her to play. But I'm sure she'll take all the hugs you can give."

"Uncle Sean and Scotty are angels now," Livvy says.

"That's a nice thought." I glance at Tony, who is listening while peeling potatoes.

Livvy nods. "So why is she sad?"

I rub her little arms and envy her innocence. "Because she misses them."

"You're not going to die soon, are you, Mommy?" Livvy's brows knit.

"No, honey. I'm healthy." My husband, on the other hand, probably disagrees.

"If I die, will I go to heaven?" she asks.

The mere thought of losing Livvy fills me with dread, driving home my sister's pain. Where is she? She must know we will worry if she's late and not answering texts. "Sweetie, let's not imagine such a thing. We'll grow old together. Can you picture me with lots of wrinkles and gray hair?"

"And a big fat tummy," she giggles.

"If that's what you like," I tease.

My parents take seats in the family room. I hope Tony can fake "normal" behavior better, pronto. I roll my shoulders and check my phone. Nothing. Dammit.

Tony takes the breakfast strata from the refrigerator and sets it in the oven.

"I wish Amy would call or text," I say to his back. "I have a bad feeling."

He looks at me, clearly bitter that I never told him about Amy's offer.

"Maybe she's in the shower," he says, thankfully not grilling me about the money. "Or getting herself in the mood to show up. She did warn us that she might not be up to this. It's not that surprising, is it?"

He's so matter of fact. So logical about the many possible explanations for her delay. Why must I always jump to the worst-case scenario? Yes, she messed up before and is grieving. But I've messed up, too, and don't want to be forevermore defined by my mistakes. Tony's right. She wouldn't do something to hurt my kids after all they've been through with her. Or with our parents waiting on her.

I wander to the family room to sit with my parents. Dad is in a dress shirt and blazer. "You two look swanky."

"We wanted to look nice for any photos." Mom pats Dad's leg.

She's as bad as Livvy with her attitude. "I don't think we should push for photographs. This isn't a party."

"Maybe it should be," she says. "When I die, don't you dare mope. I lived a long, happy life, so throw a party and talk about all the fun things you remember about me."

I can't help but smile. There would be a lifetime of memories to share—not that she'd love all the ones we might recall. She was more carefree in her middle age than she is now. Dad's asthma spooked her, and then Amy's life fell apart. Harsh realities have a way of shaping and hardening us unless we actively push back.

"Okay, Mom. But Sean and Scotty didn't get full lives, so don't expect Amy to share your sentiments. Let's just help her get through the day."

"You girls have to accept things, even when you're not ready. It's life, Kristin. Death is part of life. It's sad. We miss people. But we should still celebrate every day we're lucky enough to survive."

"Damn straight," Dad adds. A rare moment of unity between my parents, and a hint of where my sister's old attitude came from. In this way, I've been an outsider—the one always planning ahead, worrying about doing things a certain way. It was a relief to meet Tony, who felt as I did. Who had ambitions and plans and confidence.

And yet with both of us running in one direction, we lost our equilibrium. When this day ends, I hope I can repair all the damage that's caused.

CHAPTER NINETEEN

A M Y

The same morning

One year without my two favorite people.

Twelve months with only recent bouts of light breaking through the darkness. The gathering thunderclouds suggest God knows I can't tolerate sunshine today.

If I could sleep through this anniversary, I would. In fact, if I'd stayed home yesterday, I could've avoided the look on Declan's face when I asked him about sex. The recollection makes me shudder. Poor Bob also seemed disturbed by my behavior, checking in on me more than once.

When I moved here, I had a clear plan. Now, instead of finding relief by ending my sorrow today, I have to muddle through it. Logically I have good reasons to hang tough, but this morning my broken heart is beating louder than it has in weeks.

Brunch looms—another thing to grin and bear in front of others. My mother will hover like I'm a six-year-old running toward the edge of a cliff. My dad will do the opposite, sipping cocktails while shooting me mournful glances. Tony will busy himself in the kitchen to avoid uncomfortable conversations. In the center of it all will be my sister, whirling around, desperate to make everyone happy. That rarely ends the way she plans. For someone so smart, she's been slow to learn that particular lesson.

I could bail. They promised I wasn't obligated to show up. And yet, no doubt Tony has been working hard. It'd be ungrateful to no-show after everything he and Kristin did for me this year.

Rain pelts the roof. Behind me, my bed beckons like a siren, coaxing me to crawl back in and pull the covers overhead.

I can't. I must go to the cemetery, and I must do it alone to face Sean and Scotty without others' judgment. I might need a rowboat to get there, but the rain won't stop me.

Without enthusiasm, I apply lipstick the color of the burgundy Munstead Wood roses that lie on the vanity awaiting my next move. This past year has aged me tenfold. The pretender stares back from the mirror—hollow as a mannequin. I blot my lips with tissue. When I bunch it in my fist to toss in the trash, the razor-thin scar on my wrist taunts me.

Yesterday morning, I would've sworn I'd made real progress. I've shown up for Kristin and her family. We've ticked off bucket list stunts and grown closer in the process. Bob's sweet friendship proves I can still be good company. Declan has helped put me in a position to improve many lives. I can envision a future of good deeds instead of merely counting down the minutes until bedtime. All that growth now feels threatened by guilt that burns brighter this morning for having begun to move on without my guys.

I close my eyes. This time last year, after Sean and Scotty had left our suite, I'd stretched out my arms and twirled around, feeling entitled instead of regretful for fighting with Sean and abandoning our plans. Having several hours to myself had seemed the greatest luxury I could imagine. Like Cruella, I was nearly giddy with twisted glee when making my spa appointment. I even poured myself a glass of champagne and stood on the balcony, looking out over the tops of palm trees to the teal-colored Caribbean waters, intent on enjoying blissful privacy.

I savored the warmth of the sun. The rustling of colorful flowers along the resort pathways. The citrus scent of the spa. Not only that, I pampered myself by scheduling the trifecta: a mani-pedi, mud wrap, and ninety-minute massage.

I cringe now for having been thrilled to skip that boat tour and get time away from my husband and son. Hours later, the knock on the suite's door changed everything. I went numb, the edges of my vision darkening as the police officer delivered life-destroying news. A blow of self-loathing made me crumple to the ground in disbelief before I threw up. My remorse is so deeply embedded that it will never fully withdraw.

Those first few months after the funeral, I sealed myself in my house, begging for the impossible, driving myself mad with self-recriminations while Kristin and Tony alternated checking on me, bringing me food, and begging me to shower or participate with their family in any way they could think of. Instead, I lay in Scotty's toddler bed, clutching his belongings. Pored over old photos to jog free good memories to stave off the ache of loss and loneliness. Nothing worked. The pain proved too permanent.

And yet, trying to kill myself was a cop-out and another slap in Sean's and Scotty's faces. I deserve to carry this anguish forever. To suffer the loss over and over.

Another clap of thunder. My phone pings. Kristin.

Looks like we may need to skip the cemetery unless the rain lets up later. LMK if you need anything. See you soon.

I grunt an acknowledgment but have no intention of letting a little rain deter my visit. I also have no intention of having my every move today monitored, so I ignore the text. They promised me space, after all.

Outside, the scuffle of rapid footfall sounds as Bob's daughter shouts at her young son to go to the back door. I peer through the blinds and catch him jumping in puddles. He squeals before she snags him by the arm. His delight coaxes a smile from me until the pang coiled in my heart like a python squeezes with reminders of Scotty.

I pick up the bouquet and wait until they go inside, then grab an umbrella and slip quickly to my car. The blustery weather soaks through my jacket as I climb behind the wheel and start the engine.

The torrential rain is unrelenting.

While I'm stopped at a red light, doubts build. I haven't been to the graves since Christmas. Kristin was with me, although she did wait in the car after a while. I sat in the snow, my ass cold and wet, crying for thirty minutes before she came back and convinced me to leave. I found no solace that day, so I've avoided returning.

I loosen my grip on the steering wheel—the wedding band on my finger another bruise to the heart—but my arms remain heavy and tense. The phone rings. Kristin again. What doesn't she get? Surely she realizes I'm not in a social mood. They promised to let me manage this day however I must, so I refuse to answer on principle. It's time they learn to trust me.

Mental images of Sean's smiling face bombard me like a slideshow as I make my way to Route 104. By the time I reach the light near the Merritt Parkway, the rain is blinding. A sane person would turn around, but I haven't been rational since last year. The hypnotic thump of my wipers drones as I gaze straight ahead.

An impatient asshole behind me lays on his horn, but today is not a day to mess with me. I flip the driver the bird before pulling forward. Another rumble of thunder rolls overhead. I holler along with it, grateful for the privacy to release the pressure building inside.

Sheets of water pelt the window as if trying to force me to turn around. Defiantly, I pick up speed the farther north I travel. I envision myself from an outsider's perspective—a crazed woman on a pointless mission—and yet I'm drawn north as if being towed by an invisible chain.

The storm must be keeping most people indoors, because there's no one on this stretch of road. My wipers don't clear the windows fast enough. Deep puddles have begun to form on the uneven pavement. My tires skim the edge of one, tugging my car to the right. Is God trying to take me? Have three hundred and sixty-five days of living hell been ample penance for my greed?

That lottery ticket.

How thrilled I was. How little I understood. My stomach burns.

Scotty's young face breaks through my thoughts, distracting me as I zoom through another puddle where the road dips, causing my car to veer across the center line.

I squint, struggling to see out the window between the wiper blades. Thunder cracks so loud it rattles the car. I shake my head to focus. My turn is still a mile away. I accelerate as if I can outrun the storm.

If only I hadn't bought that ticket. If I hadn't prayed so hard to win. I'd give up everything to turn back the clock one year. To snuggle my boy on the shuttle to the boat, and hold his hand and pretend to be awed by swimming pigs. To die in a fiery ball with them.

But the foundation—that's important. And my family. Bob. The garden. The chance to share more adventures with Kristin. To be part of Luca's and Livvy's lives. These things can't replace what I lost, but they matter. They matter more than I understood for too long. They're reasons to keep going.

Wipers furiously thump, thump, thump.

Tears sting. In the rearview mirror I see that Piglet isn't in the corner of the back window. I unbuckle the seat belt to reach behind my seat to search for Scotty's beloved pig. As I do, I lose control of the car as the tires spin out.

Shit, I'm flying! My heart pumps up into my throat as my mouth fills with that familiar iron tang of adrenaline. One careless second and now the airborne car and I move toward the trees one frame at a time. A crash is inevitable, yet I'm suddenly unafraid. Maybe this is my destiny. A loud metallic crack rips the air just before something slams into my chest.

Mommy's coming . . .

CHAPTER TWENTY

KRISTIN

The same morning

I catch Tony glancing at the clock again. The timing of his meal pulls further off track with each minute Amy continues to be late. Not that the menu is my biggest concern.

"Call her again," Mom says.

Straight to voice mail. My hands fist as I roll my neck. I should've insisted she stay here last night. "She must've turned off her phone."

"You did say she could stay home," Dad reminds us.

"True." Yet if that were all that was going on, she'd answer one of my calls. Something is wrong. My stomach is roiling.

"What if . . . what if she's in trouble?" Mom worries aloud, hammering on my deepest fear.

"What kind of trouble?" Livvy looks up from her coloring book, her chin wobbly.

"Nothing to worry about, honey. Maybe her car won't start." I keep my voice light while making eyes at my mom. A tension headache begins to tap at the base of my skull. "I'll zip down the street to check on her."

"I'll come too," Mom says.

I don't want her to discover anything untoward, and she's probably the last person Amy wants to deal with right now if she's conscious. "I'm fine. Stay with the kids."

On my way to the mudroom, I say to Tony, "I'm sorry your meal is getting ruined."

"Seems nothing will go as planned today." Sarcasm, a taut jaw, and his cool gaze suggest he's getting angrier about this morning's revelations. Once again, I'm torn between saving my sister and my marriage.

"I hope Amy's okay." I arch a brow to highlight the stakes where Amy is concerned and then grab my keys. "Be right back."

As I pull out of the driveway, my thoughts race ahead. My sister's spent a lifetime making odd decisions, often without factoring in the consequences. We've expected a setback today, but she's also been making plans, enthusiastic about her new mission. I pray she's simply hiding under the covers or is passed out after a sleepless night.

A crack of thunder sounds overhead.

When I approach her apartment, my hands and arms tremble. What if this time I'm too late? I cannot lose my sister, especially not when I need to lean on her for a change.

Heavy rain turns the windshield into a waterfall that obscures my sight. Squinting, I pull deep into the driveway to shorten my walk. Her car is missing. She must be at the cemetery—a fool's errand in this weather—but she's not inside on the floor. My system instantly floods with relief. I dab my tears and collect myself, eyes closed and exhaling.

A knock at the window makes me yelp. Bob is huddled there beneath an umbrella, so I crack open the window. "What's up?"

"Your sister left a while ago."

Water spits at me. "Did she seem okay?"

"I didn't talk to her. She had flowers, though."

She definitely went to the cemetery. "Thank you! Have a good day."

He disappears as I back out of the driveway.

Cell service is spotty north of the Merritt. She also might've left her phone in the car. Most people wouldn't sit by a grave in this storm, but Amy's not most people. Last time we went there, she was nearly comatose while sitting in the snow, her pants soaked through by the time we left.

Surely she's on her way back now, but some roads will be flooded, possibly blocked by fallen branches. I bite my lip, shaking my head at no one in particular. All I can do is go home and wait with the others.

My mother jumps up the second I enter the house.

I hold up my hands to slow the onslaught. "I saw Bob. It seems like she went to the cemetery."

"In this weather?" Mom's eyeballs bulge.

"You know Amy." It would be easier to reassure her if my sister would simply answer a text. The nagging sense of something amiss persists, but there's nothing I can do. She's been "missing" for only two hours, so the police won't get involved. "Let's eat while it's hot. She can reheat hers when she gets here."

Mom is searching my face, seeking comfort. "I hate starting without her."

I shrug. What am I supposed to say when my husband has spent so much time preparing us all a meal?

"I'm starving!" Livvy jumps up and races to the table.

"It smells amazing." My stomach is churning, though. Tony's peering at me with questioning eyes. I give a subtle shake of the head, hoping he understands that I need his help to keep my parents calm. In truth, I wish he'd convince *me* that everything's all right, and not only when it comes to Amy.

Luca sits next to his dad, scans the various platters, and wrinkles his nose. "Can I have Cheerios?"

Tony closes his eyes. His neck swells with tension, but he's as trapped as I am by the family plans.

"Luca, Daddy worked hard all morning. Surely you can find some things to try." I don't want my son to feel pressure to always be perfect, but I also don't want him to be dismissive of others' efforts. Above all, I need Tony to know that, despite our recent trouble, we are still united.

"That looks weird." Luca points at the strata.

"It's bread, eggs, cheese, and sausage all in one. You like each of those things separately, so please just try a piece before you decide you don't like it," I implore. He reads the room and takes a small section of strata, a heap of bacon, some fruit salad, and a slice of ham.

"I mixed the meat sauce," Livvy declares, pointing at the ham.

"The glaze," Tony reminds her softly. She's probably the only person at the table who hasn't annoyed him or let him down.

"The glaze," she emphasizes while piling ham on her own plate. "It's yummy."

"Is this fresh squeezed?" Dad asks, raising the pitcher of orange juice while breaking the quiet tension at the table.

Tony nods. "Yes, sir."

"I wish you lived in Arizona," Dad teases, eliciting an appreciative smile from my husband. The first genuine one of his day.

I'm sitting, utensils in hand, yet can't move or speak because my thoughts keep misfiring. Amy's disappearing act, the pills, the money—my stomach's in knots. I want to lie down and wake up tonight having everything be okay.

"Krissy?" Tony says loudly, as if he's called my name more than once. "Everything okay?"

"Oh, sorry." This day isn't about me or us. It's about Amy's family. "I'm just . . . wishing we could turn back time."

All the adults nod. I'm about to force some bacon down my throat when my phone rings. Stamford Health? I'm suddenly cold, but instinct makes me hit "Accept."

"Hello?"

"Hello?" a woman asks. "Is this Kristin DeMarco?"

"Yes. Who's calling?" My heart sounds like it's beating in my ears.

"My name is Sandy Miller. I'm a nurse in the Stamford Hospital emergency department. Your sister, Amy Walsh, gave us your number as her emergency contact."

Everything goes hazy, and I feel like I'm fusing to my chair. Oh please, God. "What's happened?"

"There's been a car accident. She's broken some ribs and lacerated her lungs, so they're taking her for emergency surgery."

Lung damage? I start crying. Is my sister going to die?

Mom clasps her head as if it might fall off her neck, and Livvy starts to cry, which suggests I muttered that last part aloud.

"We'll do everything we can, but you might want to get here quickly in case decisions need to be made," Sandy says. "Do you know if she has a living will or other directive?"

Other directive. I've lost control over my voice. When I try to stand, it's as if I'm pushing up through quicksand.

"I don't know." I can't think. Where did she put her will when she moved? Of course, I doubt she'd want special measures taken to prolong her life. Trembling, I sink back onto my seat. Vaguely I hear my mother whimper and mutter to my dad. Tony circles the table, stroking Livvy's head before resting his hands on my shoulders. I tell the nurse, "I'll be there in fifteen minutes. May I see her before they take her to surgery?"

"Doubtful. They're prepping her now. But the surgeon will speak with you when it's over."

"I'm leaving now." I hang up without thinking. My hands tremble until I look at Tony, whose stoic expression is the life raft I need.

"What's happening, Kristin!" Mom yells at me. Dad hugs her, his face twisted with worry.

I reach for Livvy and pull her onto my lap and then gaze at Luca. "Aunt Amy's been in an accident. The doctors are operating to fix what's broken."

"Oh God," Mom cries while Dad whispers "Hush, hush" against her ear. Livvy cries in my lap, so I squeeze her and kiss her head.

"What's broken?" Luca asks, his lower lip quivering.

I dig deep to project confidence for my kids. "Some ribs. The good news is that she's right where she needs to be. Doctors do these surgeries all the time." That reminder is for myself as much as everyone else. "I'll call when I know more, okay?"

My mother rises. With an unsteady voice, she mumbles, "I'll get my purse."

"Mom, you can't come. Only one person per patient is allowed in the waiting room. I'm the designated emergency contact, so I have to go." I slide Livvy off my lap to hug my parents. "Please stay here with the kids. I promise I'll keep you updated." Tears leak from my eyes, but I blot them and hold it together.

"I'll drive you," Tony says.

"You can't stay either."

"You can't drive in this condition. I'll drop you off and then pick you up later. Let's not make things worse by you getting into an accident too." He's not going to yield.

I concede because he's right.

My mom follows us to the garage, red eyed and splotchy faced, grabbing at me. My poor parents have been through the wringer this year, and it shows. "Tell me exactly what they said."

Exactly? I can't recall it verbatim. "She broke some ribs and punctured a lung. I don't know what else, but they're rushing her into surgery. They know what they're doing. It sounds like they got her in time." My voice cracks because I'm not certain of that last part.

Even if she has an advance directive, I'm not ready to pull plugs. Adrenaline surges like it did last summer, when I found her bloody and half-dazed from drugs. The memory makes me dry heave.

"Amy's my daughter. If anyone has to make decisions, it should be me," my mom barks, her grip so tight on my arms they might bruise.

I hug her again, unwilling to hurt her with the reminder that Amy chose me. "I need you and Dad to keep the kids from getting more upset. Keep the phone handy. I'll call if there are decisions to be made, but let me go now. Please."

Tony places his hands on her shoulders and gently tugs at her until she releases me and is held against his chest. "Nancy, none of us is in control of the situation, so let's all do what we can to make it a little easier. Amy would want you to distract Livvy and Luca so they aren't scared."

She nods, slowly pulling herself together between sniffles. "All right. All right."

"I'll be back in thirty minutes," Tony tells her, and I couldn't be more grateful for his effectiveness.

Mom goes back inside, looking older and more befuddled than ever.

Tony opens the car door for me, putting our problems aside. When we back out of the garage, he asks, "What can I do?"

"Nothing. It's in the doctors' hands now." I make the mistake of googling risks and complications of lung surgery. Blood clots. Hemorrhage. Respiratory failure. My nose tingles. Parts of my body turn cold and then feel as if they're splintering. A world without Amy—even this somewhat broken version of herself—is unfathomable. I want to retch. And if she dies, I'll also lose my parents to their grief the same way we've already lost pieces of my sister. Our entire family will become half people. How will my kids cope with another year of deep mourning? I reach out to grab Tony's forearm, thankful that he is here and that, whatever happens, he will help me shepherd everyone through it.

Fifteen minutes later, we hustle from the car to the ER entrance, where I barge up to the check-in desk.

"We're here for Amy Walsh. I'm her sister, Kristin. Is she in surgery?" I ask.

The desk nurse looks at us through the clear partition. "Only one visitor is allowed in the waiting room." She's unfazed, any sense of urgency dulled by dealing with frantic family members every day. That fact doesn't keep me from wanting to slap her across the face for her lack of sympathy.

"I'll leave as soon as my wife is settled," Tony announces, daring her to remove him. They lock gazes for two seconds, but then she types some things on the keyboard and asks me some questions, taking my name and cell number.

"You'll have to take a seat. Someone will come talk to you when they get a chance." She still looks annoyed or bored, maybe both. I glance around, hoping to see another nurse or technician who might be able to supply a quick answer.

Everyone is occupied, so I relent. "Okay. Thank you."

When we step back from the counter, Tony takes my hands and kisses my knuckles. "We can sit outside on the covered benches and wait for news together."

I shake my head. "I should stay in here in case they call out my name. My parents may be too emotional to handle the kids, too, so you need to go back."

He nods. "All right."

"I'm sick, like I might throw up." I'm starting to convulse, and deep down, I know that my body isn't just reacting to this stress. I'm craving those pills to pull me through this day. My life is a mess. "What if she doesn't make it?"

He hugs me, his big hands sliding across my shoulder blades and the back of my head, snuggling me against his chest. "Have faith in the doctors, Krissy. This isn't their first rodeo. And Amy can stay with us while she recovers. We'll hire help this time. We'll do whatever we have to so you're both okay."

He rests his cheek atop my head. For a moment, soaking up his love and warmth strengthens me. Even after the damage helping Amy has inflicted on our marriage, he would open our home up to her again. That says so much about him and us. Yet our marriage is at an inflection point. Can it take another several months of stress and caring for my sister? Might I eventually need to choose between my husband and her?

He sighs. "No matter what happens or has happened this year, I love you. I'm here for you, whatever you need. You aren't alone, and you don't have to solve anything by yourself, okay?"

I cry—from gratitude and relief. Also in defeat at having to accept that I'm not superhuman. That I do need help. I squeeze him again, clinging to his certainty and strength. "Thank you."

"I hate to leave you, but that nurse keeps giving me the evil eye." He crooks his head in her direction.

"I'm okay. Go on. I'm worried about Livvy, especially."

He kisses me. "Call me as soon as you hear anything. Get some water and snacks. Stay hydrated."

"I will." I wave him off and then go find a seat. The TV feels intrusive and annoying, but another woman is watching it. Her "emergency" patient must be suffering something nonthreatening, like a broken bone or stitches. I envy her calmness to the point of anger.

Folding forward in my seat, I rest my forehead on my knees and inhale deeply with my eyes closed. This is bad. Panic courses through me, my body shuddering. For the first time in my life, I feel incapable. I've done this to myself—pretending to handle everything while self-medicating instead of seeking help or delegating. Missing out on so much, in search of what—approval, success? Those things mean nothing if I'm not healthy. Not happy. If my family suffers or fails.

"Kristin DeMarco?"

I sit up sharply. A tiny woman—short, thin, dark skin and eyes—is scanning the waiting room, searching for me. I clutch my stomach. Oh please. Please let this be good news.

I stand and wave until she sees me and comes over.

"I'm Kristin. How's my sister?" My mouth is so dry that the words sound slurred.

"She's in surgery now. Depending on what they find, it will be another two to six hours. Were you able to locate an advanced directive?"

I shake my head, almost glad I don't have one. My eyes burn. "Is that likely—I mean, do the doctors think she won't recover?"

"It's just information we like to have in case we need it. I know this is stressful, but try to stay calm. Maybe go get some tea or take a walk. We have your cell, so we'll call you when she's out of surgery."

I'm searching her eyes for a sign of something—a clue about what's going on in the bowels of the hospital. For reassurance that this is a routine surgery, I suppose, although I'm getting no hint at all. "Thank you."

"You're welcome." She smiles politely and then turns to go. I watch her leave and then take my seat again, wishing I'd had Tony stay. Six hours is a long time to be alone with my thoughts. Fear keeps glazing over me like ground frost, making me shiver.

I text Tony and my parents to let them know it will be several hours before we know anything, and then I stare into the nothingness and pray.

———

Four hours later, my head is throbbing from my drinking three cups of awful coffee, listening to the incessant blare of TV talk shows, and the sinking feeling that the longer surgery takes, the worse the situation must be. My thoughts have blurred into a thick haze, which thankfully gets interrupted when someone calls my name. This time it's a man who doesn't look much older than I am. He's short and lean, with intelligent blue eyes and sweaty blond hair sticking out from his paper cap. "Mrs. DeMarco?"

A cold sweat coats my skin as I stand. Once again, I wish I weren't here alone. I search his eyes yet read nothing in them. "Yes, are you Amy's surgeon?"

He nods. "I'm Dr. Braden, the surgeon who repaired your sister's lung."

Repaired! I shudder with relief. "So she made it?"

"Yes. We had some touch-and-go moments, but she's in recovery now."

I bend at the waist and gulp in air, as if I've been holding my breath for hours, and cry.

Dr. Braden gestures toward a few chairs in a quiet corner of the waiting room. "Why don't we sit while I explain what's happened and a bit about the recovery and prognosis."

I feel outside my body as I clumsily retake my seat. Does "touch and go" mean she flatlined at some point? As long as she's okay now, that's all that matters. My limbs soften as the fact that my sister has survived settles in. "What happens now?"

"She'll be moved to the ICU in another hour or two."

"ICU?" I frown because that means she's still in danger.

"Yes." His manner is sober but kind. "The impact of the crash broke several of your sister's ribs on her right side. Some of those fragments lacerated the distal bronchial artery and caused a large pneumothorax."

The jargon sails between my ears like an unfamiliar foreign language, making me feel lost and uncertain. "I don't understand."

"There was damage to her lungs and arteries, which caused a lot of bleeding." The mention of blood causes an instant recall of my sister's bloody arms from last summer, and I tense. The doctor continues. "We did an open thoracotomy so we could find and repair the damage." More jargon. "Your sister will remain intubated for a few more days, and the chest tube will remain in place as well until we have time to assess the tissue damage." More awful-sounding things like chest tubes. Do those hurt? Machines to keep her breathing while she recovers. Will lung damage change her life going forward? Inhibit her activities? My eyes burn. He says, "I expect her to recover, but the next few weeks will be hard. She'll likely remain in the ICU for three days; then, once we remove the tube, she'll go to a step-down unit for another couple days, and finally be moved to the surgical recovery floor for a week to ten days. We need to monitor her recovery and make sure she's moving around to prevent complications like pneumonia. She'll also need a lot of help at home for several weeks after she's released."

His voice sounds like it's traveling through a long tube, so I shake myself. "She can stay with me for however long it takes." I love Amy and will do everything I can, but this puts more pressure on my family and marriage at a time when we need a release. I place a hand on my forehead.

"That's good, but you'll need a nurse to check her dressings and show you how to properly change those for at least the first week after she goes home."

Unlike last time, this is a physical recovery, not a mental one. I'm not educated enough to understand what we're getting into here. I'll be home, at least, so I can cook and read to her and run her errands or do exercises or whatever else will help.

"Whatever she needs, we'll make it happen." Although I have many questions, the most urgent one pops out. "When can I see her?"

"Soon, but prepare yourself. She's badly bruised and swollen. She'll have multiple IVs, tubes in her nose and throat, and she'll be heavily sedated to the point where she'll appear unconscious. She won't be able to talk, but some people say patients can hear you. Once she's off the vent, she'll be awake, although it may be painful for her to talk much for a couple of days."

My head is spinning. "I wish I had a notepad. I rushed here without thinking."

"We'll be speaking with you a lot over the coming days and will give you papers that answer a lot of questions. For now, try to relax and let what I've said sink in."

I need to get his card for when I calm down and process this situation. I touch my temples. "It figures this happened today of all days."

"What's special about today?"

I drop my hands and shoulders, rolling my neck to loosen the tension that has collected there all day. "It's the anniversary of her husband's and son's deaths."

"I'm sorry to hear that." He squints, hesitating. "Did anyone talk to you about the circumstances around the crash yet?"

"No." I tip my head, only now realizing that I never once thought to ask if others were involved and hurt. Good grief, there could be legal implications on top of everything else. It was reckless to drive in the storm. Was she drinking? Heart pounding again, I will myself to focus. "Was anyone else hurt?"

"No. There were no other cars involved. No skid marks. And your sister wasn't wearing a seat belt when her car went into a tree." He stares at me as if expecting a reaction, but I'm so tired and confused that I can't put the pieces together. "We noticed evidence of past self-harm. Do you think this crash may have been another attempted suicide?"

I rock in my seat, shaking my head as if it will erase his speculation. Last week I would have been more certain, but her drinking yesterday and her refusal to respond to texts today suggest a backslide. "She's been much better lately. Really moving forward. I can't believe she'd do that again."

Even now I'm not being honest with myself, because the truth is that I have been concerned. I've wondered whether she was showing me what she wanted me to see to get me off her back. Even this morning, when I drove to her apartment, I worried about what I might find.

Could this have been prevented if I'd found the courage and stamina to confront her last night? I let her push me away because I was preoccupied with my own crises. On every front—at home, at work, and with my sister—I've failed to reach my goals. I've lied. I've hurt others. And for what? Now we will all need to start all over again. I'm not sure how to make it all work. It feels so hopeless. I cover my face and weep.

The doctor pats my shoulder. "We'll see what she remembers when she wakes up, but I'll request a psych consult too."

I nod, defeated and limp. "Thank you. So do I just wait here until she's in the ICU?"

"Visiting hours end at eight o'clock. Let's hope she gets moved in time for you to see her. Like I said, she won't be able to respond, but she may hear you." He rises. "Feel free to call my service with questions, and I or one of my team will try to get back to you as soon as possible."

I stand and shake his hand. "Thank you so much for saving her." My voice cracks. That is the one good thing to hold on to. Amy survived. There is still a chance that we will all heal. This time I'll ask for help and be braver.

"You're welcome." He smiles and then turns and disappears behind a set of doors leading to the bowels of the hospital.

I collapse on the seat and text Tony.

Can you talk privately?

Within a minute, he calls. "Hey, how are you?"

His voice is gentle, wrapping around me like a cashmere throw.

"I don't know. Amy made it through the surgery, but she'll be on a vent for a couple of days and is looking at two weeks here." I close my eyes as I relay the worst of it. "Based on the crash scene, they suspect another suicide attempt." My voice cracks.

"Oh shit. Why?"

I explain the evidence. Tears leak from my eyes again, and I'm worn out to the point of having almost no voice left.

"I'm sorry, Krissy. I wish I'd stayed with you. But let's not jump to conclusions. It was raining like hell all morning. She could've hydroplaned, plain and simple."

That's possible, but hope feels dangerous now. Especially because she wasn't wearing a seat belt. "Visiting hours end at eight, so could you pick me up then?"

"Of course."

I wipe my eyes and try to stop sniffing. "Are the kids okay?"

"Livvy's been a little off, but she's settled and is with Snickers now. Your mom and dad have been quiet—whispering between themselves. At one point they dozed off, exhausted from the tension of waiting. Do you want to talk to them or have me fill them in? You sound drained."

"I am, but let me speak to my mom. I'm not going to mention the potential-suicide part yet, just in case it isn't true. No reason to upset her more, right?"

The pause suggests he doesn't necessarily agree with yet another instance of me being less than truthful. "Whatever you think."

Secrets aren't good, I know. God, I know that today more than ever. But I want to protect Amy from judgment until we know what happened, and to protect my mom from unnecessary pain if the suspicions are wrong.

Her voice sounds weak when she picks up. "Kristin, I've been waiting all day. Tell me quick—is she okay? Please tell me Amy's okay." She starts a panicked sort of crying.

My heart breaks for her in places I didn't even know weren't already broken. "She's out of surgery and in recovery."

"Oh, thank God. Thank God. John, she's all right!" I hear her tell my dad, and then he mumbles something in the distance. Mom blows her nose before coming back on the line. "What's next?"

I recite the facts of Amy's injuries and recovery plan.

"Can I come see her now?"

It's painful to hear her suffering and not be able to ease it. "Not yet, Mom. I'm waiting in case they move her out of recovery before visiting hours end, but it's a long shot. I'm sorry."

Mom's tone gets huffy, now moving into a defiant type of anger. "I'm her mother, Kristin. You can't keep me from seeing my baby."

I get it. If one of my children were in the hospital, nothing would keep me away.

"Mom, you're overwrought, and maybe that isn't the best energy to bring here tonight. By morning, you'll be rested and calmer. Wouldn't that be better for Amy, to hear you strong and supportive instead of afraid?"

She sniffles on the other end of the line. "I guess, but if you see her, tell her why I'm not there. I don't want her to think I didn't want to come."

"Of course I will, Mom. She knows you love her."

"All right." She gets weepy again. "I'm drained. Absolutely drained."

I crack too. "We got lucky. Let's focus on that."

"You're right." She sounds less agitated.

"Get some rest. Can I speak with Livvy and Luca for a second?"

"Hang on." Mom hands the phone off, and Luca's voice comes on the line.

"Dad says Aunt Amy's okay."

"Can Livvy hear too?" I ask him.

"Yes," she says.

"Aunt Amy's out of surgery but will be in the hospital for a while. The visiting policies are strict, but you can FaceTime her in a few days."

"I'll bake her cookies," Livvy says.

"That's nice, honey, but let's see what the doctors say about her diet. Maybe it'd be better to make some soup with Daddy."

"When will you be home, Mommy?" Livvy asks.

I glance at the wall clock. "Not for a while. Listen, Nana and Pops could use a lot of hugs right now, so snuggle up with them until I get home, all right?"

"Here's Daddy," she says, handing off the phone.

"Have you eaten?" Tony asks, now in caretaker mode. He's worried about me, probably thanking God he flushed those pills.

"A terrible premade sandwich four hours ago."

"Do you want me to make you a ham and mustard sandwich on ciabatta? I can bring it now so you get something in your stomach."

"No, thanks. I'll just heat up something when I get home. I don't have much appetite anyway."

"I'll bring something at eight. You've got to take care of yourself this time. It sounds like the worst is over. She's in good hands." His voice is low and mellow, like a cello that vibrates through my soul.

"I'll try. It's just . . . I hope you're right about what happened today." I still don't want to believe that she did this on purpose. I don't know if I could stop myself from being angry if she did.

"Me too. See you in an hour."

"Thanks. Bye." I hang up and close my eyes. This day is a wake-up call. My lies exposed. My sister nearly dead. Life's fragility on full display.

Thirty minutes go by in a blink, and then, with less than twenty minutes to spare, a new nurse comes to take me to see Amy.

When I get to the ICU, she's hooked up to a million lines. The room is alive with beeps, buzzing, and clicks. Her face is distorted and practically purple, making her look impossibly frail and broken. It's hard not to burst into tears, but I need to hide my pain, fear, and guilt in case she feels them. I hug myself as I approach her bed, making a mental note to bring her a nice pillow and robe for when she's unhooked from all the equipment.

My vision blurs with fresh tears. I press my palms to my eyes and take a deep breath.

"Amy, can you hear me?" Despite knowing better, I'm crestfallen when she doesn't acknowledge me. She's sedated—comatose, basically—but I'd hoped for some glimmer of life. Eye movements beneath her lids. A twitch in her face. Something that proves she knows I'm here and she's not alone. She never has to be alone.

"Oh, Ames, I'm so sorry. You've been through so much—I hate to see you in more pain. Everyone sends their love. They wanted to come, but the doctors are only letting one of us be here at a time. We're all praying for a speedy recovery. A full recovery. Please fight your way back, okay? Don't leave us like this. We need you. We love you. There's a good life waiting for you. Hang in there and live it with us. I love you and need you more than ever. I've got a lot of work to do on myself and need your support."

I touch her lifeless hand. Cold like when I found her in July. If I feel broken, I can only imagine how she feels. I rest my head on the bedrail, pursing my lips tight to keep the sobs buried in my throat.

I've never been prone to despair until this year. Bleakness is an insidious thing, like mold. It chokes me, but I can't give in to it. I can't let life's ups and downs throw me off course or fundamentally change who I am. I won't let them turn me into a habitual liar or secretive wife, a distant parent, a prickly daughter and sister.

I lean forward and kiss my sister's forehead. "Rest up, Ames. We've got things to do, you and me."

CHAPTER TWENTY-ONE

AMY

An hour earlier

Blinding light filters through the fronds overhead. Palm trees in Connecticut? I stretch my weightless arms, then spread my fingers and wiggle them, feeling cool despite standing on a sunny beach.

Everything is saturated with color. Neon-blue stripes on the beach umbrella flap in the breeze. See-through turquoise water sparkles as if coated with crystals. Beneath my feet, a wide stretch of white sand. Exuma. I swore I'd never return. How did I get here?

The beach is empty. If the overcrowded resort had been like this instead, Scotty would've been happier. I glance over my shoulder toward the hotel but see only sand and shrubbery, punctuated by brilliant fuchsia azaleas. Overhead, a cloudless blue sky. Everything appears to extend infinitely in all directions from where I stand weightless and tranquil.

I'm confused yet unafraid. Thoughts come and go without judgment, producing an airy, curious contentment. That's unexpected, given how recollections of this island usually bring a stab of pain.

Two silhouettes materialize in the periphery—an adult and child holding hands. They're at the far end of the shore but appear to be drifting my way. Yes, drifting.

I remain still—alert yet calm. It's only then that I notice the silence. Water makes no sound as it laps the shore. Birds don't chirp from the trees. I study the drifters until their familiar shapes make my heart swell so fast it feels like I'm flying, even though I haven't moved.

"Sean! Scotty!" When I attempt to run toward them, my legs don't budge. I jerk them and then tug at them with my hands, but they're cemented in place. I glance at my family and down to my feet again, willing them to work. Impatient, I give up and open my arms wide. "You survived!"

The relief of it sinks me to my knees. Was it all a terrible dream? The months of agony. The anguish of what-might-have-beens. Is my horrible, vivid, agonizing nightmare over? I want it so badly I am shaking, and yet this feels unlike any reality I know. Something is wrong.

Sean and Scotty stop just beyond my grasp, gazing upon me with placid smiles.

"Come hug Mommy," I beg of my son, desperate to pull him close, smell his hair, and kiss his cheeks. He looks so beautiful. Glowing with a sort of peace I also feel. I blink back tears while gesturing for him to come to me.

He flaps his free hand, his gaze wandering toward the sea.

Why won't he come? Aren't they happy to see me? Sean, too, looks years younger without the harried wrinkles I remember. God, I've missed that face, his smile, the feel of being held. Why isn't either of them talking or reaching for me? They're so close. I need to touch them.

I rise and snap at Sean, "Why are you just standing there? Say something. What's going on?"

His mouth doesn't move, yet I hear his voice. "We can't touch you, Amy. You're in the in-between, but don't be scared."

"The in-between?" Suddenly off balance, I thrust my arms out in case I fall. I grab my head, trying to remember where I was before I woke up on this beach. My thoughts go to Piglet and then blur. "Am I dying?"

"Not yet," Sean says.

That's no answer, and it's definitely not his normal way of talking. He'd either tease me or be direct. Riddles were never our thing. Hold on—if this is the in-between, then there is an afterlife. I've been right all along. If I die, we'll be together again. "Do I have a choice?"

As soon as I say it, my other family members' faces crowd my thoughts, tearing me in two.

"Every single day." He looks at my wrists, a sad resignation coloring his face. "I'm glad you were saved."

I tuck my wrists beneath my armpits and look away, hating myself and ashamed that he knows what I did.

"If you do that, we'll lose you forever," he warns.

Lose me forever? I wish he'd be clearer. How I ache to touch them both.

"I don't understand." I look at my son and can't stop smiling. He's so beautiful. So unique and filled with light. "Mommy has missed you so much, Scotty."

His eyes meet mine as briefly as a butterfly kiss. I cry out in frustration.

"Let go of the pain, Amy. There's peace for us all once you do." Sean bestows a gentle smile on me. "We are always with you." Something in his tone sounds final, like he's about to go back to wherever they came from.

"Can we stay here a little longer?" If I can linger long enough to say things . . . "I love you both. I've missed you. I'm sorry I didn't come on that boat. I know I was so selfish. Please, stay here for a while and talk to me."

"It's time to rest and heal. No need to apologize. It's not your fault. We'll be together someday, but now you must live and love like you used to."

"I've tried. I have. Do you know I started a foundation in your honor? It's going to help so many people, Sean. I've made new friends, and even laughed now and then. But seeing you both again—how can I bear another goodbye so quickly when I miss you every day?" As my words tumble out, Sean and Scotty drift away, causing me to wail. "Come back! Oh, Sean, please wait. Scotty! Come back," I croak. My throat burns like I've swallowed a bucket of hot sand.

While I weep, the beach disappears bit by bit, leaving me in a dark, windowless place. I can't even tell if my eyes are open, but a distant, steady beep disrupts the silence. I try to reach into the darkness but am paralyzed, unable to move or speak.

I should be terrified, having no control over what's happening. But of all the things I could or should feel, it's restlessness that gnaws at me. I couldn't be with Sean and Scotty, but how do I get back to Kristin and the others? Am I stuck in limbo—purgatory for nearly taking my own life once? What the hell is happening? I'm too sleepy to figure it out.

I sense energy—frenetic energy hovering over me. Movement. Intense pressure in my chest.

I'm in absolute blackness. Not even a flicker of light. The faint beeping sound drones on, along with some other murmuring.

Is that Kristin's voice? What recovery? Sean said *heal*. Am I hurt?

"Kristin," I say, or at least I try. Her worry is alive, pressing against me. I want to tell her about what happened with Sean and Scotty, but she can't hear me. What's happening?

I thought I'd already lost everything, but I hadn't considered the idea of losing my mind until this minute. Would that be the worst thing? At least there'd be no more sorrow.

But Kristin's pleading, her love vibrating all around me. She needs me to wake up, and I want to leave my mark on the world by finishing what I've started. I have to do that for Sean and Scotty, and for myself.

"I'm here!" I don't think she hears me.

Stay alert. Fight to wake up.

Wake up!

CHAPTER TWENTY-TWO

KRISTIN

Later that night

At nine thirty, after filling in my parents on seeing Amy in the ICU, Tony and I retreat to our bedroom. I'm limp—a stumbling jumble of feelings, thrown out of my head and forced to acknowledge my heart. Exhaustion has me on the verge of collapsing. I'm undressing in the closet when I hear the tub filling.

"What are you doing?" I call, tossing my top in the laundry, the effort bringing home how my body aches.

Tony appears behind me. "Take ten minutes to soak and relax."

"I'm so tired, I just want to go to bed." I step out of my pants and throw them in the hamper too.

"Trust me—soak and let the warm water help loosen your muscles first. I added lavender oil to help you sleep." He rubs my biceps, his eyes reflecting concern instead of the dismay from when he found those pills. I set my head to his chest, having not realized how much I needed to be pampered. To feel loved and protected. To not be interrogated.

"All right." I grab a robe and pajamas. "Thanks."

I slip into the water in our giant soaker tub. When I picked it out, I'd fantasized about spending hours in it reading and relaxing. That was four years ago. This might be the fourth time I've ever used it. Not the best decision or return on a five-figure investment.

Tony has set a glass of water on the bath tray alongside a lit candle, and spa music plays on the Bluetooth speaker. My nose tingles for the millionth time today, but for once, it's from gratitude.

Holding my breath, I sink beneath the water's surface into silky silence. Is this how Amy feels tonight, submerged by the drugs and oxygen pumps keeping her alive? I float up until my head pops out of the water, then lie back against the porcelain, close my eyes, and try not to think about anything. Thoughts come anyway. My parents will be staying longer now—understandable, even as it creates more pressure. Neither the scented candle nor the soothing music overrides the images of my sister's broken body or shorten the lengthy recovery she faces. Nor do they erase how today I craved the pills Tony flushed. I close my eyes, embracing my discomfort in hopes of getting beyond that crutch.

I open my eyes and gaze at the door to our bedroom. Had Amy not crashed, this evening would have ended with a confrontation. Is Tony now pacing or lying in bed? Mentally planning a big conversation? Biting his tongue? I close my eyes again, as if the darkness can hide my mistakes. A bath is not a magic cure or solution, but my body feels more relaxed. I towel off and put on my pajamas, loath to leave this little sanctuary.

When I finally make it to our bed, Tony's reading his iPad. A zing of tension threatens as I brace for what comes next. I pull back the covers and lie down. He sets his device aside, turns off the lamp, and immediately slides over to spoon me. The pleasant heat from his body and the rhythm of his breath are comforting. I focus on those two things to settle my thoughts.

"Today sucked," he says quietly. I hold still because he's right, yet I have no idea what he's building up to. "We have things to work on. Compromises to find. I don't have answers, but while I'm not sure where we'll land, I know that I love you and don't want you to be unhappy, or to struggle to be someone or something only to please me. I need you to know that, too, all right?"

I nod, my heart swelling with love and gratitude. "I love you too. I'm sorry I've hurt you, and I appreciate all you've done this year for our family."

He doesn't say more, and I don't quite trust myself to say the right things after this day, so we lie there without moving. I can't tell if he's falling asleep or if, like me, he's blinking in the silence, praying for solutions. Praying for my sister.

In the safety of his arms, Amy's losses hit me again. I can't say with certainty how I'd be able to face life without Tony and the kids. They are my strength. My great loves. My reason to try. I wouldn't know how to be alone in the world after knowing this life.

If Amy tried to take her life again today, I'll be devastated. But do I have a right to be angry? It's her life. Forcing her to live it my way— or live it at all—is no less selfish than her ending it. Of course, I'll do everything I can to persuade her to keep living, but ultimately I need to accept her choices, whatever they may be, and to make sure my family is okay with them as well.

How to do all that is beyond me tonight. I hope the answers will be clearer in the morning.

———

I stop outside my sister's room and press one palm to my stomach, with my other hand gripping the artwork I commissioned. We spent the first three days postsurgery watching her sleep in the ICU while getting brief updates from the staff, much of which went over my head. She's been uncommunicative while intubated. I've taken solace in the fact that there haven't been complications so far. The staff seems to believe things are progressing normally.

Tuesday night, the doctors took her off the ventilator and roused her—a big step and first real win. She barely spoke to our dad, who was visiting at the time, and then immediately worked with occupational therapists on swallowing and eating in the step-down unit. When not working with them these past two days, she's mostly slept, so none of us has had a significant conversation with her since before the accident.

This morning she was moved to the regular surgical-recovery floor. My mother visited first, which was hard for me because I'm desperate to talk to my sister. When Mom got home, she threw her purse on the cubby bench. "It was a bust. She was still in and out of sleep and barely said a word. How long will it be before she'll talk to us?"

"Honey, one day at a time," Dad said, giving her a hug. Thank goodness for Dad, who absorbs her angst and acts as a buffer so her moods don't suffocate everyone else.

"She's alive. She's out of the ICU. Things are looking up, Mom." I set out the grilled chicken salad I'd made for lunch. "I'll run down there now so I can be back when the kids get home."

"I'll go when you get back," Dad said. "I thought I might read to her, like I used to when you girls were little." His smile seemed to emphasize that parenting is always a mix of stress and joy, of pride and frustration, of love and disagreements. More reason to learn to ask for help and to roll with the punches.

Now I stand outside Amy's door, hoping for more than my mother got earlier. There's so much to say. So much I want to understand about the crash. Knowing her delicate state keeps me from rushing in with six thousand questions. I fix my face with a smile before entering her room.

She's awake, her bed slightly elevated. It's a tremendous change to see her in a large, light-filled private room with wall-to-wall windows and million-dollar views of Long Island Sound. I hug myself and weep, overwhelmed with relief despite the patchwork of yellowing blue-and-purple facial bruises reminding me of how close we came to losing her again.

She offers a weak smile and wave. "What's that?"

I lay my purse on the sofa and hold up the painting. She and Sean are seated on the sofa, with Scotty in between. The artist rendered them with such attention to detail—Scotty's cowlick and fine copper highlights, Sean's eyes, my sister's glow. "I had it made for you for last weekend. Now I hope it'll make this place feel a little less sterile while you recover. Is this okay? If it upsets you, I'll take it away."

She shakes her head slightly. "I love it. Thank you."

"I'm so glad." I set it on a ledge under the TV, then go to her side, take her hand, and kiss her head. Each touch is a gift—this life, this love. We learned that lesson last year, but this week it's hitting home harder.

"It's good to see you alert and breathing on your own." I resist crawling into the bed and hugging her because her injuries need months to heal. I grab a tissue and blow my nose, then sit on her bed by her thigh.

It's then that I first notice another difference—a peaceful aura that's been missing all year. How is that possible, given the circumstances?

"How's the pain?" I stroke her forearm and hand, unable to stop touching her. It's like I need proof that she's still here.

"Sore everywhere. Drugs help," she rasps; her gaze drifts to the multiple IV bags, which include substantial painkillers.

It physically hurts to imagine how her body must ache. "Do you need anything? I can get the nurse."

She shakes her head and squeezes my hand. "I'm good."

Only Amy could say something so patently false with utter sincerity, a fact that makes me smile. *Things will be okay.*

"Mom says the doctors told you how long you'll need support. Tony and I want you to move back in with us for a bit. The kids will be thrilled. We'll hire some help—a nurse—so you don't need to worry about anything. Bob even offered to let you out of the lease, if that's best—he's very sweet, and genuinely concerned about you." Her fondness for her landlord has been a surprising blessing.

"Thanks." She reaches for the bed remote to raise herself into a more comfortable position. "But don't cancel the lease. I want to extend it."

A sign she plans to fight for a quick recovery. I savor that tidbit and roll my shoulders once to release the tension.

"We're so lucky, Amy. As bad as this is, it could've been worse. Much worse." I think about Dr. Braden and his description of the accident. The question in his eyes. I bite my lip, then blurt, "Why weren't you wearing a seat belt?"

"Piglet."

I frown, confused, while she shifts her body, then winces before slowly relaxing herself. I hate my helplessness, but I can't fix her. "Huh?"

"He wasn't in his spot. I undid the seat belt to fish behind my seat."

"Oh God." I rub my forehead, agitated. "It couldn't have waited until you parked the car?" I immediately regret that knee-jerk lecture and change my tone. "By the way, I've got him."

Her lips part. "How?"

"The police gave me everything from the car, which insurance declared a total loss." It looked more like an accordion than a vehicle, according to them. "When you're stronger, we'll go car shopping. You know how I love that," I tease, grateful to look forward to doing normal things with my sister one day.

"Can you bring Piglet next visit?"

"Sure. That reminds me, the kids sent lollipops to help you practice swallowing. Clear it with your doctors first." I turn to open my purse and pull out a handful of Tootsie Pops, setting them on her tray.

Amy places a hand on her collarbone in thanks, then winces again. Each movement is a reminder of the gravity of her situation. She glances out the window to the distant sparkling sea and then meets my gaze. "I didn't crash on purpose."

Her messed-up face makes it difficult to read her expressions, but the emotions reflected in her eyes are sober. I want to believe her.

"I didn't say you did."

"The doctors asked. I know you wonder." Before I can reply, she adds, "The car hydroplaned."

Tony was right. Despite my attempt to keep my emotions reined in, another relieved sob erupts. Thank goodness I kept those suspicions from Mom and Dad. I wipe my eyes, feeling apologetic for insulting her.

"I'm sorry I doubted you." We sit in silence a moment, me wrestling my guilt, her deep in her own thoughts. "I take it you were going to the cemetery."

She nods, but instead of looking sad, she smiles like a kid with a secret. "I saw them."

"The graves?" How, when her car was headed north but crashed south of the cemetery?

Amy shakes her head, tugging the bedsheet up higher. "Sean and Scotty. We spoke."

My face screws up in disbelief. This must be her head injury talking. I aim for a calm, supportive tone, knowing there will be a psych consult and additional neurology tests before she's released. I play along so I can better fill in the doctor. "Where?"

"At the beach . . . well, some in-between place . . . I'm not sure." Her eyes take on a wistful haze.

She must hear how nonsensical she sounds, yet she clearly believes what she's saying. I continue pretending this is a normal conversation so she'll stay calm. "What were they wearing?"

She snaps her gaze to me as if broadsided, but then tips her head in thought, searching her memory. "I don't remember. It was strange. I could hear them speaking, even though they weren't moving their mouths."

I hesitate. This alleged encounter made her happy, yet the elaborate hallucination makes me uneasy. "Could it have been a dream?"

"I don't think so. It was intensely visceral compared to other dreams of them. I was somewhere else. Floating, like drifting out of my body. An incredible place. Did I die during surgery or something? I forgot to ask." She takes her water cup and sips through the straw.

The doctor implied they nearly lost her at one point. Is it possible she experienced a peek at the afterlife for a few seconds? Logic rejects the idea as quickly as it surfaces, but curiosity makes me ask, "What did they say?"

Her gaze fills with amazement. "They're content. Together. The air or whatever was thick with love and peace—like, tangibly pulsing with it. I'm so grateful for that glimpse." Her eyes glaze with tears—happy ones that strangely move me, making the hairs on my arms rise.

"It must've been something to feel joy despite all this." I gesture to the IV lines and equipment surrounding her bed.

She wipes her cheeks dry. "Sean and Scotty exist somewhere, and knowing I'll be with them again someday makes everything more bearable."

She's convinced; that much is clear. It's a beautiful dream. I wish I were certain, too, but it's not my nature to believe anything without proof. I am grateful, however, for anything that brings her some peace.

"Listen," she says, letting her head fall back. She's probably getting tired. "This is important."

"All right." I lean forward.

"First, I love you."

I smile. "I love you too."

We stare at each other, and despite her swollen face, I see her at six, hanging from a low branch of the Japanese maple tree in Memaw's yard, giggling. And at thirteen, borrowing my shoes for her eighth-grade dance. At twenty-one, crying because a college boyfriend moved to Los Angeles. Then here in this hospital, holding her newborn in her arms and wearing the most adoring and fascinated expression I'd ever seen.

"I know you do," she says, "but you don't always respect me, and I really want you to believe me about seeing Sean and Scotty. I swear, it was real. I know it in my soul."

I grip her hand. "I respect you, Amy. Don't think otherwise just because we do things differently. And why do you care what I think about your experience? If you believe it, that's all that matters."

She shakes her head. "I want you to know that we all end up at the same place so you'll feel freer to live in the moment without trying to engineer a future outcome. No more pills just to make partner."

Her heart monitor ticks up a bit, making me nervous. "Please relax. I've learned my lesson with those pills. Tony knows everything, and we plan to make some changes once you're out of here and Mom and Dad go home."

Her eyes are beseeching. "Promise not to put your job ahead of your health. And please make fun as important as productivity. And ask for help when you need it."

God, I sound awful through that lens. "I promise. I'll be okay. I'm not the one in the hospital."

She nods, accepting my sincerity. "One more promise."

"Fine."

"Whoever dies first—whether next week, next year, or when we're eighty and stooped over with that hunchback that Memaw had—neither of us will be sad because we will know the other is at peace and we'll see each other again someday. Other than this year, I've mostly lived my life on my terms. I want you to do the same from now on."

"You sound like Mom now," I tease.

"I'm serious." She reaches for my hand. "We aren't put on earth to suffer or to prove anything. We're here to explore. To experience. To figure out who we are. You don't need to be a perfect everything for us all to love you and need you."

I roll my eyes. "I'm so far from perfect, it's almost funny to listen to this lecture. Almost." But her point is clear and heartfelt. I even envy her faith. If I could snap my fingers and make myself believe it, I would. "I promise to keep that all in mind."

"If I die first, I'll find some way to prove what I know. Everyone should feel this kind of peace."

"Well, that would be lovely, except for the part that you'd be dead." I shiver—all this talk about our deaths is creeping up on me with a chilling effect.

Amy nods thoughtfully. "I wasted a whole year in limbo—a regret I'll fix once I'm out of here."

"I'm glad to hear that." I clasp her hand again, heartened. Whether she saw her family or dreamed it, her mindset has shifted in a better direction. I take my first deep breath since August. "In the meantime, let's focus on your recovery so we can get the foundation off the ground. Declan sends his best wishes, by the way."

She nods. "Deal."

Her mood is light and sure, as if she hasn't a care in the world. The "supernatural" experience may account for her utter lack of concern about postsurgical risks and complications, but I remain vigilant. We're only at the beginning of her recovery, on a path as fraught as a trek through the Amazon. Even if Amy is right about the afterlife, I'd prefer for her to stay here with us awhile longer.

———

Later that night, I recite our conversation to Tony and then sink back on my pillow and study his reaction. He was raised as a practicing Catholic, whereas my family attended our Methodist church for weddings, funerals, and occasional religious holidays. Christianity, Judaism, and Islam all promise an afterlife. Perhaps the spirit ascends to heaven or, as Buddhists believe, is reborn over and over again until it reaches enlightenment. Or are atheists correct—death is simply lights out, game over? Why does it all need to be a mystery?

Throughout my life, I've cared more about living with purpose and goals than about religion. I've worked to become a good person, citizen, and family member. To meet my commitments. To cope with disappointments when they happen. Even so, I sometimes envy those who find comfort in their spiritual life. Imagine how differently all people might live their lives if they knew, with certainty, what came next.

Tony scoots lower beneath the covers. "When I was ten, my papa died." He's speaking of his father's dad, whom he looked up to. Who loved him best among all his grandkids. "A couple weeks later, he visited me one night. He didn't say anything, but I woke up sitting up in bed with my arms out as if we'd been hugging. My mom said it was a dream, so I believed her. But it was 'intensely visceral,' like Amy described. Not like other dreams. Maybe it was real. I don't know. I guess that's the point of faith."

Faith. Have I spent so much effort trying to control and fix everything because I've never had enough faith?

"Why didn't you ever tell me this before?" I'm speechless that he's embracing Amy's theory.

"It's never come up." He shrugs.

Is that because he and I spend more time talking about plans and goals than ideas and dreams? I don't want that for us. "So you don't think Amy's got brain damage?"

"Anything's possible. But face it, we don't know a lot about life, the spirit, the universe, and science. Even time is thought to be overlapping." He mimics a "mind blown" gesture with his hands and head, and then his expression warms. "If there is an afterlife, I like to think you'll be there with me."

The lovely détente makes my eyes water. He's been patient all week, never pressing for a conversation about the pills or my career plans. With Amy beginning to perk up, I feel strong enough to wade in. "It's important that you believe how sorry I am about hiding things from you and quitting without warning. I haven't been purposely avoiding this discussion. It's just been a lot to manage my parents and visit my sister."

"I get it. I hid stuff, too, and didn't see that you needed more help than I was giving. We don't need to get into this tonight. I'm just glad you're off those pills and the headaches are gone. After Amy is stable, we'll work on better communication and figure out your next career move."

He's sincere, but does he see the bigger picture—my desire for us to reevaluate the goals we both once held dear? "Does that mean you'll stay open to some lifestyle changes, if that's needed?"

He gazes at me. "I can't promise I want to give up everything, but the most important things in my life are you and the kids. So if what you need to be healthy and happy requires me to give up some things, you're worth it. Okay?"

I kiss him so fast, then hold tight. "Thank you."

"I'm sorry it took so much pain for me to see what you needed."

"It's okay. As long as we're together, we'll be okay."

Although relieved, I drift into a fitful sleep, roused by chaotic dreams rooted in an uncertain future, and then slip back into restless sleep more than once. Awake again at four o'clock, I stare at the ceiling, listening to my husband's gentle snoring.

When I was in law school, I'd wake up at four thirty to make tea and review my assignments before the newspaper arrived. It was cozy sitting in a circle of lamplight with my hot beverage, seeing my reflection in the darkened window. In spring, I'd crack open the window to let the birdsong in while the earliest streaks of pink and gold crossed the inky sky. Time moved at an unhurried pace at that hour, giving me space to breathe and to set myself for the day. I miss that routine, yet in this moment, even the allure of pleasant nostalgia can't drag me from bed.

A sudden dread glides over my skin, so I snuggle next to Tony and try to match my shallow breaths to his deep, slow ones. Within minutes, I'm being lulled, and then my phone rings, jolting me upright.

No one calls at this hour with good news.

I hesitate, staring at the phone as if it were a tarantula, my skin crawling. Tony stirs as I scramble forward to answer the phone.

He sits up as I say, "Hello?"

"Mrs. DeMarco, it's Dr. Braden."

"Yes." I'm already nauseated by the doctor's somber tone.

"I'm sorry to make this call, but your sister has passed away from the acute onset of a pulmonary embolism." I gasp, blinking into the darkness. My head is shaking, refusing to accept what he said, but reality is right there. A blood clot—one of the many postsurgical risks we'd been warned about. When I can't speak, he says, "These complications are never easy to accept, despite knowing the risks in advance. I'm very sorry for your family's loss. We'll need you to come to the hospital later this morning to sign paperwork and make transfer arrangements."

My mind goes blank, pushing away from this news with everything I have. I'm shaking so hard that Tony grabs the phone, but I can't even hear what he is saying because my ears are pulsing with static. Rocking back and forth, I cover my mouth with both hands, holding back my screams. But my body will not cooperate, and before I can stop myself, I throw up on the comforter. Holding my stomach, I fall onto my side and curl into a ball, clutching the covers and crying.

Oh, Amy. Oh, Amy, no.

It's too soon to say goodbye.

I'm not ready.

CHAPTER
TWENTY-THREE

AMY

Four days later

I never imagined attending my own funeral. Another drizzly day, although the clouds seem to be thinning. Bright diffuse light signals the promise of sun. My sense of smell and touch are lost, but my vision is more intense and expansive, and my emotional landscape utterly brimming. The soul is a wondrous force.

Almost as magnificent as the universe.

I note relationships everywhere now. Between the atmosphere and the planet. Between people and animals. Among the planets and stars. All affecting one another, feeding off each other. Pain and joy. Love and loss. A coordinated kind of chaos that's not to be controlled by humans.

I mean to walk among the pews, but it's more of a drift. Vaguely I recall hearing about how energy can't disappear and when we die, ours should get redistributed, but it feels like my spirit energy is galvanized and propelling me. Whatever the truth, it's irrelevant because I'm over-joyed to see the people I love all in one place.

It's funny how each little decision brings us closer to some and further from others we encounter as we move through the world. Our unique personalities and interests help us find kindred spirits with whom we share our life's experiences. I've been blessed to have lived mine open to possibility. Open to spontaneity. If only I'd seen sooner how that made me richer than any lottery could.

Bob is seated near the back with his daughter, who is whispering something and patting his arm. That dear man. I hope his next new tenant will finish our garden and join him for dinners. Maybe Kristin will check in on him now and then too. The middle section hosts friends from the old neighborhood, as well as my parents' and sisters' friends. Declan has come too. He seems sad for someone who didn't know me well. Perhaps he's here to support my sister, or maybe my death has picked at the scab he's put over the loss of his wife. I hope he soon finds someone worthy of that new love he wants to experience someday.

Josephina and Lillian are here, but not together. In death, I might get to watch them enjoy my gifts. There's always that chance that money won't make anything easier, like in my case. I choose to be optimistic.

Jane and Mike came. Thank goodness we began to mend fences before I died. That and working on the foundation might bring her closure. I'm proud that I got the ball rolling with that before my life ended, even if I now won't be able to see it through.

I move forward to where Luca and Livvy sit with my parents at the outer end of the first pew on the right. For a moment, I feel a pull— something like sorrow and yet not. My mother is a mess, her eyes red, her mouth pulling down at both corners. I wallowed in my grief last year, and yet now I desperately want for my mother to know it's okay. To feel only love and gratitude for the life we shared. Love is everywhere—in every breath, carried in the air like billions of dust motes. I wish everyone here could feel it with me now.

Dad seems more dazed than anything, obviously not ready to process the truth of what's happened. Luca stares straight ahead, focused on the minister. His little face is serious, reminding me so much of a young Kristin that I almost laugh—a strange sensation, given the coffin at the altar.

Livvy turns as if distracted and then smiles at me, tugging on my mother's arm. "Look, Nana. There's Aunt Amy."

Mom grabs Livvy's hand, her expression impatient. "Livvy, please, honey. Shh."

"But Nana," she says, her gaze darting back and forth between us despite the brush-off.

When I blow her a kiss, she catches it, her dimples deepening. I'm grateful she isn't frightened, and wonder how and why only she can see me. Then again, she claimed to see Scotty, too, last year. I hope this moment helps her miss me less—or at least lets her know I'll be watching over her.

Kristin rises from the pew to deliver the eulogy. A perfect hairstyle and bespoke black suit cannot mask her splotchy face and sunken eyes. Grief hangs so heavily around her that she almost stumbles on her way to the pulpit.

My sister's hands tremble as she sets out printed pages and wipes her eyes. Her sniffles echo off the cavernous church walls.

"Good morning," she begins. "My sister, Amy—" Her voice cracks, and she starts to cry.

Tony is perched at the edge of his seat, ready to catch her if she falls.

The urge to embrace her overwhelms me, driving me forward until I literally crash into her. My spirit heats and slows down as if mingling with hers. *Can you feel me, sis? It's Amy. Everything is okay, like I told you. Please live happily.* As suddenly as I stepped into her being, I'm out again and hovering.

Kristin touches her face and forearms while distractedly gazing around the altar as if hoping to see me, wearing a hint of a smile. "I believe you now," she utters as if the congregation isn't there listening.

She turns to them then, collecting herself and setting the prepared speech aside.

"I'm sorry," she says to everyone. "Not long ago, my sister shared her views on death with me. She said, no matter when she died, she'd have no regrets because she lived life on her terms. Those of us who've known her well know she never put too much stock in other people's expectations of how to live. She pursued things that interested her, like writing and Sean. She chose friends that she found funny or fascinating, even if some of them made our parents nervous with their body piercings or disdain for certain traditions. She lived her life with genuine passion and curiosity, always focused on the journey instead of setting goals. She married the man of her dreams and they had a beautiful son, both of whom were tragically taken too soon. That's the only time I saw my sister stumble, and that rocked me, probably more than I understood until right now.

"Amy spent the past six months begging me to stop worrying about tomorrow. To stop valuing things and achievements over people and relationships. Easy to say, but not so easy for many of us to do. And yet, deep down, we all know this to be true, don't we? When our time is up, what we'll miss most—what we'll wish for most—is the time spent with the people we love. It's the love, really. That's the point of everything.

"I've grown up with a reputation for perfection—or for attempting it. I'm far from perfect, but I did perfectly love my sister and will miss her every single day. It will be difficult to be in the world without her. That will never quite feel right. But I also know—because she told me more than once—that she would not want me to shut down. She begged me to believe that this earthly life is not the end of our journey, and so I'll do my best to honor that promise, and to approach the rest of my life with her philosophy.

"If you knew her—if you loved her too—I hope you'll take a piece of her outlook home with you today. I feel sure we will all live happier for having done so."

As she makes her closing remarks, I'm drifting farther away despite wishing to stay a bit longer. Snatches of images—like spliced film—flicker. Us as kids at Cove Island digging in the sand, my parents in beach chairs arguing about where to spend Thanksgiving. Playing with Barbies in our room on summer nights when our parents thought we were sleeping. Me running to her to dish about my first sexual experience, lame as it was, and her being curious because she was still a virgin. Being her maid of honor—she was the most beautiful bride—and almost forgetting my shoes. Her arriving at the hospital with a life-size stuffed teddy bear the evening Scotty was born. Shared smiles. Shared tears. Shared everything.

I am stuck, my "fingertips" grasping tightly to what I know. Then I hear Sean say, "Amy, it's time."

I turn. He and Scotty are with me again, the brightest sunlight I've ever witnessed glaring from behind them. I glance back at the pews, knowing the foundation will go on. That my family, though grieving now, will lean on each other and find ways to celebrate me and live and laugh again. That perhaps Kristin's sharing my thoughts just now will help all these wonderful humans embrace the gift of the life they are living.

It's not easy to say goodbye, and yet now I feel a new tug. I turn back to Sean and Scotty. We swim together in a swirl of love and acceptance, and I am not afraid to let go. Not for myself, and not for the people I'm leaving behind for a while.

Love multiplies the closer I move toward the light, and I can feel only blessed for my old life as well as my next adventure.

EPILOGUE

KRISTIN

Five months later

"Thanks, Jane." My gaze lands on the artwork I commissioned for Amy, which now hangs in my home office as both inspiration for my new job and a reminder of what matters most. I still choke up at times looking at it, the dull ache of missing what we never got to do together rising like the tide. Then I remind myself that she's still here in many ways, and that love never dies. "We're in good shape for the quarterly distributions. I'll email Josephina and Declan to get their final sign-off, but I need to jump off this call because the kids' bus will be at the top of the street in ten minutes."

"If remote work existed in my day, life would've been much easier," Jane muses.

"It's a great commute." I would chitchat longer if I weren't rushing. "Have a nice afternoon."

Jane has been a comfort and sort of guide for me as I've learned to accept life without my sister. When grief slams into me—often at the oddest moments—I recall Amy's earnest desire that I trust her experience and have faith. I'm sure I'd be less able to do that if I hadn't felt her at the funeral. There's no other explanation for the happiness—the buoyancy—that overcame me on the pulpit. It had to be her way of proving herself right, although I do wish she didn't have to die to convince me.

Livvy claims to have seen Amy, much like she did with Scotty. I might worry more about that if she were frightened or obsessed, but she's been remarkably calm. She says a little prayer to Amy each night and has taken comfort in the fact that she has an angel watching over her. Luca isn't sure what to make of his sister, but I think he's almost jealous that he didn't see Amy too. My parents are struggling the most with the sudden loss of their child, which is to be expected. To distract them, I took the kids for an extended summer trip to Arizona. I plan to visit them myself more regularly this year too. The kids give us all the best reason to reach for joy in spite of sorrow, which is what Amy would want.

I talk to my sister in private often, asking what she'd think or do in whatever situation I'm in, hoping for another sign that she's there. She never answers. Our otherworldly connection was a onetime thing, I guess. Still, I like to think she can still hear me. To know she and her family will never be forgotten.

I slip on my sandals and trot up the street, beating the bus by two minutes. Sunlight dapples my neighbors' flower beds with warm light as a light late-summer breeze comes off the water. The kids bound off the bus separately, Luca finishing a conversation with Tim Olson, Livvy in her own world but smiling. She clasps my hand as the three of us turn and stroll down the lane.

"I like Mrs. Scrima. She's nice. She's really pretty too." Livvy swings my hand with hers.

"I'm glad you like her. Second grade is an important year." I then ruffle Luca's hair. "How about you?"

"Mrs. Bollman is not pretty." He grimaces, ducking his head when he realizes that was unkind. "But she's pretty funny."

"Funny teachers make the year fly," I say, relieved that neither is complaining about missing their private school. They were upset at first, but Tony and I worked together this summer to set up playdates with neighborhood kids who attend the local school to help ease the transition. "The short bus ride must be a bonus."

Luca's eyes widen in agreement. "That part's great."

"Thank you for being brave about the change. I love running Aunt Amy's foundation and working from home, even though we've all had to give up a little something to make it all work." It turns out Amy had reserved around a half million dollars in her account and revised her will to leave it to me. That money is now invested in the kids' college funds.

Tony and I have committed to some lifestyle changes of our own in exchange for the chance to be more present for our family and carry on my sister's family legacy in her absence. It's not the career I envisioned for myself, but it's more personally meaningful to me than lawyering. In addition to running the foundation, which takes roughly thirty hours per week, I'm also acting as Tony's part-time in-house counsel. It saves his business some money, keeps me sharp in case I want to return to the law when my kids are older, and allows us to work together, which has been surprisingly fun.

"Me too, Mommy. Can we ride bikes now?" Livvy asks as we cross onto our driveway.

"Sure. I thought we'd visit Bob and bring him some of the brownies you made yesterday?"

They both nod.

"Get your helmets and let me change my shoes." I take their backpacks inside for them while they get their bikes set. I slip into my Kiziks; then my phone rings. "Oh hey, honey. I'm just about to take the kids for a bike ride."

"Just calling to say that I got OpTech to agree to a five-year lease with another five-year option. Bankruptcy on the office park is averted. You'll need to send them a lease to review."

"Excellent! Can we celebrate tonight? Maybe take the kids out for Thai?"

"Or maybe we eat in, put them to bed early, and celebrate in private?"

I smile. "Even better. But I've got to go right now because the kids are out in the driveway."

"See you later, hon."

I tuck my phone in my pocket, wrap some brownies in tinfoil, and return to the garage to get my bike, putting the goodies in my bike basket.

"Daddy solved a really big problem that he's been working on for a long time, so we should do something special to congratulate him tonight."

"Can we get a cake?" Livvy asks.

"Maybe we just finish the leftover brownies." I wink. "I thought you might want to make him a card or something. But right now, do we want to circle Tod's Point before visiting Bob?"

"Yeah!" Luca says, already leaving the driveway.

We cycle down Sound Beach Avenue and into the beach park.

After we circle the loop, we stop and sit in the sand, looking across the Sound toward Manhattan. On a clear day you can see bits of the skyline that consumed my former life. There will always be a little part of me that yearns for vindication and the partnership offer I never got. After considering the amount of time and effort a discrimination claim would have required, and the toll that would have taken on my family, I dropped the idea. Sadly, despite a spate of similar cases against big firms in recent years, most fade away. It's not an easy win for women, even when the facts support their theories.

But my kids and I are happier now. My marriage is stronger. I'm enmeshed in two important jobs. I have all the energy I need for my life without pharmaceuticals. When I acknowledge those wins, my old goal seems an acceptable sacrifice.

I hope my sister knows I kept my promise.

ACKNOWLEDGMENTS

It always takes a large group of people to bring my books to all of you—not the least of whom are my family and friends, who provide continued love, encouragement, and support.

This book had input from many sources. At its inception, I leaned on my MTBs, Gail Chianese, Denise Smoker, Jane Haertel, Jamie K. Schmidt, and Heidi Ulrich, to help me flesh out the spine of the story. From there I had the benefit of several excellent critique partners for different sections of the story, including Linda Avellar, Falguni Kothari, Ginger McKnight, Harmony Prom Dixon, Juliet Howe, Sarah Babb, and Laura Prior. I also could not have written this book without the wisdom and advice (and in a few cases, beta reads) from my dear friends Barbara O'Neal, Amy Liz Talley, Sonali Dev, Priscilla Oliveras, Sally Kilpatrick, Virginia Kantra, and Tracy Brogan. Our daily chats, and your patience with my many, many neurotic questions, are so appreciated!

Next, I must thank my agent, Jill Marsal, who not only talks me off many ledges but also always provides insight to refine my early drafts. My patient editors, Anh Schluep and Tiffany Yates Martin, tirelessly spent time reading and rereading through pages, helping shine a light on the story I was trying to tell so that I could do a better job. This book was no exception, and I could not be more pleased with how Amy and Kristin developed throughout that process. Of course, none of my work would find its way to readers without the entire Montlake family working so hard on my behalf. I'm indebted to the PR and marketing staff, the art department, the editorial staff, and the sales team for playing an invaluable role in my career.

Lastly, I'd like to thank Dr. Joseph Savage for the time he spent helping me plan and understand Amy's injury and what that recovery would look like. Any mistakes in how that showed up on the page are mine alone.

Finally, and most important, thank you, readers, for making the time and effort I dedicate to my work worthwhile. Considering all your options, I'm honored by your choice to spend your time with me.

ABOUT THE AUTHOR

Photo © 2016 Lorah Haskins

Jamie Beck is a *Wall Street Journal* and *USA Today* bestselling author of eighteen novels, which have been translated into multiple languages and have sold more than three million copies worldwide. She is a two-time Booksellers' Best Award finalist, a Women's Fiction Writers Association STAR Award finalist, and a National Readers' Choice Award winner, and critics at *Kirkus Reviews, Publishers Weekly*, and *Booklist* have respectively called her work "smart," "uplifting," and "entertaining." In addition to writing novels, she enjoys dancing around the kitchen while cooking and hitting the slopes in Vermont and Utah. Above all, she is a grateful wife and mother to a very patient, supportive family. Fans can get exclusive excerpts and inside scoops and be eligible for birthday-gift drawings by subscribing to her newsletter at https://bit.ly/JBeckNewsletter. To learn more about the author, visit her at www.jamiebeck.com.